RETRIEVAL

THE RETRIEVAL DUET (BOOK 1)

I proposed on our first date.
She laughed and told me I was insane. Less than a day later, she said yes.
It was a whirlwind, but we were happy…
Until we got greedy and wanted a family.

It was a life I couldn't give her, not for lack of trying. Fertility just wasn't on our side. We sought out doctors and treatments. Spent money we didn't have. Lied to our families. Smiled for our friends. Put on a brave face for a world that didn't understand.
Finally, we were successful…
Until we were forced to bury our son.

We were left broken, battered, and destroyed.
They say love is in the details, but it was the details that ruined us.

This is the story of how I took back what had always been mine.
The *retrieval* of *my* wife and *our* family.

RETRIEVAL

PROLOGUE

ROMAN

The house was dark when I quietly twisted the lock so as not to wake her. God knows she needed the sleep. I didn't know how she still functioned when her days were filled with tears and her nights weren't much better. It was precisely the reason I stayed gone as much as I did. Or so I'd thought as I'd thrown myself into work. Money couldn't solve my problems, but it might have been able to solve hers.

My body ached, and my lids barely stayed open despite the pot of coffee I'd downed not even an hour earlier. It was a miracle I had been able to drive at all. I should have just crashed at the office, but after yet another failed prototype, I'd needed an escape.

Instead, I'd gone home—the very place I'd spent so many nights trying to avoid.

Only one foot was over the threshold when I suddenly froze.

"Elisabeth?" I called, flipping the overhead light on.

My shoulders fell as I found her sitting on the sofa, her long, blond hair curtaining her face and suitcases surrounding her feet.

"What's going on?" I asked as my gut wrenched, already knowing the answer.

I had no right to be surprised. I'd all but forced her hand. If I was honest with myself, it was what I'd wanted—for her. However, none of that made the pain of reality any less agonizing.

My heart raced. "Elisabeth?" I prompted again, needing to hear her say the words almost as much as I dreaded it.

"I can't stay here anymore," she whispered at the floor.

Acid rose in my throat.

Out of habit, I dropped my keys into the basket she'd bought when we'd first moved in. "*If you fail the key basket, the key basket will fail you*," she'd announced with an infectious smile the day we had become homeowners to the two-bedroom-two-bath starter home we could barely afford. It was just seconds before I'd swept her off her feet and made love to her on the hardwood floor of our foyer in the middle of the day.

But such was life as a newlywed.

Inside that house with her was the only place I'd ever wanted to be.

Until the fantasy of forever had worn off and the walls of real life had closed in on us. Once my refuge, our home became an inescapable prison with bars built of my failures.

I couldn't breathe inside that house any more than I could look her in the eye.

We'd only been married for five years. But, seeing her now, I felt like it'd been a lifetime since I'd peered into her eyes, promising to love her in sickness and in health.

But it wasn't like she was the same woman, either.

Over the last six months, she'd wasted away both physically and mentally in front of my eyes.

And I'd done absolutely nothing to help her.

But how do you throw a lifeline when you yourself don't even have a rope to hold on to? I might have been able to keep her afloat for another day, but I'd never have been able to pull her back to me.

We merely existed on the same plane. Living under the same roof, eating meals at the same table, sleeping in the same bed. But we were far from sharing our lives together.

"Are you coming back?" I asked, not willing to accept the truth that lingered in the air around us.

Her deep-green eyes lifted to mine—the red rims and the dark circles doing nothing to hinder her beauty. Swallowing hard, she shifted her gaze to the mantel on the other side of the room. I knew what she was looking at, but I refused to follow her into the past.

That might have been our biggest problem of all.

She was still living there.

And I refused to go back.

"Elisabeth?" My voice softened, but the question remained the same. "Are you coming back?"

"No," she replied, swiping the tears from her cheeks.

A thousand arrows fell from the sky, searing into my soul. My breath hitched, and my lungs burned. This was it—the end of my life as I knew it. But, in that moment, with her shoulders hunched forward in defeat, I realized that it was the end of hers, too.

Why did that realization hurt more than the lifetime of loneliness that was awaiting me when the sun rose?

I lifted a hand and rubbed my chest, hoping to ease the mounting pressure threatening to overtake me. "Don't do this," I mumbled through the pain.

I wasn't sure who I'd meant that for though.

Was I chastising myself for having asked her to prolong the inevitable just because I wasn't ready to lose her yet? Or was I asking her to stay in this sham of a marriage for even one day longer?

Probably both.

"You'll be okay," she assured me, pushing to her feet and gathering her bag, complete with our Yorkie, Loretta, tucked in her mesh dog carrier.

My pulse quickened, nature's fight-or-flight finally kicking in. But I'd been in flight mode for entirely too long. There was no fight left.

I stepped into her path. "Elisabeth, please." I wasn't sure why I kept saying her name. I secretly hoped that it would snap her out of it, bringing her back to the reality of it all. But it was the reality that was killing us.

"I'll take off work tomorrow," I pleaded. "We can talk. Figure things out."

It was selfish. Completely and utterly selfish. But that was nothing new for me.

Her chin quivered as a steady stream of tears fell from her eyes. "Promise me something, Roman."

I would have promised her the entire fucking universe if it had made her stay one night longer. But who was I kidding?

We were over.

We both knew it.

"Anything," I whispered, reaching down to take her hand, desperate for the connection I didn't deserve.

"Remember to live." Her voice caught, and a silent sob tore through her.

Cupping the back of her head, I pulled her into my chest.

"I can fix this," I swore, but it was yet another lie. "We just need time."

Her shoulders shook as she cried in my arms. "We…we promised. We told him we'd live for him."

I closed my lids and clung to her tighter.

We were supposed to be fighting and screaming. That was what soon-to-be-divorced couples did. But that wasn't us. We didn't hate each other. Elisabeth was my soul mate on every level.

And she was paying the price for that.

Minutes later, the tears stopped and she backed out of my arms. I fought the urge to regain my hold, forcing her to stay. But her sad resolve as she hurried to the mantel and then to the door made it clear it'd be a wasted effort.

Never in a million years had I thought I'd be standing there, watching her walk away.

But, then again, I'd never expected her to have the urn of our only child cradled in her arm, either. A reminder of just how much I hadn't been able to give her. How much I'd *never* be able to give her.

My past, present, and future were walking out of my life, and I stood immobile as every fiber in my being screamed for me to drop to my knees and beg her to stay.

To take her in my arms and tell her that we'd figure it out.

To reclaim my life once and for all.

But how would that have helped *her*?

Staying wouldn't magically bring back her smile. Nor would it make her look at me with those bright-green eyes that made me feel as though I could conquer the world.

It wouldn't give me back the crazy woman who argued with her whole heart and loved with her entire soul. No. Those days were gone.

I'd lost that woman somewhere in the bitterness between grief and blame.

We'd been happy once.

But we'd gotten greedy and tried to start a family.

That was her future. Not mine. Regardless how desperately I longed to give it to her...and then selfishly take it for myself.

Sex. That's how babies are made. Children as young as elementary school are taught the simple biological facts of reproduction.

But what they never tell you is that, for one in six couples, having a baby goes a little differently.

For Elisabeth and me, it looked more like this:

Thirty-six months of crushing disappointment.

Three miscarriages.

Hundreds of tests our insurance company refused to cover because the inability to reproduce was not considered a health condition.

Countless tears.

Helplessness.

Failure.

Failure.

Failure.

Her broken heart.

My empty chest.
Thirty-seven thousand dollars we didn't have.
In vitro fertilization.
A sperm donor.
A handful of hope.
A positive pregnancy test.
Five months of utter bliss.
Earth-shattering devastation.
A funeral for a child I would never get to see grow up.
A job that became my only reprieve from reality.
And now…losing the only woman I would ever love.

I'd always been amazed by how much punishment a heart could take. I was broken, battered, and destroyed. And yet, much to my dismay, as I watched the front door close behind her, my heart kept beating.

CHAPTER ONE

ELISABETH

Two years later...

"Where are you taking me?" I laughed as Jon blindly guided me through the empty house.

His tall body pressed against my back while his callused hand covered my eyes.

"Promise me you won't freak," he said cautiously.

My body stiffened. "What did you do?" I fought against his grip, no longer willing to play his game.

He squeezed my hip to keep me in place then muttered, "Chill. And promise me."

"I will make no such promises. If you have to tell me not to freak, chances are I'm going to flip."

He chuckled. "You totally are."

I nudged an elbow back into his ribs. "This is not funny."

A grunt left his mouth, but it was followed by more laughter, which made it known that he disagreed.

Even with my objections, he continued to lead me through the carpeted rooms until my high heels clicked against tile.

"Okay." He paused. "It's not a big deal. So no more elbows. I can't hazard a broken rib. I've got work to do today."

I huffed, unwilling to agree for fear of making him a promise I couldn't keep. "Just get it over with already."

"Exactly what every man wants to hear," he teased and then dropped his hand.

I gasped, covering my mouth as I spun in a circle, taking in the newly renovated bathroom. "Oh my God. You...you did this?" I asked, moving toward the double vanity. "You did this?" I glided my fingertips over the smooth edge of the brand-new marble countertop.

He shoved his large hands into the pockets of his dirty jeans and shrugged. "You were never going to sell it with laminate countertops, Liz."

My mouth fell open when I saw the dual heads in the new shower, where a linen closet had been not even a week ago. "And a new shower?" I breathed, opening the door and stepping inside.

He smiled, leaning his shoulder against the wall and crossing his work boots at the ankle. "And a new shower," he confirmed.

I did a three-sixty and shrank when I saw the custom tile work I knew for certain he'd done with his own hands. "I...I can't pay you for this."

His deep-brown eyes narrowed. "I didn't ask you to."

"Jon," I murmured as I caught sight of the new molding butting up against the resurfaced ceiling.

His eyes followed mine. "Ah...I may have gotten carried away. But you know I can't half-ass a job. It's the eleventh commandment."

I shook my head, relief filling my chest at the same time guilt took up root in my stomach.

I'd been trying to sell that house for nearly six months, and with every passing week, it was costing me more and more to carry. I was barely keeping my books in the black as it was.

While my meager commissions as a realtor paid my monthly bills, they weren't enough to cover this place. If I wanted to continue flipping houses, I needed to get out from under it as quickly as possible. I'd dumped my life savings into that four-thousand-square-foot skeleton. And then, when that had run out, I'd taken out a loan from the bank and maxed out all of my credit cards.

It still wasn't enough.

I'd vastly underestimated how much it would cost to get that old Victorian back to something inhabitable—much less desirable.

As it stood, if I could get it sold, I'd be able to recoup my investments and possibly walk away with a few grand in my pocket to show for my hard work.

But, as appealing as the profits were, that wasn't why I loved spending my evenings covered in dust, working on whatever project I'd gotten in my head the day before. There was something about watching that house come alive around me that gave me a satisfaction I hadn't felt in years.

But, like most things in my life, I'd taken on too much too quickly.

I did the very best I could on my own, but I was only one person. As I'd learned from the fiasco while removing the fiberglass insulation, I wasn't necessarily qualified in all areas. Luckily, a friend of mine had put me in touch with Jon Hartley when I'd told her that I needed a contractor. He was a godsend who'd agreed to cut me a deal as long as he could work after five every night.

We'd quickly become friends, and his hourly wage had soon converted to beer and home-cooked meals.

He was fresh from a divorce and using any excuse to keep from going home to an empty house.

I understood him all too well. I was two years out and using one empty house to avoid another.

Jon and I had spent many nights in that old house together. But, in all of our time together, never once had any lines been crossed.

However, looking around at what had to be at least a ten-thousand-dollar bathroom renovation, I was starting to worry Jon's lines of friendship were slightly different than mine.

"Say something," he urged, walking over and then stopping directly in front of me. He wasn't touching me, but there was a certain intimacy at his proximity.

I sucked in a deep breath and swayed away in order to crane my head back. "This is too much. What the hell were you thinking?" I whispered.

"Honestly?" he asked softly. The corners of his mouth tipped up in a half smile that should have melted me. There was no denying that he was a good-looking man. But…he was *Jon*.

I bit my lip, praying for lies. I didn't want honesty. Not from him. Not about this.

"Jon," I breathed.

His hand found my hip and gave it a tight squeeze. "I was hoping that, if you sold this place, I could finally get some sleep."

I smiled, exhaling on a rush. But, when his eyes landed on my mouth, I felt no relief.

His other hand came up to my face, his thumb trailing back and forth across my cheek as he held my gaze. "And I was hoping, if you sold this place, you'd finally let me take you out and spend some time with you that doesn't require power tools."

I swallowed hard. *Shit. Damn.*

"You did this so you could ask me out?" I nervously toyed with my skirt. "That's an expensive bouquet of flowers."

He grinned. "You need out of this place, Elisabeth. And I'm not just talking the financials." Dipping his head forward, he brushed his nose with mine. "You're hiding."

"So are you," I countered, but my voice was weak.

"I was in the beginning. But, now, I only come back because of you." His lips swept mine, but I didn't reciprocate.

I wanted to though. Or, more accurately, I *wanted* to *want* to.

Jon was a good man. He'd slowly become my best friend over the last six months. And isn't that the foundation of a strong relationship? God knows that's not how it had been with Roman. And look where that had gotten us.

With Roman, he'd proposed approximately five hours into our first date. I laughed and told him he was insane. But those silver-blue eyes and that wicked grin made me breathless for the first time in my life. Our relationship was based on an overwhelming desire and an unexplainable need for one another.

It had been nearly two years since we'd last spoken, and I still felt the invisible strings binding us together. I couldn't explain my pull to that man any more than I could explain why I didn't feel it with Jon.

But maybe this was exactly what I needed. Something new and fresh but without the risk of the all-consuming kind of love I'd felt for Roman.

It didn't have to be like that with Jon. Hell, it had taken him months to even ask me out.

This was different.

Different could be good.

I *needed* different.

"Okay," I murmured, opening my lids with a newfound resolve.

"Okay?" A mixture of relief and hope danced in his gaze.

"Okay, I won't freak out about the bathroom." I paused and shyly glanced to the side. "And okay, I'll let you take me out."

A wide, white smile split his mouth. "Okay, then."

I abruptly stepped away from him and lifted a single finger in the air. "But! I'm paying you back for this."

"I don't want your money. I was trying to do—"

"No arguments. When I sell the house, I'm paying you back. I hope you kept receipts."

He smirked. "I thought you said you weren't going to freak out?"

"Yeah, well, I changed my mind. And you better agree to my caveat before I change my mind about you taking me to dinner at Harper's, too."

His tipped his head, his lips twitching as he asked, "Harper's?"

I motioned a hand around the bathroom. "You can't ask a girl out with a ten-thousand-dollar bathroom and not expect to take her to a fancy restaurant for dinner. That would be false advertising.

You've set the bar. Now, let's hope you live up to it."

He laughed, shaking his head. "Harper's it is, then. And it wasn't ten grand, but I'll let you pay me back for the materials *only*." He pointed over my shoulder. "Except for the shower. That's my gift to you."

I smiled and extended a hand in his direction. "Deal."

He stared at my hand for several seconds before clapping it and giving it a hard tug, dragging me in for a hug.

It was nice. His arms wrapped around me, securing me against his hard body as he stroked up and down my back.

So nice that I momentarily lamented the fact that I felt absolutely nothing in return.

It was just past seven when I got home from the old Victorian. Jon and I had stayed working on the guest bathroom that now looked like a hellhole compared to the master. Jesus, I couldn't believe he'd pulled that renovation off while I'd been out of town. I also couldn't believe I'd agreed to go on a date with him.

Shaking my head at myself, I tossed my keys in the basket and shut the front door. Loretta came barreling into the room as fast as her tiny legs would carry her.

"Hey, crazy girl," I cooed, bending down to give her the attention she demanded. It was rare that I went to the other house without her, but we'd just gotten back from a trip to Virginia to see my parents. "Oh, don't look at me like that. After an eight-hour car ride, we both needed a little space." I smoothed the short, gray hairs on the top of her head down.

She licked my face then wiggled from my arms. I put her back on the floor, and she immediately pranced to the back door, watching me over her shoulder the whole way.

"All right. All right. Go play," I said, sliding the back door open.

She'd missed her freedom while we'd been staying at my parents' place. It backed up to a lake, and I was terrified she'd get busy chasing one of the ducks, fall in, and drown. Poor pooch hadn't gotten a single minute off the leash over the last week.

After closing the back door, I began sifting through the stack of mail.

Bill. Bill. Bill. Advertisement. Chain letter?

I knew this because it had the words *chain letter* in handwritten block letters on the back of the envelope.

I smiled to myself as I ripped it open.

Dear Elisabeth,

I don't normally believe in things like this, but it's true! You must call your sister within the next thirty minutes or you will experience seven years of bad luck. Nancy Smith received this letter and she simply threw it away. The very next day, her hymen grew back, her cat ran away, and she slipped and fell in her bathroom.

Don't be like Nancy. Call your sister.

<3 Kristen

I didn't have a sister. And sure as hell not one as crazy as Kristen. But for the five years Roman and I had been married, I'd had her as a sister-in-law. I was an only child with parents who lived over five hundred miles away, Roman's family had become my own. His parents had been amazing, welcoming me into their lives with open arms. Never once had I felt like anything but their blood. But I'd lost them all the day I'd walked away from him.

It'd been weird not having them in my life at first, but a clean break was what we'd all needed. Or at least it was what *I'd* needed—starting anew without the memories of the past hanging over my head with every step.

For the first six months after our divorce, I couldn't stomach restaurants he and I used to frequent, much less keep a relationship with his family as they all carried on with their lives—with him.

However, the Leblanc family was a force to be reckoned with. His mom and his sister flat-out refused to accept the brush-off. In the beginning, they called daily, and when I didn't answer, they took to showing up at my house with wine and sushi. If I'm being honest, they were the only reason I made it through that first year.

As time passed, they slowly gave me my space, recognizing that moving on would probably involve another man. It hadn't. At least, not yet. Though, considering my date with Jon, that might be changing.

I reread her letter and settled on one of the wooden barstools that surrounded my large, granite island. It was a custom build—a gift from my parents when we'd first closed on our tiny starter house. I'd never forget the shock on Roman's face when the contractor had accidentally left the bill. My parents weren't loaded by any stretch, but I'd been born to them late in life, long after they'd given up the hopes of having children.

My father had spoiled the hell out of me when I was growing up. Fortunately—and unfortunately, depending on at what age you'd asked me—my mom was strict as hell, so I hadn't grown up to be a little shit. My father had been wrapped around my finger before I'd even come out of the womb, so when I was twenty-six years old, marrying a West Point graduate, Army Captain, and all-around amazing man, Daddy went over the top.

I swear I thought his smile would swallow his face as he placed my hand in Roman's on our wedding day. A day that had two hundred guests, a full dinner, an open bar, and an equally ridiculous price tag attached to it. But his little miracle only got married once, he'd said.

She apparently only got divorced once, too.

Fighting with my mind to stay grounded in the present, I grabbed the phone and dialed Kristen while I finished going through the stack of mail.

More bills. More junk mail. A Christmas card from an overachieving client seeing as we were still two weeks from Thanksgiving.

And then my body jerked as I lifted a letter from Leblanc Industries into my sights. My face flashed hot as ice formed in my veins.

I was tearing it open just as Kristen answered.

"You're alive!" she greeted enthusiastically.

"Son of a bitch," I snarled through clenched teeth as I pulled a check from the envelope.

"Shit. Did your hymen really grow back? I should have known better than to try my hand at the chain mail game."

"Your. Brother," was all I had to say.

She cursed under her breath. "What did Mr. Personality do now?"

Loretta began yipping at the back door, but I ignored her demands and headed straight for the fridge.

"Um…hello. What did Roman do?" Kristen called when I didn't immediately reply.

But I needed to get at least half of a bottle of wine in my system for this chat.

"I'm drinking," I explained.

She sighed, knowing exactly what that meant. "Shit. How much?"

I didn't bother with a glass. Instead, I yanked the cork out with my teeth and then drank directly from the bottle.

"More than the last one?" she asked when I didn't reply.

"Mmmhmm," I mumbled around the bottle.

She groaned. "Dad talked to him. I swear. We've *all* talked to him. He doesn't listen."

I swallowed the mouthful of Chardonnay, making a mental note that wine should *never* be chugged. But that didn't stop me from tipping it up once again.

Kristen waited patiently on the other end of the phone until I'd finished enough to gather my thoughts. I sucked in a deep breath, silently cursing myself for having given up the meditation bullshit I'd started when we were trying to get pregnant.

When I finally got my emotions under control, I very calmly

opened my mouth and then yelled at the top of my lungs, "He doesn't listen to anyone!"

So much for under control.

"I know," she replied somberly. "How much?"

"Two hundred thousand dollars."

"Fucking shit," she whispered.

I dug through my fridge, praying that a mini bottle of wine had gotten lost somewhere in the back behind the mass amounts of Tupperware filled with leftovers. I still hadn't mastered the art of cooking for one. A stray beer from God knows when was all I found, but I quickly twisted the top off and chugged it. Beggars can't be choosers on the hunt for intoxication in order not to kill your ex-husband.

"This has got to stop!" I said, slamming the beer on the counter. Foam bubbled from the top. "Shit. Shit. Shit!" I rushed to the sink, making it just in time to keep it from spilling.

"You okay?" she asked.

I ignored the question. I was in no way okay. I was, however, pissed off, and she was the only one around to listen. "I don't want his money. I didn't get a say when he paid off the house. But I'll be damned if I'm taking quarterly payouts."

She was quiet for a minute. And I knew what was coming. It was the same bullshit his mom had spewed when I'd first called to ask her to make him stop sending me checks over a year ago.

"He's trying to take care of you," Kristen whispered.

I barked a humorless laugh as angry tears pooled in my eyes. "Don't you dare feed me that crap. You know better than anyone that he could have taken care of me when we were married. Now, he's lost that right."

She sighed. "He started the company when y'all were still married. Technically, half of it should be yours."

"Technically?" I snapped, squeezing my eyes shut and gripping the phone so tight I feared it would break. "You want to talk technically, Kristen? Because, *technically,* Roman started that little shithole company less than twenty-four hours after Tripp died. *And, technically*, he ignored me for six months to get it up and running when I needed him the most. *Technically*, I was grief-stricken and still went back to work three weeks postpartum so he could quit his job and play scientist. *Technically*, that fucking company ruined my entire life. So, you know what? *Technically*, I don't want shit from Rubicon, Leblanc Industries, and, most of all, Roman." I stopped to catch my breath when a sob tore through me.

"Jesus Christ," she breathed.

"Just make it stop," I choked out. "It's been two *years*. Make. Him. Stop."

"Okay. Okay. Calm down. I'll talk to him again. I'll make Mom and Dad give it another go, too."

My hands shook as I pinched the bridge of my nose. "I'm trying to move on with my life, but I swear to God he won't fucking let me."

"You're right," she replied immediately, probably fearing another explosion. "I'll take care of it. I'll make it stop."

I swallowed hard and did my best to collect myself only to give up and polish the foamy beer off instead. "Thank you," I grumbled, tossing the bottle and the check into the trash can on my way to the back door to let Loretta back in. "And I'm sorry. I didn't mean to call you just to bitch about your brother."

"It's okay if you did, ya know. We all know he's a prick. It's not a newsflash. Besides, I miss you, and if you're only willing to call and bitch, I'll take what I can get."

A small smile played on my lips. "You know, I should have married you instead."

"Damn straight. I'm a freaking catch. It's a shame neither one of us swings that way."

The anxiety slowly ebbed from my system, and my smile grew. "Definitely a shame."

"Okay, now that we got the 'Roman is an asshole' out of our systems, what's new with you?"

God, I've missed Kristen.

I toyed with the ends of my hair and then mumbled, "Jon asked me on a date."

"What!" she shrieked so loud I had to pull the phone away from my ear. "Oh my God. What did you say?"

I sank down onto the stool and kicked my heels off. "I said, 'Okay.'"

CHAPTER TWO

Roman

It was past seven when I'd last checked the clock. Still at the damn office, I was beyond fed up with my so-called "meeting." With every intention of ending the bullshit once and for all, I extended my hand across my desk.

"I'm sorry to hear that."

Simon Wells, the seventy-something-year-old founding CEO of Defender Armor, stared blankly at my proffered hand. "Mr. Leblanc—"

A slow grin grew on my lips. "Simon, I believe we're way past the formalities. Please, call me Roman." I pushed my hand farther across my desk and leveled him with a menacing glare. "Then get the fuck out of my office."

His gaze jumped to mine, the corners of his eyes crinkling as they narrowed. "I'll repeat: This is my final offer."

It always was.

We'd been doing this song and dance for nearly two years. Ever since my team had created the most superior bulletproof material on the market. Rubicon, named due to its natural red coloring, was not only stronger than the competition but half the weight and thickness, making it easier to wear for long periods of time and conceal under uniforms during covert operations. In the last year, it had become the most sought-after product in the business.

I knew it.

And so did Simon Wells.

Which was precisely why he was sitting in my office for the tenth time in so many months, attempting to buy a bulk order at less than half of its current asking price.

Done with the games, I dropped my hand and stood from my chair. After fastening the top button on my suit coat, I strolled away while casually shoving a hand into the pocket of my slacks. I stopped at the door and gave him my full attention. "I hope to God this is your final offer, Simon. Because, if you come back with a number that low again, you may want to consider wearing some Rubicon of your own." Arching an eyebrow, I dared him to argue.

I should have known better. Simon lacked the ability to quit. It was annoying as fuck when you were across the table from him, but I suspected it was what kept his company on top for the last decade.

The muscles in his jaw ticked as he remained in his chair. "Cops are dying out there," he seethed through his clenched teeth.

I shrugged. "Yes. They are. Because they're wearing *your* vests. Maybe you should do something about that."

His fist slammed down on my desk as he shot to his feet. "You bastard! Have you no conscience? I know for a fact you made a deal with the military for half of what I'm offering." His hand shook as he raked it through his gray hair. "Sign the fucking contracts and let those officers dying on the streets go home to their families."

I tipped my head to the side but otherwise remained impassive. "And how exactly would you know what the bottom line on my contract with the military read?"

He squared his shoulders and attempted to regain his composure. A flicker of pride hit his eyes as he assumed he'd guessed correctly. "I'm not stupid, Leblanc. Word gets around."

He wasn't wrong. The body armor community was small.

For nearly fifty years, Kevlar had dominated the market. But, as new weapons and ammunition capable of penetrating the material began flooding our battlefields—and then, eventually, our streets—it was time for a change. Always the entrepreneur, I saw the literal and figurative gaping hole in the industry and pounced.

I wasn't a scientist though, and I quickly found myself nose-to-nose with the same brick wall most of the country was facing. Companies were pouring millions into research, knowing that the pot of gold at the end of the race was going to be astronomical.

I didn't have millions, but what I did have was a life I refused to face, a marriage I was hiding from, and the idea that dollar bills could fix it all. I threw myself into research, took a few investors on, and then hired the best team of scientists I could afford: two ex-cons with MIT degrees and my old Army NCO, who had been struggling to find a job in the civilian sector.

It wasn't exactly ideal.

But maybe that's why we were successful.

Desperation was one hell of a motivator.

For months, the four of us spent every waking moment huddled together in a makeshift lab, running on cheap coffee and fueled by hopes and dreams. Research was extensive, and failures were a daily occurrence.

Too heavy.

Too thick.

Too bulky.

Until Rubicon.

One day, I woke up miserable, alone, and broke.

The next, I woke up miserable, alone, and in the running for *Time* magazine's man of the year.

In a matter of months of going live with our product, Leblanc Industries had revolutionized the entire market—if not the world.

And it was exactly why Mr. Wells was beating my door down in order to save his own business. People weren't buying his second-rate products anymore, and as the days passed, Defender Armor fell deeper and deeper into the hole.

Now, he was hoping I could save his ass.

But I'd never been known as a philanthropist.

And his idle threats only served to piss me off.

He had no fucking clue what he was talking about when it came to my sales. Because, if he did, he'd have known that I sold Rubicon to the military for a quarter of what he was offering me. But the difference was the military wasn't using my product in flak jackets and then selling it at four times what they'd paid, which was exactly what Wells was planning to do.

The Army was using it to save lives. If I hadn't had employees who needed to be paid, I would have given it to the government at cost. I'd watched too many good soldiers die during my time in service not to want our men and women equipped with the very best. I would have loved to arm our police forces with it as well, but that did not mean giving my product away so another company could profit from it.

Unfortunately, I didn't have the facility readily available to make the body armor. And Wells didn't have my product. We were at a stalemate.

He couldn't afford me. And I couldn't go at it alone—at least, not yet.

The good news for me was that Rubicon had dozens of other uses that kept our bank accounts overflowing. And, as far as I knew, bulletproof vests were a rather niche market.

He needed me far more than I'd ever need him.

"This is ludicrous!" Wells growled.

I nodded matter-of-factly. "I agree. Now, get the hell out and don't come back unless you're ready to sign *my* contracts. No revisions."

His eyes burned into me as he finally moved toward the door, pausing just before leaving. "You know, I expected more from you. Former soldier, now CEO. I love a rags-to-riches story just as much as the next guy. It does the whole world well to be reminded that hard work pays off. But then there are men like you who disgrace us all by allowing the money and power to go to your head. It'd do you well to remember where you came from, because if you keep this up, I have a feeling you'll be back in that dingy garage lab sooner than you think."

My lips thinned, but I took a step forward, once again extending my hand for a shake. "Then perhaps it's good that I'll have you to save me a spot in the unemployment line."

The vein in his forehead bulged as he nearly vibrated with anger. "You—"

Turning, I gave him my back and strolled back to my desk. "Have a good day, Simon."

Moments later, the door to my office slammed and my whole body sagged.

"Jesus. Fucking. Christ."

The intercom on my phone buzzed immediately. "Mr. Leblanc, your sister is on line one. She's been calling for the last hour and says it's important."

Fucking great. I loved my sister, but Kristen had exactly two speeds in our relationship: bitch *at* me or bitch *to* me. And, considering we'd had dinner the night before and she'd bitched *to* me for nearly three hours about a dickhead she'd slept with and then he hadn't returned her calls, I figured her calling with something important meant I was going to get bitched *at*.

I groaned, preparing for whatever shitstorm she was about to drop at my feet.

"What's up, Kit-Kat?" I asked, after lifting the receiver to my ear.

"Oh, don't you dare 'Kit-Kat' me."

Yep. Bitch-at-me mode.

I switched the phone to my other ear and wedged it against my shoulder as I fired my computer up. "I'm seriously not in the mood to take your shit tonight. I've had an old man up my ass all fucking day. I really don't need you joining him."

"I just got off the phone with Elisabeth. She's getting remarried."

My body solidified, causing the phone to fall from my ear. Scrambling after it, I ignored the way my chest constricted.

I reminded myself that it was what I'd always wanted for her—to find someone who made her happy and could give her the things I never could. I just hadn't considered how much it'd hurt when it finally happened.

Slowly lifting the phone back to my ear, I licked my lips and opened my mouth, but not a single word escaped.

"Roman?" she probed.

I cleared my throat, strapping on the false bravado. "Good for her. This is important to me how?"

"You have to stop sending her checks. Her fiancé is livid about it."

Now, that made me smile. "Sounds like a personal problem. That money is hers. If her man has a problem with her past, I'd be happy to have a talk with him. Set him straight." Before I killed him.

I swear I heard her roll her eyes from across the line.

"Right," she said. "Just what every woman wants. The new guy having a chat with the old guy. *Especially* when the old guy is still in love with you."

"I'm *not* still in love with her," I growled. That would imply I'd ever been *out* of love with her. "And this is not my problem. So, if that's all you called to say, I need to get back to work." *Or, more likely, down a bottle of scotch.*

"Damn it, Roman. Okay. I lied. She's not getting remarried. After the shit you pulled, I'm doubting she ever will."

The second sucker-punch hit me square in the gut. I hated the idea of Elisabeth actually moving on with someone new, but I hated the idea of her being alone even more.

"Excuse me?" I bit out. "The shit *I* pulled? She left *me.* So get off your high horse and get to the point where I'm supposed to care right now. I'm not doing anything wrong by sending her money that is rightfully and legally hers."

"It's not legally hers! You made *certain* of that."

That I did. And I'd never forget the agonizing pain on her face when I'd told her that, in exchange for her fifty percent of Leblanc

Industries, she could keep everything else.

The house.

The furniture.

The cars.

The dog.

Tripp.

She had gotten our entire lives.

I'd walked away with a suitcase—and the yet-to-be-developed Rubicon.

"Yeah, well…I'm feeling generous. Besides, judging by that piece of shit she's still driving, she needs it."

"Aaaand…how the hell do you know what she drives?"

Because I've driven by our old house enough times over the last two years to wear potholes in the roads. "I saw it parked at the cemetery the other day."

She gasped. "You went to the cemetery?"

"For fuck's sake, don't sound so surprised. He was my son."

"Was he? Because, if I remember correctly, when she finally buried the urn last winter, you were nowhere to be found."

"I was working!" I defended. It was a lie. But there was no way I was copping to what I'd really been doing that day. Not even to my sister.

"You're always working, Roman! I had to make an appointment with your secretary a month ago so we could have dinner last night."

"Okay, so now you're bitching at me because I work too much?"

She drew in a sharp breath and then demanded, "Stop with the checks. She's finally getting her shit back together, and you're just making it harder. I swear to God, if you ever loved her, then you'll stop this bullshit right now. You signed the divorce papers two years ago, Roman. Let. Her. Go."

I closed my eyes and rubbed my temples. She was right, but it ate a hole through my soul to think about Elisabeth wanting for anything. Wife or not. Just because our marriage hadn't worked out didn't mean I didn't still care about her. But there was only so much I could do. I'd lucked out and been able to pay the house off, but only because she hadn't been able to afford to remove me from the deed yet. Short of dropping briefcases of cash on her porch, my options were limited.

I wasn't stupid. I knew she hadn't cashed any of the checks I'd mailed her. But there was a level of comfort in knowing that the next one was in the mail. She hated me, and she was stubborn as hell. But she was at least reasonable. If she got desperate, she'd swallow her pride and cash it. And that knowledge was the only reason I slept at night.

"I'll consider it," I lied.

"You'll consider it?" she yelled. "There's nothing to consider, Roman. Stop sending her the checks!"

I shook my head and pushed back from my desk. "Look, I need to go. See what you can do about getting her to cash that last one and I'll consider stopping."

"She's not gonna cash—"

"Then *convince* her," I ordered, standing up and digging my wallet and keys from my desk drawer. "She's shit at selling houses. I looked it up—she only sold four last year. Her specialty is interior design, not real estate. If I know her at all, she probably treats them like puppies and falls in love with each house, refusing to sell them to owners she deems unfit. Kit, she needs that money. We both know it."

She was silent for several beats, and then she let out a groan of frustration. "Were you dropped as a child?"

I grinned, knowing I'd won. Kristen was quite possibly the only person in the world who could convince Elisabeth to accept money from me. Hell, if Kristen got her mind set on it, she could negotiate world peace. The woman was pushy as shit. I credited my skills in negotiating business deals to having grown up with her. We hadn't had conversations around the dinner table—we'd had debates. And, judging by the ease in which she'd given in during this little spat, it meant she had agreed that I should have been sending Elisabeth that money before she'd even called.

"No more than you were," I smarted back.

"Shit. Maybe that's our problem," she whispered.

"Could be. Now, I *really* need to go. We'll talk soon."

"Yeah. Yeah. Yeah. I'll probably talk to your secretary first."

I shoved a hand in my pocket and smirked. "Probably."

CHAPTER THREE

Clare

"About time you showed up," Luke said, spinning in his chair as I walked into the gym with Tessa on my hip.

I peeked over my shoulder at the childcare room. "Yeah…uh…please tell me there's someone in there still."

"Yes, ma'am," he drawled, moving around the counter.

"Thank God," I breathed, my shoulders drooping in relief. "Sorry I'm late. I…um…lost track of time." I swallowed hard, fighting to keep the emotion out of my voice.

It was bad enough that my eyes were bloodshot from crying. I couldn't hide that any more than I could the gash in my hairline being held together with three butterfly bandages, but the last thing I wanted was to talk about it, so I needed to at least sound okay.

The gym was my escape. I hated working out as much as the next girl, but it was the only place I was able to erase the rest of my fucked-up life.

Tessa lunged from my arms, diving toward Luke.

He eagerly caught her and poked her belly, blowing a raspberry against her cheek. He was so good with her. Too good, probably.

I gently pulled her back into my arms and smoothed her blond curls down as I avoided his gaze. "Do you still have time for me tonight? I mean…I can always reschedule. Maybe I'll just work on cardio. I could use some time—"

He interrupted my rambling with a loud laugh. "Nope. Not happening. Give it up now, Clare. You're not getting out of leg day."

"Right. Leg day," I mumbled under my breath.

My whole body ached, my ribs were screaming just from holding Tessa, and the bruises on my thighs were probably already purple, but I would have spent my entire life doing legs if it meant I didn't have to go home.

My chin quivered as I finally looked up into his kind eyes.

He was almost successful in hiding his flinch. He sucked in a hard breath and blew it out on a curse. "Jesus, Clare," he whispered, aiming a comforting hand at my shoulder.

I ducked out of his reach. The gym might have been my sanctuary, but I wasn't free there. Someone was watching me.

Always watching.

"Legs. We should probably get started," I squeaked.

His handsome face hardened as he crossed his thick arms over his chest. "Maybe we should go to my office and go over your meal plan instead."

I shook my head and wiped a stray tear off my cheek with my shoulder. "We just made a new meal plan last week. It's leg day, Luke." I curved my lips up in something I hoped would pass as a smile. "We do legs on leg day."

The muscles on his jaw ticked as he stared at me, pity filling his eyes until he finally relented, raking a hand through his dark-blond hair. "Son of a bitch." He tipped his chin toward the childcare door. "Go. Get her settled. I'll meet you over at the mats."

Luke had been my personal trainer for three months, and in that time, he'd learned the gig. I could tell it killed him each time I came into the gym with fresh injuries or tear-stained cheeks. But he kept his opinions to himself and read between the lines, never pressuring me to spill my guts but asking just enough questions to remind me that decent people existed.

He was an incredibly nice guy. And, in another life, I would have even gone so far as to say he was sexy, too. But I didn't live in a world where I was allowed to focus on anything but keeping myself alive and my daughter safe. He was only filling in for Cindy until she got back from maternity leave. And, truthfully, Walt probably already wanted to kill him just for having contact with me, but I'd have done whatever I had to in order to keep him off my husband's radar. And that included leg day.

Walt was insistent that I keep myself in shape, but he hated when I spent too much time outside the house.

And he really hated it when I took Tessa with me.

I'd always thought he feared that, if I had her with me, I might never come back.

And he would have been absolutely correct.

There was nothing I wouldn't have done to get away from him.

Anything except actually leaving.

I'd tried that twice. And the scars of those nights still covered my body, both inside and out.

Turning him in to the police wasn't an option, either, though. He'd made sure I had more than enough of his sludge on my hands to put me away for life.

And then where would that have left Tessa? Alone with a monster.

I'd never wanted children with Walt, but he had been adamant that we start a family. And, as his wife, it had been my duty to provide him with one.

I'd cried month after month when those pregnancy tests had come back negative—they were tears of joy. I hated my life, and the thought of forcing an innocent child to join me in Hell seemed like a tragedy.

Unfortunately, Walt took our problems to the professionals.

I'd never forget how numb I felt as a reproductive endocrinologist smiled at me from across the desk, promising he'd help us.

I sobbed, hoping he couldn't.

After a round of in vitro fertilization, in which two embryos were transferred into my uterus, I prayed harder than ever before that it wouldn't take.

But I guessed God wasn't taking requests that day.

Nine months later, we welcomed Tessa into our lives.

It wasn't fair to her. But I'd have done it all over again. That little girl saved my life.

And, no matter how long it would take me, I'd find a way to save hers.

After dropping Tessa off, I stiffly made my way over to the mats.

"Change of plans. It's arm day," Luke announced.

I winced, lowering myself to the mat. "I appreciate the concern. But I assure you legs would be easier."

He frowned and then cracked his neck. "Okay. Then measurements. We haven't done your measurements yet this week. Let's go to my office and—"

"Enough!" I hissed. There were so few things within my control. I'd be damned if working out wasn't one of them. "It's fucking leg day, Luke. Can we *please* just stretch and get started?"

He blinked but otherwise remained unfazed by my outburst—until he whispered, "Clare…"

I spread my legs, folded over to one side, pressing my nose as close to my knee as my aching body would allow, and changed the subject. "I was sore yesterday. I should have taken Sunday off. Maybe we can implement yoga back into my workouts."

"Let me help you," he whispered, but we both knew he wasn't talking about stretches.

I barked a laugh. It felt just as hollow as it sounded. "I don't need a friend, Luke."

I needed a friend more than words could adequately express. But I wasn't going to find it in a personal trainer who had no idea what the hell he was getting into. And I sure as hell wasn't going to stand by while he fell down the rabbit hole trying to rescue me.

"Please. Do us both a favor and mind your own business."

The muscles at the base of his neck strained, but very slowly, he lowered himself to the mat beside me and began stretching, too.

Then he watched for over an hour as I cried through most of our workout.

It hurt like hell, but the most painful part was knowing that, when it ended, I'd be forced to get Tessa and head back home.

"There she is," he said as I pulled Tessa from her highchair.

I froze and set her back down, my entire body going on alert at the deep rumble of his voice.

He wasn't supposed to be there. His BMW wasn't in the driveway when I'd gotten home from the gym. And I hadn't heard him come in. Which meant he'd been in the house the whole time. *Oh God, what did I do that he could have seen?*

The fact that I hadn't known he'd been there sent chills down my spine. My job, as a mother, was to keep Tessa safe, and the biggest part of that was knowing where *he* was at all times.

I closed my eyes and sucked in a deep breath. My chin quivered as I plastered on a brave smile that had long since become the only one I possessed anymore.

"Hey," I whispered, turning to face him.

His green eyes lit as they landed on me, raking down my body and up again.

I'd changed after I'd gotten home. And not into the baggy T-shirt and worn-out pajamas I craved. I kept those hidden in the back of my drawer for when he was out of town. If Walter was home, I had to put effort into how I looked. Hair, makeup, jewelry. There was no such thing as comfort or lounging. He'd settle for nothing but perfection, and after our showdown earlier that afternoon, I couldn't risk pissing him off again. Not while Tessa was awake.

After my shower, in which my baby girl had pulled every toiletry I owned out of the cabinets, I'd tugged on a tight pair of white pants that accentuated my butt and a pink-and-white silk blouse I knew he loved. I'd donned the diamonds he'd given me at dinner on our one-year anniversary—not to be confused with the ones he had given me the next morning as an apology for having beaten me out of consciousness because he'd thought I had been flirting with the waiter. Though he often requested that set specifically. A quiet reminder. As though I could ever forget.

"Jesus, your face," he breathed, striding toward me.

Walter Noir was handsome. There was no denying that. I'd thought I was the luckiest girl in the world after he had seductively slid his business card across the counter at the seedy diner I'd been waitressing at when we'd first met. He'd been wearing a fitted, black suit that cost more than my car and a smile so beautiful that it hurt to look at. With his dark hair, green eyes, and olive skin, I was awestruck immediately. He was captivating in every sense.

Seven years later, I was the captive one, he struck more often than not, and the hurt was now in *my* smile.

"It's okay," I replied as he lazily stroked his thumb over the cut on my eyebrow.

He nodded in agreement then pressed his lips to my forehead and murmured, "How was the gym?"

I fought back a gag as he let the kiss linger while sliding his hands down my sides and over my ass.

"Great," I managed to squeak.

Thankfully, he stepped away, and my breath silently rushed out on a relieved sigh—until I realized where he was headed.

"Come here, baby girl," he said, stepping toward Tessa.

Panic ricocheted in my chest.

When Tessa had been a baby, she'd loved her father. And, by all accounts, he'd loved her, too. He was kind and attentive, worrying over her every peep. It was the same way he had been with me while we'd been dating. However, I knew love could turn into something ugly with Walt.

After all, he'd loved me once, too.

He had never once laid a hand on his daughter, though he'd hit me in front of her enough that she feared him all the same.

Over the last six months, things had changed with Tessa. She'd turned two and become aware of the world around her. That world being one where her father was an extremely dangerous man.

The crying any time he picked her up had started shortly after her birthday, and it infuriated Walt to the point that I spent my nights wondering how much longer she'd be safe under the same roof with him. I'd die before I let him hurt her, and as the days passed, I feared that might just be what it would come to. Time was running out. There was only so long that I could blame her reaction to him on teething or whatever mystery illness I could come up with.

"Mama," she cried, reaching out for me with both arms as he approached.

My pulse spiked as I stepped into his path.

"Can I talk to you for a minute?" I tried to distract him by placing my hands on the lean muscles of his pecs and pressing myself against his front.

He arched a menacing eyebrow. "Can I say hello to my daughter first?"

I stood on my toes and ghosted my lips across his. "Well, you could, but she skipped her nap today, so she's in a terrible mood. How about I put our girl to bed then properly apologize to you for this afternoon?"

His eyes heated as his fingers painfully gripped my hips. "What do you have in mind?"

With shaky hands, I reached behind me and took Tessa's tiny outstretched arm. She calmed instantly, so I kept my attention on Walt and seductively purred, "I'd rather hear what *you* have in mind."

He studied my face for a moment, his eyes inspecting the bruises I'd done my best to conceal with makeup. "You know, if you'd asked that question earlier, you wouldn't look like this."

"I know. Which is why I'm asking now."

He held my gaze for a minute longer then murmured against my mouth, "Get her in bed. I have a few calls to make first."

I nodded swiftly, jumping in surprise when he squeezed my ass.

He lifted his focus over my shoulder and cooed, "Night-night, princess." Then he turned his eyes back on me. "I won't be long. Go take a shower."

I'd taken a shower less than two hours ago. But that was the one thing Walt and I agreed on—I couldn't get clean enough. Not when his filth clung to me.

I kept the smile up as he left the room. Then, when he was out of sight, I sucked in a ragged breath and tamped down the overwhelming desire to vomit.

There was no time for that.

I had but one objective: keep Tessa safe.

I'd sacrifice my heart, my body, and my soul to accomplish it.

Tonight, it was my body.

CHAPTER FOUR

ELISABETH

I awoke the next morning to my phone screaming on my nightstand. Or maybe it was only ringing, but my head was splitting in half from the sound.

"Shit," I groaned when the night before came flooding back to me. I slapped my hand around until I found the offending device.

I answered only to silence it.

"Mrs. Leblanc?" the man on the other end questioned.

I threw my arm over my face and sighed. "It's Keller now, but yes, this is she."

"Oh...sorry about that. *Ms. Keller*. My name is Detective Rorke, and I'm with the Atlanta PD. I was wondering if you would be able to come by the station today and answer some questions we have for you."

"Me? You want to question me? I mean... I'm sorry. What kind of questions?"

He chuckled. "I'm sure it's nothing. Could you be here in an hour?"

An hour sure as hell didn't sound like it was nothing.

I slowly sat up, allowing my head time to adjust to being vertical again. "Uh...can you at least tell me what it's in regard to?"

"I'd rather we discuss this in person."

"In an hour? Right."

"As soon as you can get here, Ms. Leblanc," he added kindly.

"Keller," I corrected then sighed. "I'll be there as soon as I can."

"Perfect. See you soon."

As he hung up, I jumped out of bed and rushed to the shower.

I shouldn't have rushed.

Three hours later, I was still sitting in an empty hallway at the police station, no closer to finding out why I'd been brought in than I had been on the phone.

When I'd arrived, Detective Rorke hadn't been there, so a uniformed officer escorted me to a room that screamed *Law & Order* more than it did a friendly chat.

Staring at myself in what I was positive was a two-way mirror, I racked my brain for what they could possibly need to question me about. With not so much as a speeding ticket on my record, I was a rule-follower by nature. Trouble and I did not coexist.

After about an hour, a different officer came in and escorted me to a chair in the hallway. More than once over the last two hours, I'd stopped people walking by, trying to get to the bottom of why I was there. But, each time, I'd been shut down by a tight smile and some variation of, "I'm sure it's nothing."

But, as my eyes lifted and I saw Roman *fucking* Leblanc entering the mouth of the hallway, flanked by two men in suits, I knew it was definitely *something.*

I hadn't seen him in the two years since the divorce, but it could have been a thousand years and I wouldn't have forgotten him.

However, with that said, I didn't exactly recognize this man, either.

The man I'd fallen in love with didn't parade around at ten a.m. on a Thursday morning in a suit. Hell, my Roman had argued about wearing one to his own wedding. Regardless of where we had been heading, fast food or a funeral, you wouldn't have caught him in anything but jeans, a T-shirt, and a tattered ball cap.

This guy, though, was wearing that power suit as if it had

been custom-made for him. Which, judging by the way it hugged his every muscular curve, it probably had been.

I narrowed my eyes as he strode down the long hallway. It was definitely him, but not even the posture matched the man I'd vowed my life to. My Roman smiled with his whole body and could charm a popsicle from a toddler with nothing more than a wink. He was approachable, funny, laid-back, and gorgeous beyond all belief.

As I raked my eyes over him, I realized that, much to my dismay, the gorgeous part had remained intact, even if the hard set of his jaw and the resolute square of his shoulders tarnished it.

Power and money swirled in the air around him with every step.

I shouldn't have been surprised. I knew he was successful now.

I'd seen the magazine covers.

I'd heard our old friends talking.

I'd received his checks.

This was the new Roman, and it was so fucking wrong that my heart went into mourning all over again.

Suddenly, his silver eyes landed on me and, with a whoosh, the air became too thick to breathe. It was okay because my breath was trapped in my lungs, unable to escape around the newly formed lump in my throat.

He blinked for several seconds. Then his shoulders relaxed and the façade dissolved, leaving the man I had fallen in love with beautifully exposed in front of me.

The hairs on the back of my neck prickled the same way they had when we'd first met.

Back then, I'd mistaken it for love at first sight.

Now, I took it as a warning.

"Why are you here?" I accused in a low voice.

Cocking his head to the side, he returned, "Why are *you* here?"

His words hypnotically washed over me. He'd always had that effect on me. No matter how wound up I'd get, Roman could calm me with nothing more than a touch or a whisper.

Until the day he'd abandoned me.

I focused on that memory as I shot back, "I have no clue. But I'm starting to think it's probably your fault."

The corner of his lips twitched in the most annoying—and sexy—way possible. He pressed his left hand to his chest and feigned, "My fault?"

My mouth dried as the ache in my chest clawed up my throat.

His ring finger was bare.

It wasn't as though I'd expected him to be wearing his wedding ring after all this time. It was just that I'd never seen him without it. I'd given Roman that cheap gold band twenty-four hours after we'd met, when we'd gotten married at the courthouse without telling a single friend or family member.

He never took it off.

Never.

He'd still been wearing it as he'd walked out of the courtroom the day our divorce was finalized.

I swallowed hard and dropped my gaze to the floor. I couldn't do this. Not today. Maybe not ever. There was a reason I'd left him. This shit shouldn't still hurt.

And yet, it did. Agonizingly so.

"Yes, your fault," I whispered, but there was no resolve in my voice even to my own ears.

Following my lead, he gentled his voice. "I have no clue why I'm here. And, quite honestly, I'm more confused now that you're here, Lissy."

The familiar nickname made my head snap up.

As a woman with the name Elisabeth, I had no less than a dozen nicknames. Beth, Liz, Ellie, Biz, Lizzy, Bee, Elle… I'd had them all over the years. Friends, family, people I'd just met—they all abbreviated my name.

But the difference was that Roman pronounced the S.

"I'll take that," Roman said, snatching my driver's license from my hand after I'd been carded for wine on our first date. "Elisabeth with an S, huh?" He smiled, causing my heart to nearly pound out of my chest.

My cheeks must have flashed a million shades of pink, because his smile grew.

I nodded. "My parents wanted to make absolutely sure I never got one of those personalized pencils at the elementary school book fair. They're evil people like that." I shrugged. "Mission accomplished."

He blinked at me for several seconds, sporting the most breathtaking grin I'd ever experienced. Then, finally, he reached across the table and took my hand. There weren't sparks the way they flourished in romance novels or movies.

No. What I felt when Roman Leblanc took my hand was more than any poet, author, or screenwriter could describe.

It was the culmination of every emotion I'd ever experienced. The high of happy, the depths of sad, and the spine-tingling chill of ecstasy.

He continued grinning at me as my world flashed from black and white to screaming color all around me.

Then he smirked and replied, "They sound horrible, Lissy."

Not Lizzy.

Lissy.

I'd lived twenty-six years of life before that night.

But, suddenly, I was alive for the very first time.

I knew absolutely nothing about that man.

But I knew he was mine.

And I was meant to be his.

As I snapped back to the present, anger spiraled through my veins. "Don't call me that," I hissed.

He shoved his hands into the pockets of his pants and rocked forward on his toes, but he issued no apology. He just stood there arrogantly grinning at me.

Such was life with Roman Leblanc.

And, as it turned out, life *without* Roman Leblanc, too.

"Mr. and Mrs. Leblanc," a man's voice called from the end of the hall.

Roman and I both looked in the direction as an older man with salt-and-pepper hair and a Santa Claus belly approached. "I'm Detective Rorke. I apologize for your wait, Mrs.—"

"Ms. Keller," I corrected before he had the chance to go any farther. Standing in the hall with Roman was bad enough without someone else joining him in his little name game from the past.

"Right. Sorry," he said, turning sideways in order to slide past Roman. "Let's move in here." He opened the door to the room I'd originally been in before they'd relocated me to the hall.

I stood and waited for Roman and his legal entourage to enter the small room, but he swept an arm in a grand gesture for me to go first.

Always the fucking gentleman.

I rolled my eyes and walked inside. Though I did it with attitude, so flounce might be more accurate.

I heard Roman's deep throaty chuckle as I passed.

I wanted to give him hell, but more than that, I wanted this to be over with. So I kept my mouth closed and settled in a metal folding chair on one side of the table, being sure to give the chair next to me a hard shove, scooting it to the end farthest away.

Roman didn't react, but I was positive he'd noticed.

"I see you brought your lawyers, Mr. Leblanc," Rorke stated, opening a manila folder like he had all the time in the world.

Roman crossed his arms over his chest. "I was called to a police station with two hours' notice. For questioning in a matter I wasn't informed about. You'll have to excuse my caution." Judging by his tone, he didn't want to be excused at all.

What I took from that exchange was that Roman got two hours' notice. Meanwhile, I had barely been able to speed-shower, choke a bagel down, let Loretta out, and then apply makeup in the rear-view mirror on the way over.

I secretly hated him even more.

Rorke nodded, but he didn't seem placated. "Innocent men rarely travel with *two* attorneys," he said, poking the beast.

Roman's eyes darkened as his face turned to stone. "Good cops rarely drag innocent people in for questioning without allowing them time to find proper representation." His eyes pointedly flashed down to me then back to Rorke. "So, yes, I do travel with two attorneys, but now, I only have *one.* Mr. Kaplin is with me and Mr. Whitman will now be representing Elisabeth *Keller.*" He spat my last name, but that wasn't what caused me to jerk in my chair.

"What? No, he's not. I don't need *representation.*" And I sure as hell didn't need to be billed whatever hourly wage allowed Mr. Whitman to buy that expensive—albeit stylish and well-fitted—suit.

"Shut it, Lis," Roman snapped, never dragging his eyes off Rorke.

Oh. Hell. No.

I snapped right back, "You did not just tell me to shut it."

Roman continued his stare-down with the detective as he called out, "Whit, advise your client."

Whit inched over to me. "Don't say anything. I'll answer all questions for you."

"You will *not*!" I replied. "We just met. You don't *know* the answers."

He arched a challenging eyebrow and dragged a chair over to sit next to me. Then he shot me a cocky grin and said, "I know the law, which means, in this room, I know *all* the answers."

My mouth fell open, and I glanced back up at Roman.

He smirked at me, and I'll be damned if that didn't cause an unwanted, but very real, flutter in my stomach. *Shit!*

"I *don't* need an attorney," I informed the entire room.

"Well, now, you have one in case you do," Roman returned.

"I don't *need* an attorney, *Roman.*"

His lips thinned as he scowled. "Well, now, you *have* one in case you do, *Lissy*."

I clenched my teeth and ground out, "Stop calling me that."

Vaguely, I heard Detective Rorke clear his throat, but just as quickly, Roman's hand went up in the air, snapping to silence him. Then, bending at the waist, my ex-husband leaned down until he was only inches from my face and growled, "Sure thing, *Lissy*."

Yes. *Growled.* Like some sort of man-cub raised by a pack of bears.

So, clearly, I had to ask, "Did you just growl?"

The muscles on his jaw ticked as he righted himself and focused on the ceiling, muttering, "Jesus fucking Christ."

That wasn't an answer, so I pushed. "Did you *seriously* just growl at me?"

He groaned and lowered his gaze to mine, stating incredulously, "You're at a police station for questioning. I offered you a lawyer. God forbid."

My chair protested against the tile floor as I pushed away from the table and up to my feet. "I don't *want* or *need* a lawyer. I haven't done anything wrong." I was moving toward him when I suddenly remembered that we were, in fact, in the middle of a police station with at least three other people looking on—maybe more if you counted whoever could be on the other side of the two-way mirror.

Shit.

Iced by my good manners, I sucked in a calming breath. "What I do *want* is to get whatever mess you created over with so I can go home."

Roman barked a laugh. "Aaand...we're back to this being my fault."

Rorke took that moment to join our conversation. "Nobody needs a lawyer."

All eyes swung to him.

"At least, not yet," he finished. "Now, if you two will *please* just sit down and shut up, I'll explain why I asked you to come down today."

CHAPTER FIVE

ROMAN

Elisabeth Keller.

Fucking Keller.

There were no words to convey how I'd felt when I'd seen her sitting in that hallway. Time had frozen with a single glance.

She appeared tired, too thin, and her hair was still damp on the ends, which caused it to frizz out in a way I knew she hated. But, even with all of that, she was still the most beautiful woman I'd ever laid eyes on. However, that probably had more to do with the fact that she was in my veins than it did her actual appearance. But I'd never, not once, seen Elisabeth with just my eyes. My heart was just as much a part of the way I viewed her as my retinas.

And still, after all this time, my body reacted to her the same way it always had—full alert.

Atlanta was a big city, but in the last two years, I'd never seen her once. And, in the beginning, I'd tried to accidentally-on-purpose run into her more times than I'd ever admit.

Of all the places to find her, a hallway at Atlanta PD was the one location I'd never considered.

Elisabeth Keller's idea of trouble was pocketing extra packets of sugar at the coffee shop. And, even then, she would have felt guilty, tossed and turned all night, and then promptly returned them the next day.

But there she sat, all wide-eyed innocence staring at me as though she were the one seeing an oasis in the middle of the desert.

Though, as far as I was concerned, she was the mirage. A woman I needed more than water and yet couldn't reach no matter how hard I tried—at least, not anymore.

Then she had to go and catch an attitude with me. It should have pissed me off. She had no right to come out of the gate swinging, blaming me for trouble that didn't exist. But, the moment she let loose, it only made me nostalgic.

It was that same attitude that had made me fall in love with Elisabeth approximately one hour into our first date.

"They sound horrible, Lissy," I said after a story about her parents. It was a joke, but her entire face lit.

And, with just one glance, it lit something inside me, too.

I'd wanted to strip her naked when she'd opened her front door, but it wasn't until we were at dinner that I knew I'd face the wrath of a thousand gods just to make her smile.

And worse, I'd burn the world around us in order to keep it aimed at me.

I was lost in her eyes when the server asked if we were ready to order.

I quickly said yes.

She quickly said no.

She adorably narrowed her eyes.

I cocked my head and smirked.

Then I made the grave mistake of ordering for her.

My innocent angel disappeared, but the independent woman on the other side dug her hooks into me even deeper.

Using her menu to block her mouth from the waiter's view, she whisper-yelled, "I'm not eating chicken parmesan!"

"You said it sounded good a minute ago," I defended.

Her chin lifted, and she flashed her eyes around the restaurant. "It did at the time, but you have no idea how I eat it!" Again with the angry whispering.

I loved that she was standing her ground. But I especially loved that she was so obviously mortified that she was doing it in the middle of an Olive Garden, where people might possibly overhear her—including the waiter, who was watching our chat with subtle entertainment.

Mine wasn't so subtle. Therefore, I smiled huge and asked, "There's more than one way to eat chicken parmesan?"

"There is for me." She nodded confidently then tucked her long, blond hair behind her ear.

God, she was beautiful.

I sat back in my chair and stared as something inside me broke. I was twenty-seven years old. I'd had my fair share of dates and women, but not one of them had held my interest for any length of time. However, for some inexplicable reason, in a matter of minutes, I knew I wanted to argue with Elisabeth—with an S—Keller about chicken parmesan for the rest of my life.

"Oh, please, enlighten me, then," I teased.

She rolled her eyes then once again glanced around us, surveying our possible audience. "That's a second-date meal," she hissed. "Tonight, I'll have the soup and salad."

I twisted my lips. "That's it?"

"That's it," she confirmed.

I looked up at the waiter. "She'll have the chicken parmesan. Bring it out every possible way a person can order it. Pull up another table if need be."

"Roman, no!" She slapped at my arm, but I caught her hand and intertwined our fingers.

I held her gaze until the waiter walked away, at which point I seductively whispered, "Lissy, yes."

Her cheeks flushed, and then she gave me the innocent angel back. Her eyes darted to our hands before shyly sliding away. "That's a ton of food. And trust me, I'm a whack-a-doo. They'll never get it right."

That was exactly what I'd hoped. "Then I guess we'll just have to stay here until they do."

I'd have given up every possession I owned just to go back in time to that Olive Garden with her.

Even knowing how it would end.

Maybe especially knowing how it would end.

But I'd have given it all for one night where chicken parmesan was our only obstacle.

"Mr. Leblanc," Detective Rorke prompted, forcing me back to the present.

I closed my eyes and shook the memories off. "Right." I motioned for Whit to evacuate the seat next to Elisabeth.

He moved swiftly, as though he knew that his future employment depended on it.

Elisabeth scooted her chair to the left, huffing as I followed.

"Okay," Rorke started, once again digging through his file. "We just have a few questions about Peach City Reproductive Center." He kept his head down but glanced up from his papers.

"Oh, okay," Elisabeth said, knotting her hands in her lap. "We, um, did in vitro fertilization there. It was—"

A stabbing pain hit me in the gut. "Is this about a bill?" I asked roughly, cutting her off. "I paid them years ago. If anything is still outstanding, I'll personally take care of it today."

Rorke faced me, but he watched Elisabeth from the corner of his eye. "I'm no collections agency, Mr. Leblanc. Ms. Keller, please continue."

Elisabeth's sad eyes lifted to his. "It was a good place is all I was going to say."

He jotted something on the paper in front of him. "And you were under the care of Dr. Fulmer during this time. Is that right?"

"Yes. He was amazing. Very understanding. Caring. Compassionate."

"And did this procedure with him produce a child? In vitro, I mean?"

Her green eyes fluttered closed as anguish carved her smooth, white skin. "Yes, but—"

I couldn't take any more. "What is this about?" I barked, desperate to regain the control I'd never had during the actual IVF process. Or in the years that followed, leading up to that very moment when I was being forced to watch Elisabeth relive the most painful experience of our lives.

"Just a few simple questions," Rorke said, all but dismissing me from the conversation.

I slammed my palm on the table and rose to my feet. "Discussing my son is not simple for anyone in this room but you."

"Roman!" Elisabeth scolded me for my outburst. But I'd have taken whatever heat she had to offer if it kept her from getting lost in the past.

I remained focused on Rorke. "Either tell me what this is about right fucking now or this interview is over."

"A son?" His eyes flashed wide, cutting to the mirrored wall before landing back on me.

"Tripp," Elisabeth breathed, pulling Rorke's eyes back to her. "He died within an hour of being born." She looked up and offered me a weak smile. "It's okay. I can do this."

Fan-fucking-tastic. She's reassuring me.

I bit the inside of my cheek and gripped the back of my neck.

"Son of a bitch," he mumbled under his breath. "And you didn't try again?"

"None of our embryos made it to freeze," she replied.

He once again cursed then steepled his fingers under his chin. "It's my understanding you can do another cycle for more embryos. How many cycles did you do with Dr. Fulmer?"

I sucked in a sharp breath, and Elisabeth shifted in her chair, crossing then uncrossing her legs.

"We didn't have the money for another fresh cycle," she admitted. "We had to clean out our savings and then borrow the rest from my parents to pay for the first one." She paused and then blurted, "Besides, Roman and I divorced six months after Tripp was born. There was no time. Even if there was money."

Wasn't that the damn truth.

Time was never on my side. Only months after our divorce, Rubicon had been created. If only she and I had stuck it out a few more weeks, I could have filled our house with a basketball team of children. She could have stayed pregnant for the rest of her natural life if that's what she'd wanted, and I would have happily lay on the floor, acting as a human jungle gym for each and every one of those kids, content for the rest of my life knowing I had given her that.

We could have been happy…again.

Fucking time.

"Was he buried?" Rorke asked, hope filling his eyes.

"Easy," I warned.

Elisabeth answered behind me. "Cremated."

"Dammit." Rorke closed his eyes, rubbing them with his thumb and his forefinger before opening them again. "I'm sorry, Ms. Keller, Mr. Leblanc. I'm sure this is a hard topic for both of you, so I'm going to be blunt here. We were unaware your son had passed away. We were hoping…" He stopped and trained his unfocused gaze on the door. "We were hoping to get a DNA sample from your son."

"Why?" Elisabeth and I asked in unison.

He leaned forward and lifted his pen off the table, tapping it to his chin as he answered. "We have reason to believe that Dr. Fulmer or one of his technicians accepted a bribe and possibly switched embryos in the lab. Your name was brought up during the questioning of a possible witness."

Elisabeth reacted immediately, reaching up and clamping my hand in hers, squeezing hard as she gasped.

Slowly sinking down to the chair, I rumbled, "I'm sorry. What did you just say?"

Rorke continued to explain. "I honestly can't get into specifics, as we are still looking into all avenues. But we were refused the warrants for DNA on the child in question due to a lack of evidence."

Elisabeth's hand flew up to cover her mouth. "The child?"

His shoulders rolled forward in defeat, but he nodded. "Yes, there is a possibility one of your embryos survived. But the supposed birth father has denied us all access. We were hoping to take the back door on this one, proving foul play based on your child's DNA. Then get the warrant once and for all."

I was vaguely aware of Whitman and Kaplin joining the conversation, tossing Rorke a million different questions laced with legal jargon, but my mind was spinning.

Bribes?

Embryos switched?

A child?

Our child?

It was a Thursday morning. I was supposed to be in a meeting with my marketing team, and instead, I was sitting in a police station, next to my ex-wife, finding out that we might have a child laughing, smiling, and breathing on Earth.

What the fucking hell was going on?

I finally swung my head to Elisabeth. Her face was pale, and tears streamed down her cheeks. Without thought or consideration, I snaked an arm out and looped it around her shoulders, pulling her into my side. She came all too willingly, crashing into my chest just before sobs overtook her.

CHAPTER SIX

ELISABETH

It was dark outside when I woke up on my couch. My heels were gone, but I was still in the same skirt and top I'd pulled on in a hurry that morning.

Police station.

"Oh God," I croaked.

I wasn't sure how I'd gotten home, but my feet must have moved at some point, even though my mind was still rooted in the middle of that police station.

Embryos switched.

"Oh God," I croaked.

Then I heard his voice in my kitchen.

"Cancel everything tomorrow and forward all of my calls to Glen. Yeah. No." Pause. Sigh. "I don't know when I'll be back. Let's just play this by ear."

Roman.

"Oh. God." I groaned, dragging my body up to the sitting position. My head objected, but I guessed that's what you got when you cried yourself dry of tears.

A child.

"Oh God," I breathed, dropping my face into my hands and settling my elbows on my knees.

"You're awake," Roman said, stating the obvious.

Out of the corner of my eye, I caught sight of his bare feet carrying him my way.

I closed my eyes and smarted, "You're in my house."

The couch sank beside me. Then I felt his hand on my back.

His strong, kind, gentle, *soothing* hand. *Damn it.* I screwed my eyes shut.

"How ya feeling?"

"Like I woke up in the Twilight Zone."

He chuckled. "Not far from the truth."

I scrubbed my face then did my best to smooth my sleep-mussed hair down. "Thanks for, um…bringing me home."

His hand moved up to the base of my neck, where it squeezed, massaging with his thumb before repeating the process on the other side. I lacked the energy to fight it and a pleasure-filled moan escaped my throat.

He chuckled again. "I ordered takeout."

His torturous hand continued kneading my neck, leaving me unable to argue. I hadn't eaten since earlier that morning. Food, even takeout, actually sounded amazing, and my stomach growled in agreement.

However, just as quickly, I lost my appetite.

"What the hell happened today?" I sighed listlessly.

His hand spasmed. Then it stilled for a brief second before continuing. "I don't know. But my people are looking into it."

Great.

Roman had *people* now.

And they were looking into the possibility that a child with my DNA was out there, sharing a world with *other people* I did not know.

Forget food. I needed to go back to sleep and hopefully wake up in a world that made sense.

"Oh God." I moaned, finally turning to face him. "Roman," I started, but the words froze on my tongue when I got my first real look at him—up close and personal.

He was still wearing his suit pants, but he'd shed the jacket and the button-down at some point since we'd arrived home. A simple, white undershirt clung to the hard ridges of his chest, the sleeves stretching mercifully around his thick biceps. I'd been wrong earlier that morning when I'd thought he was still just as gorgeous as he'd always been.

He was better.

And, a few years ago, I hadn't known that was possible.

He no longer sported the sexy stubble he'd insisted on growing after he'd gotten out of the military. Now, he was clean-shaven, not so much as a five-o'clock shadow marring his handsome face. His once barbershop-buzzed, dark-blond hair now bore the marks of a stylist—trimmed with precision on the sides, leaving the top longer and slightly unruly.

It all looked good on him.

Very good.

But he could look as mouthwateringly beautiful as he wanted to and it wouldn't change the man inside. And I couldn't risk getting tangled in the façade again.

Just because Roman was vowing his support right now, having his *people* look into things, didn't mean he'd stay to see this clusterfuck through. I'd watched him walk away too many times to willingly sign myself up for that again.

Besides, technically, he had no reason to be there.

And worse, no reason to stay.

During our long journey to have a child, we'd discovered that Roman produced very few sperm, most of which were abnormal. Doctors had been optimistic, saying that intrauterine insemination (IUI) would be our best bet. But, three miscarriages later, they changed their tune. The same day we were told that our last hope was in vitro fertilization (IVF), it was strongly suggested that we use a sperm donor. I did not deal with this news well.

First off, I knew we couldn't afford IVF. While we lived comfortably, we didn't have thirty to forty grand just lying around.

We'd dropped most of our savings into our house when we'd gotten married and thought nothing of it. There had always been time to worry about savings later. We'd had each other. I'd like to say we were young and dumb. But what we really were was in love and eager to start a life together. A house seemed like the logical first step. We had no idea the financial burdens we'd be facing in the future. But, then again, making a baby with the man you loved was only supposed to cost a night of passion and an orgasm.

Secondly, the idea of having a child using donor sperm felt wrong on so many levels. I had a man I was madly in love with; I wanted *his* babies. Ones with his silver eyes and his mischievous smile. Little girls with his big heart and his thick lashes. I didn't just want kids; I wanted *his kids.*

I stormed out of the doctor's office that afternoon, pissed at a universe, who'd stolen the future we'd planned together, but I hadn't made it to my car before I was wrapped in his strong arms. He held my face in his neck while whispering promises that we'd find the money.

But money couldn't fix us.

A truth Roman had never fully grasped.

In the end, he was the one who insisted we move forward with a sperm donor. He smiled a gorgeous grin and told me, "Biology doesn't make families, Lissy. Love makes families."

Four months later, ten of my eggs were fertilized with a donor's sperm.

And, now, Roman was sitting on my couch, years after love had failed us, with only the biology of it all remaining.

I was the only thing tying him to this mess. I needed to cut him loose of his responsibilities once and for all.

Shifting away from him, I blurted, "I can handle this from here on out. No need for you to get involved."

His head snapped back. "Excuse me?"

"I just mean.... You know. You can go. I'll get back in touch with Detective Rorke and handle it from here. This isn't your problem."

His hand fell away from my back as he stared at me for several seconds. "This isn't my problem?"

"Well…no. This is *my* problem." I instinctively scooted over an inch, although I wasn't exactly sure why. Roman would never hurt me, but the pissed-off vibe radiating from his pores was suffocating.

He ominously swayed toward me. "*Your* problem?" His silver eyes darkened to a frightening shade of charcoal.

I leaned away. "I just meant—"

"Yeah, Lis. *Please*, tell me what you *just meant*."

"I meant…" I carefully studied his face before I found the courage to say, "We aren't together anymore?" It came out as a question. "I just figured—"

I stopped talking when he moved closer, one hand on the back of the couch, the other on the arm, caging me into the corner.

"Say the words," he ordered on a pained whisper.

"I think you should leave."

"Not the words."

"Back up," I pleaded, but he got closer. Mere inches separated our bodies—less separated our mouths.

His breath breezed over my skin as he ground out, "*Still* not the words."

My pulse spiked at the same time my mouth dried.

He was too close.

Way, way, way too…

I closed my eyes.

He was wearing a different cologne, but the underlying smell of clean soap and shampoo was still my Roman, and the smell assaulted my olfactory senses at full force. But it was the subtle hit of beer on his breath that transported me back in time to a moment that seemed as though it had been nearly a million years ago, and it felt as though it had been even longer than that.

After numerous plates of chicken parmesan—all of which were wrong—Roman and I went out dancing at a hole-in-the-wall salsa bar downtown. Neither of us knew how to salsa, but we both made fools of ourselves trying to learn. I proved myself to be a quick study. Roman not so much, but he never quit. He also never took his eyes—or his hands—off me.

On the way home, we stopped at a food cart to pick up a two a.m. snack. Roman was almost as drunk as I was, and neither of us could stop laughing long enough to order.

"Two gyros. Extra Z. Add feta," he finally got out, blindly waving a twenty at the cashier. He pulled me into his arms and kissed the top of my hair.

"Oh my God, you ordered for me again." I feigned horror, playfully pushing him away.

He grinned with pride. "Sure did."

"And what if I don't like gyros?"

He swayed toward me, gliding his hand up the back of my neck and into my hair. "Everyone likes gyros."

"Not everyone," I laughed only to be silenced when he tilted his head down and brushed his nose with mine.

He hadn't kissed me yet. I wasn't sure what the hold-up was, because God knows I'd given every signal I could think of—including a few I'd invented on the fly.

He dropped his forehead to mine and stayed close as I silently willed him closer.

When his mouth never made contact, I licked my lips and whispered, "I don't eat lamb."

His other arm hooked around my waist to bring our bodies flush. The intoxicating scent of clean sweat and beer invaded my senses. I closed my eyes and breathed deeply, holding it in for as long as my lungs would allow, engraining it into my memory so I could never lose it—lose him.

As I exhaled, I felt his breath at my ear.

"It's a food cart, Lissy. I assure you these are beef."

It wasn't a sexy statement by anyone's standard, but it still made my knees weak.

Pressing my breasts against his chest, I raked my nails up his back. Then I whispered my own unsexy reply, "Oh. Okay, then. I like beef."

He stared at me for several beats, his eyes heating despite our ridiculous conversation.

My chest heaved impatiently.

Kiss me.

As though he'd heard my silent plea, his face split into a gorgeous grin.

A nanosecond later, in front of a food cart, while a dozen hungry drunks stumbled around us, Roman Leblanc changed my life.

But it wasn't with a kiss.

"Marry me," he breathed.

My eyes popped open.

"Say the words," he growled into my face.

"Roman, please." I pressed a hand to his chest and shimmied up the couch so he was no longer looming inches from my face—and my mouth. His eyes were still scary, but the way he watched me held more than just anger.

That might have been the most terrifying part of all.

"Look, I didn't mean that you *couldn't* be involved. I only meant that you didn't *have* to be involved. You know...because—"

"The kid wouldn't be mine," he finished for me.

Yes. Exactly that. "No. That's not it."

"Then. What. Is it?"

Um...the kid's not yours, and you didn't exactly stick around after the first one.

"We aren't together anymore. I didn't figure you'd want to get—"

"I swear to God, if you say involved, I'm going to lose my mind."

I'd seen Roman lose his mind, and it was not pretty. I valued my coffee table, so I bit my lip.

His jaw clenched as he sucked in a deep—and, I hoped, calming—breath through his nose. "I'm well aware of the fact that we aren't together *anymore*. I'm also aware that *we* used a sperm donor. Not *you*. Not *me*. *We*. So whatever child was or wasn't produced from that cycle of IVF is very much *ours*." He arched an eyebrow, daring me to argue.

This was, in fact, the truth. But it wasn't as simple as he made it out to be. There were a lot of factors in play, the biggest being my heart. I feared I wouldn't be able to handle it if I gave him the only morsel of trust I had left only for him to turn his back on me—again.

But he looked really pissed, so I didn't dare fill him in on that.

Instead, I kept my mouth shut and nodded in agreement. I could write him a letter informing him of such after I'd moved to an undisclosed location where he couldn't find me and pin me to a couch.

"That means I'm *involved* in this one hundred percent," he stated.

I nodded again, fighting the urge to amend with, *Until you get too busy at work to worry about anything else—including, but not limited to, me.*

"So I'll repeat. My people are looking into it"—he paused and studied my eyes—"for *us*."

I had a million things to say to the man who had broken my heart and was now claiming he wanted to be *involved*. None of them were going to get him off me so I could think clearly though. So I went with, "What's for dinner?"

He stared for a moment longer, and then a huge grin broke across his face. "Gyros."

CHAPTER SEVEN

ROMAN

"Are you insane!" she laughed.

There was a strong possibility that I was drunk, but I wasn't insane.

I also wasn't kidding.

I'd known Elisabeth for a matter of hours, and I knew with an absolute certainty that I wanted to spend the rest of my life with her.

Sure, it was crazy and impulsive, but it was so fucking right.

So I repeated, "Marry me."

"I don't even know you. We've had one date, and you fed me the wrong chicken parmesan. That doesn't exactly scream husband material." She shot me a gleaming, white smile.

"It was only wrong because you gave up. It's not my fault you called it quits after plate number seven. I was committed to the cause."

"Your cause was wasting seven plates of chicken parmesan. You know there are starving kids in Africa, right?" She giggled and buried her face in my neck.

"Is that a yes?" I asked, sifting my fingers through the back of her hair.

Her head jerked up, those deep-green eyes smiling nearly as much as her lips. "Um, no. It's a definite no. However, despite the fact that I now think you have mental issues, I will agree to a second date."

I teasingly squinted at her, and she bit her lips to stifle a laugh.

"Fine, but you should probably head home and pack your belongings, because that date starts now and it's going to be so long it lasts a lifetime."

She barked a laugh. "So, like, say…a marriage?"

"Yes. Exactly like a marriage. Phew. I'm so glad we agree."

She shook her head and whispered, "Insane."

I trailed my lips up her neck to her ear and whispered, "Say yes."

"No."

I grazed my teeth over her earlobe. "Say yes."

"No," she gasped, throwing her head back. The ends of her long hair tickling my hand at her back.

Unable to stop myself, I placed a kiss on the soft flesh at the base of her neck. As chills spread across her skin, I murmured, "You know you feel it, too."

Fisting the back of my shirt, she moaned. "I'd like to feel more. Let's go back to my place."

I could give her more.

But I was taking forever.

I glided my hand from her hair to cup her jaw and drank her in. She wasn't particularly tall, even in heels, so at six two, I had her by several inches, but the way her body fit against mine was nothing short of perfection. Her makeup had started to melt, and her lipstick had been left on the lips of the wineglasses at the bar. But she was still stunning. I couldn't explain why I'd fallen head over heels for that woman as quickly as I had, but I knew I was never letting her go. Whether it took a month, a year, or a decade, I was going to make her say yes.

Sweeping my lips across hers, I murmured, "Fine. I'm not above coercing you into marriage with my sexual prowess."

She laughed so loud that I would have been offended—if I hadn't already been in love with her.

"Where'd you get beer?" Elisabeth asked as she scrambled

from the couch.

"Seth," I replied, hanging my head and rubbing my eyes.

Jesus, I'd wanted to kiss her. She was being a bitch, spouting shit she didn't mean just because she was too scared to let me in.

But, even through it, those plump lips were calling to me.

I'd never been able to resist that woman. Despite that we'd fallen apart, it hadn't changed. The hum for her was still in my veins. It never went away, but for two years, it had been dormant. I'd packed it down so tightly that I'd hoped it had died. But, with one look, my body began thrumming like a live wire.

"Seth?" she asked as she bent over to straighten her tight, black pencil skirt.

It was a rare occasion to catch Elisabeth in something other than a perfectly pressed skirt and a pair of heels. But she'd been sleeping all day. It was wrinkled all to hell and back. The only thing her efforts succeeded in was drawing my attention down to her legs.

Legs that had spent many nights wrapped around my hips as she came while crying my name.

Shit. I should go.

But, after the way she'd latched on to me that morning, I wasn't going anywhere.

"My assistant," I answered. "I had him pick you up a bottle of wine, too."

She blinked. "You have an assistant? Who delivers you beer? And your ex-wife wine?"

"No, I have an assistant who does whatever the fuck I need him to do. And, luckily for us, beer and wine happen to fall into the whatever-the-fuck-I-need-him-to-do category tonight." She fought back a smile as I finished, "So do gyros."

"Damn. I need to get one of those," she mumbled to herself.

I smirked. "Cash my checks and you could afford one."

It was a dick move, bringing up the money right then. But, despite her expert hand in decorating, that little starter house we'd bought with rose-colored glasses now needed a shit-ton of work.

Her back shot ramrod straight, fury crinkling the corners of her eyes as she snarled, "I'm *not* cashing your checks."

I shrugged. "Guess you'll have to figure out how to get your own wine and dinner after tonight."

"I think I can manage," she fired back.

"Suit yourself." I pushed off the couch and meandered to the kitchen.

I went to the fridge and leaned in, searching for anything I could snack on. With the exception of at least a dozen Tupperware containers, she didn't have much in the way of a quick bite.

Snagging a handful of grapes from the drawer, I made a mental note to send Seth to the grocery store after he'd delivered dinner.

Popping the grapes in my mouth one by one, I felt her watching me in what could only be defined as silent awe. I decided my best move would be to ignore it. "You know, I should have invented Tupperware. You alone could keep me in business," I told her, retrieving a beer and then shutting the door.

She scoffed then muttered, "At least then I would have benefitted from you abandoning our marriage."

Lava fresh off the volcanoes in Hell boiled in my veins.

I cocked my head to the side and questioned, "I'm sorry. Come again?"

"You should go," she snapped.

Think a-fucking-gain.

"Nah, I'm good. Got any movies?"

I tipped the bottle to my lips, doing my best to calm the storm brewing within me, all while still fighting the desire to take her to the floor, plant myself between her legs, and remind her how that fucking attitude affected me.

Clearly, she had forgotten.

My cock had not.

"Roman, it's been a crazy day. Please don't do this tonight."

"Do what?" I asked, leaning back against the huge, granite island.

She threw her hands out to the sides in frustration. "What you always do."

"What do I always do, *Lissy*?"

"This!" she yelled.

I frowned and took another pull from my beer. "Haven't been in our kitchen, drinking beer, in a long time. I hardly think it's fair to say I *always* do it."

Her eyes nearly bulged from her head. "*My* kitchen, Roman. This is *my* kitchen. Not ours. And you know good and damn well that is *not* what I'm talking about."

My lips twitched as I pointed the neck of my bottle at her. "No. What I know good and damn well is that I have *no* idea what the fuck you are talking about. Or why you're slinging unnecessary and, might I add, undeserved attitude at me like a short-order cook at the bitch house."

"He did not say that to me," she whispered to herself.

When I lifted a shoulder in a half shrug, she swung a pointed finger toward the door and yelled, "Get out!"

I grinned, crossing my legs at the ankle. "You always were cranky when you were hungry."

And that was the exact moment her head exploded.

"We are done here!" she declared, aiming her finger back at me. "Not another word more. I'll hire an attorney tomorrow, and he'll be in touch with yours regarding whatever our next step is with the cops. Hopefully, we can file something with the courts and get them to issue a DNA test or…whatever. But, in the meantime, you are *not* standing here in *my* kitchen, drinking *my* beer." She paused and sucked in a deep breath. "Yes! *My* beer, I don't give a shit if your fancy-ass assistant did deliver it. It's in m*y* fridge. In *my* house. It's *my* beer!"

I moved. And I did it so fast that she didn't have a chance to react before she was up against my chest. "I don't give a damn whose beer it is."

"Let go of me." She fought in my grasp.

"Not until you listen. While you were busy crying into *my* chest. And holding *my* shoulders like you couldn't get close enough. Then falling asleep in *my* arms like it was the only place you ever fucking belonged." I gripped the back of her hair and tipped her head back, leaning in close as I added, "Which it fucking *is*."

The fight left her. Her body sagging in my arms, even as her eyes flashed wide.

Trailing my thumb back and forth over her cheek, I finished with, "I got some information from the cops. I'm not here to fight with you, so calm down, share a meal and a much-needed glass of wine with me, and let me fill you in."

"Roman," she exhaled, her eyes flooding with tears.

I wasn't sure what part of that had softened her—or I would have repeated it.

Again.

And again.

And maybe a hundred times after that.

Because, with just the sound of my name, she gave me my innocent angel back.

And it was that moment when I realized it had been a God's-honest miracle I'd been able to breathe a single breath in the two years I'd lived without her.

It was also then that I decided those days were done.

"You know we could be civil to each other." I smiled. It was only a half lie. Because there was nothing *civil* about the things I wanted to do to her.

She would, however, enjoy them all.

"Fine. Fill me in. Eat your gyro, but then you have to leave. I seriously can't do this with you tonight."

My hand flexed on her back as I dropped my lips to her ear and murmured, "No. Then I'm sleeping on your couch."

"Roman!" she objected just as there was a knock at the door.

I kissed the top of her head and released her. "Dinner's here. Get out the plates."

She complained behind me as I sauntered to the front door before pulling it wide.

Only it wasn't Seth on the other side.

CHAPTER EIGHT

CLARE

Walter had been gone when I'd woken up.

Like I did every time he walked out our front door, I'd prayed that he wouldn't come home. Accidents happened. And, in his line of work, people died every day.

But I was never that lucky.

Walter Noir would crawl a million miles through broken glass, bleeding and dying, just to make sure he took me to Hell with him.

I'd put on my workout clothes and packed my bag first thing that morning, strategically placing it on the table closest to the door, along with my water bottle and my car keys. Then I'd gone about my day, playing with my daughter while simultaneously listening for his car to pull through the iron gates of my prison.

Around five, I heard the rumble of his BMW, so I rushed to the bag, threw it over my shoulder, grabbed Tessa off the floor, and darted out the door.

He wasn't happy that I was leaving just as he was getting home, but it wasn't as if I'd planned it that way. Or so I swore as he kissed me goodbye before I made my getaway to the gym.

Tessa was tired, so was I, but I had two hours of quasi-freedom ahead of me.

Two hours he wouldn't be around Tessa, and by the time we got home, I could feed her dinner, give her a bath, and put her straight to bed. Minimal contact was the best I could hope for when it came to Walt.

A rush of relief washed over me as I pulled into a parking spot at the gym. I slowly climbed from the car, my ribs only protesting mildly, a huge step up from the day before. My injuries were still visible, but they were thankfully starting to heal. The real agony was in the memories—and my reality.

I was unbuckling Tessa from her car seat when I heard a man call my name. I turned and found two uniformed police officers closing in on me. Panic slammed into me like a runaway truck.

In my life, the police were the only entity more frightening than Walt.

Walt could kill me, but cops could take my life by locking me away, leaving Tessa alone in the care of a monster.

I spun away with shaking hands, scrambling to get Tessa out of her seat.

"Mrs. Noir," one of them called as I collected her bag off the floor and sped toward the gym door. "Mrs. Noir," he repeated more firmly before a hand on my bicep suddenly halted me. "Mrs. Noir, a word?"

Doing my best to keep the tremor out of my voice, I replied, "I'm sorry. I don't have time." I pulled my arm from his grasp and started away.

I came to a sharp stop when the young officer smiled and reached out his hand as though he were about to touch her.

"This must be Tessa."

My soul caught fire.

The panic was gone in a blink, and a feral blaze overwhelmed me. Instinctively shifting her to my other hip, I twisted so my body was between her and the officer, blocking any possible contact.

"Don't you dare touch her," I spat.

"Jesus, Marco. Don't touch the baby," a different man scolded from behind him.

I glanced up to see an older man prowling up behind the

uniforms. Salt-and-pepper hair. Potbelly. Shiny, gold badge showing from underneath his sports coat.

Fuck.

He looked professional.

Flashing my eyes back to Marco, I stumbled back a step as the men closed in around me.

"Calm down, Clare," the older guy urged while I backed away, feeling like a caged animal. "We're not here to cause any trouble," he assured.

"Then back up," I returned.

He lifted a hand and both officers came to a sudden halt. I was able to put a few more feet between us before he spoke again.

"Better?"

"I'd be better if you left."

He pointed toward the now scabbed-over cut over my eye and said, "I don't doubt that's the truth, but we need to have a word. You're a hard woman to track down."

That's because I wasn't allowed to leave our house and it would have to be swallowed by a sinkhole in order for Walt to allow emergency personnel through the front gate.

"Not hard enough, apparently," I shot back.

He grinned and then gave a chin lift. "Boys, give us a minute."

They didn't delay in following his order.

I was far from in the clear, but I instantly felt better now that I wasn't boxed in anymore.

"Now, is *that* better?" he asked.

I didn't answer his question, but with no one at my back, I once again started toward the door.

"Mrs. Noir, we need to talk."

I didn't. I needed to get inside.

"I'm sorry. If you have something to discuss, please contact my attorney and make an appointment," I called, tucking Tessa's face into my neck.

She was oblivious to what was happening, more content to play with the small, gold chain at my neck—another of Walt's "gifts"—but I still hated that she was involved at all.

"Clare, my name is Charles Rorke. I'm a detective with the APD, and I've spoken with your husband's attorney more than I have my own wife this week. Your husband has refused to speak to us, so I'm here, attempting to talk to *you*."

"I have nothing to say." I turned to walk away.

"Not even about the fact that Tessa might not be biologically yours?" he told my back.

Cops hated me. Well, actually, they hated Walt. And then me by association. But never in my life had anyone been crueler—and that was saying a lot, considering I was married to a man who beat me on a near daily basis.

But that, whatever angle he was going for, was scraping the bottom of the barrel.

"You son of a bitch," I breathed, turning to face him. A surge of adrenaline made me strong—physically and emotionally. Taking a step toward him, I squared my shoulders. "You show up here to ask me a few questions while spouting shit like that?"

"I wish it were shit, Clare. But we're investigating the possibility of criminal activity involving Peach City Reproductive Center."

"Oh, screw you." I started to walk away when the Earth suddenly crumbled under my feet.

"We have reason to believe that Walter Noir was involved in a situation that led to embryos purposely being switched in the lab!" he shouted at my back.

I froze, my legs nearly buckling.

A meteor could have fallen from the sky and I couldn't have moved.

"*Walter Noir was involved in a situation.*"

Now, *that* I could believe. Walter Noir was involved in *every situation,* especially those that would hurt *me.* And this would rip the heart straight from my chest.

My nose began to sting as I desperately fought an onslaught

of tears back.

I dropped the gym bag from my arm and shifted Tessa to my other hip. Then, cupping my hand at the side of her head, I covered her ears as though it could stop me from hearing it all.

"What?" I croaked.

His body slacked, and his voice softened. "I see he hasn't mentioned our conversations to you."

"What?" I repeated, tears finally breaching my lids.

"We need a DNA sample from Tessa, Clare. That is the only way we can prove this once and for all." He took a step toward me before reaching out to give my shoulder a reassuring squeeze.

I didn't back away. That would have required the use of my legs, and it was a miracle they were still holding me upright.

"What?" I repeated once again, like a skipping CD unable to move forward.

I was dazed, my mind frantically trying to keep up, when I saw the giant approach out of the corner of my eye.

"Back the fuck up," he ordered.

I lifted my eyes and found Brock, one of Walt's trusty henchmen, stepping in front of me. He must have arrived for "Clare duty" just in time.

"Walt won't consent to the DNA, Clare," the detective spoke around him. "We need this from you."

"Don't fucking talk to her." Brock moved closer to Rorke.

The uniformed officers quickly reappeared.

"Not another move!" Marco shouted.

I couldn't keep up. Someone had pressed fast forward while my mind was still stuck in slow motion.

"Don't do it. Don't you fucking do it!" Marco shouted while Brock issued his own angry orders at the officers.

"Put your fucking hands up!" was the last thing I heard before I felt an arm wrap around my stomach and begin to drag me backward.

"Clare!" Rorke called just as I heard, "Come with me, Clare," whispered in my ear.

Luke.

And, finally, I crumbled.

My breath rushed from my mouth on a wail as I allowed him to pull Tessa from my arms.

"Shit," he cursed, supporting the majority of my weight on one side, Tessa on his other as he guided us into the gym and straight to his office.

Safety.

He planted me in a chair then settled Tessa in my lap long enough to unroll a yoga mat and dig a notebook and a bunch of highlighters out for her to draw with.

I was so numb that I couldn't even argue with him that I was okay.

There was no brave face anymore.

Tessa might not be your biological child, rang in my ears.

Once he had her settled, he crouched in front of me and finally asked, "What the hell is going on?"

The right answer was, *Nothing.*

The right thing to do was put a smile on, forget everything that had happened out in the parking lot, and go about the day like I hadn't just been served the most severe beating of my life.

It was the safest thing for everyone involved.

But, for reasons lost on even myself, I threw my arms around his neck and spilled it all.

Luke didn't hug me back. Instead, he kept both hands anchored to the arms of my chair as he balanced in front of me. I didn't need the physical contact; I just needed someone to listen.

I was going to get him killed, but the words wouldn't stop flowing from my mouth.

I told him about the drug trafficking.

Walt's ties to organized crime.

The murders he'd made me clean up.

The money laundering.

The beatings.

The blood.

The fear.

The prison he kept me in.

And finally.

Tessa.

Why, after all the years of having kept it locked away, I chose to unload it all on a personal trainer, I'd never understand. But finding out that my only reason to wake up the next morning might not even be mine was the final straw.

After I'd told him about what had gone down in the parking lot, I fell silent.

The weight of the world still heavily rested on my shoulders, but the load somehow felt lighter. And, for the briefest of seconds, I took a deep breath for the first time since Walter Noir had walked into my life.

Luke didn't immediately respond, and I couldn't blame him.

Finding out the scum of the Earth was doing push-ups right under your nose had to be a hard pill to swallow.

After peeling my arms from around his neck, he placed them in my lap and rocked back on his heels. His blue eyes flashed to Tessa then back to me, his face steeled with confidence as he asked, "How can I help?"

Christ, he was a good guy.

I laughed through my tears. "You can't. No one can."

He opened his mouth to reply when a booming, "Where the fuck is my wife!" came from outside the door.

I jumped, and Tessa started crying. After shooting to my feet, I plucked her off the floor and prepared for the worst.

It was Walt.

The worst was all I ever got.

CHAPTER NINE

ELISABETH

"No," Roman growled, slamming the door less than a second after he'd opened it.

"What the—" Kristen cried from the other side.

He glared at me over his shoulder, frustration floating in the air around him.

I couldn't fight my smile back.

"Elisabeth!" she yelled, shaking the door handle in an attempt to get in.

I sauntered past Roman, using my shoulder to nudge him out of the way, and yanked the door open.

As if his sister were an axe murder, he stepped close to my back, protectively looping an arm around my waist.

It was then that I worried Roman could possibly be an axe murder, because if he thought he was claiming me like that after having pinned me to the couch and proclaimed he was sleeping there that night, he had serious mental concerns that needed to be addressed ASAP.

And what better way than with his sister at my side for his intervention.

Kristen's mouth gaped as her eyes drifted down to his arm.

I grabbed his wrist and roughly removed it. "Hey," I said casually.

"Dear God, did I hit a time loop?" Her gaze went to her brother. "Quick! What year is it?"

"Better question is what the hell are you doing here?" he sniped back.

She narrowed her eyes. "No. I believe the best question is how in the hell you were able to cross this threshold without Liz lighting you on fire." Her gaze drifted back to me, her eyebrow arching in accusation. "I thought that was the plan if he showed up. Shit, Liz. Mom even bought the lighter fluid."

I giggled because she was *not* kidding. Cathy Leblanc loved her son, and when shit had gone down with Roman and me, she'd made it clear she would not be taking sides between her "children." But, the day after Roman exchanged our entire life for fifty percent of his precious company, she showed up at my door with a bottle of wine and a can of lighter fluid. About three weeks later, she must have had a change of heart, because she showed up with a bottle of wine and a fire extinguisher. "*Just in case*," were her words.

Kristen impatiently cocked her head to the side, insisting on a verbal answer.

"Some things…well, happened today," I stammered out.

Kristen was family, but I was in no rush to tell people about what had happened at the police station. We didn't know for certain if there was anything to tell. It could have been some huge mix-up nothing ever came of.

Or it could have been some huge mix-up where Roman and I had another child—one who'd lived longer than twelve minutes.

My eyes closed painfully. "Oh God," I whispered.

Roman's arm once again folded around my waist, and this time, I didn't fight. I swayed back against his chest.

"Uh, are y'all back together?" Kristen asked.

My eyes popped open as I declared, "No."

However, just as quickly, I heard Roman say, "Maybe."

I jerked from his hold on me and glanced over my shoulder. "What? No!" I insisted.

He shot me an arrogant grin then repeated, "Maybe."

"Roman!" I yelled, all but stomping my foot.

He ignored me completely and turned his attention back to his sister. "What are you doing here?"

She was watching us with a wide smile that said she really liked the idea of Roman's *maybe.*

Traitor!

Lifting a paper bag in the air, she replied to him, "Convincing her."

"Ah!" he said in understanding.

I, however, was clueless. "Convincing me of what?"

They both ignored me.

"You gonna let me in or not?" she asked.

This time, our responses were reversed.

Roman quickly snapped, "No."

While I replied, "Maybe."

Her eyebrows shot up as she suppressed a laugh. "Maybe?"

"Depends. What are you trying to convince me of?"

She shrugged. "Nothing now. Seems my little brother is going to be doing his own version of convincing."

Roman chuckled.

I swung a glare between the two of them that would have frozen normal people, but unfortunately, there was nothing normal about either one of them.

"No one is doing any convincing," I declared.

"Okay," they replied in unison.

That was a bad sign. A really fucking bad sign. It meant they were going to be secretly convincing, which was eleventy billion times worse than normal convincing, and it also guaranteed that I would ultimately *be* convinced, because I knew they wouldn't stop until I was. It was the Leblanc way.

I cursed under my breath, which earned me a mouth-watering smirk from Roman and a sugary-sweet smile from Kristen.

I groaned and moved from the doorway to allow her entry.

She didn't hesitate in accepting the invitation. "I brought sushi and wine."

"Roman's *assistant* is delivering gyros," I smarted.

She stopped midway to the kitchen, cutting her gaze to her brother, and hissed, "Seth?"

Roman rolled his eyes before tagging the bag from her hand, carrying it to the counter, and unceremoniously plopping it down. "I'm not firing the guy."

"You have *got* to be kidding!" she returned, charging after him.

"Wait." I jogged to keep up. "This is *Seth* Seth? The asshole Seth who never called back, Seth? Seth the nice cock, all night long, Seth?"

"Jesus, fuck. Seriously?" Roman grumbled. "I don't need to know that shit."

"I thought we discussed this!" she told his back.

He got busy pulling the sushi from the bag. "You talked. I listened. But what I did not do is agree to fire a man because things did not work out with my sister. This being after I told my sister not to pursue something with one of my employees."

Lasers shot from Kristen's eyes, but Roman's aura seemed impenetrable.

He lifted a pair of chopsticks in the air and asked, "Did you get extra wasabi?"

I swiftly stepped between the two of them, fearing a brawl in the middle of my kitchen. That brawl being a verbal one but no less messy.

"Okay, okay. Let's chill out."

"Where's the lighter fluid?" Kristen questioned, glowering at her brother as he shoved a piece of sashimi in his mouth, completely unaffected.

A laugh sprang from my throat, causing all eyes to swing my way.

"I'm sorry," I told Kristen. "It's just…" *I miss this.* I continued to laugh and waved the rest of my statement off.

I glanced back at Roman and found him leaning against the counter, his weight resting on his hip, his legs crossed at the ankle, a smile showing on his chewing mouth.

Gorgeous.

And comfortable.

And so fucking right.

Oh God.

I kept laughing because it felt amazing for the first time in as long as I could remember.

Do not get used to this.

"Wine?" I asked through a giggle just as another knock came.

Kristen was immediately off and stomping to the door.

I started to go after her, fearing a brawl of a different nature, when Roman caught my bicep.

"Don't," he ordered, sliding an arm around my waist.

Chills swirled down my spine as he bent to whisper in my ear.

"Just because I'm not firing Seth doesn't mean he's not an asshole. He deserves whatever fury she's about to rain down upon him." His lips swept my neck, and regardless of what my mind was screaming, my body shifted into his side and my hand moved to the firm ridges of his stomach.

It was as though the connection completed a full circuit, because the hairs on the back of my neck prickled and a heat only Roman Leblanc could give me pooled between my legs.

One simple touch and I was ready.

I'd always been that way with him though.

After we ate our "beef" gyros, we strolled to my apartment, talking, laughing, and making out in every alley we stumbled across. By the time we'd gotten to my door, his hand was down the front of my shirt and I was exploring the hard planes of his chest.

My neighbors, should they have been up at three a.m., were going to get a show. But I couldn't have cared less. Roman had that way about him. He made me forget the world around me. He was enough. And, together, we were everything. I knew that even though I'd only had him in my life for one day.

I'd laughed at his proposal. But maybe I was the crazy one for not saying yes immediately. It was wrong though; people didn't get engaged on their first date.

If only I could explain why I so badly wanted to say yes.

"Roman," I breathed, swinging my door open as he swept my panties to the side, one finger sliding inside me.

"Fuck. Me," he murmured before laving his tongue up my neck. His mouth trailed kisses up to my ear as his husky voice rumbled. "So fucking ready for me."

I was.

So fucking ready for all *of him.*

"Roman," I moaned, tipping my head to the side to allow him better access.

His finger hooked inside me, sending a rush of ecstasy through me.

"More," I pleaded, my head falling back as I struggled to stay on my feet.

His strong arm looped around my hips, keeping me upright. He removed his fingers and lifted me off my feet so I dangled inches off the ground as he sidestepped us into my apartment.

"Get the door, baby," he ordered.

Baby.

I'd have done anything he wanted if it was proceeded with the smooth sound of baby *falling from his lips.*

With a kick, I slammed the door shut.

Suddenly, we were alone, and as his mouth sealed over mine, our tongues gloriously gliding together, I wasn't sure I ever wanted to open the door again.

His frenzied hands gentled long enough to lower me to the floor. My couch was mere feet away, but we hadn't had the time nor the desire to make it that far.

His hard body covered mine, his hips falling between my open legs.

Then my shirt was off in a matter of seconds, and my skirt quickly followed.

"Fuck, Lis," he grunted, sliding down my body. His finger curled in the top of my bra, tugging it down before taking my nipple between his lips. His warm tongue swirled and his teeth nipped, shooting sparks that rivaled any orgasm I'd ever had straight to my clit.

"Roman," I moaned, arching my back and pressing more of my breast into his mouth.

He growled, the vibrations coaxing me closer to the edge. His hair was too short to thread my fingers through, so I palmed the back of his head, holding him as though he were attempting to get away. He absolutely wasn't.

I lifted my hips when I felt the tips of his fingers start their descent down my stomach.

Our groans harmonized as he dipped his fingers between my legs and pressed in just enough to taunt me.

"Please," I begged.

His head popped up to catch my gaze. "Given any more thought to that proposal?" he asked with a smirk that was all Roman Leblanc.

And, therefore, I didn't just see it—I felt it. Deep inside, where no other man had ever been.

"This is crazy," I told him, spreading my legs wide.

"I know," he whispered, holding my gaze as he slid two fingers inside me.

I writhed, driving myself down, unable to get close enough.

I needed more. Not the kind of more his body could offer.

I wanted the kind of more that spoke to my soul that only Roman had to offer.

His hand worked me, pumping in and out, taking me closer and closer to the edge.

"Roman, I—"

"Shh… It's okay, baby. Offer's on the table. Whenever you're

ready, I'll be here. All you have to do is say yes." He dropped his thumb to my clit and skillfully circled.

As an orgasm so strong that I feared I'd never be able to recover tore through me, I realized I was absolutely ready for anything and everything as long as it was with him.

"Mmm," Roman purred into the top of my hair, snapping me out of my thoughts. I was plastered against his side, my hand fisting the front of his shirt, my cheeks heated, and my legs nearly shaking. Cupping my chin, he tipped my head back so he could meet my gaze. "What are you thinking about, babe?"

Nope. No way was I answering that question.

Luckily, I didn't have to because, just as Kristen pulled open the door, ready to give Seth the tongue-lashing of his life, the air went static.

"Oh shit," Kristen mumbled, glancing back at me, her eyes wide with apology.

His gaze found mine over the top of Kristen's head. It dropped to my hand on Roman's stomach as he said, "Liz?"

CHAPTER TEN

ROMAN

"Jon. Hey!" she said in surprise, immediately evacuating her position at my side and hurrying toward the door. "Wh-what are you doing here?"

The man's eyes focused on me as he absently answered, "You didn't show up at the Victorian. Been calling for the last hour. I got worried."

I trailed after her, doing my best not to show the rage boiling in my veins or the sour churning in my gut.

For the love of all that's holy, don't let this be her boyfriend.

She stepped in front of Kristen, forcing her to move from the doorway. "Shit. I'm sorry. Today's been crazy."

Jon's gaze flashed to mine as he shifted awkwardly in the doorway. "I can see."

It hadn't exactly been said in an asshole tone, but that was up for interpretation. However, just the fact that he was standing in Elisabeth's doorway had my interpretation skewed—and not in his favor.

Shoving my hand over her shoulder to offer a shake, I smiled something that I hoped read: *Hi, how ya doing?* Meanwhile, my eyes read: *If you've ever touched her, that shit is officially over*. But it was my mouth that said, "I don't believe we've met. I'm Roman Leblanc, Elisabeth's husband."

Her body went solid before she corrected, "Ex! Ex-husband."

I shrugged and kept my eyes on *Jon* as I stated, "That's debatable."

"It's not debatable!" she yelled over her shoulder at me. Then she looked back at the asshole and said, "He's my *ex-husband*."

"We're still figuring that part out," I amended.

Jon's eyes bounced between us as he silently took us in. By the frustration and disappointment coloring his face, he was coming to the correct conclusion.

Or at least correct as far as I was concerned.

Elisabeth was on a slightly different page.

"We're not figuring anything out!" she exclaimed, shoving my unshaken hand back over her shoulder. "Come on, Jon. Let's talk on the porch."

I should have let her go. I had no reason to be jealous. The connection Elisabeth and I shared was undeniable, no matter how much she tried to pretend she hated me. Hell, she had reason to hate me, but she'd spent the day in my arms, reminding me that I'd been living half of a life for the last two years. And, moments before this guy had arrived, her face had been red, her hand had been clutching my shirt, and a soft moan had escaped her throat. There was no fucking way I was losing that.

She might have been confused about who she belonged to.

But Jon would not walk out of that house without being fully informed.

Stepping in front of her, I slid a hand up her neck and into her hair, gently fisting until it forced her head back. Her breath caught as I leaned into her face, and I took great pleasure in the goose bumps that pebbled her smooth skin.

Brushing my nose with hers, I whispered, "Hurry up, baby. Sushi's waiting."

She stared, her lips parting as I licked my own. She was in my trance. I recognized it because I'd been lost in hers for nearly a decade.

Ever so slightly, she tipped her chin up, offering me the lips I was starved for. I could have taken her right there in front of Kristen,

Jon, and the entire fucking city of Atlanta and she would have *come* willingly.

"Always so fucking ready for me," I murmured.

I wanted to kiss her—and never stop.

Unless it was to move my mouth between her legs.

At the thought, a low sound rumbled in my throat, and she suddenly came alert.

She blinked once, twice, and then I lost her.

Her hand went to my shoulder, shoving roughly as she seethed, "Let me go."

Tightening my fist in her hair, I whispered, "Never," before releasing her. Smiling at the man fuming in the doorway, I called out, "Nice to meet you, Jon," as I casually turned and walked back to the kitchen.

When I heard the front door slam behind me, my shoulders fell and I closed my eyes. Pinching the bridge of my nose, I propped myself up on a white-knuckled fist on the island.

"Wow," Kristen breathed behind me. "That was…"

Fuck. Time to be bitched at.

I lifted a hand to silence her. "I don't want to hear it. I need a fucking drink, not a lecture."

Her open hand landed hard on my shoulder, and my eyes popped open.

"Holy shit! That was incredible." She laughed.

A shy smile tipped one side of my lips. I asked nervously, "Yeah? You think?"

"Roman! She hated you yesterday, and I swear to God she just came from that whole hand-in-the-hair bit." She wrapped both hands in the front of my shirt and shook me. "Oh my God! You're gonna get Elisabeth back!"

I barked a laugh of relief. "I'm sure as hell gonna try," I told her.

She squealed, jumping into my arms like we were kids again.

Movement outside the front window caught my attention. Elisabeth's feet swayed back and forth in the porch swing, Jon's right beside her, which reminded me that we had a long way to go before we could celebrate anything.

"Okay, stop." I used her shoulders to shift her off me. "I need you to fill me in on everything about his guy so I know what I'm up against."

"Who? Jon?"

"No, the other man sitting on a swing I hung in a house that I bought and doing it all while sitting next to *my* wife."

She attempted a glare, but her smile was too wide to give it any heat.

She headed toward the fridge and pulled two beers out, passing me one before starting. "Okay, so Jon..."

Two beers later, I was sitting on the corner of the island when Elisabeth came back inside carrying a plastic bag filled with to-go boxes.

She lifted them in the air, saying, "I decided to save Seth from certain death."

"That son of a bitch," Kristen cursed.

I chuckled, tipping the beer to my lips and hopping down to meet her.

She passed the bags off to me, but her eyes never met mine as she headed straight for the glass of wine I had waiting for her on the counter.

"Soooo, how's Jon?" Kristen asked.

"He's good," she replied between gulps of her Chardonnay, not looking at either of us.

"Everything okay?" Kristen pushed.

"Yep," Elisabeth answered curtly, going to work on removing the boxes from the bags I'd set on the counter. She robotically opened each before closing it and sliding it down the counter to make room for the next. Once they were all laid out, she opened the cabinet above her and retrieved two plates.

Two.

Not three.

Two.

I felt Kristen's gaze cut to me, but I was studiously watching Elisabeth's back as she removed gyros from their boxes and delicately placed them on the blue, floral plates we'd received as a wedding gift. After she got every fry in place, she set one beside Kristen and the other beside me. Then she finally lifted her gaze.

I flinched when I got a look at the pain etched into her face. It was a look I knew well—*defeat.*

Shit. Maybe Kristen was wrong and this Jon guy actually means something to Elisabeth.

"Lissy," I breathed, reaching out to her.

She took a step away and aimed her eyes at the floor. "Y'all go ahead and eat. Just let yourself out whenever you're done. I'm gonna call it a night."

"Elisabeth," Kristen called, but she only lifted a hand in a wave and rushed from the room.

I moved to follow her but stopped at the foot of the stairs as she disappeared up to the top.

"What the hell was that?" Kristen asked after we'd both heard the bedroom door quietly close.

I raked a hand through the top of my hair. "No clue. You're sure about this Jon guy?"

"Positive. No way that's about him." Kristen appeared at my side, offering one of the plates of food my way. "Here. Go after her. I'll let the dog in and lock up."

I nodded, but my feet remained stuck. That expression on Elisabeth's face had been like a knife from the past, gutting me all over again. She had worn that look of heartbreaking despondency every time I'd seen her after Tripp died. Back then, I didn't know how to fix it. I thought that, if I could give her another baby, maybe, just maybe, I could make it all go away and bring the vibrant woman who'd stolen my heart back.

I physically couldn't do it. Fertility just wasn't on my side.

And it killed me that I wasn't financially able to do it either. I was a soldier who had gotten out of the military with hopes and dreams of starting my own consulting firm. But hopes and dreams wouldn't give us a baby. For that, I needed cold, hard cash.

So I went to work. All day. All night. Busting my ass so I could offer her the world.

Only, in the process, I lost it all.

And, in my stupidity, she lost it all, too.

Money fixed exactly zero of my problems. I could buy anything I wanted.

Except her.

Never her.

"Roman," Kristen hissed, taking my hand and wrapping it around the edge of the plate. "Go!"

I closed my eyes, sucked in a breath, and did what I should have done years earlier.

I walked up the stairs to save my wife—and our family.

Only I didn't make it far.

A man greeted me at the top of the stairway.

"Fuck!" I yelled, my hands immediately going up in defense, french fries flying everywhere. I caught the plate at the last second as my eyes adjusted and I recognized the man.

Me.

"Fucking shit!" I shouted, taking in the floor-to-ceiling mirror that covered the entirety of the wall, including the one beside it that ran parallel to the two bedroom doors on one side of the landing.

It had most definitely not been there when I'd moved out, and frankly, it was scary as hell.

The door cracked, and Elisabeth's head poked out.

"What's wrong?" she asked, her cheeks still damp from crying.

I ignored her question and pointed to the mirror with the plate. "What the fucking hell is that?"

Her head twisted to the side, her lip curling with attitude as she answered, "A mirror."

"Okay, but why?"

She swung the door open and propped a shoulder on the jamb. "Well, originally, it was an effort to make this tiny hallway feel bigger. But it didn't exactly go as planned. Now, I just feel like I live in a fun house. I've been…"

I believe there were more words spoken after that, but the blood drained from my head in a rush down south.

She'd changed clothes. Elisabeth's sleep attire was much like her fancy daily wear. No frumpy old sweats for her. She slept in short, silky dresses, nightgowns, nighties. Whatever they were called, I loved them for a myriad of reasons. Including the way they showed her legs off and the ridiculously easy access they offered in the middle of the night. But, upon seeing her now, I remembered my favorite reason of all: They left absolutely nothing to the imagination. Everything, from the swell of her breasts to the curve of her hips, was outlined in spectacular fashion.

My eyes dropped to her nipples, which were peaking behind the fabric, and just as quickly, her arms came up to cross over them.

"Anyway," she said, "did you need something?"

Yes. You. Naked and calling my name. "You need to eat."

She rolled her eyes. "No. I need to sleep."

She started to close the door, but I caught it with my free hand.

"Why were you crying?" I asked.

"I wasn't."

"Bullshit." I took a step into the room, forcing her inside with me.

Her lips went thin as I kicked the door closed behind me.

"You need to leave," she contended while I moved past her to set the plate on her nightstand.

"Tell me why you were crying and I'll see what I can do about that," I lied.

She scoffed. "Oh, I don't know, Roman. You're a smart man.

I'm sure you can figure this out without an explanation."

I glanced around the room. Not much had changed. Our wedding pictures were no longer covering the walls, but minus the khaki bedding that had been switched for a pink-and-white stripe, it all remained the same. Her closet door was wide open, shoes neatly organized over the floor, necklaces draped over hooks I'd mounted on the back of the door.

When we'd bought the place, I'd promised her that I'd expand the closet for her. It was one of the many promises I'd broken to her.

"That guy, Jon. He mean something to you?" I asked, going to the window, peeking out just in time to see Kristen's car backing out of the driveway.

She laughed, but it held no humor. "That's seriously your first guess? After the day we've had, you guess I'm up here pining over Jon?"

I glanced back in her direction and cocked an eyebrow. "Is that a no?"

She released a frustrated groan, walked to the door, and snatched it open. "Leave."

I ignored her request and sat on the side of the bed. Resting my elbows on my knees, I interlocked my fingers and let them hang between my legs. "So, you're upset about the shit that went down at the police station today?"

She blinked for several seconds, her chest heavily rising and falling. She was about to explode, but sometimes, that was the only way to break a wall down.

"Lissy," I whispered, lighting the fuse.

Three.

Two.

One.

"No! I'm upset because this is my life!"

Boom!

She gave the door a hard shove, slamming it shut before marching over to me. Crossing her arms over her chest, she snapped, "Let's see. Where should I start?" She waited for a reply that wasn't going to come before she continued. "My day began in a police station, where I found out that someone might have pulled the old switch-a-roo on my embryos. Then I woke up a second time to find my ex-husband standing in my kitchen, drinking beer, and ordering dinner. Then he pinned me to a fucking couch, declaring his one hundred percent involvement." She paused and lifted two fingers in the air. "This being said *two* goddamn *years* after he'd checked out on me. Then his sister showed up, claiming to be *convincing* me of something, which he clearly seemed to be in on. Then my *friend* showed up because he's worried about me, and you marked me like a fucking fire hydrant. Now, here you are...standing in *my bedroom*, asking why *I'm* upset. Jesus Christ, Roman!" She threw her hands out to the sides. "Take your pick!"

She wasn't wrong.

All of that had happened.

But she'd left a lot of the details out.

After rising to my feet, I closed the distance between us. Her eyes went wide as I hooked an arm around her hips and pulled her off-balance so she crashed into my chest.

"See, my day went a little differently," I started gruffly. "I woke up this morning, after I'd spent the entire night trying to figure out how to get the woman I love to take money from me. She hates me, but I fucking hate the idea that I can't take care of her."

"I don't—" she started to interrupt, but I talked over her.

"I arrived at the police station, where I saw said woman, and I felt my heart beat for the very first time in two fucking years."

Her mouth fell open, but when I cupped the back of her neck, she slammed it shut.

"*Then* I found out that some asshole I trusted enough to give my life savings to decided to sell *my* child to someone else. Yeah, I don't give a single fuck we used a sperm donor. I also don't give a damn that that child was in a petri dish when it was sold. That child is *ours*. Wherever the hell it might be right now." I paused for a breath, and she wisely remained quiet. "Then, upon hearing this news, you fell into my arms, clinging to me as if we'd never been apart. With *that*, Lis, my lungs inflated for the first time since I'd found you sitting on the couch with your bags packed around you. I walked out of that police station with you in my arms, shocked and pissed the fuck off, but I felt like someone had finally pressed play on my life again." I squeezed the back of her neck. "So, yeah, baby, you better believe I'm one hundred percent involved in *that*."

"Roman," she sighed, her stiff body finally starting to relax in my arms.

I kept going. "Then my annoying-ass sister showed up in order to convince you to keep at least some of the money I'd sent so I could get one single night of sleep where I didn't close my eyes and worry you needed something. I will *not* fucking apologize for that. That leads me to the part where a man I *do not know* showed up at your door, trying to steal that new beat in my heart and breath in my lungs, so damn straight I reacted. You aren't gonna get an apology from me about that, either. For fuck's sake, I called you my wife. I didn't beat the piss out of him. And believe me, the thought *did* cross my mind."

"Oh God," she cried, dropping her forehead to my chest. Her hand snaked up between us to rest on my pec.

After kissing the top of her head, I finished with, "So you were right about one thing. I am standing in your bedroom, asking why you are upset, because minus the bullshit going on with the cops, I see not one thing to be upset about. Also, I'm standing in your bedroom, staring at you in that fucking nightgown, and remembering how it looked the last time I took it off you."

Her head jerked up, her eyes wide and her cheeks sliding through the color spectrum of reds. "Don't," she warned, but it came out breathy.

"I won't," I assured as I slid my hands up her sides, allowing my thumbs to glide over the side of her breasts as I made my way up to her neck to cup her jaw. "Yet, anyway."

Her gaze darkened, and her hand at my chest closed, fisting my shirt. "This is crazy," she whined.

"It always was with us."

"I can't do this with you, Roman. Not again."

"Fine. Don't. But consider this your warning because…" I paused, turning us so I could back her to the bed. Bending so as not to lose the connection, I gently lowered her to the mattress and declared, "I'm checking back in."

She shook her head. "This isn't a hotel. You can't just check back in."

I battled the urge to kiss her.

To claim her.

To take back the woman who had always been mine.

Calling up every ounce of self-control I possessed, I released her, pushed off the bed, and headed to the door. After opening it, I shot her a smirk and said, "You're right. It's not. Otherwise, I wouldn't be sleeping on the fucking *couch*."

Her chin quivered as she smiled. God, she was scared to fucking death, and it broke me. But I wasn't letting go. Not again.

"It's gonna be okay. All of it," I promised.

A tear fell as she replied in a weak voice, "I'm not sure about that."

She was wrong. But I wasn't going to convince her of that right then.

"Try to eat and get some rest, okay?"

She nodded, wiping the wetness away from her cheeks.

I hated leaving her alone when she was struggling, but she needed the space, so begrudgingly, I walked away.

Then I yelled, "Son of a bitch!" when that goddamned man in the mirror scared the shit out of me for the second time.

And it was worth every second of the near heart attack when I heard Elisabeth's soft giggle from the other side of the door.

CHAPTER ELEVEN

ELISABETH

"Wake up, baby," I heard as I felt the hair being swept off my face.

It was him. Therefore, it had to be a dream.

It was a dream I'd had at least a dozen times.

However, once, it had been reality.

"Wake up, baby," he urged, sitting on the bed in the curve of my naked body. His back to my front, only a sheet dividing us. Thoughts of the night before flooded my mind—all of them starting and ending with Roman.

"Mmm," I purred, curling around him. Looping my arms at his waist, I groaned when I came in contact with his clothes. My sore, well-used body was still aching from the night before, but I was ready for more. "Why are you dressed?" I complained, teasingly patting him down, paying special attention to his zipper while searching for the length hiding behind it.

Just as I found it, he caught my wrist and pulled it away. "We need to talk."

It wasn't spoken in a tone that said, We need to talk so we can figure out where to get more condoms and then stay in the bed for the rest of the day—and maybe forever.

It was spoken in a tone that said, We need to talk because I'm married and need to get home to my wife.

I was suddenly more awake than ever.

"What's wrong?" I asked, sitting up, dragging the sheet with me.

He was no less gorgeous the next morning, but the mischievous glint in his silver eyes was now filled with worry. It was all wrong for the man who had proposed only hours earlier.

"How ya feeling?" he asked, pushing to his feet and pacing the room.

"Good," I drawled suspiciously.

He stopped moving and looked over at me. "Not sick or anything?"

I tilted my head in question and replied, "Nope. Little thirsty. Little hungover. But overall pretty good."

Scrubbing the top of his buzzed head, he breathed, "Oh, thank God."

This did not relax me in the least.

"Roman, what's going on?"

He swallowed hard then went back to pacing a path in my carpet. "I fucked up, Lis."

My already racing heart came to a screeching halt.

He'd fucked up.

Oh God.

"How?" I had no idea where the courage to ask had come from, because no one wanted to be rejected by a man who they'd fallen in love with. And that was exactly what had happened. I'd thought I had known it as he'd made love to me on the floor just inside my apartment and then again a few hours later in my bed. But, right then, staring down the barrel of losing him, I knew.

Roman Leblanc was it for me.

And he'd fucked up.

He looked at me with terrified eyes and announced, "I was drunk."

I was going to be sick. I could feel it in my stomach. I wasn't going to be able to hold it together much longer.

"Roman, I'm about to have a panic attack, so if you could just

speak in full thoughts and spit this shit out, I'd really appreciate it. What did you do?"

He balled his hands into fists, planting them on his hips as he confessed, "It was lamb!"

My head snapped back. "What?"

"I'm so fucking sorry. I've been freaking out all morning." He started pacing again. "I searched your fridge and pantry, and there's not a piece of lamb anywhere. Are you allergic? Please tell me it's not a delayed reaction. Shit. Damn. Fuck. Do we need to go to the hospital?" He gripped the back of his neck and stared at me. "Oh God, please don't tell me it's a religious thing and I knowingly fed you lamb."

My breath became lodged in my throat.

This smart, funny, and beautiful man was freaking out because he'd told me that the gyros were beef. He had a conscience so strong that it had woken him early in the morning and sent him scouring through my pantry.

The guilt was painted all over his face.

If I'd had any doubts left about Roman, that was the exact moment they vanished.

I was hopeless to stop the tears from falling.

"Say something," he whispered in absolute horror.

"Yes," I said on a half cry, half laugh.

His eyebrows pinched together. "Yes, allergic, or yes, religious?"

I sob-laughed again. "Yes, I'll marry you."

His whole body startled, and his mouth gaped open.

I quickly amended, "I mean, if the offer's still on the table."

"Oh my God," he gasped. "Are you serious?"

I nodded, wiping my cheeks and climbing to my knees.

He rushed across my bedroom faster than any non-Olympic athlete could move. Slamming into me, he wrapped his arms around my shoulders and lifted me off the bed.

"Holy shit," he breathed, planting random kisses on the top of my hair and the side of my face. "Say it again."

"Yes, I'll marry you."

"Jesus," he whispered. "I thought I was going to lose you."

I giggled. "Over lamb?"

He pinched my side. "I spent forty-five minutes searching the Internet for lamb allergies. I even held a mirror under your nose to make sure you were still breathing."

I burst out laughing as he put me back on the bed. "For the record, I eat lamb. I'm just not a fan of it in anything but a gyro."

"Noted." He pressed his lips to mine in a reverent kiss. Then he leaned away and smiled, declaring, "You're gonna be Elisabeth—with an S—Leblanc by the end of the day."

I smiled back. "Leblanc with a capital or lowercase B?"

He smirked. "Does it matter?"

I struggled to get rid of my smile, but the best I could do was cover it with my hand. "Yes, it matters. Our lives together hang in the balance of this question right here. Right now."

He chewed on his bottom lip, trying to cover his own shit-eating grin. "Lowercase."

I sucked in a deep breath and then took the biggest risk of my entire life.

And I did it knowing that it wasn't really a risk at all.

Because, regardless of my answer, I would love this man for the rest of my life.

"Okay, then. Roman Leblanc—with a lowercase B—let's get married."

I kept my eyes closed as I stretched. "What time is it?" I asked, rolling to my side and curling around him.

"Jesus," he mumbled as I felt him touch the spaghetti strap of my nightie. His thumb grazed my skin as it trailed down between my breasts. My nipples peaked in anticipation.

But then he moved the fabric to cover me. *Wrong direction.*

I groaned in disappointment when consciousness finally pulled me from my dream world.

My eyes flashed open, and I found him staring down at my

chest as he righted the material over my exposed breast.

I bolted upright and scrambled across the bed, dragging the sheet with me. "Wh-what are you doing here?" I asked, memories of the night before still lost in the early morning fog.

He twisted his lips, his eyes darkening as they slid to my hands, which were clutching the sheet, then back again. "Our legal team will be here in fifteen minutes. I thought you might like to get dressed."

With that, the world came crashing back down around me. My body sagged, and my heart wrenched. I would have rather stayed in bed all day and forget that I needed a legal team in the first place.

"Okay," I forced out.

Before I knew it, his hand was at the back of my neck, dragging me toward him. It wasn't rough, but it was demanding. He tucked my face into his neck and shifted so my chest was crushed against his side.

I didn't fight. I'd just woken up and didn't have it in me. Or so I told myself as I nuzzled closer.

"It's gonna be okay, Lissy," he whispered into my hair, his lips sealing the promise with a kiss on my crown.

"Okay," I mumbled, doing my best to tamp the overwhelming anxiety down.

"It's just a meeting with Whit and Kaplin to see what our options are."

"Okay," I agreed again.

One hand remained at the back of my neck, and he folded the other arm around my shoulders, holding me so tight that it was as if he could keep me from falling apart. And this was Roman; he might have been the only one who could. It was his superpower as far as I was concerned.

"I'm right here. One hundred percent," he said, continuing with the reassurance.

I continued with the noncommittal declarations of acceptance. "Okay."

"You want some coffee?" he asked before kissing the top of my head again.

I shouldn't have liked that as much as I did.

There were reasons Roman and I were no longer together. I needed to focus on those and not the desire to crawl into his lap and ride out the rest of the day in his arms.

Drawing in a breath, I forced myself to my feet. "I need to get dressed, but yeah, I'd love coffee. The creamer is—"

"In the cabinet. Powder. I remember," he said, scrubbing his hands over his…

Jeans?

"Where'd you get clothes?" I asked, heading to my closet—the one that used to be his.

"Seth. He dropped off my car this morning, too."

I turned and looked through the blinds to see a brand-spanking-new Range Rover sitting in my driveway. And, for reasons I didn't understand, just the sight of that fucking car sent ice through my veins. This wasn't the past where Roman was mine and he woke me up and held me in the morning while I calmed myself from the stress of the day.

This was the present where Roman had checked out on me, we'd gotten a divorce, and he'd started up a multimillion-dollar company while I'd struggled to breathe.

Anger was a worthless emotion, but bitterness and resentment were impossible to ignore.

I snapped the blinds shut as I sniped, "That's a far cry from the broke-down Honda you left in."

I couldn't see him, but I felt the air crackle around us. Then, just as quickly, everything fell flat. Glancing over my shoulder, I saw him moving toward me—fast.

His chest hit my back at the same time that fucking hand of his slid into my hair.

My body responded immediately, spiking my pulse and flushing my cheeks.

With a gentle tug, he sent chills spreading over my skin as he pulled my head back. Our eyes met. Mine were wide. His were feral.

I couldn't breathe.

I couldn't talk.

I couldn't even think.

Not with his hard body at my back, his breath on my skin, and his mouth inches away from mine.

His hand squeezed my waist as it slowly glided up my stomach, stopping just below the round of my breasts. His thumb gently swept the swell before disappearing.

My lids drooped at the contact, and my head fell back against his shoulder. As I gave him my weight, he shifted his hand from my neck around to my throat.

"There she is. My sweet Lissy," he praised softly.

As much as I needed to keep my distance, I knew it was a futile. I'd never been able to stay away from him.

And that obviously hadn't changed.

He was amazing in bed, and I was positive that hadn't changed, either.

I hadn't been with anyone since our divorce. And, the year before it, I had been pregnant, recovering, or lost in despair. Sex hadn't been very high on our list of priorities.

Maybe we could remedy this now. At least physically.

Trusting him with my body doesn't mean trusting him with my heart.

Or so I told myself during my "it's okay to sleep with your ex-husband" mental pep talk.

It was a successful one too, because seconds later, I threw in the towel with a silent, *Fuck it.*

Arching my back, I pressed my ass against his hips and circled. I heard his groan just as I closed my eyes and set aim on his mouth.

Only he didn't meet me halfway.

He didn't meet me at *all.*

He released me and walked away, saying, "I wish I could say

the same about your car. It was a piece of shit when we bought it. It's worse now. You need something new."

I blinked.

What had just happened?

Oh, that's right. I got shut the fuck down by my ex-husband after he'd basically fondled my boobs and pulled my hair.

Roman Leblanc strikes again.

"Get out!" I growled. (Yes, growled. Apparently, it was contagious.)

"Yep," he replied like I'd asked him to pass the salt. He never looked back as he headed out the door, but he paused just before closing it long enough to call over his shoulder, "After our meeting, I have to hit the office for an hour or so today. I'll bring back dinner."

He would *not* be bringing dinner back that night because I'd be staying at the dodgy motel two counties over. I didn't inform him of this information by chasing him down the stairs the way I would have liked. Instead, I took a shower, brushed my teeth, and got dressed, all the while cursing my libido.

CHAPTER TWELVE

ROMAN

Our attorneys had nothing. Not. One. Fucking. Thing. The cops weren't allowed to tell us the name of the other couple involved so we could deal with it privately. We had to sit on our hands and wait for the APD to feed us more information as it became available—*if* it became available.

I was beyond frustrated by this news, but Elisabeth was notably distraught. My attempts to soothe her only made it worse.

She was probably pissed at me for having shot her down in the bedroom when she'd all but offered me her naked body on a silver platter. But *fuck*. I'd had fifteen minutes before Whit and Kaplin arrived. There was no way, the first time I had her in what felt like an eternity—but probably calculated closer to three years—it was going to be in a quickie against the closet wall. Though, after that little grind down with her ass, I'd been tempted.

After our attorneys gave us a full briefing and left, Elisabeth locked herself away in the second bedroom, stating that she had work to do. She probably did, but the way she'd said it was more like, *Get the fuck out of my house.*

I gave her that because I did, in fact, have work to do. And the sooner I got to the office and got it done, the sooner I could get back over to her place and finish what she had started.

It was a rare day when I didn't wear a suit to the office. I hated that shit, all stiff and as comfortable as a cardboard straitjacket, but if I wanted people to believe I belonged behind the massive desk in the corner office, I had to look the part.

After my morning, though, I hadn't felt like going back to my apartment before heading in for a couple of hours. So, in a pair of jeans that were barely held together by a thread and a T-shirt that wasn't much better, I exited the elevator at Leblanc Industries.

"Mr. Leblanc?" my secretary said with surprise.

Just as fast, a man repeated, "Mr. Leblanc?"

I stopped as he moved toward me. "Can I help you?"

He was around my age, well-built, and exuding authority, so it didn't surprise me in the least when he flipped a badge my way. "Agent Heath Light, DEA. Can we have a word in private?" He tucked a manila folder under his arm in order to extend a hand.

I often had members of the force in the office; I made bullet-proof material for a living. But, with my luck, Simon Wells had sent this guy by to harass me into selling him a load of Rubicon.

I shook his outstretched hand and said, "Listen, I'm really busy today. Can you make an appointment for next week? I'd be happy to have a sit-down and discuss numbers with—"

"This is *personal*, Roman."

Personal.

Roman.

The fuck?

I arched an eyebrow as I gave him a slow nod, calling to my secretary, "Hold my calls."

I led the way to my office as he silently followed behind me. Once inside, he didn't get much more talkative. I sat in my chair and fired my computer up as he walked around, inspecting the pictures hanging around the room.

He pointed to one on the wall and said, "She's cute."

I rocked back in my chair and replied, "She's my *sister*."

"You still caught up on your ex?" he questioned like the ballsy motherfucker he clearly was.

I sat up, propped my elbows on my desk, and ignored his question. "What can I help you with today, Agent Light?"

He tipped his chin in my direction. "Lucked out. Your secretary told me you were out for the day."

"I *am* out for the day," I corrected. "So, if you could speed this up, I'd be much obliged."

He finally moved to the chair in front of my desk and sat. "Good. This way, it'll be easier to explain away that I was *never* here."

"I'm sorry?"

He slid a photo from his envelope but kept it facedown. "Roman, I'm here on a *very unofficial* capacity today. You got me?"

I narrowed my eyes, my gaze going to the photo I couldn't make out. "I got you," I replied skeptically.

"I also need your word that you're not gonna go off half-cocked and get yourself killed. That would make my life *extremely* messy right about now."

"Get to the fucking point," I demanded, quickly losing my patience with the vague bullshit.

"That your word?"

I shrugged. "It's gonna have to be. The only other ones I got for you are: Get the hell out of my office."

He stared at me for a minute before his face split in a grin. "I hear you and your woman got some news yesterday."

Now, *that* got my attention.

I steepled my fingers under my chin. "We did. You got anything in that magic envelope of yours that might be helpful to me?"

He grinned again and then demanded, "Your word."

"Never seen you in my life. I spent the day at home with Elisabeth, reuniting our marriage between the sheets."

He chuckled. "Works for me." Sliding a grainy, black-and-white surveillance picture across the desk, he said, "Walter Noir. Bad guy. And, when I say bad guy, I mean bad. Fucking. Guy. We've been keeping tabs on him for the last three years. He's the big name in drugs in the city right now. His army is strong, but worse than that, they're tight. Nobody in or out without Noir's personal approval. He's into some deep shit. You owe that man money, he's got tricks that make the old-school mob look like child's play. The blood on his hands could forge rivers."

I set the photo back on my desk. "And you're telling me this why?"

He pulled more pictures from the envelope and then slid the bottom one my way. "That's his wife Clare."

I could only see the side of her face, but that was all I needed in order to make out the wide black-and-blue bruise covering her cheek.

"Jesus," I muttered.

"That was taken outside of her gym eight months ago. It's the only place he allows her to go. The bastard keeps her on a tight leash." He passed me another picture. "This one was taken five months ago."

In this image, she was looking straight at the camera, tears flowing down her cheeks and dark bruises peeking from the neck of her tank top.

"This one was three months ago." Another image of the thin, blond, battered woman.

He started to slide another my way, but I lifted my hand in the air.

"Enough. I got it. Get to the part where you give me something helpful."

He stood and bent over my desk, slapping a picture down into the center. Then he stabbed his index finger down on the back of a little, blond head in the woman's arms and changed my entire life with one sentence. "That is the child who may or may not be your daughter."

I shot to my feet, the chair rolling from under me and slamming into the shelves that lined the wall behind me. After snatching the picture off the desk, I brought it up to my face for a closer inspection. It was nothing but a head full of white curls, but I couldn't tear my eyes away.

"Are you sure?" I asked.

"Am I sure it's your kid? No. Do I think it's a strong possibility based on the asshole who's involved? Yes."

I snatched my desk phone up and lifted it to my ear, but his hand slammed down on the base, hanging it up.

"What the fuck are you doing?"

"I'm calling the cops…or shit, my attorney…or, Christ, *someone*."

"I *am* the cops, Roman. And I assure you there is not one fucking thing we can do to help you here. If we could, I'd be off doing it rather than standing here, risking my job."

"Jesus, shit!" I yelled, raking my hand through my hair. "What the hell am I supposed to do here?" I snatched a picture of the bruised woman off the desk and lifted it his way. "He doing that to the kid?"

He cut his eyes away. "Tessa. Her name's Tessa, and I don't know."

"Bullshit! You know."

"No. I really don't fucking know. But even if he isn't. He *will*. Eventually."

"Goddamn it!" I slammed my fist down.

"You cannot go to the authorities with this."

"Then what the fuck do you expect me to do!" I yelled so loud the windows rattled.

His eyes hollowed into dark, treacherous pits. "I expect you to get *her* out."

"Kidnapping?" I laughed humorlessly. "Fan-fucking-tastic idea."

"Not the kid." He once again stabbed his finger down on my desk. Only, this time, it landed on the woman. "*Her*."

"What?" I asked in disbelief.

"She's the key to this entire investigation."

"Fuck your investigation," I shot back.

"That woman holds all the answers. Legally, she's the mother of that child. She can submit to DNA testing on herself and the girl. We find out the kid's not hers, we have ourselves a case no judge could ignore. Court order on Walter Noir plus her testimony on all the bullshit she's seen over the years. That man's done."

He made it sound so easy. But just the fact that he was standing in my office told me it was the impossible. I had a sneaking suspicion that I was about to become the DEA's sacrificial lamb.

"And what if she doesn't submit to DNA? She might be on a tight leash, but what if she doesn't want to get away? You'd be throwing me into the line of fire, keeping your hands clean, *and* getting your case. No fucking thanks."

His jaw turned to granite, and his hands flexed at his sides. "You get her away from that man, I have not one single doubt that she will sing like a fucking bird. She's scared, Leblanc. But, from what we can tell, she is *not* involved in his shit. She's just a victim. Best thing that ever happened to her is that lab tech spilling it on the doctor and Noir. She needs an out, and I need you to get off your ass, get creative, and give that to her."

"And how exactly do you expect me to do this?" I asked, my voice thick with sarcasm as I walked around the desk and settled on the corner. "Just walk into the lion's den and take his woman *and* his child?"

He crossed his arms over his chest and ignored my question. "The second best thing that happened to her was her embryo being switched with *yours*."

I scoffed and blankly gazed out the window. "Right."

"Leblanc, I've done my research on you. Prior military. Infantry. Two purple hearts and a boatload of men who respect the fuck out of you. You're smart. Fucking loaded, yet you live in a shithole apartment in the garage of an even bigger shithole house. You're charitable but run your business with a heavy hand. You wanted to be a family man, but that wasn't in the cards. Now, your ex-wife hates you, but you've been making some headway there in the last twenty-four hours, yeah?"

I pushed to my feet and took a step toward him. "You been watching me?"

He didn't hesitate to grin as he said, "Since the moment that snitch said your name."

"Right."

"Right," he replied, moving back to his chair, grabbing his envelope before riffling through it. "If there was ever a man who could handle this, it's you. You have the resources. So fucking use them. Get eyes on Clare, find a good time, and then make your approach. Be gentle. She spooks easy. She needs help, Roman. Make her understand that you can give her that." He pulled one last picture out and set it facedown on my desk. Then he passed the envelope my way. "That's as much information as I could get on her. Her address. Schedule. Gym location. All of her background. It should be a good start for whoever you hire. And should you need someone you can trust, there's the name of a protection agency in there as well. It's run by a man named Leo James. He used to be DEA. He mainly does personal security now, but you give him a call, drop my name, and he'll take care of you."

I nodded though I had no idea what I was agreeing to, but I took the envelope from his hands, knowing I had to do something.

Heath walked to the door. Then he stopped and looked back at me. "I don't think I need to remind you about the urgency of this situation, but I'm gonna do it anyway. Do *not* sit on this, Leblanc. Get on the phone, throw some money at people, and get that woman and *your daughter* out of there."

My body jerked at his definitive use of the term *your daughter*.

"Saw pictures of Elisabeth at the police station," he added, lifting his chin to the photo he'd left facedown on my desk. "It's obvious."

I immediately snatched it up and…

"Holy shit," I gasped.

But there was no way to deny it.

The oxygen drained from the room and the only thing left was a photo of a child with blond ringlets and a face I'd recognize anywhere. I'd seen it in my dreams nearly every night as we'd struggled through infertility.

She was Elisabeth's.

Absolutely. One hundred percent. Without question.

By the time I tore my gaze up, Heath was gone.

I didn't do as he'd instructed. I didn't pick the phone up and make any calls.

Instead, I grabbed my keys and stormed from the office.

One destination in mind.

And it wasn't home.

CHAPTER THIRTEEN

CLARE

I'd cried myself to sleep the night before. That wasn't anything new. However, this time, I did it in Walt's arms. I'd had no other choice. He hadn't let me out of his sight since he'd stormed into Luke's office, yanked me into his arms, and hugged me as if he hadn't seen me in decades rather than minutes. He glared at Luke only for a second before he guided me, with Tessa in my arms, out to a waiting car in the parking lot. The police were swarming, but no one could touch Walter Noir.

The entire day had been mind-boggling. I'd expected Walt to lose his shit that I'd spoken with the police—even if they had been the ones speaking to me. But the minute we arrived home, he gave me the kind, gentle, and understanding man I'd fallen in love with while we had been dating. I knew now that that man didn't exist, but as my heart struggled to beat with the newest gaping hole, I'd never been so grateful for the façade.

The moment he got me behind closed doors, he guided me up to the office, where he produced two sets of DNA results. My name at the top of one, his at the top of the other, Tessa's on both. I stared at them as he crouched in front of me, holding my hand and explaining that the police had approached him weeks earlier about the possibility of a lab error. He'd refused the DNA test because he'd feared they were using it as a ploy to once and for all get a legally surrendered sample of his DNA.

For an average man, handing the police department a sample of DNA would be no big deal and the results would end up in a dusty box in the evidence room at the end of an investigation.

For a man like Walter Noir—a money-laundering, drug-dealing, murdering low life with ties to people so bad that the government didn't even have them on a radar yet—handing his DNA over was the equivalent of a life sentence. I didn't know everything Walt was involved in, but I knew enough. I was positive there was a case file the size of a library on him, and the cops were begging for a way to tie him to it all.

So he told me that he'd had his own DNA tests performed at a private lab to ease his mind, and he hadn't told me because he hadn't wanted to upset me.

As if he'd ever cared if he upset me before.

Still in a state of shock, I listened to him while tracing my finger over Tessa's name, but never Noir. And, for the briefest of seconds, I wished that the results read differently. I couldn't live without Tessa, but if it meant she wasn't Walt's, I could die with a whole heart.

I nodded and told him that I understood.

But I understood nothing.

The truth was masked by a million lies.

The only thing I knew for sure was that Walt's "results" were worth about as much as the paper they were printed on, based on nothing more than the fact that they had come from his hands.

I wasn't sure if the cop's story held any validity, but I wasn't in any position to ask questions.

At least, not yet.

Tessa was mine no matter what a piece of paper read.

My job as her mother was to keep her safe, and that didn't end because of genetics—or the lack thereof.

Unfortunately, that job became exponentially more difficult the very next day.

Tessa and I were playing with sidewalk chalk on the driveway when a black Range Rover stopped at the front gate.

It wasn't unusual for Walt's men to show up and let themselves in, but they all had their own code to get inside, so it caught my attention when the man put the car in park and exited his vehicle.

"Mrs. Noir?" he called, moving toward the bars of the gate.

He was big, his shoulders broad, his hair perfectly styled, but he was wearing a pair of tattered jeans and a vintage T-shirt that had to be older than I was. And it should be known he was wearing it *really* well. But there was no way a man like that could afford a car like the one he rolled up in. He had to be one of Walt's men. I didn't care what the old slogan said—crime definitely paid.

"Did you forget your code?" I called out, using my hand to shield the sun from my eyes.

"I…ah… Yeah. Any chance you could let me in?"

Not if I value my life. I strolled closer, figuring he must be new. "Sorry, man. You know the rules. Call one of the guys."

"I…don't have my phone," he replied. "Any chance I can borrow yours?"

I barked a laugh. Clearly, he didn't value *his* life. I was off-limits to all of Walt's guys. This conversation alone was borderline dangerous.

I stopped in front of the gate and shook my head. "What's your name? I'll text Brock and see if he can help you out."

I was pulling my phone from my pocket when it happened. His hand darted through the bars, and he grabbed my forearm and slammed me into the gate.

My heart lurched as my face pressed against the metal bars.

"Listen to me," he demanded in a rough and scary whisper.

My eyes darted back to Tessa, who was still thankfully focused on her sidewalk chalk Picasso of Dora the Explorer. "Let me go! He'll kill you if he sees you touching me!" I said quietly so as not to startle her.

His voice was low and desperate as he said, "My name is Roman Leblanc. My wife and I did in vitro fertilization at Peach

City Reproductive Center three years ago. The police recently informed us that our embryos might have been switched. And I'm here because I believe they were switched with yours, and I also believe your husband is responsible."

My lungs burned at the same time my nose began to sting. What was a nightmare within a nightmare called? Because I was currently living one.

"You're wrong." I lied. "Let me go." I attempted to shake his hand off, but his grip tightened.

"I also believe you, much like my wife and I, are an innocent party in this. I've heard about your husband, Clare. I know he puts his hands on you. On her."

As I struggled against his hold on me, Tessa decided to finally look up.

"Mama!" she cried, and his hold on me momentarily loosened at the sound.

I took the opportunity to yank my arm from his grasp, but just as quickly, he caught the front of my shirt.

"I'm a man of resources, Clare. I can save you. I can save Tessa," he swore, his desperate, gray eyes shining the truth. He believed he could do it.

I believed something a little different. "You're about to get us both killed! Let me go. Walk away. And forget this address. *Now,*" I spat back at him.

Tessa careened into my legs, sobbing. I patted her hair down and held Roman's stare. "Shhh… Mama's okay. The scary man was just leaving."

His face was stone, but I saw the wince before he could hide it.

"Leave before he sees you here," I begged.

He shook his head. "Two choices. You pick her up and get in my car right this fucking second. Or, the next time you see me, I will be taking her *without* you."

The blood roared in my ears, and my vision tunneled.

I'd spent my life protecting her from one asshole. I sure as hell wasn't going to allow another to take her from me.

Years of pain and fear all joined forces in the span of a second, igniting my adrenaline into a fiery rage. My fist flew through the bars of the gate, slamming into his face as I shrieked, "You will not touch my daughter! Ever."

Surprise registered on his face as he dodged my second scrambled blow. "Then help me get her away from him!" he implored. "I'm here to help you, Clare. I swear on my life I would never let anything happen to her. *Or you.* Just open the fucking gate and get in my goddamn car." Anguish filled his voice, but again, even through my fury, I knew he was being honest.

But Walt had held that same truth in his eyes once, and look where that had gotten me.

His hand was still wrapped in the front of my shirt, and even with the adrenaline fueling me, I was no match for him, so I drew in a breath and used the only resource I possessed.

It was wrong, and it felt filthy to utilize it on what seemed like a decent man, but much like the rest of my life, I was out of options. Opening my mouth, I screamed Walt's name at the top of my lungs.

His eyes grew wide as he started shaking his head. "No!" he growled. Then his anger morphed into pleas. "Come with me. Please." His eyes flashed to the door behind me.

Tears rolled down my cheeks as I waited for my dark knight to appear, swoop me off my feet, and carry me back to the dungeons of Hell.

"Clare, please," he said, digging into his back pocket and retrieving his wallet. Without releasing me, he flipped it open and shoved it in my face. "This is my wife. Look at her!"

It took a second for my eyes to focus, but when they did, I wasn't sure I'd be able to see anything else ever again.

Tessa's eyes.

Tessa's nose.

Tessa's hair.

Tessa's smile.

"No," I breathed.

With the exception of my eyes, I'd always thought Tessa looked like me. But, with one glance at that woman, I realized just how wrong I'd been.

"Her name's Elisabeth, and she's a good woman. I scared you. I'm sorry. But please hear me when I say I *can* help you. And if you don't believe me, fine. Give me the DNA. Get the police involved. They can help you. I'm not here to take her away from you. I'm here to get you *both* someplace safe."

I couldn't have answered if I'd tried.

But I never even got the chance.

"Fuck!" Roman barked, letting me go and then hauling ass back to his car.

Walter must have finally shown up to save me—from a man who was actually trying to *save* me.

No.

No.

No.

No.

No.

No.

No!

CHAPTER FOURTEEN

ELISABETH

I spent the day finding things to do in order to keep my mind off… well, my life.

I returned phone calls from clients who had zero intention of actually buying a house. Replied to emails from other clients who were concerned about why their overpriced, smelly house had been on the market for over twenty-four hours. And then I had lunch with Jon where I had the unfortunate task of informing him that Roman was back in my life. At least temporarily.

He smiled. Lied and said he was happy for me. I felt like a total heel. After a quick hug in front of a sandwich shop, I watched a good friend walk away for what I hoped wouldn't be the last time.

Roman was in a mood when he got home. Unfortunately, so was I, considering my house was not his home and he had used a key, which I had not given him, to get in the front door. He'd at least had the good manners to toss it in the key basket when he'd slammed the door behind himself. I made a mental note to remove it from his key ring before kicking him out.

"What are you doing here?" I snapped, rising off the couch as he marched to the back door to let a tap-dancing Loretta outside.

It should be said that she was not the best guard dog.

"Change of plans. I'll have Seth deliver dinner again. Figure out what you want. I need a shower," he said before heading to the stairs.

"Um, maybe we should try that again? What are you doing here?" I asked his back while following him up.

"Anything but Chinese and I'll be cool."

"Roman," I called. I was hot on his heels as he walked past my bedroom door and yanked the door to the hall closet open.

"Actually, I could do a good burger."

"Roman!" I finally yelled when it was clear he had no intentions of answering my question.

He lifted his gaze to mine and said, "What?"

"What?" I repeated, dumbfounded.

"Yeah. *What*, Lis? You got something to say? Let's hear it, because right now, I need a shower, a beer, and, if it's good with you, a fucking burger."

Roman was officially off his rocker, so I gave it to him gently. Which meant I only used minimal sarcasm when I *gave* it to him.

"Okay. Well, then you better hurry home and get on that."

"That's what I'm trying to do." He bent down to the bottom of the closet and retrieved a gym bag that was busting at the seams.

He's leaving. Praise the Lord!

He squeezed my hip as he walked past me...

Directly.

Into.

My.

Room.

"What are you doing?" I asked a little louder than I had planned, but it was still below a shriek, so I chalked it up as a huge demonstration of self-restraint.

He tossed the bag into the corner by the bed, and it slid across the hardwood until coming to rest against the wall. "Jesus Christ, Lis. We *just* discussed this."

"No. What we discussed was you going home to *your* house, taking a shower, drinking a beer, and ordering a burger. I'm not sure why I'd have to agree to said burger seeing as how I *won't* be eating dinner with you. But, if you need that approval, you got it!"

His eyes narrowed and the muscles in his sexy, sexy jaw began to tick as he ground out, "I know you heard me say I was checking back in last night."

I threw my arms out to my sides. "Still not a hotel!"

He sucked in a hard breath, his chest expanding, and just like his jaw, it was sexy squared. "I had a shit day, Lis," he warned, scrubbing a hand over his smooth chin. "I'm not coming home to more shit. So check your attitude before I check it for you."

My mouth fell open as I gasped. "You did *not* just threaten me."

"For fuck's sake," was all he said before he was on the move.

And, as it seemed he only had one speed when he was pissed, he did it *fast.*

One of his hands went to my ass, the other into the back of my hair, and he had me pinned against the wall beside the door before I could even protest.

My body heated from head to toe as his fingers in my hair curled into a fist like he had done so many other times over the last twenty-four hours.

It was clear I needed to either shave my head or find a way to amputate his arms, because the sparks that fired off inside me had become progressively more intense each time. I feared I'd spontaneously combust if there was a next time.

"Roman," I breathed, though I should have been fighting against him.

Coulda. Shoulda. Woulda.

"I'm not fucking leaving. There is a shitstorm brewing around us, and I'm gonna take care of it. But, in that, I'm gonna take care of you, too. You gotta trust me on that, Lis. I fucked up in the past. I thought I was doing the right thing, but I see now that I wasn't. I'll explain that to you later. But do not for one second think that you are going to melt for me the way you did yesterday, again last night, and then again this morning after two fucking years and then you're gonna take it away."

"I don't know what you're talking about," I said, feigning innocence, though I knew exactly what he was talking about. I had melted for him. I just wasn't ready to acknowledge it. Not even to myself, and certainly not to him.

He twisted his lips. Then he proved his point by using my ass to grind me against his thickening length, which drew a moan from my throat.

"You feel it between us," he declared.

"Roman, you're very well…um…endowed," I informed in a sugary-sweet tone before finishing with a snap. "Of course I fucking feel it." It was a last-ditch effort to keep from falling under his spell.

It failed.

He grinned arrogantly and gave my ass a squeeze.

I moaned, and this time, I ground into *him.*

He dropped his elbow to the wall. "Christ, Lis."

That small victory allowed me to take some of the power back. I couldn't lie: I wanted Roman. I'd been physically and mentally strung out all afternoon as I'd sat on the couch, waiting for him to come back while equally hoping he didn't.

But the fact remained. He did come back. And, now, he had me pinned against the wall, only two layers of clothes separating me from what I knew would be an incredible night of ecstasy. And, through all of this, he hadn't kissed me yet.

And I couldn't bring myself to care.

"Fine. If we're gonna do this, we're doing it my way. One night. You leave when we're done."

"Done?" He laughed. And not just a chuckle. I'm talking an all out belly laugh like I'd taken up a side gig as a stand-up comedienne.

"I'm serious," I defended.

"You're a lot of things. But serious is not one of them. I get inside you, I'll have my ring back on your finger by tomorrow night."

Oh, hell no! We are not going back down that road.

I gave him a hard shove. "You will *not.* Don't even think about it. That is not what this is about."

He smirked. "Don't worry, baby. I'm not proposing."

That mildly relaxed me.

Well, until his lips descended upon mine and he said, "But you'll still say yes," a half second before taking my mouth.

Oh God.

Yes.

Without hesitation, I opened like the desperate woman I was, welcoming him home. His tongue greedily swirled with mine, and I circled my arms around his neck, taking him deeper, my nipples tingling as they met his chest.

After releasing my hair, he moved his hand down to the other side of my ass and lifted me off the floor. I took the cue and wrapped my legs around his waist. My dress gave way and his straining hard-on made contact with my lace-covered core, forcing a cry from my lips.

It had been too long.

Too long without him.

Too long since I'd reached for the toy tucked into the back of my bedside table.

Too long since I'd dropped my finger between my legs in the shower.

Part of that was because it paled in comparison to the real thing.

The other part being that I couldn't close my eyes without imagining it was *him.*

No matter how much I'd told myself to let him go, he was always in the forefront of my mind.

But there he was, in the flesh, carrying me to a bed that had once been ours, and I was ready to let him take me in any and every way he wanted.

He set me on the edge of the mattress and then followed me down. His hands landed on either side of my head, his mouth still moving with a practiced ease over mine.

I kept my legs around his hips, locking my feet at the ankle and using them as leverage to circle myself against him.

"Fuck, baby," he grumbled into my mouth.

I made fast work of peeling his shirt over his head then sat up off the bed long enough for him to tug the zipper at the back of my dress down. He didn't delay in pulling it over my head.

As much as I'd lied to myself about what was going to happen if he showed back up tonight, deep down, I'd known. And it was that knowledge that left me sitting in front of him in only a pair of black lace panties and a matching bra that were not only beautiful, but the pattern was so wide that it was damn near invisible. Everything from my nipples to my slit was on display.

With an approving rumble, he raked his eyes over me. Licking his lips, he pushed me back flat and sank to his knees between my legs, which were hanging over the side of the bed.

"Repeat after me," he ordered, gliding his hands up my chest, gripping both of my breasts, and then smoothing his palms back down my stomach.

I moaned, arching off the bed while seductively sliding my bare foot up his side.

"This is not one night. You will not shut down on me. I get you're scared. We'll figure out that part later. After I make you come, fast and hard against my mouth. After I shower. After I drink a beer. After my burger. But before I fuck you."

Drunk on the promise of feeling him between my legs, I would have agreed to anything, but something he'd said required discussion.

Brazenly, I sat up and threaded a hand into the top of his hair, using it to pull him back to my mouth for a toe-curling kiss. When I released his mouth, I corrected him. "*After* you fuck me."

"No," he replied firmly.

I had no choice but to move my assault farther south. Dragging my tongue down the corded muscles of his neck, I pushed my argument. "We'll talk *after*, Roman."

His hand moved into the back of my hair again, and it wasn't helping his case in the least. My entire nervous system lit up like the New York City power grid.

And then the most incredible thing happened.

For the first time since he'd come back into my life, Roman Leblanc didn't argue.

"Okay. *After*," he rumbled, thrusting a hand into my panties then pressing a single finger inside me.

"Yes," I panted against his shoulder while spreading my legs wider.

"Take off your bra, baby," he ordered, giving my hair a gentle pull and adding another finger.

"Oh God," I cried at the beautiful bite at my scalp.

"Off," he repeated, guiding my mouth back to his.

As his tongue stroked mine, I obeyed and unclasped the back of my bra, allowing it to fall from my arms.

I groaned in remorse when his hand left my hair, but then I groaned for a different reason as it landed on my breast. I rolled my shoulders back to encourage him to take more. I didn't have the biggest breasts, and truth be told, they'd been fuller when we'd first met, but his large hand more than covered all of me. Yet, if there was even a millimeter he wasn't touching, I wanted him to find it.

His hand disappeared from between my legs at the same time he released my mouth and roughly pushed me to the bed. I went down easily, knowing what was next: Roman's order of operation.

First, he stripped my panties down my legs.

Second, he stripped his jeans down his legs and palmed his heavy cock as he stepped out of them.

Third, my personal favorite part, he dropped to his knees and sealed his hungry mouth over my clit.

A strangled cry escaped my lips, the pressure climbing high within me.

Fourth, one arm snaked up my chest, gripping my breast and

sending the perfect balance of pain and pleasure searing through me.

And, lastly, when I was perilously close to falling over the edge, he thrust two fingers deep, coaxing the orgasm from the inside.

"Roman!" I moaned, fisting his hair as I rode my release out against his mouth.

When I stopped pulsing around his fingers, he lifted his head and rose to his feet.

"Back up," he ordered, prowling toward me, his hand glistening with my release as it pumped his cock.

Still in a post-orgasm high, I sluggishly shimmied up the bed, dropping my legs open as he followed me up on his knees.

Using my thighs, he stopped my ascent and dragged me back toward him. "Far enough."

"Condom," I breathed as he hovered over me.

His response was fast and final. "No."

"But—" I started.

He cut me off. "I'm not using a fucking condom with my wife."

"I'm not—"

"I swear to God, Elisabeth. Do not fucking finish that sentence."

And then the most incredible thing happened.

For the first time since Roman Leblanc had come back into my life, *I* didn't argue.

"I'm clean," I whispered.

"I know you are, baby, and so am I, okay?" he said, positioning himself at my opening.

"Okay." My eyes fluttered closed with anticipation.

And then he drove in with a gentle dominance that spurred orgasm number two to mercilessly rear up. The feeling of finally being full again overwhelmed me. My body shook as I fought a second release back. I wanted to ride it out with him, but emotions were scrambling my resolve, leaving me unable to hold back.

"Roman," I whispered, a single tear escaping the corner of my eye.

All at once, his arms slid under me and lifted me so he was on his knees, our chests smashed together, and my face tucked into his neck. "Shhh. Stay with me."

I folded my legs around his back while he used his upper-body strength to lift me up and down, setting a relentless rhythm that would have us both finishing in seconds rather than minutes.

I finally lost the battle and came as he speared into me, his arms squeezing me painfully tight. His speed increased, and then he planted himself to the hilt, groaning, "Lis," as he emptied inside me.

I clung to his shoulders as he lowered me back down to the mattress, our connection remaining until he shifted to my side. He was still holding me, but the loss was staggering.

He gathered me in his arms, tucked my face back into his neck, and brushed the hair off my neck.

We sat in silence for somewhere between a second and a century, his fingers lazily drawing patterns on my shoulder, before I finally found the courage to confess, "I miss you."

He sighed. "You have no idea."

My heart wrenched, and I couldn't keep the ache from my voice as I asked, "What happened to us?"

His arms spasmed around me, and then he kissed me hard on the top of my head, letting it linger for so long that I wasn't sure he was going to reply.

But, when he finally did, I still wasn't ready for the answer.

"Do you remember the lamb gyro?"

I stopped breathing, and he must have taken that as confirmation.

"Well, this time, I really fucked up. I actually lost you, and now, I'm lying here, praying that you'll let me fix it. Otherwise, I'm gonna look like a real ass when I propose tomorrow night and you say no."

A sound registering between a laugh and a sob came out, and I hugged him tight. "Please don't."

"I won't," he promised. "But you have to understand I will eventually."

"Roman," I pleaded.

"I can fix this," he declared.

"Stop."

"I can fix *us*," he swore.

"Please, stop."

"I *can* fix us."

"Hush." I kissed his chest.

"I *will* fix us, Elisabeth," he vowed. "Mark my words. I will not spend my life without you."

How do you argue with that?

"Okay," I agreed, completely unconvinced.

The sun had barely set when his body slacked under my cheek. "Okay," he repeated.

Minutes later, Roman fell asleep.

I listened to his breathing even out until I eventually followed him into dreamland.

And, in my dreamland, he was always there.

Even when he wasn't.

CHAPTER FIFTEEN

ROMAN

I woke up alone, just as I had every morning since she'd left. The hollow ache in my chest was my only company. I rolled to the side to check my alarm clock, and then my mind finally woke, too.

I was at home.

And not the piece-of-shit garage apartment I'd rented from an elderly couple when we'd first split.

I was *home.*

The room was dark, but the clock on her nightstand read only nine p.m. I couldn't have been asleep for more than an hour or two.

The day came back in a rush.

Heath Light

Walter Noir.

Clare.

Dread soured my gut.

And then…

Elisabeth.

Elisabeth.

Elisabeth.

My cock stirred to life as a smile split my mouth.

I scrubbed my hands over my face and pushed myself from the bed. The light in the bathroom was off, so I knew she had to be downstairs.

I dragged my jeans on, leaving my shirt discarded on the bedroom floor, then set about finding her.

The stairs of the old house creaked as I quietly made my way down. I froze in the middle when I heard her whispering in the kitchen.

"Because I'm freaking the fuck out!" she said quietly.

I could see her lower body pacing around the kitchen, the hem of a blue, silk nightgown brushing the tops of her thighs. It didn't appear that anyone else was in the house, so she had to have been on the phone.

I sank down to my ass and stayed out of sight. It was a familiar position for me. I'd done it numerous times in the six months after we'd lost Tripp. But, back then, it wasn't out of curiosity; it was out of desperation. I spent hours sitting on that step, listening to her laugh on the phone with one of her friends. She didn't laugh anymore back then—at least, not with me. I knew that, as soon as I hit the bottom step, she'd hang up and fall back into the pits of despair.

She needed the laughs. And my soul needed to hear her have them.

So, every Saturday morning before I darted off to work in an effort to create a way that I hoped would buy her smile back, I fed like a leech on the soft giggles that were no longer mine. And, when she'd finally hang up, I'd draw in a breath, walk the rest of the way down, and watch her smile slide away.

And then, like the coward I'd been, I'd leave.

Today would be different.

Tomorrow would be different.

Forever would be different.

She could fight me all she wanted. She could vent and freak the fuck out to whoever she was on the phone with. But, when I hit the bottom stair, I would *not* be leaving.

Ever.

I'd lived that life for two years, and I was done with it.

"He said he's checking back in. What does that even mean?"

she whispered. "He doesn't just get to waltz back into my life and decide he's ready to start over. I'm pretty sure I get a say in this, too." She paused. "Oh, shut up! Sex is sex. It's totally different."

I bit my knuckle to stifle my laugh.

"He's an attractive man. I'm a woman with needs. And let's be honest—his cock is huge." I heard her giggle. "Then, if you don't want to hear about it, Kristen, don't bring up sex in the first place."

Dear Lord, it was Kristen. The good news was I knew she'd have my back. The bad news was I was starving, the smell of meat cooking was wafting up the stairs, and a conversation between those two could easily last all night.

Standing, I made my decision and then jogged down the last few stairs.

She was facing me with terrified eyes as I rounded the banister.

"Hey," I said, raking a hand through my hair to get it out of my face, throwing an ab curl and a bicep flex in for good measure.

Clutching the phone at her ear, she stared at my chest and bit her bottom lip.

When I smirked, I swear to God the woman squeaked.

"Kristen, I have to go." She didn't say goodbye before hanging up.

My smile grew.

"Hey," she said, dropping the phone to the counter. Her eyes once again flashed down to my chest. "Do you…uh…need to borrow a T-shirt?"

I shook my head. "Nah. I've got clothes in my bag."

"Right," she said stiffly. Giving me her back, she turned toward the oven. "I…um…don't have an assistant to call for dinner delivery, so I made some burgers. You hungry? They're still warm. I was gonna come wake you up in a minute." She pulled a cookie sheet out of the oven and placed it on top of the stove.

Half of the pan was covered with my favorite seasoned sweet potato fries, and the other side had two handmade beef patties.

I snagged a fry, popped it in my mouth, then spoke around

it. "Was this before or after you told Kristen about my huge cock?"

Her back shot ramrod straight. "I...don't know what you're talking about."

Chuckling, I slid a hand around to her stomach from behind and placed a kiss at the curve of her neck. "Fine. But you wanna tell me why you're freaking the fuck out?"

She sighed, her chin falling to her chest, her hand lifting to cover mine. "Oh, I don't know. Maybe because you're half naked in my kitchen right now after we had mind-blowing sex and where I confessed I miss you and you swore you were going to eventually propose again?"

"Mmm." I hooked my arm over her chest and pulled her flush against my front. "Yeah, but I said I missed you, too. And that I was gonna fix us. And then you made me burgers in a little, blue nightgown."

"I'm serious, Roman. This is too much. Combined with the embryo thing, I can't handle this right now. We need to slow down."

I inhaled deeply, filling my lungs with her sweet, floral scent, then kissed the other side of her neck. "How long did I wait the first time?"

She tried to step out of my grasp as she huffed, "This isn't the first time anymore."

"No. But, baby, you have to understand—we're creeping on two days since I got you back. This *is* me taking it slow."

"Roman, please. You can't fix years' worth of problems in minutes. I need time."

But she'd had two fucking years of time. I wasn't waiting even a minute longer. My life was with her. It always had been. It always would be.

I released her long enough to step in front of her. Then I shoved my hands under her arms and lifted her to sit on the counter beside the stove. Parting her legs, I stepped between them, resting my hands on her bare thighs and announced, "Shit went down today. And I really need to fill you in, but I need your head straight on where *we* are before *we* can move forward to that."

"What went down today?" she asked, worry flashing over her face.

"Your head straight on what's happening between us yet?"

She scoffed. "No. But at least I'd know what shit went down today and won't be lost on both accounts."

I bent at the knees so we were eye level and said, "Let's get you straight. *Then* we'll talk about the shit."

She rolled her eyes. "Money has made you bossy."

"No. Living without you has made me realize that time's wasting. And I'm done watching the clock."

She opened her mouth to reply, but I silenced her with a kiss.

Her mouth was stiff at first, but it was Elisabeth. She soon became pliable.

And then she came alive.

Her arms wrapped around my neck, bringing me closer. I forced myself away when I felt the tip of her tongue touch my bottom lip.

I had minutes.

Not years—which is what it was going to take if her tongue entered the equation.

"I got out of the military because it wasn't ever going to provide me with the life I wanted for myself. I was a single, twenty-seven-year-old guy, and I wasn't getting any younger. When my time came up, the decision was easy. Between deployments, I had saved up around a hundred grand, so I moved home and dropped it all in a little building in downtown Atlanta in order to open Leblanc Consulting. I made twenty-two thousand dollars that first year. It was a fucking joke. But I had no doubt it could have been a success with time."

She raised an eyebrow. "I know all of this, Roman."

And she did.

But she didn't know the whys of my decisions back then—the same whys that had led me to make the decisions that had ultimately ruined us.

"When I met you, my entire world changed in one night. You were the best thing that had ever happened to me. But Leblanc Consulting wasn't going to enable me to give you everything I wanted to. I literally went from the bachelor life to a family man over night. You needed insurance, food, a house, and clothes. So I sold the building, took that entry-level corporate job in the city, put down a chunk of money on this house, finally bought you a diamond a quarter the size of the one I wanted, and then I made a life with you."

Betrayal sparkled in her deep-green eyes. "You told me you wanted that job in the city. You told me Leblanc Consulting was failing and you *needed* an out."

"I *needed* you to be happy."

"What?" Her voice broke as though I'd maimed her.

I quickly assured, "And I have never once regretted that decision. Because part of me giving you those things that made you happy made *me* happy. Watching you fall asleep with a smile on your face in a life I made for us was the most gratifying thing I'd ever done."

She stared at me in disbelief, her head shaking as she said, "Roman, I wasn't falling asleep with a smile on my face because of the life you made for us. I was falling asleep with a smile on my face because I was doing it next to *you.*"

"Right. And I got that even back then, baby. But, for a man, it's different. I can't expect you to understand, but I'm asking you to accept it. For a man, success is measured by your ability to provide a good life for your family. It doesn't have to be money, just a quality of life where your wife can fall asleep with a smile and doing it saying she's happy just to be doing it with you."

I thought she understood what I was saying when she stared at me for several beats without a response.

This was Elisabeth though.

I should have known better.

"Yeah. That makes no sense," she said. "This is why men get a bad rap. Y'all do stupid shit then try to justify it by saying crap like, 'For a man, it's different.' Sorry to be the one to break it to you, but if a man is kind, loving, respectful, makes a woman laugh, knows how to open the pickle jar, and change a flat tire, we really don't need much else. If I needed insurance, food, a house, or clothes, I would get off my ass, get a job, and get that stuff myself. What I can't get on my own is a good, kind, loving, respectful man who makes me laugh, knows how to open a pickle jar, and change a flat tire." She glared at me with an arched eyebrow.

I grinned and added. "With a huge cock."

She shrugged. "Doesn't hurt. But I could still make do if you didn't."

I threw my head back and laughed. God, I'd missed her.

Her fingers traced over my abs as she giggled right along with me.

When I finally sobered, I pressed a closed-mouth, but no less deep, kiss to her smart-ass mouth. Then I got serious again.

I didn't want to do it.

What I really wanted to do was take a shower, drink a fucking beer, eat a homemade burger that was currently getting cold, then go to bed and make love to my wife before she fell asleep with a smile on her face, content to be doing it next to *me*.

But, again…I had minutes.

And years to make up for.

Palming each side of her face, I tipped my forehead to hers and got to it. "Lis, I spent my whole life thinking that, if you wanted something, you work hard and make it happen. And then, one day, I had to face the harsh reality that some things were out of my reach no matter how hard I tried. I couldn't give you a family, and it was the first time I ever felt like I'd failed you."

"Roman," she gasped, but I kept talking.

"It was a such a basic biological function, and I just couldn't do it. Do you have any idea how hard it was as a man to, month after month, watch the woman you wanted to give the world fall apart over pregnancy tests that just wouldn't turn positive? And then the miscarriages." I cleared my throat when a thick, gritty knot took up root.

"Roman," she breathed regretfully. "We both—"

"No, let me say this. It's been too long."

Tears welled in her eyes, but she closed her mouth and gave me a short nod.

I sucked in a breath and let five years of pent-up anxiety fly. "That fucking roller coaster of euphoria when you finally got pregnant, the constant nerves during those first few weeks, then the crash down into utter devastation when you'd start bleeding. Jesus, Lis. It destroyed me. I know it killed you too, but you were stronger than I was. You always got back up and wanted to try again. You have no idea how many times I wanted to tell you no. I couldn't handle it. I wanted it to stop so we could just go back to being us—being happy. But then I'd see that glimmer of hope in your eyes. So I'd pull my shit together and set about giving you the world, regardless that it was shredding me."

"Why didn't you say anything?" she accused, leaning away from me.

I was breaking her. I could see it in her eyes. Everything I'd shielded her from during those years we were trying to conceive was crushing her all over again.

I gave her space and swayed my torso back, but I kept my hips between her legs. "Because, if you wanted it, I wanted to be the one to give it to you."

She chewed on the inside of her cheek, tears streaming from her eyes. "I…I thought we were a team."

"We were!" I swore. "But, baby, infertility is an impossible sport. Everyone loses."

"Until they win," she replied sharply. "You're standing here, talking about our struggle to get pregnant and how that affected you. But you seem to forget the fact that we beat it. We got Tripp."

My eyebrows pinched together. I didn't know how to reply. I'd loved that little boy from the moment Elisabeth had told me she was pregnant. I'd never forget the first time I'd felt him kick. It was the first time I believed in miracles. I'd also never forget the day we found out he was a boy—and then, minutes later, found out about the fluid on his brain and that he probably wouldn't make it to delivery. It'd felt like I'd been hit by freight train. I wasn't sure we could consider that kind of tragedy a victory.

She closed her eyes and whispered, "You never connected with him, but I never thought you'd turn your back on me."

"I never connected with him?" I repeated on a violent whisper. "Have you lost your fucking mind? He died in my arms!"

"And then you left!" she yelled, pushing me back and hopping off the counter. "Like it meant nothing. Like those twelve minutes he was alive weren't worth it. You woke up the next morning while I was still in the hospital, grieving our little boy, and declared you were quitting your job and starting Leblanc Industries."

"So I could give you another child!" I roared.

Her face turned red as she screamed, "I didn't need another child! I needed *you*!" She began pacing the length of the granite island. "God, Roman. What is wrong with you? You act like I was some baby-crazed woman who wouldn't stop until I got a basketball team. I had just lost our son. The last thing on my mind was replacing him."

I stepped toward her, blocking her path. "But you would have wanted to try again eventually, Lis. And nothing had changed. I wouldn't have been able to give it to you. I couldn't do it physically, and it destroyed me when we had to borrow money from your parents the first time. That was my job to provide that for you. And I just couldn't! I started the company, and I did everything I fucking could to earn the money to pay for another IVF cycle." I pinched the bridge of my nose and stared at the floor. "I fucked up. I fucked up. I *fucked* up. I know this now. I should have talked to you. But, in the throes of failing the only woman I've ever loved, the words didn't come easily. I take full responsibility for that."

"God, Roman! You have no idea how often I used to lie awake in that bed, all hours of the night, just praying you'd come home and talk to me."

I slowly lifted my gaze to hers and admitted, "Yeah, I do. Because I used to sit in my car, down the street, waiting for your bedroom light to go off."

"What?" she whispered, a sob catching in her throat.

I reached for her hand, but she snatched it away.

"I couldn't stand watching you cry anymore and I couldn't fix it. I came home a few times and found you talking to my mom or one of your girlfriends, and for those moments, you were okay. Happy, even. But, as soon as your eyes met mine, they filled with tears. I figured staying away was better."

She shoved me as hard as she could. "You dumbass. I missed you. I missed our life. I missed being your wife. That's why I'd cry, because even when you did come home, you *still* weren't there!"

I lifted my hands palm up and, at a loss for more words, said, "I'm sorry."

"You're sorry? You're sorry? That's it?"

Was that it?

Not even fucking close.

I strode toward her, but she backed away just as quickly.

"Don't you dare come near me," she said. "Keep your hands to yourself and out of my hair so I can actually think for once."

This was not how this conversation was supposed to go.

"Lis, stop. Please. Let's just take a deep breath."

But she was far from done. "And I'm sorry, but I'm calling bullshit on your little give-me-another-baby excuse when it comes to your company. You signed over our entire life in the divorce in exchange for my half of your company." She marched forward and stabbed a finger in my direction. "Half that I never wanted! I fucking hate that company. I swear to God it's like the other woman in our relationship. I don't want your fucking money." Another step toward me. "I don't want any-fucking-thing that comes from that company or your precious little Rubicon." Her chest heaved when she finished. She kept her gaze locked on me as she glared expectantly.

Oh, I had a response. But she wasn't going to like it any more than I was going to like telling it.

"Three hundred and seventy-two"—I paused, bending at the waist before finishing—"*thousand dollars.*"

"What?"

"That's how much debt Leblanc Industries was in the day our divorce was finalized."

She gaped and repeated, "What?"

"You think I was eager to saddle you with half of that debt? Fuck that! I had nothing, Lis. But the woman I loved walked away with a house. Furniture to sit on. A bed to sleep in. A piece-of-shit car, but at least she had wheels. It wasn't much. But it was all I could give you."

Her face contorted murderously as she yelled, "Stop being such a goddamn martyr!"

I closed the distance between us in one long stride, catching her just as she crumbled.

Crawling even closer into my chest, she cried, "I hate you so much."

"I know," I breathed, kissing her temple.

"I spent two years of my life without you because you couldn't figure out how to open your fucking mouth and talk to me."

I hugged her as though I could absorb her pain. "I know. But I'm talking now."

"I don't wanna talk now." She whined. "I wanted to talk two years ago. I wanted you to stop me before I ever got to the door."

"I know. And I'm sorry." I kissed every inch of her face and hair that I could reach, her body shaking in my arms, the tiny remnant of my heart shattering all over again.

CHAPTER SIXTEEN

ELISABETH

My chest was tight, the ache lingering. I'd always been confused by the way our marriage had ended. However, hearing Roman's side of it definitely took some of the sting out. Even if I still couldn't completely wrap my mind around it.

I didn't know what all of it meant for us—as far as a future went.

To use Roman's words, my head was definitely not "straight" about what was happening with us.

But I knew with my whole heart that Roman still loved me.

And I knew with my entire being that I'd always loved him.

He was a bossy, suit-wearing, Range-Rover-driving, rich guy I barely recognized. But beneath it all was still my smart, funny, and gentle husband. So I didn't fight as he picked me up off my feet and carried me up the stairs to our bedroom, whispering a million apologies into my hair as we went.

He was still in jeans as he settled us both on the bed, and he wasted no time curling me into his chest. He combed his fingers through my hair until I relaxed on top of him. As I listened to the steady beat of his heart pounding out my favorite lullaby, my tears eventually stopped.

Then, in a bed we had bought together.

A bed where we'd spent countless nights laughing and talking about our days.

A bed where he'd made love to me with his hands, his mouth, and his body.

A bed where our children had been conceived.

A bed where he'd held me after we'd lost them.

A bed where he'd brought me breakfast and flowers every single Mother's Day.

A bed I'd fought the urge to burn on a near daily basis after we'd divorced.

A bed I realized I never wanted him to leave.

I finally got my head straight.

As I lifted my eyes, he looked down to meet my gaze.

"So, um…I guess you can keep the house key. Even though you stole it."

He grinned, and it lit his entire face, his perfect lips to his mischievous eyes.

I tipped my chin up, silently asking for a kiss—an offer he did *not* decline.

It was short but no less meaningful, and it caused a peace I hadn't felt in years to wash over me.

But a tinge of worry still lingered in the back of my mind.

"This isn't over. You know that, right? It's gonna take time to rebuild," I informed him just before he kissed me again.

With our lips still connected, he rolled us so we were on our sides, sharing a pillow. "Patience isn't my strong suit, Lis," he grunted, sliding a hand over my ass.

"Then you're gonna have to figure it out, because things happened, and they cut us both deep. It's gonna take time to heal." I brushed the hair off his forehead. "Now, I'm all for trying to do that healing together, but in order to do that, you're gonna have to find the strength to keep whatever twenty-pound diamond you've probably already bought tucked in your pocket."

This got me another blinding, full-face grin.

I leaned in to kiss his smiling mouth, but by the time I got there, it was no longer smiling.

It was open and sealing over mine.

He swallowed my moan when his tongue glided against mine. Then he fed me a groan as I threw a leg over his hips and ground against his cock.

Lifting my nightie, he shoved his hand inside the back of my panties, gripping hard and rocking me against him.

I lost his mouth as he knifed up, stripped the silk over my head, and threw it across the room. I found his mouth again seconds later as it landed on my breast, sucking my nipple deep and swirling around it with his tongue.

When I arched off the bed, he shoved an arm under my back, lifting me closer to his mouth.

"Oh God, Roman," I cried, writhing beneath him.

He shifted his attention to my other breast, setting off an explosion that traveled to my clit. My legs scissored beneath his heavy weight, but he was too lost in his feast on my chest to catch my silent plea for more.

His mouth was torturous. It took me high, but nowhere near high enough to fall. And, as he flicked his tongue over my peaked nipple, my body craved the release. I took the initiative and slid my fingers between my legs.

He growled and pushed up when he felt my hand move between us.

"Keep going," he demanded, rising off the bed, snatching my panties down my legs as he stood.

I dropped my knees to the sides, his eyes honing in on my fingers playing between my legs.

"Jesus, fuck, you're beautiful," he rumbled, dragging the tips of his fingers up my thigh, over my stomach, and then down the other side.

"Touch me," I begged.

Still staring down, he licked his lips then made the path up my other thigh, over, and down again.

"Haven't been with anyone else," he muttered.

"No one," I confirmed. "Touch me."

"Two fucking years and no one."

Up one thigh.

Down the other.

"No one," I repeated.

Up one thigh.

Down the other.

"I couldn't do it. I knew I'd get back here one day, and I was not bringing another woman with me," he confessed.

My hand stilled as my mouth fell open.

He hadn't been talking about me.

He had been talking about himself.

Oh.

My.

God.

For the first few months after our divorce, I had become physically ill at the idea of Roman being with someone else. Then, after Rubicon had taken off, I'd accepted it as fact. On top of the sexy, smart, and charming man he'd always been, he'd become wildly successful and wealthy to boot. I'd figured women were probably lining up outside his office.

Now, hearing him say that he hadn't been able do it blanketed me in love.

"Keep going," he ordered, his hand still traveling up one thigh and down the other as he stood beside the bed, staring down at me.

My fingers went back to moving, but I was blinking tears back.

"No one?" I squeaked.

He finally lifted his eyes to mine. "I work a lot, but I could've made time. To date or whatever the hell people tell you to do after a divorce. But I always knew it wasn't over with us, and I refused to tarnish that with someone else."

Oh.

My.

God.

My throat closed, and that love flooding my system turned into an all-out wildfire.

Roman Leblanc was mine.

All of him.

Even when he wasn't.

Moving my hand to catch his wrist, I gave him a tug. "Come here, Roman."

He didn't move. He just continued to stare down at me, his face unreadable.

Swinging my legs over the edge of the bed, I sat up and kissed just above his navel.

Going for the button on his jeans, I told him, "I want to feel you, baby. Now's not the night for you to watch." I undid his zipper and pushed the denim down his legs, his thick erection springing free. "However, I'm gonna taste you first. So you can watch for a few minutes longer."

His abs rippled as I wrapped my palm around his cock and guided it to my lips.

"Fuck," he rumbled when I took him to the back of my throat.

I used my hand to work his shaft, my mouth paying special attention to his sensitive crown. His cock twitched with every swirl of my tongue. As I continued to slide him in and out of my mouth, one of his hands dipped to my breast, tugging on my nipple and shooting a tingle down my spine.

He brushed my long hair away from one side of my face, and I glanced up to find him watching, his gaze so intense that it caused goose bumps to pebble my skin.

"Missed your mouth, Lis," he said, fisting the back of my hair.

I cried out as he gave it a sharp, but still in-fucking-credible, tug and popped himself free of my mouth.

"Missed watching you ride my cock more."

"Yes," I moaned.

I'd missed that, too. A hell of a lot.

He smirked. "You ready, baby, or you need me to help with that?"

If help meant his dexterous fingers finally finding their way inside me, then yes, I absolutely wanted help. But I didn't need it. I was more than wet and completely ready. And, judging by the glint in his smoky eyes, he wasn't just going to watch me ride him.

I knew that look well, and I was usually naked before he ever touched me whenever he wore it. He was going to take me from the bottom after he drove me to sheer insanity with his thumb at my clit.

It was *one* of his favorite ways to fuck me.

But it was my *absolute* favorite of all.

Because of this, I did not delay in standing, rolling up to my toes, ghosting my lips across his, and confirming, "I'm ready."

The side of his mouth hiked as he released the back of my hair and gave the bed a chin lift.

I followed his unspoken order and climbed up, watching him step out of his jeans and then prowl up after me.

He didn't touch me as he passed, but I shivered all the same as he settled his muscular body with his back to the headboard. My core clenched as he wrapped his large hand around his cock and gave it a firm stroke.

His gaze lifted to mine, his eyes so dark that they were barely recognizable. "Gotta say I love the way you're looking at me, but all I've had is my hand for the last few years. I'm gonna need you to get your ass over here, climb on top, and give me that pussy."

He did not have to tell me twice.

I moved at near pissed-off-Roman-Leblanc speeds (but not quite) and did exactly as he'd said. I climbed onto his lap, lined us up, and slowly sank down on his cock.

We both bit a curse back when I took him to the hilt. One of his hands went to my ass and rocked me back and forth as if he were trying to make sure I'd taken every last millimeter of him. It was not a hardship because my clit found much-needed friction on his stomach.

I closed my eyes, threw my head back, and ground down harder.

His hands found my breasts and began kneading and plucking as I glided up and down his length.

I set my pace and stuck with it even as his hands became frenzied.

"Find it, Lis," he growled.

I moaned an unintelligible response, leisurely enjoying the hunt.

Suddenly, his hips thrust up, slamming in deep and snatching my orgasm before I could even prepare.

"Roman," I cried, my body shaking as my release tore through me. My hands flew to his pecs for balance, but just as quickly, his arms folded around me, holding me still as he drove up inside me.

It wasn't his usual MO, but it was no less amazing. Thrust after thrust, his strong arms held me to his chest as he fucked me hard and fast. It was feral, and had it been any other man in the world, it would have been punishing.

But it was Roman, and he was back.

He was mine.

And I had always been his.

No one else.

I clung to his shoulders, biting and sucking up and down his neck as he bucked beneath me, slamming in deeper.

It didn't take long before another orgasm started to build, my entire body going tense as it rose within me.

"You gonna give me another one?" he asked on a pant.

"Yes," I breathed.

"Then hurry up," he ordered, driving back in.

As though I had a choice.

And I *really* didn't have a choice as he bottomed out inside me and circled his hips in an overwhelming combination I couldn't fight.

With my face buried in his neck, I let go and came apart in his arms.

He held me tight, gliding in and out for a few more strokes before he let go, too.

"Fuck, Lis," he hissed, his cock jerking as he emptied inside me.

I'd had sex with Roman more times than I could count, but never once had I felt like I'd lost a piece of myself in the process.

I was scared he couldn't say the same, because as I collapsed on his chest, his arms slack at his side, I knew with an absolute certainty I'd taken a piece of Roman Leblanc, and it filled me in immeasurable ways.

Something had broken between us.

But, in the process, something had also been repaired.

CHAPTER SEVENTEEN

ROMAN

Never in all of our years together had I taken Elisabeth so savagely. With the exception of having her hair pulled, she was a slow-build kind of girl. But it had been too long without her—I couldn't keep myself in check. She didn't complain though, and as her body sagged on my chest, sated and spent, I didn't figure she was going to.

"You good?" I asked the top of her hair.

"Mmmm," was her only reply.

I chuckled. "You gonna get cleaned up?"

"Can I say no?" she mumbled.

"You could. But you know you'll get up in the middle of the night and do it anyway."

She groaned but didn't move a muscle.

I gave her ass a squeeze and urged, "Come on, baby. I'll go down and lock up and get Loretta in. Meet you back here in a minute."

"You know, you never got your shower. Or beer. Or burger."

I smiled and gave her ass another squeeze. "No, but I got my fill of you. I'll survive."

She giggled, rolling off me.

I rose from the bed and went to my bag in the corner. My entire life was in that bag. I'd given Seth strict instructions about what to pack. All the clothes from my dressers—and my laundry hamper—sneakers, boots, and flip-flops from the closet, the gun from my nightstand, and a single picture of Elisabeth and Tripp taken minutes before he had taken his last breath. They were the only things I wanted from that shitty garage apartment. Sure, I had a closet full of suits and expensive shoes. There were also two computers, a big-screen TV, a ratty-ass couch, and about a million stacks of papers that had somehow migrated from the office over the years.

But I didn't care about any of that. I could lose everything else tomorrow, and as long as that bag sat in the corner of Elisabeth's bedroom, I'd have everything I'd ever need.

And, as I pulled a pair of boxer briefs on, looking at her as she sat naked and pink-cheeked on the bed while staring back at me, I decided I didn't even need the bag.

I walked back over to her and planted a fist on the bed. After a brief kiss, I said, "Clean up, baby. Two minutes. Want you right back here."

"Okay," she replied.

I kissed her again then headed for the door.

"Roman," she called.

I looked over my shoulder. "Yeah?"

"I'm sorry," she whispered.

My throat tightened. "Nothing—"

"For not seeing how deeply you were affected by the infertility stuff. For not understanding your reaction to losing Tripp. And, most of all, for not fighting harder for us."

"Lis…" I shook my head. "That is *not* on you."

"But it is. And I'm sorry."

I raked a hand through my hair and looked at her.

All innocent angel staring back at me.

My chest ached for the past even as my heart sped with possibilities of the future.

I opened my mouth to say…something. What, I didn't know.

It probably would have been, *I love you*, but I feared it would be, *Marry me*.

I would have meant both, but it was too soon for either.

She finally broke the moment with a soft, "Go get Loretta, baby. Two minutes."

I nodded but didn't move. I needed to say something. I wanted her to understand I didn't need an apology from her but I appreciated the fact that she had still given it to me.

"Two minutes," she repeated with a gentle and understanding smile.

I loved her so damn much that it physically pained me. I didn't want to wait to start our lives all over again. Elisabeth Keller had been born to be a Leblanc.

To be mine.

But, if she wanted to take this slow, I'd figure out a fucking way to make that happen—for her.

I tossed her a weak smile and finally got my feet moving.

After a brief standoff with the man in the hall mirror, I jogged down the stairs, let Loretta in, locked up, and then headed back up to spend the night with Elisabeth wrapped in my arms.

My wife.

The sound of the gunshot woke me from a deep content sleep. Elisabeth jerked on my chest, sucking in a deep breath in what I knew would become a scream. I slapped a hand over her mouth and rolled us both to the floor just as the second shot sounded outside the bedroom door. Loretta went nuts barking, and I heard feet scrambling down on the steps.

"Get in the fucking closet. Call nine-one-one. Do not come out until I come back to get you," I ordered.

Behind my hand, she wildly shook her head as her eyes bulged.

"Go. Now," I growled, releasing her and heading straight for my bag to retrieve my gun from the side pocket. "Phone, Lis," I said, sliding it across the floor.

She caught it and then scooped the dog up and rushed to the closet.

I didn't move to the door until I heard her shut herself in and her panicked voice say, "Yes, I need to report a break-in. There were gunshots inside my house."

With my back to the wall, my gun held high and ready, I swung the bedroom door open. I listened for a moment, but the house was silent. Still cloaked in darkness, I reached a hand around the corner to flip the hall light on, readying for an attack as my eyes adjusted to the light. As the hall came into focus, the man in the mirror didn't greet me. A million tiny cracks formed shards still held together but shattered completely, webbing out from two holes.

It seemed the man in the mirror put up one hell of a fight against whoever had made his way up the stairs, probably with his gun held high and darkness masking his true identity.

Slowly, I made my way down the stairs and found the place empty, the back door standing wide open. It was completely intact, nothing broken, nothing splintered. Just. Open.

It had been less than a minute since I'd left Elisabeth upstairs, and the sounds of sirens were already screaming in the distance. In a city the size of Atlanta, that was a miracle the likes of Moses splitting the Red Sea.

A loud boom at the front door made me spin, my finger poised at the trigger.

The door busted open, and it was only a nanosecond of hesitation that saved his life.

We stared, our guns trained on each other, when Agent Light said, "Gun down, Leblanc."

"Son of a fuck," I ground out, slowly lowering my weapon.

He kept his up. "You okay?" he asked, scanning the house.

"Yeah, we're good. What the fuck are you doing here?"

He didn't reply as he rushed past me, clearing the house, and shutting the back door. When he was finally content that we were alone, he tucked his gun into his shoulder holster and stormed toward me. "You dumb fuck!"

"Excuse me?" I asked, my shoulders rolling back in defense.

The sirens drew closer.

"What the fuck did I tell you? Do not go off half-cocked!" he yelled.

"Light," I started, not in the mood for whatever bullshit he was about to sling. Elisabeth was upstairs in a closet, scared out of her gourd. I did *not* have time for his shit.

"You could have gotten her killed!" he roared, stabbing a finger in my direction. "Clare. Tessa." He paused, his face contorting with fury. "Elisabeth! Goddammit, Roman, I told you Noir was not to be fucked with. So you haul your ass over to his *house* and engage his *wife*? Who, by the way, I will fucking add, if you ever lay a finger on again, I will slit your goddamn throat myself."

"What did you expect me to do after you show me a picture of my child and tell me that she's in the arms of an abusive criminal?"

The muscles in his jaw clicked as he seethed, "I expected you to keep your shit together! But no, I had to sit my ass in a fucking car, watching *your* house all night long to keep Noir from coming in here and snuffing you out."

I took a step toward him, bringing us nose-to-nose, and whispered, "This was one of Noir's guys?"

He barked a humorless laugh. "Fuck, Leblanc. You signed your death certificate by showing up at that man's house today. Putting your hands on *his* wife. Trying to take *his* family. I want you to imagine for a second some man showing up at your house and pulling that shit. You'd fucking kill them. Now, I want you to imagine a piece of shit like Noir, who's killed men for innocently sitting in the same room as his woman." He leaned in close, his eyes flashing malevolent as he whispered, "He's gonna extinguish your entire family."

"Fuck you!" I spat, bile rising in my throat.

He shook his head and backed away. "No. You fucked us both."

Another surge of adrenaline hit me, causing my vision to tunnel. I didn't give one fuck who this Noir guy was. I'd set fire to his world if he thought he was going to lay one fucking finger on Elisabeth.

"Put your hands up," came from the front door, uniformed officers flooding in.

Heath kept his attention on me, his back to the door. "You need to get her away from here. You won't be this lucky next time," he said, slowly lifting his hands in the air. "Remember. Never seen me in your life."

"Right," I mumbled.

He nodded then called out, "Agent Heath Light. DEA. The suspect escaped out the back door."

"Drop your weapons!" the uniforms yelled in a round of chaos.

"Right," I mumbled again, squatting to set my gun on the floor.

Heath pulled his from his holster and did the same before retrieving his badge from his pocket. Once the cops were satisfied with his identity, he took over, passing orders out then getting on his phone to bark out more.

I didn't waste a single second before sprinting back up the stairs to Elisabeth.

The closet door was thankfully still shut, and it was only that sight that finally made my heart slow.

"Lis," I murmured quietly. "It's okay, baby. You can come out."

The door nearly clocked me in the face as it burst open and she came flying out. She launched herself into my arms, her green eyes consumed by fear. "Are…are you okay?"

"I'm good," I assured, holding her tight.

Her body trembled in my arms, so I scooped her off her feet and carried her to the bed, sitting on the edge with her securely in my lap.

She was terrified, but she was putting up one hell of a fight. Her chin quivered, but not a single tear fell from her eyes.

"The police are here," I told her, then kissed her forehead.

"I was so scared," she replied.

I guided her face into my neck, struggling with the knowledge that I'd inadvertently caused all of this. "I know, but it's over now. And everyone's safe, okay?" Judging by what Heath had told me, it was a lie, but I'd make it the truth. Somehow. Someway.

"What the hell happened?" she mumbled against my skin.

This time, I only half lied. "I don't know. You think you can get it together enough to come down and talk to the cops?"

She nodded then hugged me tighter, not budging off my lap. "I just got you back. I can't..." She trailed off.

My gut twisted. It was a sentiment I shared. If anything had happened to her... Fuck that. I was not going down that road.

I glided a hand up the back of her neck and tilted her head to force her eyes to mine. "No one. And I mean *no one* will take you from me. Or me from you, okay? I swear on my life I'll make us safe."

Her eyes suddenly narrowed. "Make us safe? It was just a break-in, right?"

"We'll talk later," I said, shifting her off my lap. "I need to get dressed."

"What aren't you telling me?" she asked my back as I headed toward my bag to pull on jeans and a T-shirt over my boxer briefs.

I ignored her and said, "You need to get..." I stopped when I glanced back and saw her standing there in what could only be described as a church dress. White. Floral. Hideous. "That is a seriously ugly-ass dress." A smile tipped one side of my lips.

She glowered. "I was naked and hiding in my closet from a gun-wielding burglar while my husband took off after him. I pulled on the first thing my hand landed on."

My smile grew as I arched an eyebrow and asked, "Your husband?"

"Don't you dare try to change the subject. What aren't you telling me?" she snapped.

"Later," I said, tugging the tee over my head.

"Roman!"

I leveled her with a glare. "I don't have the energy to deal with your attitude right now. The cops are crawling all over the downstairs, and they're gonna be making their way up here soon. We can talk *later* because, right now, I need to get *my wife* down there so they can take her statement while I make some phone calls and get our shit sorted for the next couple of weeks."

"Couple of weeks?" she questioned incredulously while crossing her arms over her chest.

Fuck, she was cute.

Cute was yet another thing I did not have time to deal with at the moment.

I didn't say a word as I walked over, took her hand, and dragged her to the door.

She quickly gave up with her argument when we got into the hall and she took in the broken mirrors. "Oh God," she gasped, covering her mouth with a hand.

Looping an arm around her waist, I took some of her weight and led her down.

Just as we got to the base, I saw an irate Detective Rorke standing close to a completely unfazed Heath Light.

"And you just *happened* to be passing by the Leblancs' house tonight when you heard gunshots," Rorke accused.

"Yep," Heath replied curtly.

"Seems awful convenient, Light."

"Sure does, considering no one ended up dead." He lifted his head when he saw us come down. His eyes landed on Elisabeth and stayed there as something eerie sifted across his features. "Excuse me," he told Rorke, already on the move in our direction. He stopped in front of Elisabeth, his eyes so intently studying her face that it unnerved me.

She must have felt the same, because she lifted a hand to rest on my stomach and shifted deeper into my side. "Um, hi?"

"Agent Heath Light, DEA," he said robotically.

"Elisabeth Keller."

"Leblanc," I corrected, then snapped my fingers at Light.

His gaze slowly cut to mine.

I stepped around Elisabeth and tucked her into my back. Lowering my voice, I said, "I need the number of your security guy again."

He nodded, digging into his back pocket and pulling a card out while mumbling, "Finally, he does something smart." He passed the card my way. "Shoot me a text when you get free of this shit, and I'll forward you all of his info. He's in Chicago, but drop my name and he should be able to get some guys down here tomorrow. Get someplace safe until then. Yeah?"

"Yeah," I agreed immediately.

Elisabeth's hand tensed at my back, and I swung an arm back to pat her side.

It wasn't much, but in that moment, I had nothing else to offer her.

It was a common trend in our relationship.

But it was one I was planning to break.

I could fix this.

I would fix this.

I will fix this.

CHAPTER EIGHTEEN

CLARE

I woke up the next morning feeling run down and achy. I'd cried myself sick over the last few days.

When Walt had finally gotten to me the day before, I'd collapsed onto the driveway as I'd watched Roman speed away.

Walt held me, making my skin crawl as I protectively wrapped myself around Tessa. Both of us sobbing.

She was scared, and I couldn't blame her.

I was terrified, too.

Walt led us both inside and got us settled on the couch. Then he immediately retreated to his office. Over the next hour, a steady stream of his men came through the front gates, flooding in the back door, and going straight up to join him.

A man had come to help me. And I'd thrown him to the wolves.

And, as I sat on my couch the next day, Walt walking around in nothing more than a pair of slacks, not a trace of anger on his hideous face, I knew that that man was now dead.

I'd seen that picture Roman had thrust in my face. He had a wife, probably a child, and if his assumptions were correct and our embryos had been switched, it was *my* child. And I'd all but pulled the trigger myself.

The father of my daughter was dead.

But it was the wrong man. It was the kind and decent one

who'd put his life on the line to save me—and Tessa.

And I'd killed him.

A tear escaped my eye, and I quickly swiped it away for fear of Walt noticing. I had a million reasons to blame it on after the last few days of drama, but I was all out of lies.

I couldn't help Roman anymore, but there was one man I could still save. I'd selfishly told Luke everything, putting his life at risk to make myself feel a moment of relief. I needed to stop him from repeating any of it before he was gone, too.

"I'm going to the gym this afternoon. I'll figure out dinner when I get home," I said as Walt started up the stairs to his office.

He stilled, one foot on the bottom stair. "I don't want you going back to that gym."

My heart leapt into my throat. "What... Why?"

"Why?" he asked incredulously, changing direction and heading back to me.

I steeled myself for an explosion and glanced to the kitchen, where Tessa was sitting at the table, playing with a giant ball of Play-Doh.

I stayed silent as Walt approached.

His knee landed beside me on the couch. The smell of his cologne made vomit rise in my throat. His hand went to my throat, sliding up and tilting my head back so I was forced to look at him.

My gaze flashed back to Tessa as panic ricocheted inside me.

Then, much to my surprise, he bent, kissing me chastely before saying, "Because, after the last few days, I don't want you out of my sight. There are men out there who think they can put their hands on my wife and still wake up breathing. You gotta know, sweetheart, that that shit does not fly. You're a Noir."

And I hated it more than anything else in the world. Carrying his last name was a punishment worse than any he'd ever doled out with his fists.

He gave my throat a gentle squeeze and trailed his other fingers down my chest, between my breasts, and down my stomach before stopping just short of between my legs.

I fought off the dry heave and did my best to control my breathing.

Walt was like a bear in the woods. He wanted dominance, and he demanded that you gave it to him. But, if you showed him fear, it only fueled him. He fed off the power.

I knew this game well. He wasn't going to hurt me—at least, not right then. But he wanted me to remember that he could.

However, victims often became the smartest players in the game of survival.

Puckering my lips, I silently asked for another kiss. He gave it to me then smiled menacingly.

I lifted my hand and teased the bare flesh at his stomach. "I'm yours, Walt. They touch me, they touch you."

"They touch you, Clare, they *die*."

"I'm yours," I murmured.

His eyes heated, so I kept talking.

"No one would be stupid enough to challenge you again."

He licked his lips.

Raking my nails up his sides, I pushed further. "You're Walter Noir. And I'm your wife. I'm untouchable, and I dare them to try."

"Fuck," he breathed, dropping his forehead to mine.

"It's just the gym, honey. A couple of hours on a treadmill to get my mind off the last few days." I slid my hand over his shoulder and into the hairs at the nape of his neck and whispered, "Don't let them win."

He stared at me, his eyes becoming soft at the corners. His stiff body uncoiling under my affection.

"Please," I added for good measure.

He gave in on a huff. "One hour. And Brock drives you."

It wasn't ideal. But it was something. And I *needed* to get to Luke and make sure he kept his mouth shut about everything I'd unloaded on him. Both of our lives depended on it.

I faked a grin. "Okay."

His hand tightened at my throat. "You run into any trouble whatsoever, I'll be there in a blink."

"I know."

He closed his eyes and inhaled deeply, breathing an, "I love you," on his exhale.

I fucking hate you. "I love you, too."

The ride to the gym that afternoon was a silent one.

Brock pulled up in front. Then he got out and opened the back door so I could get Tessa out of her seat. When I had her on my hip, he slammed the door and grunted, "One hour." He then pulled around to a parking spot with clear visibility of the front door.

At least he isn't coming in.

"Hey, Clare!" the front desk girl, whose name I could never remember, chirped.

"Hey," I said, glancing around her toward the row of offices. "Luke in the back?"

"Uh," she stalled. "Actually, Luke didn't show this morning, but don't worry. I called in—"

The world stopped spinning.

I interrupted her on a nearly desperate cry. "What do you mean he didn't show?"

Her eyebrows shot up in surprise. "I mean…he didn't show up this morning."

My hands began to shake, and I shifted Tessa onto my other hip in order to lean my elbow on the counter for balance. "Did you try calling him?" I snapped.

"I did," she replied cautiously, "but he didn't answer."

My mouth dried. "Has…" I cleared my throat when the emotion prevented me from finishing. "Has he ever done this before? The not showing up thing?"

She shook her head. "No. He's usually here early. Let's just say

Maxine was not excited to be called into work this morning to cover for him. She closed up last night after a full day of back-to-back clients…"

She continued to talk, but my ears were ringing, which left me unable to focus.

Please, God, don't let this be happening.

"Can you try to call him again? It's an emergency. I need to talk to him," I choked out. *To make sure he isn't dead.*

She frowned, eyeing me warily, but picked the receiver up and started to dial. "Sure," she drawled.

Please pick up. Please, just let him pick up.

I never tore my eyes off her as she did her best to avoid my gaze.

After a few seconds, she shook her head and hung up. She offered me a tight smile.

Oh my God.

It was not a coincidence that, only days ago, he'd met Walter Noir and, now, he was missing.

Fear and guilt mingled in the acid that replaced the blood in my veins.

Walt's words from that morning flashed into my mind. "*There are men out there who think they can put their hands on my wife and still wake up breathing.*"

Men.

Not man.

Not just Roman.

And not just because I'd felt threatened.

Luke.

Because he'd cared. Walt must have sensed it when he'd stormed into the office.

Oh my God. He's gone.

"Clare!" I heard yelled.

Then, all at once, the Earth dropped out of orbit, taking me with it.

My knees gave out. The darkness closed in. My life flashed on the backs of my lids. My last thoughts were of Tessa. My only instinct still in tact was to protect her. As I hit the floor with a crash, she landed squarely on top of me, secured in my arms—the only place she was ever safe.

I was vaguely aware of voices clamoring around me and then Brock storming in.

But all I could see was the blood of innocent men pooling around me.

CHAPTER NINETEEN

ROMAN

After the cops had come and gone, Elisabeth and I had packed a few bags and the dog and headed for a hotel. The sun was starting to rise by the time we arrived. And, though we were both exhausted, adrenaline having burned through whatever rest we'd gotten, sleep wasn't going to be found.

Before our bags were even on the floor, I was on the phone with Heath's contact, Leo James. Elisabeth was listening with her mouth hanging wide open as I filled him in on all things Walter and Clare Noir. I wasn't far into the story when she began to tremble. I wrapped her in my arms, her heart thundering so hard that I could feel it in my chest.

Leo did not delay in telling me that he and a group of his men were catching the first flight down to Atlanta. It made me feel marginally better, but judging by the terror on Elisabeth's face, she did not share the sentiment.

When I hung up, she was plastered to my front and staring up at me expectantly.

"It's okay. Just breathe," I told her.

"She looks like me?" she squeaked.

I smiled and brushed the hair off her neck. "She's yours, baby. No question about it." I took her face between my palms. "We have a daughter, Lis."

"Oh God," she whispered.

"It's okay," I repeated, kissing her forehead. "Now that we know who they are, things should be easier. We'll have our attorneys petition the courts. See about getting the DNA then ultimately custody—"

She jerked in my arms. "Excuse me?"

"It's going to be time consuming, but I'll stop at nothing, Lis."

"We aren't taking that baby from her," she announced, stepping out of my grasp.

This time, I jerked. "Come again?"

"Roman, we *aren't* snatching that child away from the only mother she's ever known. *Especially* if what Heath told you was true and Clare's a victim in all of this too."

"Yeah, baby. She's a victim, but I saw her. You cannot help someone who doesn't want to be saved."

"You probably just scared the shit out of her, Roman! Some man shows up at my house. Grabs me in front of my child. I wouldn't be real keen to jump in his car, either."

"Maybe. But I tried. And she screamed for the man who beats the shit out of her. That does not say scared to me. That says fucking *lost*."

She flinched. "We can't just storm in there and strip the child from her arms. As a mother, I would never be able to live with that."

I released her and made my way over to the pile of shit we'd brought with us. I dug through it until I found what I was looking for then headed back to her.

Lifting Heath's picture of a battered Clare Noir in her direction, I said, "He does that to her." I dropped it to the floor then lifted another. "And that."

Her body turned to stone as she slapped a hand over her mouth.

"And our daughter lives under the same roof with that man, Lis. This whole fucking situation sucks. Hell, the fact that a man like that is sharing the same oxygen we breathe is fucked. But there is nothing I can do about that, either. I know this is hard for you to understand. You're a good person with a good heart. Your gut instinct is to save the world. And, usually, I'm right there with you. But you need to hear me on this. I have no control over Clare. The only thing I can do in this situation is keep my *family* safe." I lifted one final picture in her direction and finished, "That family now consists of you, me, and *this* little girl."

Her eyes flashed wide, and just as quickly, the picture of Tessa was snatched from my hand. She stumbled back until she hit the bed. Then she slowly sank down, her eyes glued to the photograph.

I sat beside her and slid an arm around her back. "Let me worry about her. I don't like the idea of snatching her away from the life she knows, either. But, Lis, that life is *dangerous*. I gotta tell you I'd be just as hell-bent on getting her out even if I wasn't sure she was ours. No kid deserves to grow up like that. But the fact is no one can deny that that little girl is yours. So I will fight like hell to get her someplace safe—that place being with *us*. And when, and only when, we make that happen, we'll see what we can do about Clare."

Her tear-filled eyes lifted to mine. She was looking at me, but I knew she was still seeing Tessa's face.

"Okay?" I prompted.

She nodded and looked back at the picture. Her fingers glided over the curves of the child's face. "Okay, Roman."

I breathed a relieved sigh and squeezed her shoulder. "Now, baby, I know you've had a lot dumped on you, but we gotta figure out where we're gonna live for a little while. I'm not taking you back to our house, and my place is shit."

"My Victorian," she whispered at the picture.

"Say again?"

"I own an old Victorian house. I flipped it. I've been trying to sell it, but it's currently empty. All the utilities are hooked up. And I'd feel safe there."

"It furnished?"

She shook her head.

"Right. Okay. I want a bed, couch, TV, some kind of table we can eat at, and whatever the hell else you need to feel comfortable." I dug my wallet from my back pocket and pulled my credit card out before offering it her way.

She glanced down at the card then up at me. "All of that's going to be expensive, Roman."

I grinned. "I think I'm good for it."

"We really don't need that much stuff. I've got an air mattress and a couple of chairs there already."

"An air mattress and a couple of chairs?" I repeated incredulously.

She bobbed her head eagerly. "We can make do."

No fucking way was Elisabeth ever *making do* again. I'd worked my ass off and even lost her for over two years to ensure that.

"Seven point four million dollars," I announced.

Her mouth fell open, and her eyebrows pinched together. "Holy shit. Is that how much you're worth?"

I chuckled and waved my credit card at her. "That's what I made last month. Buy some furniture, Lis."

She clamped her mouth shut and blinked, but a few seconds later, she took the card.

After a shower, which had been just as mentally cleansing as it had been physically, I got to work calling our attorneys. Kaplin was still unsure of our next move. However, Whit was hitting the ground running. He had Detective Rorke on the phone before he'd even hung up with me.

During this time, Lis alternated between staring at the picture of Tessa, petting Loretta, and scrolling through furniture on the Internet. She was lost in her thoughts—and her pain.

I never strayed far from her. Not for fear, but rather for comfort. If she needed me, I was mere feet away. I kissed her every chance I got. And, as I paced the room, trying to figure out the best solution for…well, anything, I'd paused to drag my fingertips over her shoulders, reminding her that she wasn't alone.

She'd glance up at me with a forced smile that broke me every time.

But I was there.

And she was with me.

We'd figure out the rest together.

Around two p.m., Leo James, along with three of his men—Aidan Johnson, Alex Pearson, and Devon Grant—arrived at the hotel. I was a big guy. But fuck, Alex and Devon were giants. And Johnson was just flat-out scary—tattoos running up and down both arms, black gauges in his ears, brute terror in his eyes.

"Leo, nice to meet you," I greeted, ushering them to the sitting area of the suite. "Gentlemen, this is my wife, Elisabeth Leblanc."

Her gaze jumped to mine, but she didn't argue with my use of my last name. I shot her a wink then continued with the introductions. When I finished, she smiled blankly and offered a soft, "Hi."

I settled beside her on the couch, hooking her legs at the knees and dragging them into my lap so they draped over my thigh.

She inched closer and dropped her head to my shoulder.

"Mrs. Leblanc," Leo said, settling in a chair across from us. "I hear you guys have been having some trouble recently?"

"I'm not sure *trouble* is the right word," she replied.

"Well, I'm here to help you two take care of that." He grinned warmly, leaning toward her, propping an elbow on his knee, and leveling his dark-brown eyes on hers. He lowered his voice and soothed, "I promise, Elisabeth, I've gone toe-to-toe with far bigger men than Walter Noir. I know what I'm doing here, so I need you to trust that me and my men are gonna keep you two safe. That way, you can focus your energy on getting your little girl out. Leave the rest to us. Can you do that?"

Her body relaxed for the first time all day, sinking deeper into my side.

Even if he did absolutely nothing else, this guy was officially worth every fucking penny of the six figures I'd already paid him.

"Yeah, Leo," she whispered.

He gave her a chin jerk then turned his attention back to me. "I don't have a ton of time here, Roman. Johnson and I have to head back to Chicago tomorrow. I'm leaving Alex and Devon for you to use at your disposal. Get them a schedule of places you need to go ahead of time, and they'll handle the logistics of the whens and hows to get you there safely. In the meantime, we need to discuss this house I understand you two will be staying at."

"The Victorian," Elisabeth added.

Leo looked back at her, grinned, then all but motherfucking purred, "Yeah, that one, babe."

Babe?

"James," I warned. My lips thinned, and I cocked my head to the side while shooting him a dangerous glare.

The corners of his twitched as he leaned back in his chair, holding my gaze while pointedly rotating a gold wedding band around his ring finger with his thumb. "Anyway, the Victorian," he said. "I'll need the keys. Johnson and I will be working with a security company to get it wired up before we leave. I want you guys to stay here tonight. You're gonna need to call down to the front desk. I want my guys in the room next door. If it's not available, you're gonna need to change rooms, hotels, or, fuck, cities if need be. But I want my boys in earshot in case anything goes down."

"I can do that," I replied.

At the same time, Elisabeth sat forward and gasped, "You think something else is going to go down?"

Every man in the room spoke at the same time. "No."

I pulled her back into my side and kissed her temple. "Baby, I swear you're safe."

She looked up at me, her eyes filled with fear, but when she opened her mouth, a familiar attitude came out. "I'm sorry, Mr. Lock Me In A Closet Then Run Out With A Gun Chasing The Man

Who Broke Into Our House In The Middle Of The Night And Put Two Bullets In Our Wall. You'll have to excuse me. But it's not *me* I'm worried about here."

I scowled at her while I listened to the guys chuckle. "You worried I can't handle myself?"

Her lips formed a hard line as she adamantly shook her head. "No. I'm scared that *you* would not hesitate in getting yourself killed if it meant keeping *me* safe."

"Not even for a second," I confirmed curtly.

Her eyes narrowed, and her eyebrows pinched. "Then, *clearly*, you understand why I'm afraid here."

I twisted toward her, forcing her back against the couch with my upper body. "Nothing's going to happen to me, but if it does, you'll deal. But make no mistake about it, Lis—you will do it with a pulse."

"Roman!" she objected, shoving at my chest.

"Okay," Leo interrupted. "Let's calm down. This is just precautionary stuff at the house. But let's make a deal here. Elisabeth, your man, Mr. Lock You In A Closet Whatever The Fuck You Called Him, will make sure no one touches you. And Alex and Devon will make sure no one touches your man. Everyone's covered. Okay?"

After a second, she grumbled a quiet, "Deal." Glowering at me, she added, "But you should know—you pin me to a damn couch again, Roman, you are going to need men far bigger than those two to keep you safe."

This received a chorus of deep chuckles—one of them being mine.

I casually righted myself on the couch and gave Leo my attention. "So, what's next?"

He smiled and shook his head, glancing over at the three guys looming around us. "Get your rooms for the night settled. Assuming all goes well with the security system, I should be able to get you into the house before I leave tomorrow night."

"Elisabeth needs to go shopping for furniture," I informed.

Leo arched an eyebrow. "You going with her?"

I replied by stating, "She was looking at floral throw pillows earlier."

"Technically, they were damask," she corrected.

Leo glanced from me to her and then back again. "Right. Alex. Devon. Take the lady shopping. Roman, you're with Johnson and me at the Victorian."

I grinned.

Johnson laughed.

Alex and Devon mumbled curses.

Elisabeth giggled.

Leo grinned back.

Yeah. Worth. Every. Fucking. Penny.

CHAPTER TWENTY

CLARE

True to his word, Walt rushed to my side when he found out that I'd collapsed at the gym.

I'd cracked the back of my head on the floor, splitting it open, but despite the urging of the gym staff, I'd refused to go to the hospital and have it stitched up. I'd taken care of far worse injuries on my own, and going to the hospital meant leaving Tessa with Walt.

No. Fucking. Way.

I assured everyone that I was okay, and then, as Walt and Brock shared angry whispers at the door, I quietly asked the front desk girl to call me immediately if Luke happened to show up.

He wouldn't. But the only thing I could do was hold on to a shred of hope.

My head was aching as I strapped Tessa into her highchair for dinner.

She was chasing blueberries around her tray with two wooden spoons as I finished up the lasagna I'd insisted on cooking as a way to keep my mind off all things Roman and Luke.

It hadn't worked. If anything, it had given me entirely too much time to obsess as I mindlessly prepared dinner.

By the time the oven timer went off, my guilt had become poisonous, which was causing my hands to shake and my stomach to knot.

"Hey," Walt greeted, folding his arms around me from behind.

My body turned solid, and tears flooded my eyes.

"What's wrong, sweetheart?" he murmured, placing a kiss at my neck.

It was one of the many times in my life I should have kept my mouth shut. The first being the day Walter Noir had asked me out on our first date. The second being the day he'd slid his ring on my finger. But, just like in those instances, the words flew from my mouth before my mind could intervene.

"Did you kill that man who came to the gate yesterday?"

His head popped up and he squeezed me tightly. "So that's what's going on inside your head. You're worried about that piece of shit?"

I couldn't tell if he was pissed or concerned, so I stuttered, "I...I just—"

He turned me around and used my chin to force my gaze up to his.

I sucked in a sharp breath when I found his face soft, a comforting grin tipping one side of his mouth.

"Not yet," he whispered. "But I swear to you he will be taken care of *very* soon. You'll never have to deal with him again. No one touches you, remember?"

A shot of adrenaline jumpstarted my system.

Not yet.

Not yet.

Not. Yet.

A sob of relief tore from my throat, my body shaking in his arms.

Roman was still alive.

"Jesus," he breathed, tucking my face into his neck. "I had no idea you were this scared." He rubbed his hand up and down my back.

It was one of the only moments of solace I ever got. I hated him and wished he'd die on a daily basis, but I was so starved for comfort that I'd accept whatever I could get—even from him.

His gentleness made me momentarily forget the monster in disguise, and I asked, "What about Luke?"

His hands stilled, and I realized I'd made a huge mistake.

I could have been scared of Roman, but I had absolutely no reason to fear Luke. So my asking about him could only be construed as interest in Walt's warped mind.

"Luke? Your personal trainer?" he whispered maliciously.

My mind scrambled for a cover. "I…I was just trying to figure out if I needed to hire someone new. That's all," I said, attempting to move away.

But his once gentle hands turned punishing in the span of a second.

I was still wrapped in his arms when he squeezed me painfully tight, my lungs protesting and my tender ribs screaming. "I… can't…breathe…" I choked.

He nuzzled his jaw against the side of my face and drawled, "Good."

I struggled in his arms, the combination of fear and his grip making it nearly impossible for me to breathe. I was on the verge of passing out again when he suddenly released me. He didn't move away as he watched me fight to draw air into my lungs. He hovered over me, a venomous glint in his eyes.

"Please," I begged, stumbling away, drawing him away from Tessa, knowing from experience what would follow.

I hadn't gotten far when he caught me, the tips of his fingers biting into the backs of my arms.

"He's dead," he sneered, rearing one of his hands back.

I closed my eyes preparing for the blow, but it never came.

I pried my eyes open, and he grinned, brushing the back of his hand down my cheek. A moan of approval rumbled in his chest when I flinched.

"I gutted him with my own hands," he said, trailing his fingers down my eyes, my nose, and then my chin. "You should have heard him screaming to God for help. Such a fucking coward, that one." He kept his eyes locked on me as he asked, "You don't have a problem with that, do you, sweetheart?"

I hid my wince and fought the vomit crawling up the back of my throat, keeping my shield firmly in place as I replied, "Not at all, honey."

It was the wrong thing to say.

But I'd learned with Walt that there was never a *right* thing to say.

"Not at all, honey?" he whispered, gripping my neck and lifting me to where I could barely keep my tiptoes on the floor. "Not at all, honey?" He laughed, dropping me back down. "Not at all, honey!" He yelled at the top of his lungs, spit flying from his mouth as a heavy hand struck my face.

I stumbled back as pain exploded within me.

Tessa screamed from her chair as Walt roared, "Liar!"

"I'm not lying about anything," I cried, my hand covering my swelling cheek.

"You fucked him. You whore!"

I adamantly shook my head. "I didn't! I swear. He never laid a finger on me."

He stormed forward, and I retreated as fast as I could, stopping only when my back hit a wall.

He slammed his palm on the wall beside my head and leaned in, snarling, "Trust me, he wanted to."

"No," I stated firmly.

He held my gaze and searched my eyes.

My heart raced, blood thundering in my ears, and I had to hold my breath to keep from exposing my fear, but I finally managed to repeat, "No."

Anger still radiating off him, he shoved off the wall and backed up a step. "Well, then I have some good news for you, Clare. As far as I know, Luke is alive and well." He cracked his neck. "For the next half hour, anyway. What's his last name?"

Any relief I'd had when I'd heard he was alive morphed into paralyzing fear. "Walt, no," I gasped, shaking my head.

"If this guy means nothing to you, give me his fucking last name."

Frantically trying to come up with a distraction, I stepped forward and rested my hands on his chest. "I swear to you he means nothing to me, Walt. But that doesn't mean he needs to die."

He swatted my hands away. "Name. Now. Or you *will* regret this."

But I already regretted everything. I couldn't add Luke's death to that—not again.

"Please don't do this," I pleaded, reaching out for him once more.

Suddenly, he turned on a toe, giving me his back as he headed toward Tessa.

My heart constricted as I flew after him. "Walt! Stop!"

"Mama!" she shrieked, fighting to get out of her seat as he approached.

I rushed around him, blocking him from advancing any farther.

I fully expected him to plow over me. But he came to a halt, his hand stabbing into his pocket to retrieve his phone. He quickly dialed a number and lifted it to his ear.

"His name, Clare. Right. Fucking. Now." He pointedly glanced over my shoulder at a now hysterical Tessa.

Walt had never gone after Tessa before, so I had no idea what he was trying to insinuate, but it was my daughter, so I wasn't about to wait to find out.

It was the exact moment my soul broke in two.

One part would forever be with Tessa, and the other would be buried in a shallow grave with a man whose only mistake was being kind.

"Cosgrove," I whispered, the pain searing through me.

He barked, "Luke Cosgrove," into the phone. Then he turned on a heel and strode out the front door, slamming it behind him.

Tears sprang from my eyes, and the heave of my stomach threatened to overtake me. I managed to get Tessa out of her chair and both of us locked in my bedroom and then locked in the bathroom before I lost it.

She crawled into my lap, curling as close as possible as I threw up in the toilet.

How is this my life?

I couldn't do it anymore, but I knew with a certainty I could feel in my bones that Walt would never let me go.

He was going to kill me one day.

The only thing I could do was make sure Tessa wasn't there to witness it.

It would gut me, and I'd live the rest of my short life soulless and empty, the promise of dying being my only reward.

But I now had it in my power to make sure she wouldn't suffer the same fate.

She was young; she'd forget me eventually.

I never would though.

At least, this way, I could let go and allow death to swallow me with the vision of her smiling branded on the backs of my eyelids.

Sobbing, I rose to my feet with her snuggled in my arms. "Mama's gonna take care of this, baby," I whispered, carrying her to my bed. "You're gonna be okay."

I climbed into bed, held her impossibly tight, and cried myself to sleep, mourning the loss of my only child.

CHAPTER TWENTY-ONE

ELISABETH

Ten days later...

"Calm down," Roman urged.

"Oh God. Oh God. Oh God."

"Elisabeth," he called, shaking my shoulders.

I clung to his shirt, fighting for breath, as an all-out panic attack tore through me. It wasn't my finest hour. It was, however, thirty minutes before the entire Leblanc family was set to descend upon my old Victorian for Thanksgiving dinner and I had just burned the bottom of the sweet potatoes.

Roman and I had been taking it slow. Which, for us, meant we'd furnished an entire house together, he'd moved in, we'd taken two full weeks off work so we could spend every day together, he'd made love to me every night, and I'd fallen in love with him all over again. Not that I'd ever fallen out of love with him, but it was different this time.

Time had changed both of us.

But, dare I say, this version of Roman Leblanc was even better. He pissed me off with his bossiness, but it only made the moments when he was tender that much sweeter.

We had bodyguards watching us twenty-four-seven, but he never made me feel like I was trapped inside the house. He worried about me—I could see it in his eyes. But, if I wanted to go somewhere, I went. And, depending on the task, he sometimes came, too.

Not everything had changed though. We still laughed like maniacs, slow-danced in the shower, and occasionally ate dinner on a blanket on the dining room floor instead of at the table.

It wasn't all a walk in the park though. I was still struggling with the past and our new reality. Our attorneys were working around the clock, and we waited with bated breath for a judge to sign off on our request for DNA testing. It wasn't an easy sell, but with Rorke and his team working on their end, we had hope someone would come through for us.

Tessa weighed heavily on our minds. I prayed that she was safe. And, if I was being honest, I prayed the same for Clare. I couldn't imagine what she was living through, but Roman was right. Our first responsibility had to be Tessa, but that didn't mean I'd give Clare up.

I'd framed the grainy surveillance photo of Tessa and placed it on the nightstand next to a picture of Tripp. Then I promptly lost it when I realized, if Tessa was ours, it probably meant that Tripp wasn't.

Roman held me until I was out of tears and eventually fell asleep in his arms. The next morning, I awoke and found him fully dressed, sitting in bed, holding a scrapbook that I knew had still been in my nightstand at the old house.

I'd started it when we'd first decided to do IVF. In that book was everything from the beginning to the end: ultrasound follicle pictures from when I was in the stimulation phase. Pictures of Roman and me wearing those hair nets doctors wear in surgery—it was taken just minutes before they'd put me under for our egg retrieval. There was another picture of us in the exact same pose taken five days later as we held a tiny picture of two beautiful embryos while waited for them to be transferred back into my uterus.

Then the images changed. There was a picture of us holding

a positive pregnancy test, both of our eyes filled with tears. It was followed with weekly belly pictures leading up to our twenty-week ultrasound, where we found out about Tripp's condition. But, even through my grief, I still documented every moment of our little boy's life.

On the last page was a picture of his tiny body snuggled into my chest, Roman's hand on his back, a huge smile on both of our faces. The name *Roman Daniel Leblanc, III "Tripp"* in huge letters at the bottom of the page.

Roman smiled as he placed the album in my lap then kissed my forehead. "Lis, he was ours in every way that mattered. He was created with love, born with love, and died with love. Not everyone can say that."

Oh, yes. I loved Roman Leblanc.

So, with tears in my eyes and a photo album of our baby clutched to my chest, I filled him in. "I love you."

He grinned, the twinkle of the man I'd first met all those years ago dancing in his silver eyes as he said, "I love you, too. I never stopped, and I never will."

That afternoon, we went to visit Tripp's grave together for the first time ever.

The peace I felt while standing in Roman's arms as we both spoke softly to our little man was indescribable. When we got home later that night, just before we fell asleep, Roman confessed that, the day I'd buried Tripp's ashes at the cemetery, he'd spent the afternoon in my empty house, sitting on the edge of our old bed, trying to figure out how that had become his life.

It broke my heart, but I held him tight and assured him that that life was over for both of us. And I meant it. I wasn't a fortune teller, but I still knew that Roman was here to stay. Mainly, because I flat-out refused to ever let him go again.

After that, he sat in bed, laughing, as I gave him a ration of shit because, if he had been sitting on my bed a year ago, he had clearly broken in.

We both fell asleep with smiles on our faces.

Content for no other reason than we were doing it together.

Which brings us back to the now. Thanksgiving Day. Burnt sweet potatoes. Me in an all-out panic about that—but mainly about spending a holiday with Roman's family for the first time in years.

"Chill out," he said, palming each side of my face and dipping his forehead to rest on mine.

"Oh God. Oh God. Oh God," I replied.

Then I chilled out because his hand slid into the back of my hair and he tipped my head back so his mouth could cover mine.

I moaned as his other hand made it down to my ass.

He kissed me just long enough for me to forget my potatoes, but not his family. Therefore, when he released my mouth, I only said, "Oh God," once.

"Baby," he started. A man like Roman Leblanc did not roll his eyes, but right then, I could sense that he was fighting the urge. "I'll go to the store and buy some more fucking potatoes."

"It's Thanksgiving, Roman. Nowhere is going to be open."

"Then I'll find a fucking field and dig 'em up myself. Just calm the hell down, Lis."

"Screw the potatoes. Your family is coming over!" I gripped the front of his T-shirt.

Yeah, Roman was back to his old uniform. I hadn't seen him in a suit since that day at the police station. Albeit his old uniform had gotten a seriously pricey overhaul, but they were still jeans and T-shirts, so I could deal with it. My man was sexy all the time, but something about him in washed-out denim did it for me.

He eyed me skeptically. "That's usually what happens after you invite family over and then spend a week hashing out the details of who is bringing what."

I scowled as his lips twitched with humor. "I know this, *Roman*. But I haven't seen your family in years."

"You saw Kristen yesterday."

"Yes, but—"

"And I know you've seen my mom semi-recently. She loves to rub that shit in my face every time she sees you."

"She rubs it in your face?"

He nodded. "Lis, I've been in love with you for years. Moms have a knack for reading between the bullshit. She loved you and made no secret of the fact that she wanted us back together. So yeah—every single time she saw you, I got a phone call the next day telling me how beautiful and happy you looked. And how you did whatever-the-fuck nice thing you happened to do while she was with you. And, because she's my mother, I couldn't even hang up on her."

I giggled. I loved Cathy Leblanc. And I loved that she loved me enough to punish her own son for being a dumbass. "Your mom is amazing."

He grinned. "So, basically, you're worried about my dad?"

"No. Rome has always loved me."

And he had. He hadn't batted an eye when he'd found out Roman and I were already married when he first met me, which was only approximately forty-eight hours after I'd met Roman. He'd just slapped his son on the back and congratulated him for recognizing a good woman when he'd found one. Simple as that.

"Okay, baby, I don't have any long-lost brothers you don't know about. Kristen, Mom, and Dad are the only ones coming over. And you've already admitted that you love them all. Care to let me in on what exactly you're flipping your shit about?"

"It's not just Kristen. Or Cathy. Or Rome. It's all of them. At the same time. And I don't even know what the current state of our relationship is."

His eyebrows furrowed together as he frowned. "Okay, now, we have a problem. What in the ever-loving hell do you mean you don't even know 'the current state of our relationship'?"

Yep. He totally tossed me a pair of air quotes.

I rolled my eyes. "I mean…how are we presenting this to them? Am I your ex-wife? Girlfriend? Wife?"

He stared at me blankly before grunting, "Yes."

"Yes. What?" I threw my hands out to the sides in frustration.

I was up off the floor before I knew it. My ass landed on the counter, Roman wedged between my legs, his hands on my hips.

"Was I inside you last night?"

He had been. And we both knew it.

"Jesus, Roman." I glanced around to make sure Devon and Alex weren't in earshot.

I guessed he took that as my answer, because he continued. "You love me?"

"Of course," I replied immediately.

"You planning to make a life with me?"

"I…I…" I stuttered in surprise.

He arched an eyebrow.

"I mean…yeah. I was kinda hoping to." I began chewing on my bottom lip.

We hadn't talked about the future yet. Though it was kind of a given.

He smiled and moved his hands to the counter, one on either side of me, and kissed me—hard.

My body responded immediately, my nipples tingling, my toes curling, sparks igniting.

Ya know, the usual when it came to Roman.

I slid a hand around his neck and slanted my head to take it deeper. His tongue glided with mine as I shimmied to the edge of the counter and locked my legs around his hips.

He continued to kiss me, but I became vaguely aware of him digging something out of his back pocket.

My stomach fluttered in the best possible way.

Oh. God. This was it.

He was going to propose again.

I was actually impressed he'd made it nearly two weeks.

My heart pounded in my chest as I asked, "W-what are you doing?"

I felt something land on my thigh, both of his hands fumbling with it.

I pried my lips from his and glanced down to see his hands digging in his wallet.

Then out came a ring.

Only he slid it onto his own finger.

"Uh…" I dodged his lips as he attempted to catch my mouth again. "Did you just give yourself a ring?"

"No. I just put the ring you gave me back on," he said, moving in for another kiss, but I turned my head, so his lips landed on my cheek instead.

"You keep your wedding ring in your wallet?" I had no idea why *that* was the part that had surprised me most.

"I only took it off to get people at the office to stop asking questions. But you gave me that ring. I sure as fuck wasn't going to hide it away in some box at the top of my closet. Why? Where's yours?"

I bit my lip and looked away sheepishly. "In a box at the top of my closet."

Chuckling, he pressed his lips to my temple. "I'll send Devon to go get it. You need to at least be wearing your engagement ring when my parents get here. Considering I already told them we were getting remarried."

I swung my head to face him, my eyes bulging in disbelief. "You did not!"

He shrugged.

"You didn't even ask me yet. I have the right to refuse."

He twisted his lips and gave me a teasing side-eye. "You were gonna say yes."

"You don't know! I could totally say no."

This time, he laughed, throwing his head back and everything.

"Roman, I'm serious," I scolded.

Still laughing, he looked back at me and said, "I have no doubt that you are, Lissy. But I also know you would have said yes at the police station if I'd asked."

"I would not!"

"You would."

"I would not."

"You would."

"I would *not*!"

He leaned in close. "You *would*."

"Roman…" I was preparing to let him know exactly what I thought of his proposal assumptions when he suddenly produced a huge diamond ring out of thin air and lifted it into my line of sight.

Any further objections died in my mouth.

"Like I said." He smirked, taking my hand and sliding the ring on my finger. "You should probably put on your engagement ring before my parents get here."

My vision swam, and my lungs seized.

He'd proposed—kinda.

He wanted to be my husband again.

And I wanted to be his wife more than I'd ever wanted anything.

It might have taken us some time to figure it out.

But we'd fallen in love in less than a day.

Not even utter devastation and two years apart could erase that.

A love like ours wasn't measured in years, distance, or time apart.

It was never-ending.

An electrical current traveled through me, prickling the hairs on the back of my neck the same way it had the first time I'd laid eyes on him and then again that day at the police station.

Only, this time, I realized that it was the overwhelming sensation of *right*.

The diamond was gorgeous, but that feeling had less to do with the stone and more to do with the man who had given it to me.

He was right.

We were right.

We'd *always* been right.

So, with absolute certainty—and despite the fact that he hadn't asked—I laughed a throaty, "Yes."

His smile grew exponentially. Then he pressed his smiling mouth to mine and taunted, "See? I told you you'd say yes."

I slapped his arms and wiped a stray tear on my shoulder. "Don't be an ass right now. I'm too happy to give you any attitude."

"Okay, Elisabeth Leblanc—with an S and a lowercase B—I won't be an ass right now while you're feeling happy."

The familiar words turned the waterworks on full force. "God, don't be sweet, either. Just stand there and tell me you love me."

"I love you."

He did. I had not one single doubt about that.

I threw my arms around his neck, buried my face in his neck, and mumbled, "Never mind. That just made it worse."

His shoulders shook as he laughed, and he smoothed his hands up and down my back, his lips peppering kisses anywhere his mouth could reach.

It was then that I understood what he'd meant when he'd said that his lungs had inflated for the first time since he'd found me sitting on the couch the night I left.

Because, for the first time since I'd made the decision to leave, I took my first real breath. I clung to his shoulders and basked in the beauty of it all.

After a few minutes, he murmured, "Baby, you gotta let me go if I still need to go dig up some sweet potatoes."

I sniffled and sat up, staring down at my ring. "Nah. I think this will be enough to distract them from the lack of carbohydrates on the table."

"Probably." He grinned just as the front door swung wide open and Kristen sauntered in with Devon on her heels, carrying a huge tray of pies.

"Damn it, Kristen," Roman barked, shoving away from me and striding toward his sister. "He's a bodyguard, not a bellhop."

"Oh, shut up, Roman. He offered to help. Besides, he's going to be eating some of it, too." She batted her eyelashes. "I made extra since I'm sure a big, strong guy like Devon has quite an appetite." She bit her lip and shot Roman an exaggerated wink.

While Kristen did think Devon was hot (and he was), she really just enjoyed screwing with her brother.

"Oh, for fuck's sake," he bit out, snatching the tray from Devon's hands.

"Roman!" Cathy scolded as she came through the front door. "It's Thanksgiving. Can you give the cursing a rest?" Her hands were filled with a million bags, and a huge smile covered her face as her gaze met mine.

I hopped off the counter, straightened my dress, and headed to help her. I was pulling bags from her hands when I was wrapped in a hug from behind.

"My girl came home," Rome mumbled to himself before releasing me. Taking the bags from my hands, he grumbled at his wife, "Woman, I told you I'd get the bags."

"And I told you..." She kept talking, but I lost her words as she bustled to the kitchen.

As I watched the man I loved—who, only minutes earlier, had slipped a ring on my finger—as he argued with his sister in the kitchen, his parents chattering under their breath, and one lost and confused bodyguard skillfully trying to make his escape out the back door, I realized that Rome was not wrong.

I was home.

CHAPTER TWENTY-TWO

ROMAN

"Shelly," I called to my secretary. "Where is the new offer from Wells?"

She peeked her head around the corner. "I'm assuming it's on the table with the rest of your mail. I didn't open anything that was personally addressed to you."

I groaned, cutting my eyes to the table that had to be moved into my office sometime over the last week, for no other purpose than to hold all of the mail I'd received while I'd been out.

I quietly cursed myself for having made the rule about mail after Shelly had opened a blow-up doll Kristen had sent to the office for my birthday. Only it hadn't been my birthday and she'd only done it because she was pissed and knew that my secretary opened all my mail. She'd ordered it on her cell phone while impatiently sitting in the chair across from the desk, waiting for me to get off a business call.

Taking two weeks off to spend time with Elisabeth had been amazing. Part of it had been spent working with attorneys to figure out the best course of action in getting custody of a child who I couldn't even prove was mine. However, the other part, where I'd gotten to know Elisabeth again and then convinced her to marry me again, had been worth every minute of coming back to mountains of work at the office.

Less than two seconds after walking into my office, I made the decision that I needed to hire someone to help me run things.

I'd worked a lot since starting Leblanc Industries, but now that I had Elisabeth back, I had no interest in spending eighteen hours a day away from her. It was time I started living again, and what better way than with the woman I loved at my side.

"Thanks, Shelly," I said, dismissing her and moving toward an only slightly smaller version of the Alps made out of unopened boxes and envelopes.

Twenty minutes later, I was still searching for a more-than-likely-shit offer from Wells when my hand landed on a padded envelope with no return address. I flipped it over to check the back, but besides my address and a postmark from nine days ago, it was completely blank.

Curious, I ripped the top off, slid the contents out, and then stopped breathing.

My entire body turned to granite when I realized what I was holding.

Two plastic baggies filled with four Q-tips each.

Another filled with curly, blond hairs.

Another with darker-blond locks.

And, finally, a toothbrush.

I frantically tore the two pieces of folded paper open.

One was a generic consent to DNA testing that had to have been printed off the Internet, but the only thing that mattered was that it had Tessa's name at the top and it had been signed by Clare Noir.

The second paper caused a heavy weight to sink in my stomach.

Hand-written on an otherwise blank piece of paper was a note that said:

Roman,

You were right. I should have gotten in the car. Unfortunately, you were wrong too. There's nothing that can be done to help me anymore, but I'm begging you to use this DNA and do what I can't.

Save Tessa. Get her as far away from Walt as you can, even if that means away from me too.

I wasn't sure exactly what you'd need, so I swabbed each of our mouths with the Q-tips. The toothbrush is Walt's.

All I ask is that, one day, when I'm gone, you'll remind her how much I loved her.

Please hurry.
-Clare

I felt like someone had kicked me in the stomach even as my mind celebrated the breakthrough.

That woman was handing me a child she loved.

My child.

Elisabeth's child

Clare's child.

Despite the fact that it meant losing her.

My stomach wrenched at such a selfless sacrifice.

My conscience exploded with guilt.

I couldn't leave her hanging in the breeze.

But I had no idea what the fuck I could do.

I slid the contents back in the envelope and marched over to my desk. Then I snatched the receiver up as I dragged my wallet from my pocket and found his card.

"Light," he growled in greeting.

"I just got a package in the mail from Clare Noir. A legal consent for testing, baggies full of possible DNA for her, Tessa, and Walter, and a letter begging me to save the girl."

Silence.

"Heath! Did you hear me?"

"Walt's DNA won't be admissible in court," he said, emotionless.

"Hers will though. And, if we can confirm that Tessa is Elisabeth's, that's all we need to prove foul play, right?"

He didn't answer my question. "You at the office?"

"Yeah."

"Hang tight. I'm on my way." Then he hung up.

Keeping the phone to my ear, I hit the button with my hand then released it and dialed again. "I need to speak with Detective Rorke immediately. It's an emergency."

After I'd relayed the story to him, he too stated that he was on his way over to my office then disconnected.

I debated calling Elisabeth, but I didn't want to get her hopes up. I had no fucking idea what the hell this meant for us. Yes, we now had the DNA, but I had a feeling getting custody of that little girl wasn't going to be an overnight process.

With restless legs, I spent the next fifteen minutes pacing my office as I reread the letter from Clare over and over again. Each time I finished, my anxiety and my resolve to help her grew stronger.

By the time Heath came striding through my door, I was roaring with adrenaline.

"Letter!" he demanded.

I handed it his way then fisted my hands on my hips and watched him read, recounting each word by memory as his eyes scanned the page. His jaw clenched, the muscles twitching as he ground his teeth.

I waited. And waited. And waited.

He had to have read it at least four times. But he never looked up.

"What are my options here?" I finally asked.

He said not a single word as he dropped the letter to the floor and headed right back out my door.

"Light," I called after him.

His long legs swallowed up the distance to the elevator as I marched after him.

"Where the fuck are you going? I need some help here."

His blue gaze swung to mine, causing me to flinch when I caught sight of the hollow orbs staring back at me. He shook his head, raked a hand through his hair, and boomed, "Fuck!" His fist slammed into the metal doors just before they slid open and revealed Rorke standing inside.

The air turned thick as the two men saw each other.

"You are not here," Heath said dangerously.

"Light," Rorke warned.

He took a giant step into the elevator, bumping his chest with Rorke's. "*You* are not *fucking* here!"

I caught the elevator door before it closed and climbed inside. "What the fuck is going on?" I rumbled, squeezing in front of Heath, who had passed the point of anger and was teetering precariously on the edge of blinding rage.

"This man just cost you your daughter," he growled.

My body jerked. "Excuse me?" I planted a hand on his chest and turned to face Rorke.

"I did not!" the detective assured, visibly shaken.

"You smoke your mole out yet?" Heath shot over my shoulder. "Because I guarantee Walter Noir has heard that his wife gave up DNA to the police and they are both probably dead or dying by now."

Rorke cocked his head to the side and spat, "I kept it quiet."

Heath turned and jabbed the L button, muttering under his breath, "If *you* know, it's not quiet enough."

My mind was spinning, and I couldn't keep up. Finally, I'd had enough. "Somebody tell me what the fuck is going on right fucking now!" I seethed in a volatile whisper.

Rorke started with, "Light thinks—"

He didn't get another word out before Heath dove around me, grabbed the front of his shirt, and slammed him up against the back of the elevator, snarling, "I *know*! I don't *think*! I fucking know! You have a goddamn cop feeding Noir our every move. Now, once again, I have to figure out a way to clean up your mess."

"You're not cleaning up shit, Light. You go anywhere near that house, you'll blow the entire investigation."

"Fuck you. Fuck your department. Fuck your entire jacked-up investigation." He gave him another hard slam into the elevator. "I swear to God, Rorke. One fucking uniform follows me, I'll have your badge."

"Really? Because it sounds like you're about to lose yours." Rorke pushed back.

Heath's lips formed an angry snarl. "What's he gonna do? Call the cops?"

The elevator dinged, and the doors opened to the lobby. Heath stomped out but stopped only a few feet away to turn back and look at me. "You coming with me or what?"

I was. I so was.

Even though I had no idea what the hell was about to go down.

CHAPTER TWENTY-THREE

CLARE

It had been nine days since I'd mailed the DNA to Roman.

I hadn't heard anything back.

I didn't know if that was a good or a bad thing.

His face wasn't on the news as a missing person.

But the cops hadn't showed up to take my daughter yet, either.

I wasn't positive that was the way it would work, but every night as I fell asleep with her in my arms, a knife under my mattress, Walt curled up behind me, I had the sweetest dreams about that moment.

It would kill me to tell her goodbye.

But the relief of knowing she was finally out of his reach would make it all worth it.

It was the day after Thanksgiving, and I was decorating the house for Christmas when I heard Walt coming down the stairs.

Tessa froze when she heard him, but I gave her a smile and a wink and tossed her a few of the plastic ornaments I'd managed to untangle from the lights.

I kept my back to him, hoping he'd ignore me.

I'd never been more wrong.

I felt him get close, and I steeled myself for his usual hug and kiss.

Only, this time, I felt his hand wrap around my neck, cutting my air off, as he spun me and slammed my back against the wall.

My scream was unable to escape past his grip on my throat.

I had always been afraid of Walt, but I'd never, not once, seen him as angry as he was in that moment.

His face was nearly vibrating as he exploded. "You gave the police our DNA!"

That was it.

The time had come.

It was my day to die.

And, as my eyes frantically flashed to Tessa, who was screaming on the floor, my only thoughts were that I'd failed her for the first, and ultimately last, time.

Roman

"What are you planning to do?" I asked, sitting in the passenger's seat of Heath's white Explorer as he gunned it toward the Noir residence.

"Haven't made it that far," he grunted, swerving around traffic.

Fuck. This does not sound good.

"Then maybe we should pull the fuck over and develop some sort of plan of action here," I argued.

He ignored me and lifted a phone to his ear. "It's Light. I need surveillance at Noir's temporarily shut off for about an hour." Pause. "Well, that's up to you, but there's about to be a fuck-ton of my face up in that shit." Pause. "Then that's on you. But I'd suggest you do it now." Pause. "Right. I've got Leblanc with me."

I heard the man on the other end of the phone shouting as Heath pulled the phone away and pressed the end button.

Fuck. That sounds even worse.

"Heath, man...I'm not sure about this. I want this done too, but I don't think this is the way to—"

He cut me off. "He's gonna kill her. If he hasn't already."

"Tessa?" I asked, my heart lurching into my throat.

He shook his head, keeping his eyes on the road. "*Clare*. Then he's gonna pack up your kid and leave the city. We might find him again." His haunting gaze flashed to mine. "But we might not. The one thing I can swear to you is that we do *not* have time to pull over and work out a plan of action. Now, I can pull over, drop you off, and you can walk away from all of this here and now. Or you can reach into my back seat, dig out my vest, put that motherfucker on, and follow me into the pits of Hell to retrieve your daughter."

I gritted my teeth.

It wasn't a choice at all.

If he was right, this might have been my only shot to bring her home to Elisabeth.

So I stayed silent, leaned into the back seat, and pulled a fucking *Kevlar* vest on, vowing to arm our boys in blue with Rubicon the first chance I got. And then I prepared to take back my family.

Clare

"You stupid cunt!" Walt yelled into my face.

His hand was still around my throat, and I struggled to pry his fingers away.

I couldn't breathe, and I was precariously close to losing consciousness.

But knowing that, if I let go, I'd probably never wake up again gave me the strength to slam my knee into his groin.

His body jerked and his grip loosened long enough for me suck in a sweet gasp of oxygen.

He regained his hold on me, but with fresh air in my lungs and a lifetime of fear fueling me, I threw my fists into his face and another knee into his groin, and then I shoved him as hard as I could. Desperation made me strong, and he stumbled back.

Suddenly free, I took off at a dead sprint. Snatching Tessa off the floor and then darting to the front door.

My pulse was roaring in my ears, but I could hear his footsteps echoing behind me.

I pushed myself faster.

I struggled with the door before swinging it open and racing out front.

I only made it two steps before pain detonated at the back my head, forcing me to a sharp halt before snatching me backward.

"No!" I screamed as Tessa fell from my arms.

Roman

Heath parked one street over, and we jogged the rest of the way up to the Noirs' front gate. His gun was drawn as he scanned the perimeter. The sun was just starting to set, and the pink Georgia sky made for a picturesque view. From the outside, it looked just like any other Atlanta mansion. No one could have imagined the evil residing inside.

However, as a man's vicious yell came from inside the house, I jolted into a reality I'd never wanted to be a part of.

"Fuck!" Heath growled. "I'm going around the side to see if I can get in. You stay here," he ordered before bolting away.

The man yelled again, and this time, I heard the shrill of a child screaming too. An icy rage sent a shiver down my back, and fire shot through my veins. Shaking the tall, metal structure, I furiously tried to find a way inside. The steel wouldn't budge no matter how hard I fought. Refusing to stop until I got to Tessa, I attempted to squeeze my bulky body between the bars, but it was useless.

"Fuck. Fuck. Fuck!" I snarled, using my weight to try to pry the bars apart.

I'd managed to wedge my shoulder between two of them when I saw the front door swing open. Clare came flying out, Tessa in her arms, Walter Noir directly behind her.

"Clare!" I yelled as Walter snatched the back of her hair, pulling her to an abrupt halt and sending Tessa to the ground.

"No!" Clare screamed as she fell.

I shoved an arm through the bars, frantically trying to reach her, but she was yards away. "Tessa!" I shouted next, hoping I could get her to come to me. Her small body would have fit through the bars.

Terror churned in my gut as Walter slammed Clare into the ground then charged after the child.

I rammed my shoulder into the gate again, yelling, "Don't you fucking touch her!"

I swear to God I was going to rip that son of a bitch in half.

If *only* I could get my hands on him.

CLARE

I twisted, diving for Walt's ankle as he went after Tessa. I caught him with one hand and sent him stumbling to the ground just as I heard a man yelling. I glanced up, fear consuming me at the possibility of it being one of Walt's men.

Only for my heart to burst when I saw Roman Leblanc standing like a white knight coming to rescue Tessa from the dragon's lair.

He was there.

Someone had come.

The sob tore through me as I fought to keep Walt down.

"Take her!" I shrieked. "Take her!"

"I can't reach her!" he shouted, thrusting his arm through the metal bars of my prison.

Walt reached back, ripping my hand off his leg.

"Tessa, go!" I screamed when he got back to his feet.

She was hysterical, tears streaming down her face, blood dripping from her scraped knees and elbows.

"Mama!" she cried, running from Walt but too afraid to go to Roman.

She was so close to being free. I couldn't allow him to get his hands on her again. Drawing up the remainder of my strength, I pushed to my feet and sprinted after him. Slamming into his back, I once again took him to the ground.

"Goddamn it!" he barked, rolling over, his fists flying at my face.

"Tessa, go!" I ordered, doing my best to defend myself from Walt's blows.

Even through the struggle, I heard Roman trying to coax her over to him.

"Tessa, don't you fucking move!" Walt barked, his hands momentarily slowing their assault.

I couldn't see her from my position, but I prayed that Walt's reaction meant she was heading to Roman.

I couldn't do anything but hurry her along and try to ease her into the arms of a stranger. "Tessa, it's okay. Please, baby, go to him."

Then, suddenly, the chaos stopped.

Everyone stopped yelling.

Tessa's cries fell quiet.

And, in the silence, I actually heard the Earth begin spinning again.

She had to have gone to Roman.

He had to have finally gotten her.

She was safe.

She was safe.

Oh my God. She's finally safe.

Tears poured from my eyes.

My job was done, and within a second, my entire battered, beaten, and exhausted body finally gave out. Gravity finally defeated me as I sagged on the concrete driveway.

My arms and legs were limp as one more of Walt's fists landed on my face, but I didn't feel it amongst the euphoria and relief.

"She's safe," I found myself repeating as I felt Walt rise up off me.

Keeping my eyes closed, I waited for the final blow that would end it all.

I smiled, eager for the darkness.

But it never came.

The familiar sound of my name made my eyes flutter open.

Walt was standing there. A gun to his temple.

A long, muscular arm at the other end of the trigger. My daughter safely tucked into his side. Warm, blue eyes I immediately recognized stared back at me.

"Heath, give me the girl!" Roman called.

Heath?

I blinked as he dug the gun into Walt's temple. Then he whispered something in Tessa's ear and set her down.

Glancing back at me over her shoulder, she reluctantly ran to Roman and clung to his neck as he gently guided her between the bars of the gate.

"Just get her out of here," I begged.

"Oh, I am, but I'm taking you, too," he said.

Oh my God. It has to be a dream.

But not even my mind could have conjured a moment that beautiful.

"Okay, Luke," I whispered.

TRANSFER

THE RETRIEVAL DUET (BOOK 2)

I fell in love with a man who didn't exist.

What started out as romance ended in hell.
His words turned to razor blades.
His kisses converted to fists.
His embrace became my cage.
His body transformed into a weapon, stealing parts of me until ultimately....
I broke.

I hated him.
My sole job in life became to protect our daughter.

I wasn't sure I'd ever escape the prison he'd skillfully crafted from my fears.
Until the day our savior arrived.

This is the story of how I escaped the man who thought he owned me.
The transfer of my life and my family.

TRANSFER

CHAPTER ONE

HEATH

"Okay, Luke," Clare breathed.

Never had more beautiful words been spoken.

Her eyes shined bright with life, staring up at me as if she'd just witnessed a miracle.

I knew I had. I'd spent the last half hour with fire consuming my soul, fearing she was already gone.

I'd spent over three months being devoured by that possibility.

"Okay, Luke," she repeated when I failed to form a single syllable in response.

It was the wrong name.

But she could call me whatever the fuck she wanted. Just the sound of her voice would have kick-started my heart to beat for another century.

"Luke?" Noir whispered, a flash of recognition hitting his face just before he exploded. "You motherfucker!" Ducking under my arm, he knocked the gun from my hand, sending it skittering across the concrete.

But I didn't need a weapon for what I was going to do to him.

I had three years of watching that piece of shit from afar. Months of watching Clare drag herself to a fucking gym with bruises covering half of her body while tears poured from her hopeless, blue eyes. And weeks since one of his men had killed Atwood.

I'd dreamed about the moment when I could get my hands on him—and not while wearing a badge, when the best I could do was subdue him and then haul his ass to jail.

No. I wanted Walter Noir to suffer a thousand slow deaths before his toxic, black heart fell motionless.

And I wanted nothing more than to be the man responsible.

I'd seen too many tears fall from her eyes.

Too many times she'd flinched when I'd reached for her as though she didn't understand that hands could be gentle.

The bite marks he'd left on her shoulders and the bruises on her swollen face had slashed through me in a way I knew I'd never heal.

I'd fought the overwhelming desire to tell her who I was on a daily basis. To force her and Tessa to come with me.

But, every day, as I helplessly stood at that gym door and watched her walk to her car, fearful she wouldn't make it back, it had broken something inside me.

Fuck the investigation. That's what I'd said the day I had taken it upon myself to involve Roman Leblanc. I couldn't sit by and do nothing any longer.

I'd be damned if a bitch like Walter Noir was going to fight me over her now.

He would lose for no other reason than I refused to fail her.

Catching him around the waist, I lifted him high before slamming him down to the concrete face first.

His head cracked, but like a rabid dog, he got right back up.

At six four, two twenty, I had the clear advantage in size, but whatever he lacked in that department, he made up for with mental instability. That crazy bastard had no respect for his own life, much less those around him. He'd happily battle to the death before surrendering.

"Luke!" Clare cried, pushing herself to her knees and then crawling toward us.

"Get out of here," I growled at her, landing a hard fist to the side of his head.

His knuckles found my face, splitting my lip wide. The pain didn't even register amongst the chaos, and the sight of my blood dripping down lit me ablaze further.

That would have been Clare's blood if we hadn't arrived in time.

It would have been her face rather than mine taking the brunt of his anger. All while Tessa innocently stood by, watching him brutally murder her mother.

Just the thought multiplied my strength.

Smashing his head into the concrete, I dove over him, going for my gun, but he caught me around the waist.

"Son of a bitch," I huffed when a heavy punch landed on my ribs.

However, with his hands down, I was able to hook an arm around his neck and squeeze impossibly tight while wrapping a leg around his torso for leverage.

My vision had long since tunneled, but as he bucked beneath me, it was images of Clare smiling that kept me holding on. The sound of her laugh drowning out the blood thundering in my ears. The memory of her shaking body as she clung to my neck and confessed the depth of Walter's depravity was like a lit match to my adrenaline.

This was *my* fight—*hers.*

When his body sagged, it took self-restraint only years in the DEA could engrain into a person to release him while he still had a pulse.

Killing Noir was on the top of my list of priorities, but I knew, for the Administration, he was a small fish in a big pond. We needed him alive.

Finally satisfied that he was out cold, I let go and rolled off. My chest heaved from exertion, but I immediately searched for Clare, only she was no longer there.

Anxiety rooted in my stomach, but thankfully, less than a second later, I found her.

Or, more accurately, her foot found Walter Noir's face as he lay unconscious on the driveway.

"I hate you!" she screamed, landing another kick before I could get to her.

Wrapping her in a bear hug from behind, I lifted her off her feet and dragged her back.

"I fucking hate you!" she yelled at him, fighting like a hellcat to get back at him.

A large part of me wanted to give that to her. She'd more than earned it. The other part of me needed to get her out of there before any of his men showed up.

"Chill," I growled, but if she was even aware I was holding her, I couldn't be sure.

The tighter I held her, the harder she fought. And I began to fear I was going to hurt her if she didn't stop. Her face was already swollen, and God knows what the rest of her frail body looked like.

She needed to get to a hospital, not go another round with Noir's limp body.

I placed her on her feet only long enough to wrap her back up, this time chest to chest, her arms pinned between us.

She twisted her head around to keep him in her sight. "I hate you!"

"Clare," I barked.

Finally, her attention snapped to mine. Her body stilled, and she closed her mouth while she scanned my face in awestruck disbelief.

"I can't believe you're alive," she said, her chin quivering.

Fuck. Me.

She was alive.

"Chill," I ordered, holding her gaze, her left eye barely visible beneath the swelling. "We only have a minute before he wakes up. I need you to listen to me."

She blinked but didn't reply.

"You listening?" I asked just as I felt the tremble begin to work its way up from her legs.

"How are you here?" she whispered on a shaky breath.

She was about to crash. Emotionally. Mentally. Physically.

Fuck.

"Stay with me, okay?" I urged. "You're safe. Tessa's safe. And I'm gonna get you out of here. Can you walk for me?"

She vigorously shook her head as a sob tore from her throat.

She started struggling again, but this time, it was to get closer.

"Shh, it's okay. I got you," I soothed, loosening my hold and allowing her the space to move her arms from between us.

They quickly circled around my neck, her legs doing the same at my hips.

Holding her with one arm, I dug my phone from my pocket and dialed. "Tomlinson? I've got a woman and a child, both of which need medical attention. Tell me you're close."

"Our eyes on Brock Nolan say he is en route, Light. Get them the fuck out of there. I've got units on the way to head Nolan off, but you need to leave."

My head snapped up so I could scan the perimeter, but I did not waste time before striding over to where my gun was on the driveway. "Roger that. I'm out." I hung up and then tucked my phone away. Keeping a hand on her back, I leaned over to retrieve my weapon. I spared one last glance at Walter, who was still out cold, and then jogged with her in my arms over to the gate.

Roman watched us with haggard eyes as we approached. He had Tessa's face tucked into his neck, one hand over her ear, her tiny body flush with his.

I rubbed a hand up Clare's back and asked, "What's the code, babe?"

"Eighteen-eleven-two," she replied.

Roman went to work typing the numbers in.

As the gate came to life, the most amazing sense of relief fell over me.

It had slid open only a foot before I turned sideways and carried her out.

She was free.

They were free.

We were free.

With her in my arms and Tessa in Roman's, side by side, we guided them from Walter Noir's darkness.

And into the light.

CHAPTER TWO

Clare

Sometimes, when I dreamed, I'd travel back in time to the days when I'd *thought* my life was hard.

When paying bills and eating ramen noodles three meals a day had been my biggest challenges.

Back then, I'd feared I'd end up homeless. Now, I feared going home.

Back then, I'd balked at the idea of spending my life washing dishes and waitressing to make an honest living. Now, I worried I'd be ordered to clean up another hideout after Walt had murdered a man for crossing him.

Back then, I'd longed for designer clothes, jewelry, and expensive handbags. Now, I just wanted my heart to still be beating when I finally escaped.

Funny how things could change in the blink of an eye.

My head was down as I approached the table, a pen stuck into the back of my hair, a pad tucked in my apron, and an exhausted smile pulling at my lips. I'd been on my feet for well over ten hours, and if the crowd didn't die down before the breakfast rush, it was going to be at least four more before I could go home.

"What can I get you?" I asked, placing two napkins followed by forks and spoons on the table.

A hand roughly caught my wrist as I started to pull it away.

It wasn't the nicest of diners in Atlanta. Shit *was actually the term that had come to mind when I'd interviewed six weeks earlier. However, I lived in a trailer two blocks over. I was more than accustomed to shit.*

I jerked my attention to the guy holding my arm. Typical for this time of night. Young. Dumb. Broke. My tip would be whatever change was left after he'd paid his bill, assuming he didn't dine and ditch.

Drunken brown eyes stared back at me as he slurred, "Well, hello there, gorgeous."

"Dude, let her go," his buddy laughed.

I snatched my hand back, but his grip stayed tight.

"You should really listen to your friend," I warned.

"Clare?" he purred, reading my nametag. "Sweet name for an even sweeter ass." He snaked his grimy hand around and grabbed my butt.

My body jerked. This wasn't the first time some douchebag had put his hands on me since I had taken the job. At three a.m., the customers were always the same—intoxicated. But, if I wanted to keep my job, I could only do so much—well, besides rolling his dinner around on the bathroom floor.

"What can I get you, boys?" I gritted through clenched teeth.

"Oh, trust me. I ain't no boy." He gripped what would probably be the world's smallest dick through his filthy denim.

I arched an eyebrow. "A eunuch then?"

He smiled, showing off a mouth full of crooked teeth. "Does that mean big cock? Because hell yeah."

"It means no balls, you dumb fuck." I pulled a steak knife from my apron and pressed the tip into the laminate tabletop. "Now, let me go before I make it your new reality."

His smarmy grin fell flat, and his friend barked a loud laugh.

"Bitch has jokes," he mumbled, finally releasing my arm

I smiled to myself, but it was short-lived. Not a second later, he caught me around my waist and dragged me down onto his lap.

"Hey!" I shouted, struggling against him.

A deep, raspy voice came from behind us. "Let the lady—"

He didn't have a chance to finish before I slammed my elbow into the douchebag's nose.

"Oh fuck!" the asshole yelled.

"Don't you ever touch me," I seethed, the busy restaurant getting quiet as everyone looked our way.

"Stupid bitch," he growled, grabbing napkins off the table and trying to stop the blood pouring from his nose.

I snatched the rag from my back pocket and threw it at him. It hit his chest before falling into his lap. "You can call me stupid, but I'm not the bitch here. Clean up after yourself, and then get the fuck out of my restaurant before I call the cops." I turned on a toe and marched back behind the counter.

When I heard the last of his curses and the bell on the door noting his departure, I allowed my shoulders to slouch forward. Jesus, I had to get a new job. My bills were not going to pay themselves. I'd lived in my car for a few weeks after my dad had passed away the year before, and there was no way I was going back to that crap. But even the pits of Hell had to be better than this place.

I was wiping the counter down when a man's large frame filled my peripheral vision. Out of habit, I didn't even look up before setting a napkin and silverware in front of him. "What can I get you?"

"Your number," he stated confidently.

I internally groaned. Not this bullshit again.

I glanced up, my mouth locked and loaded with an attitude that would probably get me fired, but not a single syllable came out.

Dear heavenly father, he was beautiful.

Wearing a fitted, black suit that cost more than my car and a smile so sexy that I nearly broke a sweat, he was nothing short of perfection. With thick, dark hair and eyes so green that I swear they glowed. I was awestruck.

His smile grew as I gaped at him. "You know, you really made the whole Prince Charming coming to a damsel in distress difficult on me back there."

"Sorry," I apologized breathily.

He chuckled. "It's okay. I really like that you can handle yourself."

My cheeks heated as his gaze dropped to my mouth.

"So, your number?" he prompted.

"I, uh, don't have a phone," I admitted, more than a little embarrassed.

His eyebrows shot up in disbelief, but his smile never wavered. "Okay, then I guess we'll have to set up our date now."

"Our date." I had intended for it to come off as a mocking question, but I'd failed. It had been spoken in total agreement.

"How about this?" he said, pulling a card from his wallet and sliding it across the counter. "Call me when you get off. I'll meet you up here and then take you out for breakfast."

I worked at a restaurant and got free food at the end of every shift, but there was no way I was turning down an offer from a man like him—money and power oozed from his gorgeous body.

I was dead on my feet, but as I took his card, our fingers brushed, awakening me with a single touch.

"Okay…" I drawled, asking him for his name.

"Walt." He paused, smiling salaciously as he grazed his brilliant, white teeth over his bottom lip. "Walter Noir."

"Sounds like a plan, Walter Noir," I replied breathily.

That was the moment my world tilted on its axis and everything I thought I knew about myself was thrown off balance.

And, as the days passed, I feared I'd never find solid ground again.

"Mrs. Noir? I need you to stay with us," a woman's voice called to me.

My aching body refused to cooperate, and my sluggish brain honed in on one word.

"Clare. Not Noir. Just Clare," I mumbled lazily, forging through the darkness that had constricted my thoughts.

"Okay, Clare. Stay awake, okay?"

I felt hands under my arms, lifting and jostling me, before I found myself horizontal.

What the fuck happened to me?

My mind scanned the memories, but it felt as though I were searching for a word resting on the tip of my tongue yet still completely out of reach. The thoughts floated through my mind, but I couldn't grasp any of them.

With one sound, a lifetime of memories crashed down like a tidal wave.

"Mama!"

My entire body came alive.

I bolted upright. "Tessa!" I screamed, slapping the hands of doctors and nurses off as I scrambled toward her voice.

Chaos broke out around me. A police officer appeared, grabbing my wrists to restrain me.

"Mrs. Noir—"

"Tessa!" I rose to my knees and searched over his shoulder, but she was nowhere in sight.

"Get your fucking hands off her."

I heard the familiar voice just as his strong, muscular back separated me from the officer.

Oh, thank God.

I lurched toward him. "Luke! I need Tessa. Please help me."

He guided his hand back and patted my leg. "You lay a hand on her again and I'm gonna rip them off your wrists, yeah?" he told the officer.

"Light, calm down. I was just—"

His body angled forward as he growled, "Your only warning. Do. Not. Test. Me."

Another of her cries assaulted my ears. "Tessa!" I grabbed the back of his shirt. "Luke, please. Where is she?"

He spun to face me, pure wrath filling his strong features. I jerked in surprise. Never had he appeared even remotely menacing at the gym. Sure, he was always big, but he had worn such a kind smile that I couldn't help but be put at ease.

But, right then, with the hard set of his jaw and murder dancing in his eyes, he looked flat-out terrifying.

"Luke," I whispered, swaying away.

His face softened and his wide shoulders curled forward as he lifted a hand to cup my jaw.

I dodged it on instinct.

Shaking his head in frustration, he lowered his hand back to his side and turned his gaze to the floor. "She's safe. She's with Roman."

That wasn't enough. If Walt wanted his daughter back, no one—not even a man like Roman Leblanc—could stand in his way.

Panic spiraled within me. "No. I need her!" I fisted the front of his tight, black T-shirt, pulling him toward me.

His gaze jumped back to mine.

"He…he's going to come for her. She has to stay with me. Walt…. He…" My voice broke. "He'll take her. He'll find us, and he'll *take* her. Luke. Please."

His eyes turned dark—ominous, even—as he held my gaze so deeply that I feared he could see the holes Walt had carved into my soul.

"I'll go get her," he replied softly. "But call me Heath. Not Luke."

I nodded multiple times. I'd have called him Rumpelstiltskin as long as he got me my daughter.

He pointedly looked down at my hands, which were still clutching the front of his shirt. "You gotta let me go, babe."

But, as much as I wanted Tessa, I was terrified to let go.

I'd been alone in my fight against Walt for so long, I couldn't bear the thought of going back to that. For seven years, he had bled me dry of my desire to live. I had nothing left to give. The tiniest taste of having someone to share that burden with made me an addict.

"You're coming back with her?" I asked weakly.

"Yeah, Clare. I'm coming back with her."

"You…you'll stay with me?" I pushed in case he had misunderstood the question.

One side of his mouth lifted in a sad smile. "For as long as you want."

I caught sight of his hand flexing at his side.

"Let go, Clare."

I wasn't sure I could. "I'm really scared right now," I admitted on a whisper.

His body jolted, and he leaned against my fists, his chest pressing into my hands, but he made no further move to touch me.

"I know," he said. "And that's okay for you to feel. But I swear I'm not going anywhere. I just gotta get your girl. Settle down and let the doctors take a look at you while I'm gone. And I'll be back in a flash."

I swallowed hard, willing my hands and legs to stop shaking, but they refused to obey, and it wasn't long before the tremor had worked its way up to my chin.

"Hey," he soothed. "No one's gonna hurt you ever again," he assured as if it were an absolute fact.

I didn't agree. Walt would never quit until he destroyed me.

"Okay," I whimpered.

He kept his gaze locked with mine. "You're still holding on."

"I am," I confirmed without releasing him.

He nodded in understanding. "Then we'll wait until you're ready."

"I don't know that I can do this." I bit my lip as twin rivers dripped from my chin.

"You don't have to do anything anymore, Clare. You already did the impossible. You kept yourself and that little girl alive. I swear on my life, from here on out, I'll keep you that way. You just let go and trust me to get Tessa. I'll handle the rest."

I was genuinely confused when I first felt the warmth. His hands remained at his sides, so I knew he wasn't touching me. But, as I stared into his promising, blue eyes, a blanket of security wrapped around me.

"Luke," I breathed, dropping my forehead to his chest.

"Heath," he corrected.

"Heath," I repeated.

"Jesus," he whispered, inching even closer so his front became flush with mine, forcing me to move my head to the crook of his neck. He didn't embrace me as he stood there, allowing me to desperately cling to his shirt—to hope. However, his promise meant more than anything he could have ever physically offered me.

I didn't need a man to coddle me.

I needed *help*.

And, somehow, someway, after what felt like an eternity of living in Satan's lair, God had finally heard my prayers.

I felt his cheek on the top of my head, but it was the warmth of his skin against my battered face that offered the most comfort. I'd been cold for too long.

A man's voice interrupted my breakdown. "Can we at least move her out of the hallway?"

Heath's hand flew out to the side, snapping him to silence. "When she's ready," he declared gruffly.

The fact of the matter was I was never going to be ready.

But I needed my baby girl.

And I needed Heath's blanket of security wrapped around us both.

Drawing in a ragged breath, I released him and settled back on the gurney. When I finally took in my surroundings, there were at least three doctors and nurses waiting against the wall. We were in the middle of a hallway, barely inside the doors of what I imagined was the emergency room, two uniformed police officers hovering nearby and another guarding the door.

The sense of alarm hung heavily in the air around us.

They, too, were waiting for Walt to show up to reclaim his family.

He would.

Absolutely.

I only prayed that Heath's blanket would be thick enough to hide us all.

"Right back," he assured.

A cold chill slid up my spine as I watched him walk away.

CHAPTER THREE

HEATH

Tessa was quietly crying when I made it to the room. Roman was doing his best to console her as he held her on his lap. Back at the house, I'd promised her that Roman was a good guy. But reassurances only lasted so long for a terrified little girl in the arms of a stranger.

"Luke!" she shrieked when she caught sight of me.

Over the past three months, I'd worked my ass off to gain that little girl's trust. In the beginning, I had done it hoping Clare's would follow as a result. But, as the days had turned into weeks, I had done it because…well, somewhere along the line, being with them stopped being about an investigation and became everything to do with showing a little girl and her mother that there was a world that didn't involve beatings and tears.

Whether it was tickling her as Clare fought a breakdown or tossing her in the air while Clare battled for the ability to breathe, I did my best to distract them both from the madness that was their lives. I would be lying if I didn't admit that I'd loved every fucking minute of watching them emerge from their cocoons of fear.

Before I had been assigned to go undercover as Clare's personal trainer, I'd seen at least a dozen images of her. Not once had she ever been smiling. After I'd met her, I realized that her smile was one of the world's best-kept secrets, because if any man experienced one, they would wage wars to hold on to it. It was life changing.

And my federally issued badge did not make me immune.

As a man—and a decent fucking human being—I'd ached to help her from the start. She was beautiful; no one could deny that. But she had this glimmer in her defeated eyes that spoke to my soul in ways others could never understand. It was a subtle flicker that danced even during the day as the flames of abuse consumed her from the inside. The bruises didn't have to be present physically. It was as obvious as a beacon shining from her ocean-blue eyes. Not even the greatest actress could hide that unmistakable inferno.

The DEA hadn't known much about Clare Noir at first. Walter had kept her under lock and key for years. It wasn't until after Tessa had turned one that he'd started allowing her out of the house to go to the gym. Surveillance on her had started immediately, but it had taken years for us to develop enough of a case to send an agent in. And, even then, all we had known was that she was married to Atlanta's enemy number one. My job had been to find out if she was enemy number two or, hopefully, bring her in as the final nail in the coffin in our case against Walter Noir.

But, within weeks, I'd found myself with a different objective altogether.

"One more, Clare," I demanded, using one hand to help her lift the bar.

She groaned, struggling to get it up before finally catching it in the cups.

"Nice!" I praised halfheartedly.

She'd shown up with a busted lip and a fresh bruise peeking out from under her tank top. I'd excused myself under the pretenses of making a call and then spent ten minutes pacing my office in an effort to keep myself from demanding she tell me what the fuck had happened.

I needed to know she was okay.

But, if I asked, she would have just said yes.

The answer would have been no, especially not with marks like that.

Scars on her wrists.

Bruises on her thighs.

A gash through her eyebrow.

And there was not one fucking thing I could do to stop it from happening again without compromising the entire investigation.

For almost a month, I'd been patiently working with her, but she hadn't opened up yet. And it felt like acid to my soul each time I had to ignore what that scum was doing to her.

"You do know I'm not trying to become a bodybuilder, right?" she smarted as she sat up on the bench, giving me a full view of the bite mark on the back of her shoulder.

Gritting my teeth, I flexed my hands at my sides and pasted on a grin that I prayed passed as something more than a grimace. "Which is exactly why you're only lifting the bar."

"Ten reps though? Walt's going to lose his mind if I start putting on muscle."

"Fuck Walt," I shot back before I could catch myself.

She barked a laugh. "I can't say I disagree. But you're not the one who has to live with him."

I meandered toward the free weights and pretended to be interested in a set of fifteen-pounders. "You know you don't have to live with him, either."

I chanced a glance up and found her eyes locked on mine in the mirror. "Unfortunately, that's not true," she said matter-of-factly.

"I could help—"

She cut me off. "So, what's next, Luke? I feel like I need manly shoulders to go with my new manly biceps."

I chuckled, but it was completely for her benefit. I found not one thing humorous.

When I faced her, I caught a glimpse of her dipping her mouth to her wrist.

My forehead crinkled as I asked, "Did you just kiss your watch?"

She smirked. "It's 11:11. You have to kiss the clock or you don't get a wish."

"You are aware that you're twenty-eight years old, right?"

"And?" She grinned, her eyes temporarily extinguishing the flame as they lit with pure, breathtaking happiness.

No makeup, blond hair pulled back in a sweaty ponytail, gray jogging shorts with a matching pink-and-gray tank that exposed countless black-and-blue patches, and a smile so genuine that I didn't just see it—I felt it deep inside my chest, in a place a subject of interest had no business being.

Clearing my throat, I attempted to shake off my stupor. "Okay, well, what'd you wish for?"

She curled her lip and gawked as though I were insane. "I can't tell you that!"

"Come on. You don't seriously believe that crap."

She tipped her head to the side. "Um…I kiss the clock at 11:11 in order to make a wish. I think it's fair to assume I absolutely believe that crap." Another of her Earth-shaking grins assaulted me.

At that moment, I didn't care what the hell she'd wished for. I'd have made a deal with the devil to make it come true. And we were dealing with Walter Noir, so that might have been exactly what I had to do.

I rounded her side of the bench and snagged my bottle of water off the floor. "Well, maybe we can swap. I had a birthday last week, so I have a wish of my own. I'm sure a trade wouldn't be against the cosmic rules of wishes."

She dramatically clutched her chest. "Come on. That's not fair! You know I won't be able to resist the temptation of knowing big, bad Luke Cosgrove's birthday wish."

I laughed at her blatant sarcasm before taunting, "Your loss, because it was a really badass one this year, too."

Her nose crinkled adorably as she tapped her chin in mock consideration. She might have been joking, but her curiosity was real, and eventually, it got the best of her.

"Okay, fine. But you go first." She anxiously rolled her fingers together, and I swear to God the woman was damn near giddy as she stared at me with rapt excitement.

My birthday wasn't actually for another month, and I hadn't blown candles out since my little sister Maggie had turned fifteen and become too cool to bake her big brother birthday cakes anymore. I had no actual wish to share with her. But, if I could make her laugh, I'd happily forgo all birthday wishes for the rest of my life.

I shrugged. "Fine with me, but just to be clear, I don't have to pinkie promise or share my diary combination first, right? I mean, we are taking our BFF status to a whole new level sharing wishes and all."

"So funny," she deadpanned. "Besides, if I thought you had a diary that consisted of anything more than a list of ways for you to torture your clients, I would have stolen it weeks ago. Combination or not."

We were supposed to be working out, but like so often in my time with Clare, it had dissolved into us standing around a piece of equipment, bullshitting about anything I could think of in order to keep her talking and out of her own head.

"Come on, Cosgrove. Spill it," she prompted impatiently.

My gaze dropped to her mouth as I ached to correct her with my real name. What I wouldn't have given to hear Heath *tumble from those pink, crescent lips.*

I forced my attention from her mouth and said, "New jockstrap."

Her lips twisted and her shoulders sagged in disappointment. "You have got to be kidding me! That's your amazing birthday wish?"

I laughed and defended, "Hey! Do not underestimate the chafing a worn-out jockstrap can cause!"

"Oh, yeah? Well, in that case, I hope it's chafing you right now. You're ridiculous, and that's not fair. No way I'm spilling my wish in exchange for your gross underwear."

Using the end of my water bottle, I pointed at her. "Don't you dare try to back out now, woman. We made a deal. I told you mine—you tell me yours."

"What are you, twelve?"

"Asks the woman who kisses her watch at 11:11," I retorted.

"Nope. I'm not telling you." She shook her head and started to walk away, but I absentmindedly reached up and caught her arm.

She instantly froze at the contact, her face draining of all color.

Guilt slammed into my ribs with an alarming velocity. I hadn't been thinking. I never touched Clare, no matter how I longed to. And, sometimes, when she was laughing and cracking jokes, it became easy to forget how fragile she really was.

"Shit." I released her immediately. "I'm sorry."

"It's okay," she murmured softly, hurrying to the free weights.

She kept her back to me, but as I stood, I could see her chest heaving in the mirror. Her brave mask made her face unreadable, but her body's physical reaction to such an innocent touch told the real story.

"Clare," I apologized, striding toward her. "I shouldn't have grabbed you, but I'd never hurt you."

She nodded, picking a set of weights up while avoiding my gaze. "Really, it's okay. I'm just jumpy sometimes."

"You want to talk about it?" I asked cautiously, praying that she'd finally let me in.

Her gaze slowly lifted to mine in the mirror, that fucking glimmer of pain once again dancing within. "I wished that I'll catch 11:11 again tomorrow."

"What?" I took a step toward her.

She blinked tears back as she held my gaze, her mask slipping away. The emptiness appearing in its place viciously sliced through me.

With a shaky voice, she confessed, "I don't really believe in wishes, but somehow, I've found myself in a situation where a silly wish is all I have left. If I'm lucky enough to catch 11:11 again tomorrow, it means we've survived another day."

My stomach lurched at her honesty. It was the first time she'd opened up even the slightest bit.

And it wrecked me.

I couldn't have spoken around the lump in my throat if I'd tried. I didn't try though; I just stared at her in absolute awe.

Words couldn't help her.

But I could.

That was the moment I officially threw in the towel as an undercover DEA agent. Fuck my job. Fuck the entire investigation. I wasn't quitting on Clare Noir no matter how things ended. And, whether it was legal or not, I was going to find a way to make her safe.

So she'd never need another goddamn wish again.

Of course I'd wanted to help and protect her.

But the way I felt for Clare had gotten way the fuck out of hand over the last few weeks.

My job was to get her to talk about her life, find out all the dark, dirty secrets about Walter's operations she'd hopefully slip and tell us. But, secretly, I was trying to figure out a way to get her the fuck out. So I started asking her about the past in hopes she had a family she could go back to.

During those conversations, she told me about Clare.

Not the wife of a criminal.

Not the frightened victim of domestic abuse.

Not even the mother.

She gave me the real woman.

And I drank her in like a man on the brink of dehydration.

It was wrong on so many levels. She did *not* need me, the man who'd been sent to investigate her, to develop feelings for her. It'd happened anyway.

And here I was, going to get her daughter while wishing I never had to let them go.

"Hey, Tessi," I cooed.

She dove out of Roman's lap and into my open arms. I caught her just before she fell.

"Easy there," I whispered into the top of her hair.

When she'd seen me prowling up behind Walt and Clare while they'd been fighting in the driveway, she'd sprinted to me. That alone validated every repercussion I'd face with the DEA for having passed Roman information about the Noir family.

In a lot of ways, I was just as selfish as Walter when it came to Clare. I wanted her as my own. But I'd never hurt her—hurt *them*. My heart had crossed the line as far as she was concerned, but I wouldn't allow my body or my mind to follow suit.

She'd had too much taken from her already—physically and emotionally.

If I'd made any kind of move on her while she was at her weakest, that's exactly what I'd have been doing—*taking*.

For Clare, I'd *give*.

I'd pack it all down. Make sure she got out of this alive and without any more scars than she'd already acquired. And then I'd walk away so she could find a better life. One where she smiled every day and graced the world with the masterpiece that was her laughter.

"Where's Mama?" Tessa asked, dropping her head to my shoulder, her little arms circling around my neck.

By God, it was going to hurt like hell to let them go.

I smoothed her unruly curls down. "Let's go find her, sweet girl."

CHAPTER FOUR

ELISABETH

I'd been trying to get in touch with Roman for over an hour. He was late. Though it was the first time he'd been back to the office since we'd rekindled our relationship. So my idea of late might not have been his. It was creeping on eight, and the dinner I'd made was getting cold for the third time. I was about to give up rewarming it.

"Alex," I called to the bodyguard who had been assigned to me after one of Noir's men had broken into our house.

We still hadn't been back to that place, but after a massive shopping spree, my old Victorian was starting to feel like a home. I'd been making a list of things I needed to retrieve from the old house, and Roman had been sending Devon, our other bodyguard, over to pick them up. I'm sure it was a pain in the ass, and I'd decided earlier that afternoon, when I'd had to strain spaghetti with a dishtowel, that we just needed to make the decision to move once and for all.

I'd had no intentions of ever leaving our old house. We'd made so many memories there. But maybe a fresh start was exactly what we needed.

Roman had only proposed the day before, but I suspected he'd have me at the courthouse as soon as it opened back up after the Thanksgiving holiday.

Same man.

New life together.

Maybe a new house wouldn't hurt, either.

"Yeah, Elisabeth," Alex answered, peeking his head out from the closed-off dining room that had been converted into the security room. He had a phone to his ear, but it was angled away from his mouth, which let me know I had his full attention.

"You want some chicken parmesan?" I asked, tipping my head at the pot on the stove. "I mean…I use alfredo sauce, so it's really just breaded chicken with white sauce and parmesan. But same thing."

Alex never refused a meal. Both guys ate a lot, but Alex was a machine. I'd never seen a human capable of downing that much food in one sitting and then, an hour later, come back for an equally impressive second serving. But I guessed, when you were six six and wore a suit of rock-hard muscles, you had to find fuel somewhere.

"I'm good. Thanks though," he said, quickly closing the door.

"Well, okay, then," I mumbled to myself and bent to the bottom cabinet to grab a stack of Tupperware.

He'd eat it eventually. Either that or four chickens had sacrificed their breasts for nothing.

As I got the food situated, I struggled to keep my head straight and tell myself Roman wasn't throwing himself back into the office twenty-four-seven the way he had before we'd divorced.

This was different.

Or so I chanted as I tidied the kitchen up and got ready to spend the rest of the night on the couch—alone, with a book. The familiarity settled heavily in my stomach.

"Elisabeth?" Alex said, emerging from his room a little while later.

I couldn't pinpoint it, but there was something in his tone that set me on alert.

My heart sped as he closed the distance between us. Squatting in front of me on the couch, he extended his phone my way.

I braced, not wanting to take it, and the wariness in his eyes told me he was bracing, too.

"It's Roman," he said softly.

A rush hit me, and I snatched the phone from his hand and lifted it to my ear. "Are you okay?"

"Lis," he breathed. It was a single syllable, but a palpable mixture of relief and anxiety poured through the phone.

"What's going on?" I asked, pushing to my feet, Alex following me up.

"Everything's fine. Calm down, baby."

"Then why are you calling me on Alex's phone? And why do you sound like you're about to drop some seriously bad news?"

"Alex is gonna hang with you the rest of the night. I'm not sure when I can get home. And I don't want you to be alone."

My insides coiled tighter. "Roman, please tell me what's going on."

"We got her, Lis."

A shudder shook my shoulders. "Who?" *God, please let it be who I'm hoping it is.*

"Tessa, baby."

My hand flew to my mouth, and tears pricked the backs of my lids. "You got her?"

"Yeah. And Clare, too," he added.

"Oh God," I whispered with burning lungs.

"Listen to me. Everything is fine. They're safe now. But they were a little banged up, so we're up at the hospital."

He hadn't even finished before I was darting toward the door. Alex suddenly stepped in front of me.

"Move," I ordered, not interested in any further conversation.

A daughter I had never met and the woman who had been raising her were currently at the hospital. In a few minutes, I was going to be there, too.

"Elisabeth," Roman called.

I was more focused on Alex. "Move!" I barked, snatching my keys from the basket next to the door.

"Talk to Roman," he replied.

"I'm talking to *you*. And I said move!"

"Elisabeth!" Roman yelled, catching my attention.

Narrowing my eyes on Alex, I snapped into the phone, "What?"

"You can*not* come up here," he answered.

Roman being bossy wasn't exactly something new. However, the conviction in his voice took me aback.

"What?" I repeated—sans the attitude.

"Baby, it's not safe. I need you to hang tight there and stay close to Alex. Devon's on his way up here now, and I'm gonna call Leo and see about getting a few more guys sent down tomorrow."

My heart sank, and a swarm of angry bumblebees came alive in my belly. "Wh…what do you mean it's not safe? You're there, Roman."

"And I'll be okay. I swear. But I can't have you up here right now. Things did not exactly go as planned, and I have a feeling getting them away from Noir was just the beginning. This could go two ways: the DEA got him and he's currently on his way to jail, or he could show up here, guns drawn, ready to reclaim a family that is *not* his anymore."

None of that sounded good. It actually sounded really fucking bad.

"Roman, maybe you should come home."

"I carried Tessa out, Lis."

"Okay," I drawled in confusion.

"She was terrified. Shaking and bleeding in my arms. But she held onto my neck and trusted me to take care of her."

The ache in my chest grew as I imagined that scene. I hated that Roman could possibly be in danger, but knowing he had been there when she had been scared and bleeding did some serious things to my heart. Tears finally made their way from the corners of my eyes.

He continued. “If that maniac shows his face up here, trying to get to her, he will have to go through *me*. And, Lis, when I say that, I mean he will die trying to get through me, because I’m coming home, baby. And I’m bringing Tessa with me.”

“And Clare?” I choked out immediately.

His voice softened. “And Clare, as long as you feel comfortable with that.”

“Absolutely.”

“Jesus, you’re an amazing woman,” he breathed as though he’d been worried I would say no.

I wasn’t an amazing woman. I was just a mother. Who understood that losing your child was the most agonizing experience a person could experience. And, regardless of whose DNA was coursing through that little girl’s veins, Clare was her mother. I wouldn’t take that away from her. *Ever.*

“Roman, listen to me. Tessa may or may not be biologically ours, but regardless, she’s Clare’s daughter. Do not go in there barking at her and ordering her around, telling her how it’s going to be. Ask her if she wants to come here. She might have family or someone she’d feel more comfortable with right now. And that’s okay—”

“Bullshit!” he interrupted. “That is not fucking okay. She’s away from Walter. But she is far from out of the woods. So they’re coming to stay with us, and we’re gonna make them safe.”

While he had an excellent point, I didn’t figure that his attitude was going to go over well with anyone else.

I made a suggestion. “Perhaps you shouldn’t be the one to talk to her.”

“No, I should *definitely* be the one to talk to her. However, Light’s head might explode if I raise my voice above a whisper in her presence. He’s been all over anyone who has so much as looked in her direction. So I’ll go out on a very short limb and say it’s gonna be him who talks to her. But it’s gonna be *me* who talks to *him*.”

Interesting about Heath and Clare.

And good.

I'd only met Heath Light once, so I couldn't be sure of what kind of bedside manner he had in the face of a crisis, but I knew Roman Leblanc well enough to know he needed to stay the hell out of it.

So, with that decision made, I replied, "Okay, Roman."

"Now, where's your head at right now? You straight with all of this?"

"I don't know. I've had about thirty seconds to process it."

"Okay, how about this? You got any questions or concerns? Let me put your mind at ease, and then I need to get back in there."

"Um…" I had a million.

What does it feel like to hold her? What does she sound like? Is she still scared? Why was she bleeding? Is she going to be okay? What about Clare? How did he even end up with them?

However, I was certain I wasn't going to get the answers to any of those questions right then.

But the fact that he was dealing with all of that and had still taken the time to make sure my head was straight was crazy sweet. My heart overflowed with love for that man.

I needed to be strong. For him. For Tessa. For Clare.

I glanced up at Alex, who was hovering beside me. I shot him an apologetic smile and said, "I'm good, Roman. And I'd be better if you don't come home with bullet holes."

He chuckled. "I'll do my best."

"I love you. Call me back when you can."

"Love you, too. Stay tight with Alex, okay?"

"Okay. I'm about to force-feed him some chicken parmesan."

"Alfredo?" he asked, a content smile in his voice.

"You know it."

He laughed. "Utilize some of that Tupperware you hoard and save your man a plate."

"Okay."

"I'll update soon."

"Okay."

"Love you, Lis."

"Love you, too."

I listened for a few minutes longer, but he'd hung up.

With our connection severed, my courage evaporated. Regardless of what I'd told Roman, I was not okay.

I was basically freaking the hell out.

Get it together, Elisabeth.

Sucking in a shaky breath and pasting on a smile, I turned to Alex and passed him his phone back. "So, you want to eat first or tell me who you were talking to on the phone earlier who was so important that you were able to perform the unfathomable feat of turning down food?"

He grinned. "Eat."

I headed to the fridge to unpack the food. "Okay. Then, after that, since it seems we are stuck together, you can fill me in on your mystery woman."

He frowned.

"Or man," I corrected.

He frowned deeper.

I shrugged and added, "Or you can help me pick out furniture for the guest rooms we need to miraculously have furnished by tomorrow."

I honestly didn't know that it was possible, but at the prospect of online furniture shopping, he frowned *even deeper.*

He propped his hip on the counter and studied me as I prepared his plate. I did my best to keep up the façade while dishing noodles out, but just as I handed it over, he caught my elbow to stop me from backing away.

I dramatically craned my head up.

Alex was a handsome man. The strong, silent type. Devon would have given me a pep talk and assured me that everything was okay. It was Alex though, so all I got was an arm squeeze. But, despite how hard I was trying to keep it together, that simple gesture was more than enough to break me.

Bursting into tears, I face-planted against his barrel chest.

I vaguely heard him mutter a curse as he awkwardly patted my back.

But I was lost in a world where I had a daughter and I'd just had to ask my ex-husband-fiancé-love-of-my-life not to come home with bullet holes.

Yeah. I had questions for Roman, all right.

How the hell was this my life?

CHAPTER FIVE

CLARE

After a team of doctors and nurses had poked, prodded, and inspected every inch of me, they decided to keep me overnight. I assumed that it was more for a mental evaluation than anything to do with my physical injuries. I couldn't blame them; I was a mess.

After Heath brought back Tessa, I spent the next two hours holding her while staring off into space and trying to put the puzzle pieces together to figure out how I'd ended up there.

Shock was what the doctors had called it as I'd listened to them assure an extremely concerned Heath that I'd be okay after I'd gotten some rest. I'd refused the sedatives and pain medications they'd offered. I didn't need to be drugged up or asleep when Walt finally showed up.

Roman occasionally poked his head into the room to check on us, and I caught sight of uniformed officers guarding the door, but Heath wouldn't allow any of them to come inside.

He sat stoically in a chair at the foot of the bed, staring at me as though he were afraid I'd disappear if he so much as blinked. His long legs stretched out in front of him and his broad shoulders reclined against the back of the chair, but he was as far from relaxed as a person could get. His jaw clenched, his lips pursed tightly, and his hands constantly opened and closed at his sides. It appeared as though it were taking a great deal of effort to keep his ass in the chair and not up pacing the room. Or pulling me into his arms—but that was only wishful thinking, considering he hadn't actually touched me since we had gotten to the hospital.

Tessa had fallen asleep in my arms, and though the nurses had rolled a bed in for her, I refused to put her down.

With the day's drama finally slowing, my mind began to churn with questions. Most importantly, who exactly was Heath Light/ Luke Cosgrove? It didn't take a rocket scientist to figure out he was some sort of law enforcement officer. Rarely did normal guys walk around with two different identities. Not that I was an expert on normal anymore.

I was dying to know how much of this man sitting at the foot of my bed was Heath—the cop.

And how much of him was Luke—my only friend.

As the clock ticked past midnight and into a new day, I found the courage to finally open my mouth.

"So, you're a cop?" I accused, Tessa's head rising and falling with every heave of my chest.

"I'm a DEA Agent," he answered, leaning forward and propping his elbows on his knees, his gaze never shifting from mine.

I cut my gaze to the wall as they filled with tears of betrayal. I knew it, but hearing him confirm it burned in ways I never could have anticipated.

He was just my personal trainer. It wasn't like we'd forged an everlasting bond over squats and crunches in the gym. But, when you're completely alone in life, surrounded by darkness on all sides, it doesn't take much more than a warm smile and simple conversation to convince yourself that maybe there was more.

But it had all been a lie.

He was a DEA agent trying to make his case, and I was left to mourn a good man who had never even existed.

It was too much.

"Get out," I ordered, keeping my eyes anchored to the pale-yellow hospital room wall.

"Let me explain," he replied, but I couldn't stomach being fed any more bullshit.

God knows Walt had filled me with enough over the years. I sure as hell wasn't volunteering to take it from someone else.

"I'm not interested in any explanation, *Heath*." I seethed his name as though it said everything. And, in some ways, it did.

"Clare," he called, his voice so kind and familiar that it shattered me even further.

Luke was gone even as he stood directly in front of me.

As a silent sob ricocheted in my chest, I wrapped my arms around Tessa and squeezed her tight. "Are...are you here to arrest me?" I stuttered.

He pushed to his feet and took a step toward me, but when I scooted away from him, he froze. His baby-blue eyes turned angry, and his hands fisted so hard at his sides that the veins on his tan forearms bulged.

"No," he stated firmly.

"Then *leave*."

I didn't believe him. I'd confessed to *Luke* every one of my deepest, darkest secrets the day the cops had shown up at the gym. He knew all about the blood on my hands and the sludge Walt had all but smothered me in. There was no way *Heath* could turn a blind eye to that. He was going to arrest me, and I was going to lose Tessa once and for all.

"Oh my God," I choked.

Days earlier, I'd been ready to let her go if it meant getting her someplace safe. I'd ripped my heart out with goodbyes to her every night since I'd mailed our DNA to Roman. But the moment *Heath* had lifted me into his arms, I'd dared to hope that I could keep her.

He had come for me.

And, now, he was going to take her away.

"I thought I could trust you," I accused, dropping my chin to my hollow chest to kiss the top of her head. "Will you at least tell me how much longer I have with her?"

"Clare, look at me," he ordered.

My vision swam as I lifted my gaze to his.

His shoulders were square, and his tall body pulsed with anger, but his voice remained gentle. "You *can* trust me. It's still me, Clare. You know who I am."

I adamantly shook my head. "No. I know Luke Cosgrove."

"Different name. Same person," he growled.

"No!" I seethed on a whisper. "You're a cop who manipulated me to get shit on Walt. And I'd personally like to express my thanks in that matter. Honestly, if you'd told me the truth, I would have spent my days spilling every detail about him rather than staring at your abs. But, just so we're clear, you are *not* the same person as Luke."

His face lit. "No. I'm better than Luke." He grinned.

Grinned.

Like a huge, gleaming-white, butterfly-inducing grin.

I was about to lose my daughter and spend the rest of my life in a jail cell, and he was grinning.

"You're an asshole," I snapped.

"Nope. I'm not that, either." He bent over, propping himself on two fists at the foot of the bed.

I curled my legs to avoid touching him. Though a part of me still ached to climb from the bed, with Tessa in my arms, and cling to his neck—to Luke's neck.

This guy though…

"I'm not Luke. And thank fucking God for that. I'm *Agent* Heath Light, and I'm going to make sure no one ever touches you or that little girl again. Luke Cosgrove was a bitch who couldn't do one fucking thing to help you except take a daily inventory of whatever bruises you came in with and whatever trivial fact you let slip about your home life. I, on the other hand, will use every fucking resource I possess in order to secure your safety. Even if that means raining down the entire federal government on that piece-of-shit husband of yours. So, no, I'm not your fucking personal trainer, but

I *am* your friend. And you *can* trust me when I say no one is going to arrest you, nor are they going to take Tessa. Not the cops. Not the DEA. And sure as fuck not Walter Noir." He pushed himself upright and moved back to the chair. Then he slowly sank down, his eyes locked on mine. Once he got settled with his legs crossed ankle to knee, he finished with, "Questions?"

It sounded good, but if I'd learned anything by marrying Walt, it was that too good to be true was often just that.

"You're a liar."

His eyebrows shot up. "Oh, I am?"

"Yes. You are!" I sat up, taking Tessa with me. She was knocked out, and her sleeping body folded to the side, her weight sending her toward the floor.

He lurched from the chair, his arms extended to catch her, but I caught her and dragged her back onto my chest first.

"Don't you touch her!"

His eyes narrowed, and he ran a hand through his thick, blond hair. "Don't touch her?" he asked in utter disbelief.

I didn't reply. He might have been the only man I'd ever trusted to touch her. Or at least Luke was.

"Don't *touch* her?" he repeated incredulously.

"You played me for months."

He nodded multiple times, his scruff-covered jaw ticking as he struggled to keep his composure. "I sure did," he replied, cracking his neck. "But I did it for *you*." He tipped his chin at Tessa. "For *her*. The man you met that first day at the gym was a lie. I'll admit that. But the person you got every single day after that was *me*." He stabbed a thumb at his chest before pointing a finger at me. "And the woman you gave me was not the fraud you put on for everyone else. It was *you*, Clare Cornwell."

I sucked in a deep breath at the use of my maiden name.

He wasn't wrong. I had given that to him. He was the only person I'd felt comfortable enough with to be myself around. I hadn't understood it then, but I'd felt it all the same.

"Luke," I whispered.

"Heath," he corrected. "It's still me, Clare. Your favorite color is green, like Tessa's eyes. It took approximately two weeks before it became my favorite color, too."

Oh my God. My heart stopped.

"Your favorite hobby is gardening, and I wished like hell every day that I could take you outside and just watch you lose yourself in a pile of dirt and an endless supply of flowers."

"Heath," I sighed.

"Your favorite food is pizza, and you could wax poetic for hours about what toppings you were planning for your monthly cheat day. I used to fake a laugh and urge you to stick to your meal plan, but it took every ounce of restraint I had not to start sneaking pizza into the gym and forcing you to actually eat. You're too thin, Clare. And, for fuck's sake, everyone deserves pizza more than once a month."

A strangled laugh bubbled up my throat, and a sad, but very real Luke Cosgrove smile split his mouth. Or maybe that grin had always belonged to Heath Light. I couldn't be sure.

He took a cautious step toward me, and this time, my heart raced for a different reason.

"I get it," he said. "You've had total shit dished out to you by men. But those men are not me. Look at me, Clare. You know who I am. You know you can trust me. I was pulled off your case the day Walter saw you in my office. Yet, today, I risked my job to get to you. That had not one thing to do with the investigation and everything to do with *you*. And I would do it a million times over as long as it got you here. Right now. With *me*. And I'm gonna take care of you both." He nodded to Tessa. "I give you my word, regardless of how I have to make it happen, that life is over for you." He inched even closer until he was looming over me. His hands were still at his sides, but his proximity was possessive—and not in a scary way.

No, the way Heath's warmth wrapped around me sent a shiver down my spine at the same time it drained the fear from my tense body.

"Walt…he always told me the cops would arrest me if they knew what I'd done for him. And I told you everything."

"No one is here to arrest you. Especially not me. We all know you're an innocent in Noir's bullshit."

I could do nothing but stare. Had I woken up in an alternate dimension where criminals were issued sentries for protection rather than orange jumpsuits and public defenders?

"Do you believe that?" I asked. Initially, I hadn't understood why it mattered to me what Heath believed. But it did. So much. I wasn't a criminal, and I *needed* him to know that.

He replied immediately. "Probably more than you do right now."

"Are you sure?" I squeaked.

He grinned again. "I was sure of that within the first week of getting to know you."

I tried to laugh, but it came out as a cry. "Does your boss know you're making these promises?"

"He will. We're taking Walter down. And guess what? You're going to help us."

My eyes flashed wide as bile rolled in my stomach. "I…I—" I stammered.

"And I'm going to be there to help *you*. The whole way. Every step. Every day. Whatever you need. I'm there."

My heart soared as his blanket of warmth wrapped around me even tighter.

I still wasn't positive I could completely trust him, but I knew with my whole heart I was going to try.

"Yeah?" he prompted, his blue eyes holding me captive.

"Yeah," I agreed breathily.

He smiled. "Okay. Now. What do you need right now?"

A new life where you walked into my diner before Walt.

"Can I have a hug?" I asked, using my shoulder to wipe my tears away.

"You can have whatever you want from me, Clare. But you're

gonna have to come take it." He bent at the waist, over the bed, offering me his upper body without really offering me a hug.

But it was more than anyone had given me in as long as I could remember, so without hesitation, I took it.

Rising to my knees, with Tessa held to my chest, I hooked an arm around his neck and shoved my face against his throat. His arms instantly folded around us both as he squeezed me, Tessa tucked between us.

"I'm scared," I whispered, not sure what else to say.

"I've got you." He nuzzled his jaw against the side of my face. "I swear on my life I've got you."

CHAPTER SIX

HEATH

After I insisted she try to get some rest, Clare *insisted* I move my chair next to her bed. I didn't argue. Sleep wasn't going to find me that night, but having them within my arms' reach would do wonders for my ability to relax.

It was well past three when her breathing finally evened out while she clung to my forearm.

I'd blown off nearly a dozen calls and texts—and even more than that if I included those from Roman. As much as it killed me to leave her alone for even a few minutes, I needed to get caught up on what the hell was going on with Walter as well as figure out what the hell was going to happen when Clare and Tessa were released. They needed to be taken into protective custody, and I needed to make it clear that I was going with them.

She stirred only the slightest bit when I inched my arm out from under her hand. Very quietly, I snuck out of the room, my phone already poised at my ear. It was rendered useless when I found eight men waiting in the hall, all of them coming alert with the click of the door.

"Light," my lieutenant, Mark Tomlinson, called, stepping toward me.

My fellow agent and close friend, Shane McIntyre, was right behind him.

"Heath," Roman said, scrambling up from the tile floor next to the door. A huge guy with dark hair I'd never seen before loomed beside him.

"Agent Light," Rorke called, two of his uniformed henchmen closing in from the right.

"You." I pointed my finger at Rorke. "Get the fuck out of here."

"Light," Tomlinson warned. "They're local."

I kept my gaze glued on the overweight detective as I shot back at my boss, "They sure as hell are. They're also the reason Atwood is in the ground. I don't want them anywhere near her."

"We had nothing to do with one of your boys getting dead," a uniform started. "Maybe you—"

He was quickly—and wisely—silenced by Rorke.

"Marco, enough!" Rorke jacked his pants up and straightened his tie. "We were just hoping to question Clare and offer whatever protection we could until Noir is taken into custody."

I must have missed the memo that Hell had frozen over.

"Unless you've showed up here today with irrefutable proof that your mole is in custody, you can fuck off."

Tomlinson started cussing under his breath. But I had nothing to gain by being respectful to Rorke or any of the APD. Yet, with Clare and Tessa on the other side of the door, I had everything to lose.

I stood my ground, my body swelling as I swung my gaze through the men surrounding me. "No one gets near her without my permission," I declared. "And, in case I haven't been clear enough, Rorke, your boys will *never* get that. I highly suggest you find the fucking door and utilize it. We've got it from here." I turned my attention back to Tomlinson.

He was young for his position in the Administration, but he'd more than earned every single one of his promotions. The man was well respected—especially by me. And, as far as I knew, the feeling was mutual.

"You gonna back me up here?" I asked him.

He rested a hand on his hip and used his thumb to wipe the corner of his mouth. "It's politics, Light. We can't just—"

"You have got to be shitting me." I swept a finger in Rorke's direction. "Not even a month ago, someone in *his department* hung Atwood out to dry. He was days away from being inducted into Noir's army, and within hours of his identity being released to the Atlanta Police Department, he was found with a bullet in the back of his brain. Politics have no place in this anymore."

His gaze turned hard as he took an authoritative step toward me and lowered his voice. "I don't know what the hell is going on with you and that woman, but you are not thinking straight. Do not make more enemies for us. Jesus Christ, it's gonna take me a fucking year to bury the surveillance footage of you storming Noir's gate."

I shrugged arrogantly. "Not my problem. I warned you to turn it off. Besides, I showed up there, witnessed that asshole putting his hands on her. If that's not probable cause to enter his residence, I don't know what is."

He arched an eyebrow. "Don't bullshit me. You should have waited for backup."

I laughed humorlessly. "Wait? You wanted me to fucking standby while he killed the key witness in our investigation?" *The woman who has worked her way so fucking deep under my skin that I can't even remember what it felt like not to have her there anymore.* I kept that to myself.

A symphony of questions fired from multiple directions, all of which were along the lines of, "She's going to testify against him?"

I angled forward and arrogantly whispered, "She is now."

Tomlinson's eyes nearly bulged from his head, and his whole body stiffened.

I tilted my head toward Rorke in a silent demand.

His eyes stayed glued to mine as he announced, "Rorke, you and your men are officially released from this investigation. The DEA appreciates your support in the matter, but we will be handling the Noir case from here on out."

"You cannot be serious," Rorke groaned.

Tomlinson finished with, "Please turn over any and all case files by end of day tomorrow."

"This is ludicrous. You don't have the resources to handle this kind of operation without the aid of the APD," Rorke continued to protest, but McIntyre began herding him and his men toward the elevator.

Once the doors had slid closed behind them, Tomlinson's body sagged and he pinched the bridge of his nose. "He's right, I absolutely do not have the resources to handle this, Light. So I'm gonna need you to get in there and find out exactly what she's got on Noir that I can use as leverage to get additional manpower and funding."

"I can do that," I replied. "But, first, I want your word that we're taking her and the girl into protective custody. And, in doing that, you're also going to assign me as her number one."

He scoffed and shook his head. "No. No fucking way. After your bullshit today, it's obvious you are way too attached to this one."

If he thought scaling the fortress wall was bad, he didn't even know the half of it. If he had any idea how I really felt about her, I'd be not only off the case, but also out of a job before I could even explain—assuming I could think of an explanation.

My only saving grace was that no one, not even Clare, knew how I felt about her. And it was one secret I'd take to my grave.

"Too involved?" I asked incredulously. "You sent me in to gain her trust and get her talking. I did both—and took it two steps further by bringing her in and convincing her to testify. You think a shattered woman like that is gonna be real keen to put her life on the line after you take away the only badge she's ever trusted?" Not even to mention the hell I was going to cause if they tried to take her away from *me*.

"I'm sorry. I can't approve it," he stated matter-of-factly.

"I'm not thinking you have a choice."

"Well, I'm thinking, if she wants protective custody for her and her daughter, she's gonna find a way to get on without you."

My blood began to boil at a nearly explosive temperature, but before I had the chance to utter a word, Roman joined the conversation.

"Come again?" he said, closing in on Tomlinson. "You're going to deny her protection if she insists on staying with Heath?"

"I didn't—" Tomlinson started.

Roman boomed, "That woman has been through hell without you manipulating her in exchange for her safety!"

"Stay out of this, Leblanc," Tomlinson ordered. "You have no idea—"

"Fuck you. I know enough. You're asking her to risk her life to make *your case* and you're planning to use *her life* as leverage to convince her." He paused and barked a loud humorless laugh. "You and the rest of the DEA can suck my cock. She's coming home with me."

I whipped my head in his direction, my hackles instantly raised. "Excuse me?"

He met my gaze. "I've got the space. The security—Leo's sending in more men tomorrow. And we both know what those DNA results on Tessa are going to read when I have them ordered tomorrow. Elisabeth isn't real excited about taking the little girl from Clare, so yeah, you heard me. They're *both* coming home with me." He turned his attention back to Tomlinson, but his words were aimed at me. "And, the way I see it, she needs all the people she can get at her back, so you are more than welcome to come with her, Heath."

While I would have felt miles better with the DEA watching her ass rather than whoever Leo James had sent Roman, options were never a bad thing to have.

I smirked at Tomlinson. "Sounds like she won't be talking after all."

"Light," he warned. "You try to pull this shit on me and you might as well turn in your badge now."

Digging in my back pocket, I retrieved my badge and then offered it his way. "Not a problem if this is the kind of man you are, using an innocent woman and kid to get a conviction."

My woman. My kid.

Jesus fuck.

I needed my head examined.

He crossed his arms over his chest and glowered, making it known he wasn't accepting my half-assed resignation.

Our gazes were fused in a stare-down. He was my boss, but I didn't back down. Not even an inch. Not when it came to Clare and Tessa.

Never when it came to them.

"Either take my badge or give me your word," I demanded, breaking the silence.

His gaze flashed to my outstretched hand then back again. "Fuck, Light. What are you doing? This isn't like you."

He definitely wasn't wrong about that. I was known to be steady and emotionally detached. I thrived on well-thought-out strategies. But, then again, I'd never met Clare.

"I will ask you one more time," I replied evenly. "And *only* because I respect the hell out of you and I know you're working on a snap judgment of what you saw on that video from Noir's place. You have a man she trusts, Lieutenant. *Use me.* I won't cross any lines. I'm not sleeping with her. It's not like that." And, as much as it burned on my tongue, I had to remind myself that it never would be. I cleared my throat and forged ahead. "I've spent the last three months getting to know her. We have the same goal here—her survival. There's nothing, and I mean *nothing,* I won't do to ensure that. You could put a dozen different agents with her and none of them would keep her safe like I will." I held his gaze but shoved my badge back in my pocket. "Put me with her and let me do my job."

He closed his eyes and grumbled.

Hope swirled in my veins.

"Shit." He groaned. "You better get me something good here, Light. I'm putting my ass on the line."

A victorious smile split my face. "She hates him. I won't have to get you anything. She'll gladly give it all."

"You know he was gone when our boys got there," he informed me.

I'd figured as much. We had surveillance on the Noir house, but it wasn't like the old-school movies where we had guys around the corner in an unmarked van.

"Yet another reason we need to be vigilant here," I retorted.

He nodded and pinched the bridge of his nose. "I'll send a team out to Leblanc's as soon as she's released." He turned his attention to Roman. "You working with Leo James?"

Roman nodded curtly, the big guy behind him relaxing a fraction.

"I can't imagine where you got his name," he said sarcastically. "I'm sure you had nothing to do with that, Light."

I grinned. "Nope. Pure luck."

"Right. Well, Leo was my team leader before he left the Administration. You're in good hands. I'll give him a call and get things set up. Now, if you'll excuse me, I got a shitstorm of phone calls to return." He turned on a toe and walked away, leaving me smiling like a maniac in the middle of the hospital hallway.

Roman waited for Tomlinson to round the corner before asking, "She asleep?"

"They both are."

"Good. They need it." He tipped his chin to where Tomlinson had disappeared. "He gonna send someone to guard the door?"

"If I had to guess, there's a sea of men downstairs, but yeah. I'll shoot him a text about getting someone up here," I muttered and offered him a hand.

He clasped his with mine but didn't immediately let go. When I looked up, his eyes filled with a determination that matched my own.

"We're gonna do right by them," he vowed.

"Fuck yeah," I agreed.

"No. Heath. *We* are gonna do *right* by them. No matter the cost. No matter the sacrifice. Priority number one and two are behind that door. The way we rank those priorities might be a little different, but that does not mean we aren't in this together. You got me?"

I nodded and gripped his hand even tighter. "They're *both* my priority number one, Roman. But yeah, I got you."

"Good. Devon and I will be out here all night. You go ahead and get back in there before she wakes up."

Good fucking plan. It was a sad day when I was already jonesing after having been away from her for ten minutes.

Christ, I was fucked.

CHAPTER SEVEN

CLARE

"Where are we going?" I nervously asked as Heath made another trip around the 285 loop.

He kept his eyes on the road as he replied, "We're just taking the scenic route to make sure no one is tailing us."

I turned and looked out the back window to see traffic as usual, no sign of Walt or any of his guys—as far as I could tell, anyway.

"Turn around and relax," he ordered.

"Sure thing," I smarted, righting myself in my seat and once again adjusting the oversized scrubs the hospital had given me to wear.

Relaxing was easier said than done. I didn't get to experience it often, and after my briefing this morning from a salt-and-peppered Richard Gere–lookalike named Mark Tomlinson, it wasn't something I figured I'd be experiencing much of any time soon.

No one had seen or heard from Walt since Heath had left him unconscious on our driveway. But I knew Walt; he was off somewhere, licking his wounds. I could only pray that we were safe at the Leblancs' house, under the watchful eye of the DEA and Roman's private security team, by the time he decided to make his move.

"Hey," Heath called to catch my attention. "We're good, ya know? We've got a car in front of us leading the way and a car behind us watching for anything suspicious. I'm just waiting for the all clear before making our way to Roman's place."

"Oh," I said softly. Something akin to relief but much less relaxing washed over me. At least, if what he'd said was true, we probably wouldn't be gunned down in the middle of the highway.

"Luke!" Tessa yelled.

I nearly jumped out of my skin as I attempted to scramble over the center console to get to her before Heath's arm went up between the two seats and blocked me in the front.

"You all right back there, Tessi?" he asked the rearview mirror. Cool, calm, and collected. Everything I was *not*.

"I spilled my fish," she replied as grief-stricken as an almost-three-year-old could be about having spilled their favorite snack.

"Well, quick! Catch 'em before they swim away." Heath chuckled.

She giggled. "They can't swim, Luke!"

I'd told her that morning to call him Heath, but I still called him Luke on occasion. There was definitely going to be a learning curve involved for both of us.

"Oh! You mean your crackers," he teased. "I thought you might have brought your pet fish with you."

She cackled louder. "I don't have no fish!"

She'd never had any kind of pet. Animals weren't allowed in Walt's house. Excluding him, of course.

"Clare." Heath's voice was low so she couldn't hear him. "You need to calm down and show her there's nothing to be afraid of."

I swallowed hard and did my best to slow my pounding heart. "Yeah. I might need a step-by-step instructional video on how to do that."

He turned his head my way, flashing me his blue eyes and one of his signature smiles that transformed his entire face from the badass Heath Light to the friendly and easygoing Luke Cosgrove.

"I'm not sure they make YouTube tutorials for that," he joked.

I rubbed my sweaty palms over my thighs. "Yeah, I can't imagine 'how to relax while on the run from your neurotic crime lord husband' has much of an audience."

"Probably not," he replied, flashing me another one of those smiles as he flipped his blinker on and switched into the exit lane.

"Are we getting off here?" I asked.

"Yep."

A second round of nerves took up root in my stomach, but for a completely different reason. "How far out are we?"

"'Bout fifteen minutes still, depending on traffic."

I pulled the visor down and used the mirror to inspect my face for the first time since we'd arrived at the hospital. Based on the impaired vision, I'd known my eye was going to look bad, but I wasn't prepared for the rest of it. The doctors had glued numerous gashes on my face, and they were all starting to bruise. My lips were swollen, and dried blood still stained the corner of my jaw from the split on my ear despite the thirty-second shower I'd taken while Tessa had played peek-a-boo with the shower curtain.

Heath had offered to watch her while she'd sat in his lap, watching videos on an iPad he'd magically produced. However, I hadn't been anywhere near ready for there to be a door dividing us if Walt showed up.

Closing the visor, I gave up on the lost cause that was my face. I looked like hell, but there was not one thing I could do to fix it.

The nerves rolled all over again.

"You good?" he asked the windshield.

I glanced back at Tessa then asked him, "Have you met her?"

"Who?"

"Elisabeth Leblanc."

He sighed. "Yeah. Once."

"What's she like? I mean…is she nice?" I mentally chastised myself for sounding like a high school girl. I was twenty-eight years old, but I'd never been good with women. Though, given my current predicament, I wasn't all that great with men, either. "Never mind. Don't answer that. I'm sure she's great. She's opening her home up to us."

"She looks like Tessa." His eyes flashed to mine then back to the road. "I just want you to be prepared for that."

I focused on my lap. "Yeah. I've seen a picture of her."

"It's eerie though. First time I saw her, I couldn't drag my eyes away."

My stomach wrenched. Why did that hurt? And not the idea of her looking like Tessa—I'd accepted that fun fact weeks ago. But the idea of Heath gawking at her seared in a way I had no right to feel.

"I'm sure she's beautiful," I mumbled and shifted awkwardly in my seat.

His head swung in my direction, his lips tight and an eyebrow arched in curiosity.

"I just mean, if she looks like Tessa, she has to be gorgeous." I smiled.

His hands tensed around the steering wheel. "Don't do that," he said roughly.

My head snapped back at his tone. "Do what?"

"Put on that fake-ass smile and lie to me."

"I'm sorry. What?" I snipped, glancing back at Tessa and finding her astutely listening to our conversation. I smiled and tossed her a wink.

She smiled back, but it never reached her eyes.

"See? You're even teaching her to do it," he said—again roughly.

I cocked my head to the side, leaned an elbow on the console, and hissed, "What is your problem?"

"Don't placate me with a smile," he replied curtly. "Open your mouth and tell me what's bothering you."

"Nothing is bothering me except your attitude."

Tipping his gaze to the rearview mirror, he asked, "And what about you, sweet girl? You worried about something back there?"

She looked at me with wide eyes and instantly shook her head. "No."

Crap. She was scared. Guilt pooled in my stomach. She'd seen way too much in her young life. If I wanted her to feel comfortable with Heath, it was definitely going to be a lead-by-example kind of thing.

I sucked in a deep breath as he pulled to a stop at a red light.

"I wasn't placating you with a smile," I lied.

He twisted in his seat to face me, resting his muscular forearm on the steering wheel.

I focused on Tessa to avoid his gaze—and his sexy forearm—before continuing. "I'm just nervous about meeting Elisabeth, and I look like…well." I waved my hands over my face and down my scrub-covered body. "Like this."

I cautioned a glance back in his direction, but his face was unreadable.

Slowly and purposely, he raked his eyes over me from head to toe, a chill spreading over my skin in their wake.

When he got back to my face, he licked his lips and told me, "You look like a survivor, Clare. And the minute you find something ugly in that is the moment we have problems."

Shit. That felt good. And, if he had stopped there, I probably could have made it the rest of the way without tears. But he didn't stop there.

"Tessa," he called. "How do you think your mama looks today?"

"She beautiful," she answered.

He smiled and tossed me a wink. "Your girl's got good taste."

She did. But only because she'd always liked him.

My chin began to quiver as I fought tears back. "Thanks, Heath."

"You can't thank me for the truth."

He was wrong. But I didn't have the words to correct him.

The light turned green and he slowly accelerated. However, a dirty and broken piece of me would forever be left at that stoplight. He'd taken it from me and replaced it with something to be proud of. The tiniest smile pulled at my lips as a single tear rolled down my cheek.

"Elisabeth and Roman are both good people, Clare," he said, misreading my overflowing emotions. "I wouldn't be taking you there if I didn't know that."

I nodded and peered out the window. I felt his eyes on me every so often, but he didn't speak the rest of the drive, allowing me my own moment of privacy even as he sat directly beside me. It was the kindest thing he could have done. And it stripped another piece of my filth and left it on the side of a Georgia road.

Right where it belonged.

Ten minutes later, Heath followed an identical black SUV down a private drive. I found immediate comfort in the lack of a gate.

Sure, there was nothing to keep someone out.

But there was also nothing to keep me locked inside.

A large but somewhat modest, considering who Roman was, old, white Victorian house with dark-blue accents stood tall in the middle of a decent-sized private lot. The yard was far bigger than ours—no, Walt's—but the grass and the flowerbed needed some serious help.

And then I saw her. Standing on the front porch, her arms folded over her chest to ward off the November chill, her side pressed into Roman's chest, his mouth at her temple, anxiety etched in her face.

I hadn't been wrong; she was beautiful. And I'd be lying if I didn't admit that a pang of jealousy hit me. This was her life. The worst that had probably ever happened to her was having shitty grass and an overgrown flowerbed. I didn't want her to see my baby. To be able to offer her something I couldn't—stability.

There she stood, in her designer dress and heels, with a man who adored her and had probably never lifted a hand to her.

She was a better version of me—better than I'd ever be.

My heart lurched into my throat. "I can't do this."

"Then we'll wait until you can," Heath said, putting the car in park, but he left the engine running.

I kept my eyes glued to her as she turned and asked Roman something.

Even from yards away, her resemblance to Tessa was uncanny, and it hurt so fucking badly. In that moment, regardless of what I'd wished over the last few weeks, I selfishly didn't want her to be Tessa's biological mother anymore.

That was *my* job.

The anxiety started in my hands, gradually working its way up until it engulfed my entire body.

"Breathe," I heard Heath say, and I momentarily managed to drag my eyes off Elisabeth.

Concern painted his handsome face, but it was his comforting blue eyes that cut through my panic.

I exhaled on a sob as I threw my arms around his neck. "I can't do this."

"Shit," I heard him mutter as I buried my face in his neck. His left arm wrapped around my shoulders, but I felt his body angle forward and his right arm reach into the back seat. "It's okay, sweet girl," he soothed. "Everything's fine."

I lifted my head an inch and saw his hand patting Tessa's leg. The silent tears streaming from her eyes immediately sobered me.

"Hey. Hey. Hey," I cooed, sitting up and drying my eyes. "What's wrong?"

"You cryin'," she squeaked, swiping her cheeks with the backs of her hands.

Shit. Shit. Shit.

I lifted my gaze to Heath, who was studying us both warily.

"Right. Well…" I took a deep breath and did my best to collect myself. "I'm happy, baby. This is where we'll be staying for a while." I motioned out the window. "We'll be safe here. Remember Roman? He's going to let us stay with him and his wife."

She looked out the window then to Heath for a beat before looking back at me. "Luke, too?"

I smiled, and it wasn't even fake. "Yeah, baby. Heath is going to stay too."

She nodded, her little body visibly relaxing into her car seat.

I sighed and squeezed his arm.

Then I jumped seven hundred feet in the air—though that might be an exaggeration—when Tessa screamed, "Dog!"

"Easy," Heath urged, pointing out the window to where a little Yorkie was trotting toward our SUV, yipping with every step.

I closed my eyes and wrung my hands in my lap. "I suck at this calm thing."

"Maybe we should check YouTube, just in case."

My eyes popped open and I found him watching me with a sly grin.

"It couldn't hurt." I offered him a weak smile.

"You ready?"

I shook my head and sucked in a deep breath. "No," I sighed. "But I guess I can't live in a government-issued SUV forever."

He grinned wider, causing a flutter in my stomach. "Oh, I don't know. It doesn't have a bathroom. But I could run you through the carwash once a week."

I unbuckled my seat belt. "Watch out. You find a way to rig up Wi-Fi for Tessa's iPad and I might take you up on that."

He shrugged and offered, "She can use my phone."

There weren't even words to express what a good guy he was. And not just because he was taking care of me and my daughter, but because he found moments to make me forget that I needed anyone to take care of me and my daughter at all.

"Mama! Dog!" Tessa squealed.

I held his gaze and felt another damaged piece of myself fall away. "I think I'm ready," I whispered.

His smile faded as he searched my face. "Be sure, Clare. We're in no rush."

I jerked a thumb toward Tessa. "I think Cesar Millan back there would disagree with you."

"Mama! Dog. Look, Luke. Dog!"

His eyes danced with humor. "I have no idea who that is."

I laughed and shoved my door open. "Then you should probably leave the dog whispering to me."

He turned the ignition off and opened his door. After folding out, he stretched his bulky frame before leaning back into the car, asking, "You sure you're good?"

Another broken piece of me hit the ground as I stood on my own two feet.

"I am now."

CHAPTER EIGHT

ELISABETH

"Loretta!" I called after the dog as she jogged toward Clare's car.

"Let her go," Roman mumbled into my hair. "She can be the welcoming committee."

"What if they don't like dogs?"

His shoulders shook as he chuckled. "I'm relatively sure Light can hold his own against a twelve-pound Yorkie."

He had a point, but I was about to lose my mind. They'd been sitting in the car for a solid five minutes. My nerves were shot. What if Clare had changed her mind?

The DEA had been at our house all morning, inspecting the security and chatting with Leo, who had somehow managed to arrive at my front door before I'd even rolled out of bed. Not that I'd slept. I'd spent the night fretting about Roman. Despite that I hadn't had him back for long, that bed felt entirely too big without him.

When he arrived home only an hour earlier, I was a wreck. It was Roman though. He wrapped me in his arms and talked me off the ledge of insanity. I was still a nervous wreck, but it was at least manageable with him at my side.

"Oh God," I mumbled when I saw the passenger's door to the SUV open, which was quickly followed by the driver's side.

"Play it cool, Lis. She's skittish."

Right. Cool. I could do cool.

A child's voice came from inside the SUV. "Look! Look, Mama. Dog!"

I could so *not* do cool. I couldn't even do kinda cool. Big, fat, ugly tears sprang from my eyes.

"Not exactly what I meant, baby," Roman said, pulling me into his chest.

"I'm sorry. I just…" The words died in my mouth as I caught sight of a woman who was only recognizable as a woman by her shoulder-length, blond hair, and her small frame. "Holy shit," I breathed, bile creeping up the back of my throat.

"She's fine," Roman assured.

I stepped out of his arms. "She is *not* fine," I corrected, starting toward her.

I only made it a few steps before her eyes—or at least I assumed it was her eyes, as one was so swollen I couldn't even see the whites—landed on me.

For the way she looked, I had no idea how it was possible, but a blinding smile covered her face. It only faltered for the briefest of seconds when our gazes met.

I returned her smile and awkwardly lifted my hand in a finger wave.

She looked up at Heath as I heard the rumble of his deep voice, but I couldn't make out what he said to her.

She nodded, shut the car door, and then headed my way.

With every step she took in my direction, my nerves intensified. What started as a knot in my stomach quickly became a raging ache that threatened to overtake me.

By the time she stopped a few feet in front of me, I wasn't sure I would even be able to speak past the lump in my throat.

Somehow, I managed. "I think I might puke."

Yep. I was the queen of first impressions.

She blinked.

"I mean, I'm really nervous right now."

Her swollen lips twitched. "Me too."

"Oh, thank God," I breathed, extending a hand. "I'm Elisabeth."

She took it in a gentle shake. "Clare."

Her voice was so soft and feminine, but not at all timid like I'd expected. Actually, she seemed to be keeping her shit together better than I was.

Still holding her hand, I said, "So, Roman told me to play it cool, but I'm not going to lie—I have no idea how to do that. I'm failing miserably."

Her mouth curved up. "I'm no expert, either. I lost it in the SUV when we pulled up."

I smiled. "Is it wrong for me to admit that you saying that makes me feel better?"

She giggled before it caught in her throat. She nervously toyed with the bottom of her oversized scrub top. "I know I'm supposed to be introducing myself and saying thank you for having us at your home. But is it wrong for me to admit that the only thing I want to know is if and when you're planning to take her away from me?" Her chin quivered as tears filled her eyes.

"No," I gasped, adamantly shaking my head. I released her hand and folded her into a hug.

She came willingly, both of us bursting into tears.

"I won't take her from you. I swear on my life," I vowed.

Her body shook, but she held me tight.

I backed away and carefully palmed each side of her battered face, her blue gaze meeting my green. "I lost my son, Clare. No mother deserves that."

"She's all I have," she pleaded unnecessarily.

"We will *not* take her from you," I swore.

"It's just—"

"I give you my word. We will *not* take her from you. We want her safe, but I promise you we want the same thing for you. Roman told me a long time ago that biology doesn't make families. Love makes families. She's your daughter. You carried her. You've kept her safe. We just want to be part of her life."

She sucked in a shaky breath and searched my face. "I always thought she looked like me."

I lowered a hand and tapped a finger over her heart. "She does in here. Everything she is on the inside is your doing."

She laughed without humor and backed out of my reach. "I'm not sure that's a good thing at this point. She's been through a lot."

"But she's here now. And that was your doing, too."

She reverently closed her eyes. "Christ, how are you people so nice?"

I smiled. "I guess, what God forgot to give me in cool, he made up for with nice."

She laughed and opened her eyes. "Thank you. For, you know, opening your home to us and being so kind. This could be really awkward and you're making it…well, easy."

"The same goes for you, ya know."

She focused on the ground and tucked a stray hair behind her ear. "So, you wanna meet her?"

My smile grew. "I would love to."

Her head lifted, and a shy smile played on her lips. She pointed over my shoulder. "She likes your dog."

I didn't know how I'd missed her getting out of the car, but as I spun around, the entire world disappeared except for a little, blond girl with ringlet curls, blazing, green eyes, and the most amazing smile I had ever seen.

Heath had her on his shoulders, and Roman was holding Loretta up for her to pet.

I didn't care one bit that four armed DEA agents were looming around us.

Or that my dining room had been converted into a security room that now housed bodyguards.

Nor did I care that Leo James and two new guys named Jude and Ethan were waiting on the other side of my door to give us all a security briefing.

No. I couldn't have cared less.

That moment was perfect.

Just like her.

"She's gorgeous." I whispered.

"Inside and out," Clare replied. "Come on. I'll introduce you."

She walked away, but I couldn't move.

"Mama! Her name Retta," she told Clare as she dove off Heath's shoulders and into her mother's arms.

Clare smiled over her shoulder at me before whispering something in Tessa's ear.

Then my heart burst with absolute love.

"Hey, Lisbeth," she called out in an angelic voice.

And she'd pronounced the S. I was sure it was because she couldn't say her Zs yet. But I took it as a sign.

Roman's face lit when we made eye contact. He lifted his chin in a silent order for me to join them, but that wasn't what got my feet moving.

"Wanna see da dog?" Tessa yelled, pointing at Loretta.

I'd had, and loved, that dog for five years, but I'd never been so excited to "see" her in my entire life.

"I'd love to," I laughed, walking over, my heels sinking into the grass.

"She like balls?" Tessa asked Roman.

He chuckled. "Nah. Loretta's only trick is not spilling a drop as she pees inside my shoes."

"It was one time when she was a puppy, Roman. It's time you let that grudge go," I teased, sidling up beside him. "She doesn't like balls," I informed Tessa. "But she has squeaky toys inside that she likes to chew on. Wanna see?"

She cautiously looked up at her mom and then over to Heath. "We go inside?"

"Yeah, sweet girl," Heath answered, lifting his hand for a high-five Tessa enthusiastically returned.

"I made cookies," I blurted as everyone started toward the door. "Well, it's more like a cookie bar. I didn't have a cookie sheet and they all melted together, but we can cut it into cookies."

"Yes!" Tessa shrieked, patting Clare on the shoulder. "Can we have cookies, Mama? Please. Please. Pleeeeeease."

Clare tightened her lips as she gave me a side eye, but her words were for her daughter. "I don't know. It depends on what kind they are."

"Uh…Chocolate chip?" I said nervously.

What if Clare was some kind of health nut and didn't allow Tessa to have sweets? I really should have broached this topic with her before offering her kid cookies. Damn.

Clare frowned at Tessa. "Sorry, baby."

Only the little girl didn't look even remotely upset. She laughed wildly. "You can't eat dem all!"

Clare poked out an exaggerated pouty lip. "But, but, they're my favorite."

Tessa continued to giggle, and my worries drifted away.

"How about you grab Mrs. Elisabeth's hand and the three of us will race and see who gets there first?"

My breath hitched, and a chill prickled the hairs on the back of my neck.

Oh God.

Tessa cautiously looked up at me as if weighing her decision. She once again looked over to Heath, who gave her a smile and a short nod, before she lifted her tiny hand up in my direction.

I had been wrong earlier. *That* was the moment when my heart burst with absolute love.

I took her hand in mine and tried to keep the moisture swimming behind my lids at bay.

She grinned. "I hope you fast. Mama loves chocolate chip cookies."

I barked a laugh and the tears spilled out. I did my best to hide them, but they wouldn't stop.

She was perfect.

Head to toe.

Inside and out.

Clare gave me an understanding smile and put me out of my misery by issuing a, "One, two, three, go."

She pulled up on Tessa's arm, and I did the same, swinging her off her feet as we headed to the front door, Heath and Roman on our heels.

Those might have been the saddest, most tragic chocolate chip cookies I'd ever baked.

But sitting on a barstool, listening to Tessa giggle when Clare pretended to be Cookie Monster, cry when she spilled her milk, then laugh again when Roman let Loretta lick some of it off the floor made them the most incredible chocolate chip cookies I'd ever eaten.

CHAPTER NINE

Heath

"Well, as you can see, this room…is rather…um, bare," Elisabeth said, pushing the door directly across the hall from Clare's room open.

She wasn't kidding. The room was empty with the exception of an air mattress and a small nightstand beside it.

"Oh, and this one doesn't have a private bath. You'll have to share the hall one with Devon and Alex." She paused. "Shit…and I guess all the other new guys too." She worried with her thin, gold necklace. "I figured it'd be best to give Clare and Tessa the one with the bathroom. Even if it does look like shit. I'm gonna have someone come in to renovate it soon. It's really ugly right now."

"I'm sure it's fine," I said, putting the bag my sister, Maggie, had dropped off on the floor.

"New furniture will be here on Monday," she added.

"Dis you room, Luke?" Tessa asked, squeezing past me, Clare in tow.

While I was impressed with how well Tessa was adjusting, Clare was starting to worry me. Somewhere around dinnertime, her brave smile had melted away and she'd shut down. She hadn't eaten anything, and when I'd asked if she wanted to go lie down, she'd shaken her head and diverted her eyes.

She hadn't let Tessa go since we'd arrived. And I mean, not at all. If she wasn't carrying her, she was holding her hand. Tessa had tried to break free at least a hundred times, but Clare had refused and redirected her attention to something else.

Roman and Elisabeth were chomping at the bit to get their hands on her, but Clare never gave them a second. She'd included them in conversations with Tessa and urged her to talk to them, but not once had she let her go. I understood her caution, but this was something different. Something more was going on in her head, but I couldn't pinpoint exactly what it was.

"Whoa! Dat you bed?" Tessa asked, belly-flopping on the air mattress. "It's bouncy!"

Clare grimaced and scooped her up, planting her on her hip. "Don't, baby. You'll put a hole in it."

"It's okay," Elisabeth said, watching Tessa with a warm smile. "I have an extra downstairs."

Clare cut her eyes to Elisabeth and clipped, "No. It's not okay."

Elisabeth's back shot ramrod straight as Clare rushed from the room, Tessa in her arms.

I watched with narrowed eyes as she crossed the hall and closed the door to her room behind her.

"Did I say something wrong?" Elisabeth asked.

I shook my head. "Don't worry about it. I'll go check on her. They're both just exhausted."

"Yeah," Elisabeth whispered, unconvinced.

I squeezed her shoulder. "The last few days have been hard on everyone. We could all use a good night of sleep."

"Right." She swallowed hard, staring at the closed bedroom door.

"Go find Roman, Elisabeth. I'll take care of this."

She didn't say anything, but she started toward the stairs. "You'll let me know…if y'all…you know, need anything?"

"Of course."

She glanced back at Clare's door and sighed before finally going down the stairs.

After digging through my bag, I pulled out the pair of headphones I'd asked Maggie to pack and then walked to the door.

With a soft knock, I called, "Clare? It's me."

She didn't respond, so I knocked again.

"Clare?"

No answer.

"Don't shut me out," I told the door. "You need time alone, that's fine, but you gotta let me know you're okay."

I heard her humorless laugh.

"I'm not sure I'll ever be okay," she said.

I rested my palms on either side of the doorjamb. "Then let me in so I can help."

"Go away, Heath."

I groaned, testing the doorknob and finding it locked. "You want to be alone? Why don't you let me watch Tessa for a little while? You can take a shower, do whatever you gotta do."

"No one is watching Tessa but me."

There was something in her tone that bothered me, just the slightest hint of an edge I'd never heard before.

I skimmed my hand over the top of the doorframe and, *bingo,* found one of those universal pins for opening locks. "Clare, I'm coming in. You dressed?"

"Nope," she snipped, that fucking edge more prominent.

Worry soured in my gut.

"Then I suggest you get that way fast because I'm coming in." I poked the key into the tiny hole on the knob until it released the lock. "Let me know when you're covered," I said, cracking the door but not swinging it open.

"Jesus Christ, Heath. Yes. I'm dressed." She snatched the door from my hand, causing the key to fall to the carpeted floor.

We both bent to pick it up at the same time, our heads nearly cracking together.

"Shit. Sorry." I jumped back up, but she remained hunched over. "Clare?" I questioned, reaching out for her but stopping at the last second.

She folded an arm across her stomach and then used her other to prop herself up on her knee. Her back rounded as a painful moan escaped her mouth.

"Mama?" Tessa cried from the bed, promptly abandoning the iPad I'd loaned her and scrambling over the side.

"I'm fine," Clare said in a broken voice that told me she was anything but fine.

I squatted in front of her at the same time Tessa careened into her legs.

She winced and an agonizing wail shot from her mouth before she moved the arm at her stomach to wrap it around Tessa's back. "I'm fine," she repeated.

"What's wrong?" I asked, desperately fighting the urge to take her into my arms.

She groaned, using a great deal of effort to stand up straight. "Nothing. I'm good," she panted as though she'd just run a marathon.

"You're in pain."

"I'm just a little sore."

"Bull—" I didn't finish the curse strictly for Tessa's benefit. "Hey, sweet girl. Go get the iPad. I brought you some headphones."

She looked up at Clare warily but reluctantly followed my direction.

Once I had her set up on the bed, watching one of the princess movies I'd downloaded for her, I refocused on Clare. "Hall. Now," I ordered.

"Don't tell me what to do," she mumbled as she walked past me in a gait that could only be compared to that of an eighty-year-old recovering from a hip replacement. She stopped at the door without crossing the threshold into the hall.

"How bad is it?" I asked.

She glanced over her shoulder at Tessa. "I'm fine, Heath. We just need some sleep."

"Don't feed me that shit."

She was still wearing the scrubs the hospital had given her that morning despite the fact that Elisabeth had placed several bags of clothes on the armchair in her bedroom.

"Why don't you go take a long bath and get changed?"

"Into what?" she snapped, slapping her hands on her thighs in frustration before wincing again.

I crossed my arms over my chest and rocked back on my heels. "Maybe something in one of those bags."

She scoffed and glanced to the floor. "I'm fine in this."

"Yeah, but you've been wearing it all day. And you need a shower. I'm not saying you stink or anything, but..." I trailed off and tossed her a smirk.

One she did not return.

Her whole face crumbled, which sent off a chain reaction through her body. She threw a hand out and caught herself on the door.

I would have given anything to take that from her. To make things better. But I couldn't be sure she even wanted the comfort from me. And, if she didn't, I would have been no better than any other man who had put his hands on her without her permission.

I pinched the bridge of my nose and ground out, "Talk to me."

Her breathing sped rapidly as emotions ravaged her, but she kept them locked away.

Pressure mounted in my chest because there was not one damn thing I could do to ease her agony unless she trusted me enough to open up. I couldn't force her. It was something she had to decide on her own. And it fucking killed me.

She screwed her eyes shut but didn't move.

"Clare, I'm gonna be real honest here. I'm on the verge of spontaneously combusting. I refuse to be one of those men in your life who puts my hands on you when you have no say in it. But, if you don't stop being such a hard-ass and lean on me, I'm going to lose my mind. If you want to be left alone, I'll completely understand. But, for the love of God, babe, open your mouth and tell me what the hell is going on in your head."

Her sad, blue eyes lifted to mine; the pain shining within was staggering.

I loomed forward, thrumming with need to hold her. "It's me, Clare. Whatever you need, you know I'll give it to you. You just have to *tell* me."

Finally, fucking finally, she closed the distance between us, folded her arms around my waist, and pressed her cheek to my chest. "I wanna go home, Heath. I can't stay here. I can't…"

That was all the permission I needed. I'd promised myself that I'd only *give* to Clare, but as I wrapped her into a gentle hug, I had to admit that it was for me. My heart slowed immediately as I filled my lungs with her scent.

"I can't let you go back to that."

"No," she corrected. "Not back to Walt's. I mean *home.* To the shitty trailer I lived in before I met him." She paused and then softly finished with, "Before my life ended."

"I can't let you go back to that either, babe."

Her shoulders shook as her breathing shuttered. Her fingers tensed at my back as she clung to me.

"I know this is hard," I told the top of her head. "But we're all here for you. Me. Roman. Elisabeth. The DEA. Everyone."

"I don't belong here," she squeaked.

She was so fucking wrong. She belonged exactly where she was—safe and in my arms.

"This isn't permanent."

She lifted her head off my chest and tilted it back to catch my gaze. "That's the problem. I don't belong anywhere. A woman I only met hours ago bought me underwear today, Heath." Her voice hitched. "I don't even have my own underwear," she choked out. "What happens when this is over? I have no family. My parents are dead, and my aunts and uncles, who I haven't spoken to in over a decade, could barely take care of themselves back then. I can't imagine that anyone is going to be rushing to my aid when this is all said and done. I have nowhere to go. No money. No clothes. No way to take care of Tessa. No job. No experience. No nothing."

"You've got me," I replied without hesitation. And I fucking meant it.

I wouldn't abandon her.

Even if I couldn't stay.

"You're a really sweet guy. But come on… Eventually, the DEA is going to stop paying you to take care of me."

I cocked my head to the side. "You think I'm only here because it's my job?"

"I don't think it's the *only* reason you're here. But, Heath, two days ago, I still thought your name was Luke."

"And…" I drawled.

She sighed. "And…it's hard to believe that next time you go undercover and your name becomes Gino that you'll still be my Luke."

My Luke.

Wrong name, but I could live with it as long as it was preceded by "my" and it came from her mouth.

"Okay, let me stop you right there. One, I have blond hair and blue eyes. I'm willing to assume no one is going to buy me as a Gino. So we're both safe there." I smirked.

She half laughed, half cried.

"Two, I already told you this, but it seems it needs repeating." I smoothed a hand up her back and stared down into her swollen and battered, but no less beautiful, blue eyes. "I don't want to be your *Luke*. Not anymore. I'm Heath. I've always been Heath. I'll always be Heath. But, regardless of what my name is, I'm not going anywhere."

Not until you're ready anyway. I ignored the stabbing pain in my chest.

Her lashes fluttered as her eyes closed just before she rested her forehead on my chest. "Why?"

Because I wouldn't be able to breathe without knowing you're safe.

Because I'm drawn to you in ways that would ruin us both.

Because it's irrational, illogical, and so fucked up that I feel like I'm going insane, but I can't stop feeling like you and Tessa are mine.

"We're friends, Clare. That's what friends do."

She hugged me tight then mumbled something I couldn't quite make out into my chest. I assumed it was some variation of thank-you. So I gently returned her squeeze.

Until she suddenly stepped out of my arms, embarrassment and horror covering her face. "Oh God, you are."

I narrowed my eyes in confusion. "I am what?"

"Shit. I'm sorry."

I inched toward her and impatiently repeated, "I am what?"

"Married," she replied, lifting her gaze to mine. "Shit. Your wife probably wants to claw my eyes out. You should have introduced us when she dropped off your bag today. Maybe I could have talked to her and smoothed things out for you," she rambled adorably.

Her disappointment was unmistakable, and that alone did some seriously good things in my chest. Really fucking *good* things.

I barked a laugh. "My wife doesn't want to claw your eyes out." I swayed my head from side to side in consideration. "I mean, she might, but seeing as to how she doesn't exist, I don't think she's an immediate threat."

One side of her mouth tipped up in a grin.

"I'm not married, Clare. The girl who dropped my bag off today was my little sister, Maggie. And I would have introduced you, if I hadn't thought she'd embarrass the ever-loving shit out of me." I flashed her a smile and winked. "I've got a reputation to uphold here."

Her smile spread. "You have a sister?"

"Four," I replied, my smile growing to match hers.

Her mouth fell open. "Four?"

I laughed at her surprise. "Yep. Jenna, Laurie, Melanie, and

Maggie. I'm the oldest, and they have an ongoing competition to see who can fuck with me the most. Laurie currently holds the title after she ran into me out on a date last year. She was eight months pregnant at the time and came over to our table, fake-crying and asking me if I was at least going to show up for *our son's* birth. My date took off, never to be seen again, and my sisters all got a big laugh. We're tight. And I love 'em. But they are serious assholes sometimes."

She cupped a hand over her mouth to stifle her laugh. "Wow."

And that's when it hit me. I'd always *acted* like Heath when I was with her, but as far as my past was concerned, I'd only been able to give her Luke Cosgrove—twenty-nine-year-old only child from Orlando, working as a personal trainer until I was able to open my own gym. Lies. Lies. And more lies. Yet I wanted her to trust me.

"Hey, I've got an idea," I said, shoving my hands in my pockets to keep from pulling her back into my arms. "Why don't you let me take Tessa downstairs while you take a long bath and get ready for bed? We'll come back up in thirty minutes with some food and ibuprofen, and I'll tell you anything you want to know about me."

Her smile fell, and she uncomfortably cut her eyes to the side. "Tessa stays with me."

"Okay," I replied immediately. "Then get in there, take a bath, put on some of the clothes Elisabeth bought you, and *I'll* be back up in thirty minutes with some food and ibuprofen to answer anything you want to know about me." I grinned.

A shy smile played on her lips as she continued to look off to the side. "Okay."

"Thirty minutes," I reminded her, backing away.

"Thirty minutes," she repeated before biting her bottom lip.

She didn't move. Nor did she look at me.

However, I kept backing toward the stairs because it was either that or bite that fucking bottom lip of hers, too.

Thirty *long* minutes later, I headed back up the stairs with a bottle of ibuprofen, a large Italian-sausage-and-onion pizza, two cups, and a two-liter of Coke—and not the diet shit she drank.

I rapped softly on the door, and seconds later, she pulled it open an inch.

Literally. One inch.

"It's just me," I assured, but she didn't open it wider.

She put her lips to the crack. "Do you remember when you told me about your sisters and how they liked to embarrass you?"

I twisted my lips. "Uh…it was thirty minutes ago, Clare. Can't exactly forget."

"Right. Well, I think Elisabeth might be my long-lost sister because this is what she bought me to sleep in." She swung the door open, and it was all I could do not to drop the pizza.

The box bumbled in my hand as I raked my eyes over her from head to toe—then again for good measure. Then *again* because… well, I was a man and she was wearing a tiny, black, silky dress that clung to every curve of her petite body. She was still wearing a bra, but the swells of her breasts were exposed at the top, a fucking perfect line of cleavage taunting me.

I was going to lose my mind if I had to sit and talk to her while she was wearing that.

"I see your point," I mumbled, raking my eyes over her one last time before pulling my shit together.

"This is all she bought!" she exclaimed on a whisper. "Twelve of them to be exact. All in different colors and styles. Not even so much as a pair of yoga pants."

Well, there was one positive. I'd stared at her ass in those enough to know they weren't much better than this little nightgown thingy. Though I feared that Clare in a potato sack would still have the same effect on me.

"Okay. We can fix this," I declared, walking into the room and setting the pizza and the Coke on the foot of the bed, where Tessa was sound asleep, headphones still on, iPad still curled against her chest.

I glanced back at Clare, biting the inside of my cheek to suppress the groan when I got another eyeful. Then I stripped my T-shirt over my head and tossed it in her direction. "Here. Put this on."

My groan finally escaped as her eyes lingered on my abs just before she tugged it on.

Offering her that shirt was quite possibly the worst decision I'd ever made.

Because, while my shirt covered her exposed chest, it left her standing in front of me, in a bedroom, wearing *my shirt.*

Do not go there, Light.

She is not yours.

But she could be…

"Jesus fuck," I mumbled, searching around the room.

Surely, Elisabeth had to have bought her a robe—or, if I was really lucky, a burka.

No such luck, but I found a throw blanket hanging over the chair in the corner.

I tortured myself with one last glance at her before offering the blanket in her direction. "Maybe you should cover up with that."

"I'm sorry," she apologized, her face flashing bright red as she wrapped the blanket around her shoulders.

I gripped the back of my neck. "You're beautiful, Clare. Nothing to apologize for." *For fuck's sake, what is wrong with me?*

She cleared her throat and then pointedly dropped her gaze to my chest. "Well…um…with that same sentiment in mind, perhaps you should go grab another shirt."

And take a cold shower.

And bleach my retinas to forget how goddamn sexy she was in that nightgown and even more so in my shirt.

I'd promised I wouldn't *take* from Clare, but I was willing to bet that jerking my dick to visions of her would most definitely fall into that category. Son of a bitch, I was an asshole.

"Yeah. I'll be right back," I replied, hauling ass from the room.

What was I doing? I'd been able to contain myself for three fucking months with this woman. And, after one night and sleeping in an uncomfortable hospital chair at her side, I was losing it?

Or maybe it had more to do with the fact that she was finally away from that maniac and my head wasn't filled with worry and fear that something would happen to her.

Or maybe I was a head case who was falling in love with a witness who had worked her way under my skin with nothing more than a brave heart and a smile I felt all the way down to the marrow in my bones.

Fuck. Fuck. Fuck.

It was a good five minutes before I'd collected myself enough to make my way back over.

"Hey," I said, fully intent on telling her I was going to call it a night. We could talk later…after my lobotomy…and my castration.

"You bought me a sausage-and-onion pizza," she stated with sparkling eyes as I entered the room. The blanket was thankfully wrapped tight around her shoulders as she perched on the corner of the bed.

I shrugged. "Actually, Roman's assistant, Seth, bought you a sausage-and-onion pizza, but yeah, I asked him to get it."

Her lips pursed, and for a split second, I thought she was upset.

A tear rolled from the corner of her eye.

My whole body came online as I searched her face. "What's wrong?"

She dried her cheek. "You hate sausage. You gagged when I told you this was my favorite."

I chuckled as relief flooded me. "I can pick sausage off. And besides, I ate that weird pork stuff Elisabeth made." I tipped my chin to the box beside her. "That pizza's for you. Well, half of it, anyway. That weird pork stuff Elisabeth cooked was shit."

She giggled, and just the sound soothed my exposed nerves.

"How old are you?" she asked out of the blue as she started picking sausage off a slice.

"Thirty-four," I answered.

Her eyebrows popped up. "Wow, gramps."

"Ass," I teased, walking over to Tessa. I gently removed the headphones and tucked her under the blankets.

When I turned back to face Clare, she was smiling.

"Thanks for the pizza, Heath."

"Thank me by passing me a slice."

"Are you sure you should be eating pizza? My grandpa always got indigestion if he ate too late."

"Aren't you just hilarious," I deadpanned.

She giggled again, and I knew there was not a chance in Hell I was calling it a night.

Not when I had the opportunity to spend even a minute with her.

Snagging the sausage-free piece she was working on from the box, I asked, "All right, what else do you want to know about me?"

"Where are you from?"

"Augusta." I took a bite and settled in the chair across the room.

"Parents?"

"Mom died when I was sixteen. Breast cancer. Dad didn't take it so well, became a drunk. He and I don't get along so well. Next."

"How old are your sisters?"

"Shit. You gonna make me do math while I'm enjoying some onion pizza?"

She laughed before taking a bite. A sexy-as-hell moan rumbled in her throat as she chewed.

Christ, she was beautiful. The blanket was doing its job up top, but her petite feet crossed at the ankle drew my attention up to her toned thighs.

Yep, time to talk about my sisters.

"So…Jenna's three years younger than me, thirty-one. That

would make Laurie twenty-nine, Melanie twenty-five, and Maggie twenty-two. Despite the age gap, I'm closest with Maggie. She came to live with me after high school so she could go to Georgia Tech without having to sell her organs to pay for room and board. She graduated last May and moved into her own apartment over the summer."

"Where do you live?" She took a bite.

"House in the northeast burbs." I took a bite.

She finished chewing. "College?"

I finished chewing. "University of Georgia."

"How'd you become a DEA agent?" Another bite.

My hand froze in midair, the pizza halfway to my mouth as a slow grin pulled at my lips. "A 'show me your titties' sign."

Her chin snapped to the side as she laughed. "Um. What?"

"St. Patrick's Day, downtown. I was a rookie cop, and we'd gotten word from the Captain that we were cracking down on the Mardi Gras–style flashing for beads that year. You know, trying to keep the biggest drinking day of the year family friendly and all," I joked.

She rewarded me with another soul-soothing giggle.

"Anyway, I concocted a plan. Captain agreed. I drove my truck down and parked along one of the main strips with a fuck-ton of beads and a handwritten 'show me your titties' sign. Chicks walked by, showed me their titties, then my boys picked 'em up for indecent exposure. Eighty-seven arrests. Captain was so impressed he threw my name out to the DEA. Rest is history."

"You did not," she gasped.

I smirked with pride. "Can't make that shit up. I got paid to sit around and be flashed all day. Best job a man could have." I took another bite of pizza, talking around it as I said, "But that was before I found out I could get paid for sitting around, bullshitting with you."

Her eyes lit at the compliment. "Well, in the nightie Elisabeth bought, it's practically the same thing."

I pointed at her with my crust and winked. "This is not a bad thing."

Aaaaaaannnnd…now, I'm flirting.

Fuck. Me.

But, as she started picking sausage off another piece of pizza for me, I realized I was already fucked when it came to Clare.

And, Christ, it felt good.

CHAPTER TEN

CLARE

"Mr. and Mrs. Noir. It's so nice to see you again," Doctor Fulmer said as he entered the room. His balding, gray head was down as he flipped through the pages of a medical chart.

I had an overwhelming urge to light it on fire and pray that the flames would engulf me too.

I was flat on my back, an IV in my hand, a paper blanket covering my lap, and tears rolling from my eyes.

"Don't be nervous, sweetheart," Walter purred before placing a chilling kiss to my forehead.

I wasn't nervous.

I was devastated.

It was the day of my egg retrieval. The day my eggs would be paired with Walt's sperm and innocent children would be created. When I'd been a little girl, I'd had dreams of having sweet, little babies with my eyes. But not like this.

During the IVF process, I'd prayed every night as Walt gave me my shots that my ovaries wouldn't stimulate. However, the monitoring ultrasounds revealed three "beautiful" follicles steadily maturing.

I hadn't given up all hope. From what I'd read on the Internet, not all follicles contained eggs and three was an extremely small number for the amount of medication they'd given me. But Doctor Fulmer had assured us that he'd been successful with less.

Just that morning, I'd dropped to my knees in our bathroom and begged whatever God was out there that he'd fail.

The doctor reassuringly squeezed my foot and glanced up to Walt. "We're all set."

"Perfect," he replied sinisterly.

"All right, Mrs. Noir. The anesthesiologist is going to get you sedated and then we'll wheel you to the back, retrieve those beauties, and you'll be right back at your husband's side before you know it."

That only made the tears fall harder, and a loud sob tore from my throat.

"Clare," Walt scolded, sliding his hand under my neck and squeezing painfully hard. "Get it together," he seethed.

"Sorry," I said to him before looking to the doctor and lying. "I'm just nervous. That's all."

His eyebrows regretfully pinched together, but his gaze darted back to Walt. "Okay, then. I'll just give you a moment to collect yourself, and then we'll get things started."

"Just send them in now. She's fine," Walt replied, his hidden fingers biting into the back of my neck.

More tears spilled from my eyes, but I managed to squeak out, "Yes. Send them in."

Doctor Fulmer shook his head but didn't say anything else before exiting the room.

No sooner had the door clicked than Walt was in my face. One of his hands slapped over my mouth. The other twisted in the back of my hair, forcing my head to the side.

"I swear to God I will fucking kill you if you pull that shit again." The veins on his forehead bulged from the exertion.

Panic thundered in my chest. I had no doubt he was telling the truth. Just a week earlier, I'd heard him say those exact words to a man he'd considered his best friend since childhood as he'd sat on our couch as a welcomed guest. An hour later, I'd been on my knees, cleaning his skull fragments off my living room wall.

I nodded vigorously.

He studied my frightened eyes for a few beats longer before finally releasing me. "I'd appreciate it if you tried to be a little more grateful here." He sauntered over to the door and peeked outside. "It's not my fucking fault we're in this situation. It'd do you well to remember that. My shit tested just fine. It's your white-trash, inbred ovaries that's costing us thirty fucking thousand dollars." He raked a frustrated hand through his dark-brown hair before smoothing it back into place. "A 'thank you' and 'I love you' would go a long fucking way right now, Clare."

"Thank you and I love you," I repeated immediately, vomit creeping up the back of my throat.

He glared at me and cracked his neck. "You're fucking lucky I love you. If I was a different kind of man, I would drop you and move the fuck on. Your kind's a dime a dozen, and most of them aren't broken like you. Don't fucking forget that."

Oh, how I'd wished he were a different kind of man. I wouldn't wish a life with Walter Noir on my worst enemy, but that didn't mean I wouldn't enjoy walking away if he found someone new to torment.

"I know," I whispered to keep the shake out of my voice.

He scoffed and planted his fists on his hips. "Then fucking act like it. I'm sick and tired of these doctor's appointments. Any other woman I'd be able to fuck in the ass and still knock her up. You though? I had to jerk my own cock into a cup to make a baby. Something is seriously wrong with that bullshit."

A few years ago, that rant would have destroyed me. But I'd become numb to his verbal abuse. Nothing he could say could hurt me as much as living at his side.

Being forced to carry his baby, though, would be a close second.

"I'm sorry," I said, using the back of my arm to dry my cheeks.

He rolled his eyes, snatching a tissue from the box on the counter. "Clean up your face." He waved it in my direction.

I followed his order and dug down deep in order to keep fresh tears from reappearing.

Crying was useless.

But, then again, so was breathing when you were married to a monster.

A knock sounded at the door just seconds before a middle-aged man pushed a cart inside.

"You ready?" he asked.

Walt quickly moved to my side and took my hand.

My pulse sped to a near marathon pace and my body began to tremble as I told the biggest lie of my entire life. "Yes."

"You ready?" Heath asked, sitting beside me on the bed.

"No," I whispered.

He nodded and rested his elbows on his knees.

It had been a week, and no one had heard from Walt.

Was I unnerved that he'd all but disappeared? Unquestionably.

Did I feel like I was finally living for the first time since he'd slid his ring on my finger? Abso-fucking-lutely.

After my first night at Roman and Elisabeth's, I'd learned something from the sexy and impossibly sweet Heath Light. Being forced to depend on people wasn't such a bad thing after all. So what if Elisabeth had bought me underwear and ridiculous nighties to sleep in? She'd also baked my baby cookies and provided me with a fully furnished bedroom where we could sleep safely and soundly while DEA agents and personal security guarded us. She hadn't had to do that any more than Heath had had to order me pizza and stay up until the wee hours of the morning, filling my head with his past until I'd finally managed to drift off.

The following day, after Heath had mentioned something to Elisabeth over a breakfast she'd cooked for us, I'd found a bag full of yoga pants and oversized T-shirts on my bed.

I'd cried as I'd pulled them on.

They felt like me. But not Clare Noir. Walt never would have allowed me to wear that to bed.

They felt like *me*. Clare Cynthia Cornwell. The woman I'd lost the day I'd signed my life away on the dotted line of a marriage certificate.

That night, after I got out of the shower, I found Heath sitting in my room, lounging on the bed, while Tessa explained to him all things Surprise Eggs and Shopkins. He listened intently with bright eyes and a wide smile that made my stomach dip.

That was Heath.

He was oddly reminiscent of Luke—but better.

After Tessa had fallen asleep, we stayed up all night, talking again and watching old reruns of *Wheel of Fortune*. He was exhausted and yawned repeatedly, but he stayed until my lids fluttered closed. I wasn't sure when he'd snuck out, but he was gone by the next morning.

He *always* came back the following night though.

When I was with Heath, I didn't feel like I was drowning. For those hours locked in a bedroom with him while Tessa slept soundly beside me, I was the happiest I'd been in years. The expansive world outside paled in comparison to the beauty inside those four walls. He made sure of that.

I would have lived in the confines of that safe haven forever as long as I had them beside me.

Heath had taken so many of my dirty and broken pieces away over the last week that it was a wonder I wasn't transparent. The holes left behind weren't always as easy to fill. But, each time I fell apart, he was there.

It'd taken a few days, but I'd relaxed when it came to Tessa. I'd been encouraging her to spend more time alone with Elisabeth and Roman. They were good people. And God knows she hadn't had many of those in her life. The smile on her face as she found comfort with others was worth every minute of my anxiety. And the peace I felt when I leaned back against Heath's chest as we watched her from the window while she raced through the backyard, Loretta hot on her heels, made it worth it in a different way.

My relationship with the Leblancs was evolving as well. I was no expert on friendship, but it felt like Elisabeth and I had developed one. We laughed a lot and had shared quite a few tears too. She was candid about her and Roman's relationship. How they had gotten a divorce and it wasn't until they found out about the possibility of the embryos having been switched that they rekindled things. Their story of love and loss wasn't an easy one, but as sad as it may sound, I was jealous.

Roman was an amazing man—albeit bossy and stubborn. But it was obvious he was madly in love with her and her with him.

It was a concept my mind couldn't quite grasp.

Walt had proven that love wasn't always hearts and flowers. It could be dark and dirty, defined by power and pain, and filled with anguish and agony.

But, even knowing that, I still longed for a connection. Like the magical spark I felt when I was with Heath—even when he had been Luke.

Swallowing hard, I snuck a peek at him as he crossed his thick arms over his chest and kicked his legs out in front of him. Beautifully relaxed. His blond hair was styled away from his face, and a thin layer of scruff covered his jaw. My stealthy gaze drifted to his lips, where they lingered for entirely too long. I had no right to wonder what they would feel like pressed against my own. But that didn't stop me.

It was not the day to be daydreaming about Heath.

Tessa's DNA test had come in and a doctor from the lab was driving out to give us the results in person. We all knew what they were going to read, but apprehension had still hovered in the air over breakfast.

Desperate to feel something—anything—except the nerves rolling in my stomach, I rested my hand on his thigh.

"What do you need, Clare?" he murmured the same way he had so many times over the last week.

My answer was always the same. "You."

"Then get over here and take it," he replied as usual.

It was an offer I never refused.

His blanket of warmth was often the only thing that could ward off the chill of reality.

"I'm nervous," I admitted, leaning into his side.

Curling an arm around my shoulders, he reclined on the bed, taking me down with him.

"You should be," he said dryly. "I've decided today is going to be the day I finally beat you at *Wheel of Fortune*."

An evil laugh bubbled in my throat. "Good luck with that."

"I'm serious. I know you're cheating."

"Oh please!" I rolled my eyes. "You guessed *The Old Man and the Bee* as a famous book. It doesn't require cheating to beat you."

"Hey!" He feigned injury. "It was a brilliant piece of satire."

"A brilliant piece of fake satire is more like it. I Googled it. It's not real."

He teasingly gasped. "You used the Google against me? How dare you!"

I squealed as he tickled my side.

Tessa's attention snapped to us, concern in her deep-green eyes.

Heath sat up a fraction to flash her a huge grin before saying, "Your mama thinks she's funny."

Her eyes lit. "Mama's funny when she dances."

Oh shit.

Heath's head swung to me, his mouth hanging open in amusement. "You dance?"

I bulged my eyes at Tessa. "No!"

And I didn't—unless I was alone in a room with Tessa. And then I became Michael freaking Flatley—assuming he was drunk, deaf, and rhythmless. But there was no way Heath would ever get to witness a tragedy like that.

"You do!" Tessa argued. "Like dis." She got to her feet and flailed her arms and legs in probably a much better impression of my dancing.

Heath laughed loudly.

I rolled to my side and buried my face in his chest. "You're never going to let this go, are you?"

His head dipped, his lips going to my ear as he rumbled, "Change of plans, babe." Chills prickled on my neck as his warm breath breezed over my skin. "Tonight we're forgoing *Wheel of Fortune* so you can show me these famous moves."

I giggled and stretched my arm across his stomach, letting my hand splay over the hard ridges of his abs.

Heath and I weren't exactly cuddlers, but true to his word, if I needed something, he gave it to me. And, truth be told, sometimes, I didn't need it at all—I *wanted* it.

And I was quickly realizing that, when it came to Heath, I wanted it all.

I decided a change of topic would be better than discussing my "famous moves" any further. "What should we do with her while we hear the results?"

"I trust her with Alex," he said, squeezing me tight.

"I don't know."

"She likes Ethan a lot," he suggested.

"I know," I replied, lifting my head to check on Tessa, who had gone back to quietly drawing in one of the activity books Elisabeth had bought her. "What about if I just let her wear the headphones and watch a movie?"

He gave me a tight squeeze. "You gonna be able to keep it together? It'll freak her out if you get upset. She feeds off your emotions."

I sighed. "I already know the results."

"What about me?" he suggested. "I could sit with her."

I sucked in a sharp breath. I trusted her with Heath. Completely.

But I didn't trust myself without him when those results were read.

"Headphones. I'll keep it together," I decided immediately.

He nodded, and while I couldn't be positive, I swear I felt his lips press against the top of my head before he mumbled, "Okay."

God, it felt good to have him. He might not have agreed with my decision. But he supported me no matter what.

"Luke! Look!" Tessa yelled, holding up a picture she'd drawn.

He lifted his head off the bed, keeping me held tight to his side as he praised, "Good job, sweet girl. Is that a snowman?"

She burst out laughing. "No! Dat's you!"

"Well, shit," he mumbled, glancing down at me with a playful grin. "I think that might be my cue to get back in the gym."

I laughed, and there was no mistaking it that time. A huge smile split his mouth just as it came down on my forehead. He kissed me chastely, like it was the most natural thing in the world.

And maybe it was.

It didn't hurt. It wouldn't be followed by demands of sex. Nor would my reaction determine how many bruises I would end up with.

It was just a simple show of affection.

And it came from Heath.

My heart swelled and my nose began to sting, but I refused to cry. Tears had no business between us anymore.

"You ready?" he whispered.

No. Absolutely not. Because ready meant leaving that moment with him and facing the reality that loomed on the other side of the bedroom door. However, I was certain the doctor had already arrived, assuming he'd made it through our security detail.

"Two minutes?" I asked.

This got me a, "Yeah, babe," which was followed by a tight squeeze and another lip touch on my forehead.

And that made me regret not asking for two *days*.

We sat in silence, watching Tessa search through every crayon for the perfect shade to color a pig.

Two minutes turned into ten, but he never pressured me.

He was incredible like that.

Patient.

Kind.

Thoughtful.

Heath.

Finally, I forced myself to sit up, his blanket of warmth sticking with me as he followed me.

"We should probably go downstairs," I said softly, staring up through my lashes.

His eyes flashed dark as he licked his lips. "You sure?" He smoothed a hand down my back before reassuringly gripping my hip.

This. Man.

I swayed into him. "No. But, if I want to escape back up here with you for the rest of the night, it's a necessity."

He smiled, tucking a stray hair behind my ear and peeling another shattered piece of my soul away. "I like that plan. Then let's get this over with."

"Okay, Heath," I whispered. My eyes flashed to his mouth, and he must have noticed, because his smile grew tenfold.

Holding my gaze, he called out, "Tessi, grab your headphones and iPad. We're going down."

"Yeehaw!" she squealed for reasons that could only be described as My Little Pony overload.

Heath laughed loudly, and I couldn't help but join him.

And, looking back, I was glad I did.

It was only those memories with him that pulled me through the darkness.

Again.

Tessa held my hand as we rounded the corner to the living room, her eyes glued to the iPad, her headphones already in place. I hated how much time she spent on that thing, but when you were on the run from a tyrant, little girls got extra screen time.

Elisabeth and Roman were already sitting on the leather sofa flanked by Alex and Ethan at either end. A middle-aged man with horn-rimmed glasses pushed to his feet when he saw us.

"Mrs. Noir, I'm Doctor Hurly," he greeted.

Just the sound of Walt's name slashed through me.

"Just Clare. Please," I corrected.

"Of course. Clare, come have a seat," he invited, but my feet didn't budge.

Suddenly, a rush of nerves swirled in my stomach as it all became too real.

I swallowed hard, trying to pack it down, and then Heath stepped in front of me and whispered, "We can wait."

"I'm okay," I lied.

Which he easily read. "Try that again."

I reached out and rested a hand on his chest. "Fine. This sucks."

He grinned and leaned toward me. A subtle offer for comfort in Heath Light style. I'd take whatever I could get and swayed into him. One of his hands found my hip before sliding around to my lower back, warmth radiating out from his touch.

Bending his head down, he murmured in my ear, "Elisabeth cooked."

My eyebrows pinched together in question as I craned my head back. "Um…okay?"

"That means, after this bullshit is done, it's you, me, Tessa, and a pizza. And, this time, I vote we add beer."

"Oh my God," I breathed, beaming with excitement. "It's like you're speaking to my soul."

He gave a deep, masculine chuckle, and I did my best not to gawk at his sexy mouth. Well, at least not repeatedly. And failed. Tragically.

His eyes heated as he rumbled, "So let's try this again: We can wait."

"I'm okay," I replied, this time honestly. And I really was.

He was there.

It was time we put this to rest. Tessa was my daughter. She was also Elisabeth's. Most importantly, together, we could keep her away from Walt.

I drew in a sharp breath and patted Heath's chest before moving around him.

Ethan lifted his hand for a high five as we passed, and Tessa did not leave him hanging.

Elisabeth was on her feet and wrapping me into a bear hug before I knew what had hit me.

"This changes nothing," she vowed.

She was wrong; it changed everything. But different could be good. Nothing was worse than standing immobile in Walt's fiery inferno, waiting to die. And that was exactly what I'd been doing for the last seven years.

I backed out of her hug and lifted Tessa into my arms. "I know. I'm okay. Really. It is what it is at this point. I just want it over with so we can all move on with our lives. This is step one."

"You're incredible," Elisabeth gasped, tears filling her eyes.

I wasn't. I was just making the best of the shit hand I'd been dealt.

Grinning, I sat down in an oversized chair and arranged Tessa and her iPad on my lap. I reached up and caught Heath's hand from where he was standing behind me. "Let's do this. Rip the Band-Aid off, Doc."

Elisabeth shuffled back to her position with Roman and nodded at Doctor Hurly to carry on.

He cleared his throat. "Of course. Let's get to it. Mr. Leblanc asked me here today in case there were any questions from either party. However, the results of our testing are quite straightforward." He flipped through the papers in his hand before passing one to me and another copy to Elisabeth. "First off, our tests were performed—"

I interrupted him. "Please save your explanations for later. Just tell us what you found."

"Right." He smiled tightly, glancing around the room. "In the case of maternity, we have found to a degree of a 99.8 percent certainty that Tessa Noir is the daughter of Elisabeth Leblanc."

My lungs seized for the briefest of seconds.

Quick. Fast. And to the point.

The truth still took my breath away, but then it was done.

I could live with done. Done meant I'd lived through it and come out on the other side. Done meant moving forward.

And then the floor opened up and the demons of Hell attacked me from all angles.

"It also proved to a 99.8 percent certainty that Walter Noir is her father."

Quick. Fast. And to the point.

I was stabbed in the heart with a verbal blow so painful that I wished I hadn't lived to see the other side.

The room fell silent to my ears even as chaos broke out around me. Roman shot to his feet, Elisabeth right beside him.

And I stared ahead, utterly numb.

I was vaguely aware of Heath plucking Tessa from my lap. I didn't have it in me to fight him. My arms fell to my sides, limp and empty. So fucking empty. Just like the gaping hole in my chest where my heart had once been.

Elisabeth is her mother.

Walt is her father.

Embryos hadn't been swapped.

They'd been created.

Walter fucking Noir had paid someone to give him the egg I couldn't.

And then he'd used me as nothing more than a vessel to deliver her into Satan's lair.

I blinked, my entire life flashing on the backs of my lids.

His words slicing me like razor blades.

His hands pounding me unconsciousness because I had the audacity to breathe without his permission.

His insecurities keeping me caged like an animal.

His body becoming a weapon, stealing bits of me until, ultimately, I broke.

Yet, not one of those things came even close to the pain he'd just inflicted.

Walt didn't even have to be present to destroy me.

I'd only thought I'd gotten free of him the day Heath and Roman had carried us out.

The truth was…there was no escape.

He would never stop.

He'd ruined every last part of me.

And, now, he was going to ruin her too.

The most God-awful, agonizing scream I'd ever heard hit my ears.

It wasn't until Heath appeared in front of me that I realized it was coming from my mouth.

CHAPTER ELEVEN

HEATH

The scream tore from her throat just as Ethan raced Tessa into another room. It wasn't far enough. There wasn't a person in a hundred-yard radius of that house who could have missed her tortured cry.

The visceral devastation gutted me.

I rushed to her, wrapping her in a hug, but she fought against me until I was forced to release her.

Her fists hammered against my chest as she screamed, "No!" at the top of her lungs.

"Clare!" I yelled in an attempt to snap her out of it, but she was inconsolable. Her feral eyes stared right through me.

"No. No. No. No," she repeated through broken cries and angry screams.

"Breathe, babe," I urged as she backed away from me.

"He's going to kill me," she sobbed, tripping over the chair and falling on her ass.

I lunged to catch her, but she swatted my hands away.

She scrambled on all fours until her back hit the wall and she threw a hand up to stop me. "He'll kill us all!"

My body went solid, and despite every fiber of my being demanding I force her to take comfort from me, I managed to take a step back. "He can't hurt you anymore," I swore, slowly lifting my hands in surrender.

"He can *always* hurt me!" Her voice broke as she drew her knees to her chest. "He won't stop." Her hands trembled as she swung her unfocused gaze around the room. "He'll come for her. He'll kill me, and then he'll *take* her."

"Babe, look at me," I pushed, careful to keep my voice even. "He won't. I won't let him."

"He will, and he'll kill you too. He won't stop until everyone I care about is gone. He'll kill Roman, he'll kill Elisabeth, he'll kill you, and then he'll kill me and *take her.*"

After this shit, I wished like hell Walter Noir would come for me so I could end this for her once and for all. I should have killed him that day on his driveway. I wouldn't make that mistake again. The next time I saw that coward, he would leave in a body bag—*my* bullet in his head.

"Breathe, Clare."

"This is not happening," she choked out, covering her mouth with her hand. "Please, God, tell me this is not happening."

"What do you need, Clare?" I asked for no other reason than I knew her answer and I needed her to let me in before my arms tore free of my body in order to get to her.

"He's going to take you both from me."

"He won't. I swear to God. Nothing. No one, not ever, will take me from you. Or her from *us*," I swore, dropping into a squat to bring our eyes level.

Her wild gaze bounced to mine, but she didn't see me. Hollow orbs so far from the woman I knew stared back at me. I couldn't even be sure my Clare was still in there. But I would forage through the pits of Hell to bring her back.

"Clare!" I barked, slamming my palms down on the hardwood floor, desperation overriding my patience.

And, finally, fucking finally, Clare reappeared in the depths of her blue eyes.

But it was Clare the frightened and tortured woman I'd met

all those months ago.

It shattered me.

"Get. Over. Here," I ordered, hating myself for being so rough, but nothing else was getting through to her.

A flash of recognition hit her face for only a second before she tore off the floor, flew across the room, and dove into my arms.

She collided with my chest, knocking me back onto my heels before I was able to right myself.

Sobs shook her chest as she buried her face in my neck, her nails digging into my back.

And, even still, I breathed a ragged sigh of relief.

"I've got you," I swore, rising to my feet.

Her legs encircled my hips the way she had just over a week ago when I'd carried her out of Walter's gate. Only, this time, I couldn't carry her out of the darkness.

The best I could do was carry her upstairs, get Tessa, and then shut the door on the entire fucking world.

It wasn't enough.

She deserved so much fucking more.

But it was all I could do.

That and rip Noir's head from his spineless body the first chance I got.

That "giving" bullshit was becoming impossible.

Clare had been curled into my side, blankly staring into space, for over an hour. I wanted to force her to talk to me so I could get into her head. I'd told myself to be patient, to let her open up when she was ready, but it was breaking me.

"Say something," I urged when the silence had become too much.

"Something," she whispered.

"I'm serious, Clare."

"I'm fine," she replied with absolutely zero conviction.

"Do you want me to get Tessa?"

"Is she with Elisabeth?"

"Yeah."

"Then no."

I groaned.

"You want to eat?"

"No."

"You want—"

"Please stop."

I closed my eyes and sighed.

For seven days, I'd watched her bruises fade and a completely different woman emerge.

For seven days, I'd listened to her laugh with abandon and watched her smile as if her mouth had never known anything else.

For seven days, I watched her rise up stronger and more confident than ever before.

Or so I'd hoped.

It had taken one sentence to crush her.

Maybe I was delusional thinking I could fix her so easily.

But that fucking cloud of denial we'd been living on was the sweetest thing I'd ever experienced.

I hadn't laughed as much in my entire life as I did when I was with her. And, every night as I watched her fall asleep, her lips curled in a serene smile, it filled me in unimaginable ways.

The first time I'd kissed her forehead as she'd slept, I had known it was wrong. It was *taking* at its finest. But I couldn't stop myself. My body ached to touch her and not just when she needed me. Sometimes, I needed her. And, as the days passed, the ache became agonizing. It sure as fuck didn't help when she stared at my mouth as though the ache had found her too.

No lines had been crossed. *Yet.*

But they would be eventually. A fact that taunted my dreams on a nightly basis.

I was fucked.

And not in a good way.

I'd managed to keep my hands off her for a full seven days.

Swear to God, I deserved a medal of honor for that act of heroism.

One thing had become blatantly obvious to me in that time: Letting her go was no longer an option.

But, after today, it was clear keeping her wasn't going to be easy, either.

Yes, I could make her laugh and keep her safe. But I couldn't fix her, no matter how much I wanted to. She needed help that I just couldn't offer. She and Tessa both.

"I think it's time you talk to a therapist," I announced.

"I think it's time I talk to the police."

I jerked my head back so I could get a read on her face. "What?"

Despite the fact that the DEA had offered Clare full immunity in exchange for her testimony and cooperation in their case against Noir, she was still a nervous wreck about it. After a fair amount of talking in circles, I'd convinced Tomlinson to give us time for her to heal physically before dragging her through questioning. I'd yet to tell her that that time had run out—days ago. It was all I could do to keep them off her back until we had gotten the results of Tessa's DNA.

"He's going to kill me, Heath. It's better we get everything documented before he does," she stated emotionlessly.

My body tensed. "He's not—"

She suddenly pushed up on an elbow and looked at me. "You know what I don't get? How the hell a disgusting piece of shit like Walter creates something as perfect as Tessa." She sat all the way up and folded her legs to crisscross between us. "I mean, *how* does that happen? Meanwhile, I can't have kids. Roman, either, ya know? When we did in vitro, I was twenty-five years old, in tip-top health, with shit for eggs. And, somehow, drug-dealing, slime-of-the-Earth Walter fucking Noir can jerk his dick in a cup and create something as perfect as my baby girl."

I would have rather gouged my eyes out with a rusty coat hanger than think of Walter "jerking" anything into a cup. But that wasn't her question, and at least she was talking.

"She's perfect because of you."

"She was perfect when she came out." She leaned forward, her blond hair slipping from behind her ear. "*How* did *he* do that?"

"I don't know." I reached up, caught the lock of her hair, and twisted it between my fingers. "I honestly have no fucking idea." I gave her hair a gentle tug, pulling her down as I rose up on an elbow to bring us nose-to-nose. "But one thing I can tell you is that his role in her life is over. I don't give a fuck what that DNA test reads. He is *not* her father. He's not even a sperm donor. That man is nothing to her. Nothing to you, either. You two do not exist for him anymore."

She scoffed, so I released her hair and caught the back of her neck.

"Swear to God, Clare. You do *not* exist for him. At all. Ever again. He won't kill you. He won't take Tessa. Because I will have his head on a stake before he so much as looks at either of you."

Her lips thinned in a patronizing smile. "You're sweet."

I arched an incredulous eyebrow. "I'm *sweet*?"

"I know you believe that—"

I didn't give her a chance to finish. Releasing her neck, I caught her at the back of the legs and forced her back to the mattress.

She squeaked as I followed her down, landing my hands on either side of her head, my body hovering above her as I supported myself on my knees.

"Do you trust me?"

She blinked a few times before nodding.

"This is serious. Do not lie to me. Do. You. Trust. Me?"

She licked her lips then nodded again.

Slowly, I lowered myself down on top of her, her legs parting and my hips falling between them. I kept my weight on one elbow but brought my other hand up to cup her jaw.

"Tessa *believes* in Santa Claus. And the Easter Bunny. And the Tooth Fairy. You *believe* Walt is going to kill you. And he *believes* you belong to him. But, Clare, I don't *believe* any of that. Beliefs are bullshit. *I know* for a fucking fact that you do *not* exist for him. Because, I'll repeat: I *will* have his head on a stake before he so much as looks at either of you. That is my word."

She stared up at me, tears filling her eyes. "Heath," she sighed, wrapping her arms around my neck, bringing our chests flush.

I held her gaze as I swore, "There is nothing in this world that I will not do to protect you two. And, if you think for one second that I can't do it, you are highly underestimating the depths of my selfishness when it comes to you and your girl."

I shouldn't have done it.

Not even two hours ago, she'd had a complete mental breakdown.

But she was so fucking close.

Her mouth inches away from mine.

Her sweet breath mingling with mine.

Her soft breasts pressed against my chest and her heated core resting against my zipper, only two layers of denim dividing us.

Three months of tension in desperate need of release.

Three months of anxiety making me weak.

Before I could stop myself, I dipped my head and caught her mouth. It was meant to be gentle. It didn't stay that way.

Her mouth opened hastily, her tongue snaking out to tangle with mine. I groaned as her fingers threaded into the back of my hair and she slanted her head, taking me deeper.

A kiss wasn't *taking*? Right?

Now, if I stripped her naked and buried myself inside her, that would be a little different. I wanted her fiercely, but I had the strength to control myself.

At least that's what I'd told myself—until she hooked her leg around my hip and ground against me.

"Fuck," I bit out.

I did *not* have the strength for *that.*

"Clare, wait," I mumbled.

She didn't. She rolled to the side, pulling me with her until she was straddling my hips. Her mouth disappeared but only long enough for her to peel her pale-purple sweater over her head and toss it off the side of the bed.

Her round breasts thrust toward me as she reached around to undo the hook at her back.

If she got that bra off, I was done for. I would be inside her without any further conversation or consideration.

Entire fucking armies didn't have that kind of strength.

CHAPTER TWELVE

CLARE

"Jesus. Wait." He gripped my shoulders to still me, but his eyes drifted down to my chest.

"Don't stop," I pleaded, wiggling in his grasp.

Something had happened inside me when his lips had met mine. A hunger I hadn't felt in years had surged through me.

Passion. Longing. Desire.

I could barely remember a time when I'd wanted Walt to touch me.

But, with a single taste, I *needed* Heath—everywhere.

His mouth.

His fingers.

His length, swelling between my legs as his eyes focused on my nipples, which were peaking beneath the thin, white cotton of my bra.

I wished it had been something sexier. Something deserving of his appraisal. Maybe one of those little nighties hanging in the closet. But, if he noticed my bra at all, he didn't let on. His eyes were dark, and his fingers bit into the flesh of my shoulders as if he were clinging to the edge of self-control.

An edge I desperately needed him to let go of.

I folded down, mumbling against his lips, "Heath, please."

As I circled my hips over his cock, he groaned, "You're killing me here."

"Ask me the question," I whispered, palming either side of his face before taking his mouth again.

His hands slid down to my hips, where he rocked me in his lap. "What question?"

Moving my assault from his mouth to his neck, I traced my tongue up to his ear and then prompted, "What do you need, Clare?" punctuating it by raking my teeth over his earlobe.

His entire body tensed as he moaned his approval with a curse. I glided my hands down to the waistband on his jeans, popping open the button before tugging at the hem of his T-shirt. His arms lifted as I dragged it over his head.

Heat pooled between my legs as his shirt joined mine on the floor.

Heath was beautiful. All raw power and defined muscle. But it was just window dressing for the man hiding inside.

Gentle hands. Kind heart. Gorgeous smile.

My nipples tingled as I traced my finger down the soft, blond trail of hair that disappeared into the waistband of his boxers.

He sucked in a breath and closed his eyes. "Clare," he exhaled.

I kissed over his heart. "Ask me."

His eyes popped open, uncertainty still lingering in his gaze. "This is a bad—"

I didn't allow him to finish before I reached back and unfastened my bra, letting it fall down my arms.

His fiery gaze locked on my chest.

"Jesus," he cursed, but his hands moved to palm my breasts.

My head fell back and my mouth slacked open as sparks fired to my clit, adding to the electricity already roaring within me. "Yes," I cried, rocking against him.

Sitting all the way up, he swayed me backward in his arms and sucked my nipple between his lips.

I balanced one hand on his thigh, the other threading into his hair, holding him close as he devoured my breast. His tongue swirled and his teeth nipped, growls rumbling in his throat.

He thrust a hand down the back of my jeans, kneading my ass as he ground me against his hard length.

God, I needed him inside me.

"Ask me," I ordered, giving his hair a sharp tug.

"What do you need, Clare?" he mumbled against my chest.

I smiled victoriously. "You."

His eyes lifted, an inferno brewing within as he finally gave me the only permission I would ever need. "Then take it."

I was off the bed, stripping my pants off, before the final syllable had even cleared his lips. He did the same, peeling out of his denim and his boxers. His hand went to his thick cock, stroking as I climbed back onto the bed and straddled him.

His hand caught my chin, forcing my eyes to his. "This is all you, babe. But, just so you know, there is not one thing I don't want from you."

I held his stare as I reached between us and brazenly wrapped my palm around his fingers working his shaft.

He glided his hand around to the back of my neck and hauled me toward him. His lips touched mine, the tip of his tongue hitting my bottom lip as he said, "I'm yours, Clare. Take it all." He moved his fingers between my legs, grazing my clit before pressing inside.

"Yes," I hissed, releasing him to balance myself with his shoulders.

"You're wet, babe," he stated before kissing me with a cocky grin.

I could have told him that. It had happened the second he'd asked me if I trusted him. Never had four simple words been so arousing. And not because he'd said them in that deep baritone that could drive a woman mad. But, rather, because it was the moment when I'd realized that I did trust him. Unequivocally. Completely. Utterly. Mind. Body. And soul.

"I am," I confirmed breathily.

His finger curled, pressing deeper and causing me to cry out.

“Then guide me home, Clare,” he ordered against my mouth.

Pushing up on my knees, I inched forward. He removed his hand and rested it on my hip, but that was the only move he made. He didn’t urge me down or press up into me as I aligned our bodies. He sat there, impossibly still, his eyes burning into mine, searching my face for any sign of hesitance.

He would find none.

“Kiss me,” I urged, slowly sinking down on his cock, relishing in the way he stretched me.

He groaned into my mouth as a million broken pieces crashed to the floor.

And then I *took* from Heath. Repeatedly.

I threw my head back and closed my eyes, letting the world around us go and getting lost in him.

His warm mouth on my neck.

His strong hands on my ass.

His hard cock filling me.

Nothing between us.

Not even words.

And he *gave* with his entire body.

Sex wasn’t going to fix my life. But those minutes of peace when we were joined as one reminded me why it was all worth the fight.

I had no idea how long I’d been riding him when he rumbled, “Hurry up, or I’m takin’ over.”

My legs were beginning to ache, and a sheen of sweat covered us both.

But I was in no hurry to find my release.

I could have stayed in that moment forever.

However, his “takin’ over” definitely held some promise.

So I replied, “Take over, honey.”

Tucking my knee under his arm, he flipped us. I lost his cock on the way over, but I gained so much more as his large body covered me.

“You trust me?”

"Always."

"You sore yet?" he asked, easing back inside me and then draping my legs over his shoulders.

I shook my head,

"That's about to change," he declared.

And then.

Heath.

Took.

Over.

Hard and fast. Rough and raw. A man on a mission, my body being his only way home.

"Fuck, Clare," he growled, driving in and banging the headboard against the wall.

"Yes!" I cried out, my back arching off the bed and my nails raking down his chest as I tried to hold on.

He thoroughly worked me over. His hips bucked, creating a relentless pace as his thumb found my clit and drove me toward the edge. But, as the minutes wore on, I couldn't step off.

He buried himself at the hilt and growled, "Get out of your head."

If only it were that easy. He was hitting all the right spots. My body was thrumming with need, but I couldn't fall.

Falling meant letting go, a novelty I'd never been afforded.

"Heath!" I objected when he suddenly stilled, just the tip of his length nestled inside me.

He shrugged my legs off his shoulders and pressed in slowly as he bent to kiss me. "Give it to me, babe."

"I was trying," I complained.

"Then stop *trying* and give me whatever burden has got you so blocked in your head you can't even get off."

I had no fucking idea how to do that. "I…I'm not sure…"

He shook his head and stared deep into my eyes, his thumb trailing over my cheekbone. "Listen to me. That burden is not yours anymore. *Internalize* it. *Accept* it. Then let it fucking go and trust me to take care of it. Of you. Of your girl. Of everything. I've got you, Clare. From here on out, it's you and *me*."

I blinked. Then blinked again. In a lot of ways, it had always been him and me.

Me and Luke.

Me and Agent Light.

And, now, me and Heath.

Ever since the day I'd met him, he'd taken care of me.

Even when I hadn't known who he was.

And, at that realization, the strangest thing happened.

I breathed and my lungs weren't constricted by the vise that had been smothering me for most of my life. Even before Walt.

Warm blood rushed into my veins, not a trace of the chill of reality.

For the first time in as long as I could remember, my pulse slowed and my tunnel vision expanded, which revealed a new dimension of clarity surrounding me.

"Oh my God," I choked.

"There she is," he breathed, brushing the sweat-soaked hair off my forehead.

I wrapped my arms around his neck and my legs around his hips, unable to get close enough.

"That's it," he groaned, his hips beginning to move again.

Slow and shallow this time, but it was more than enough. We'd been going for what felt like forever, but for the way my body reacted, he might as well have been touching me for the very first time.

My release climbed within me, his gentle thrusts coaxing me higher.

"I've got you," he rasped, the muscles on his back flexing as he surged inside me.

"Me and you, Clare."

A second later, Heath didn't just take another broken piece of my soul—he took them *all*.

And I gave them freely, knowing only he had the power to put them back together.

"Heath!" I cried as I fell apart in his arms.

My muscles pulsed around him as he twitched and jerked, emptying inside me, the deep groan of my name on his lips.

I was lying flat on my back as I came down from my orgasmic high, but I knew with absolute certainty that the Earth had tilted back on its axis, and when I stood up off that bed, I'd find solid ground again.

With Heath.

CHAPTER THIRTEEN

ELISABETH

"That piece of shit," Roman growled, pacing the back porch.

He'd been repeating the same phrase for nearly two hours.

I was doing my best to relax in one of our new rocking chairs while watching Tessa play in the grass with Loretta. My stomach ached as I clutched a glass of wine to my chest.

It was barely five o'clock and I was already a half a bottle in. Day-drinking had never been more necessary.

"What do we do now?" I asked, flashing Tessa a forced smile when she turned to make sure I was still there.

Tessa had been asking for her mom, but after the way Clare had exploded when the DNA results were read, I'd figured it was best to give her some time alone.

I understood. I'd wanted to explode too. It was hard enough to swallow that our embryos had been swapped. But to find out my egg had been knowingly used to create a totally different embryo had hit me like a ton of bricks.

"Now?" Roman asked rhetorically. "Now, I'm gonna find that son of a bitch and murder him."

I swirled the Chardonnay in my glass as I asked, "He's her biological father. What if he tries to get custody of her?"

Roman stopped and turned to face me, both hands planted on

his hips. "He's a wanted man, Lis. No judge is gonna give that coward custody. But, above and beyond that, he would have to pry her from my lifeless arms. And that's assuming he was still breathing after Light got done with him."

This was all true. Roman was…well, Roman when it came to Tessa.

And, over the last week, I'd seen just how much Heath loved both Clare and Tessa too. He tried to play it cool and kept his hands to himself for the most part, but his eyes told another story. He always watched them—studying Clare's mood and anticipating her every need. It was really sweet to witness. He was such a hard-ass with Roman and the rest of the security team, demanding to be in on every decision and raising immortal hell when something didn't go his way. But, the moment Clare entered a room, a wide smile would cover his face and his entire demeanor would shift, changing him into a gentle giant.

And Tessa? Forget about it. He was a lost cause for her. She had him wrapped around every single one of her tiny fingers—and probably even her toes. There was nothing Heath wouldn't do for that little girl.

"You're right," I said to Roman, though my stomach remained in a knot.

"She's your daughter too, baby."

"She's Clare's daughter," I corrected, staring down at the wooden slats on the deck, hating myself for wishing that were different.

He walked over and stopped my chair from rocking as he squatted in front of me. "I just meant, if Walter tried anything, you're her biological mother. We'll fight him."

My vision swam as I admitted, "I don't want to fight him. I want this to be over."

His arms were around me before a single tear fell. "I know. And it will be soon enough. I swear."

"It just won't stop. All of this. It has to—" I was cut off as Alex opened the sliding back door.

"Leblanc, we got a problem," he informed us, a murderous glint in his eyes.

I immediately scrambled out of the chair after Tessa.

"Elisabeth, chill!" Alex called, but my feet were already moving.

Whatever the problem might have been, she'd be safer inside.

"You have *got* to be kidding me," Roman boomed just as I got to Tessa and scooped her up.

I spun around, my heart racing, and found Kristen, Cathy, and Rome Leblanc all standing on the other side of the glass door, their mouths gaping as they stared at me like I'd grown a second head.

And, as I glanced down at Tessa while she sat on my hip, I realized that, as far as they were concerned, I had.

"Shit," I mumbled under my breath, anxiety ebbing from my body.

"You say shit!" Tessa giggled, oblivious to my near panic attack.

I clamped my mouth shut and looked down at her. Doing my best to be stern and not laugh as I said, "I did, sweetheart. But you shouldn't."

"Why not? Roman say shit. Mama say shit, too. Luke say fuck though."

I bit my lip. He did say fuck—a lot. "Yeah, *Heath* does say… um…that word. But, again, you shouldn't."

She blinked. "Can I have cake?"

If it would distract her from saying shit and fuck before I had to carry her in to meet her kinda-sorta grandparents and her aunt, who we had not told about her yet, she could have whatever the hell she wanted.

"Yes, ma'am," I replied, heading back to the house.

As we got closer to Roman and the rest of the security guys, their conversation grew louder.

Tessa's eyes flashed wide, and her little body tensed when a

DEA agent boomed, "They were on the list!"

"What fucking list?" Roman barked back, his face turning red and a scary vein on his forehead twitching.

Ethan rounded the corner and planted a hand on his chest just as another DEA agent shoved his way out the door to join the argument.

"And, now, we're all here! I hope someone rolled out the fucking red carpet for Noir before leaving your stations," Roman snarled.

I frowned and made a mental note to lose my damn mind on every single one of them, including Roman, for having this argument in front of Tessa. But that would have to wait until later, when she wasn't scared and clinging to my neck.

Rushing past them, I made my way into the house and then slid the door shut behind them.

"It's okay," I whispered in her ear. "They're just talking."

"Uhhh," Kristen drawled. "What in the hell is going on?" Her surprised gaze flashed between me and Tessa then out to the glass door, where her little brother was shoving his finger in the chest of an armed federal officer.

"Well…" I started only to trail off.

I'd need to write an entire book to explain how we'd gotten to this point, which was precisely why we hadn't told any of them yet. Neither of us knew what the hell to say. We'd been waiting on the DNA confirmation before dragging anyone else into this mess. Only, now, the mess was even bigger.

"So this is Tessa," I introduced, but that was as far as I got before I realized I'd probably have to write two books.

Suddenly, Heath came barreling down the stairs in nothing but a pair of jeans, his gun drawn, his hair disheveled, claw marks covering his chest.

"Don't move!" he yelled.

Rome barked a surprised curse and spread his arms wide, protectively shielding Cathy and Kristen.

"No. No. No!" I yelled, rushing toward Heath. "We're fine! Everyone's fine!"

His gaze swung around the room, but he never lowered his weapon as he growled, "What the hell is going on?"

"Luke!" Tessa cried, popping her head up and wiggling in my arms to get to him.

"Please. Put the gun down." I begged. "This is Roman's family. We weren't expecting them, and Roman's upset because one of the guys let them in. That's all. Nothing's going on."

And then I decided it would take at least three books to explain this to the Leblancs as Clare came running down the stairs in absolutely nothing except Heath's T-shirt, shouting, "Tessa!"

Of course in response, Tessa yelled, "Mama!" and struggled even harder.

Heath scanned the room one last time before reluctantly tucking his gun into the back of his jeans.

My shoulders sagged in relief, though I wasn't quite sure I'd ever get my heart to slow.

"Come here, sweet girl," Heath cooed to Tessa.

I'd barely put her on her feet before she was sprinting into his arms.

He scooped her up, gave her a quick once-over, flashed her a wide grin, and then handed her off to a notably frazzled—and equally disheveled—Clare.

He glanced around the room and then ran a hand through his hair as he extended the other in Rome's direction announcing, "Heath Light." Casual, as if he'd just bumped into him at the grocery store on a fucking Tuesday afternoon.

"Rome Leblanc," he mumbled, cautiously taking Heath's proffered hand.

How was this my life?

"I need more wine," I declared.

"I could do wine," Cathy called out.

Kristen kept her eyes leveled on Heath's naked chest as she

said, "I hope you've got a vineyard."

I didn't. But I'd give Roman's assistant, Seth, a call.

"Clare?" I questioned.

She peeked around Heath. "Um...I should...probably get dressed."

"Right. Well, I'll have a glass ready if you change your mind."

I didn't waste a single second longer before heading for the wine.

"How are you doing?" I asked Clare as we sat on the couch, watching Rome and Cathy Leblanc play blocks on the floor with Tessa.

Roman had given the abridged version of what was going to be my three-book series to his family once he'd finally calmed down. As to be expected, they were all surprised. Rome's surprise was expressed in a string of angry expletives similar to those of his son, but Cathy cried, exclaiming that she had a granddaughter before launching all of her pent-up Grandma energy on Tessa. Kristen spent half an hour trying to formulate a proper response. Though she did it while googly-eyed staring at Heath and Ethan.

Clare glanced up at Heath, who was leaning against the wall, hovering like a sentinel watching over his girls. Her cheeks were bright red when she turned her attention back my way, a shy smile playing on her lips. "I think I'm good."

As it turned out, Heath was the one who had made this mysterious list of approved visitors. It consisted of Roman's family, my parents, and his sisters. I thought it was crazy sweet that he trusted us enough to include people he'd never met on his list. However, after listening to him and Roman argue, I found out that he didn't trust anyone. He'd just done extensive research on both of us before he'd first approached Roman.

I wasn't sure how I felt about someone investigating my parents. However, my wine told me not to worry about it.

And who was I to argue with wine? It had never steered me wrong before.

"You sure? I'm really sorry about all of this." I motioned a hand around the room. "I would have asked them to leave, but not even the DEA has the manpower to deal with Cathy Leblanc's wrath."

She flashed me an understanding smile. "It's okay, really."

"Sex makes everything okay," Kristen stated, flopping down on the other side of Clare.

"Kristen!" I scolded in a whisper.

Clare giggled, tipping her beer to her lips before glancing up at Heath again.

"What?" Kristen defended. "We all saw those two hoofing it down the stairs." She jerked her chin in Heath's direction. "Is the bottom half as hot as the top?"

"Oh God," I groaned, dropping my head back against the back of the couch.

Clare didn't answer. At least, not verbally. But her smile grew wide as she became enthralled with the label on her beer.

Kristen clutched her imaginary pearls. "Oh, sweet Jesus. It is. On that note, I need more wine."

"We're out. But *Seth* should be here soon," I said, waggling my eyebrows.

Her smile curled down into a frown. "That hot-ass son of a bitch."

I leaned into Clare, bumping her with my shoulder. "Just to get you up to speed, Kristen slept with Roman's assistant. He hasn't called her back."

"Ouch," she told Kristen sympathetically.

Kristen emphatically nodded. "Yeah, and worse, I'm stuck seeing him every single time I go out of my way to stalk him down at Roman's office. The least Roman could do is fire him and make it challenging for me."

Clare's eyebrows shot up, her lips thinning as she suppressed a laugh.

As Kristen sauntered away, I told her, “You can laugh. We all know she’s insane.”

“She really is. Don’t take this the wrong way, but I can’t believe she and Roman are related.”

I looked up to where Roman was standing with Alex and Ethan, discussing something quietly. His handsome face contorted with anger. I, again, listened to my wine and took the last sip instead of trying to figure out what was wrong now.

“Oh, Roman’s crazy too. He’s just better at keeping it hidden than Kristen.”

Her gaze drifted up, following mine to Roman. “I’m sorry,” she apologized.

I snapped my attention back to hers. “For what?”

She shook her head and went back to peeling the label on her beer. “That Walt did this to you.”

My chest tightened, and I reached out and took her hand before giving it a reassuring squeeze. “He didn’t do this to *me*. He did it to all of *us*. That includes you. You don’t owe anyone any apologies.”

She smiled but kept her gaze aimed at her lap. “Do you think he was mine?”

“Who?”

Her sad eyes lifted to mine. “Your son…Tripp. I mean, my egg quality was bad, which is why we had to do IVF to begin with. But the doctors told us after my egg retrieval that they got three. Do you think maybe Walt had someone switch the eggs and you got mine, and that’s why he died?”

God, my heart ached at the mention of Tripp. I hadn’t had him for long, but that little boy was my life. I missed him every minute of every day and probably would for the rest of my life.

“I don’t know whose egg it was, but I know that wasn’t why he died. It was just one of those things,” I replied, glancing back to Roman, who was now studying me from across the room.

Reading my mood, he tipped his head in question, but I shot him a smile to let him know I was good.

I turned back to Clare. "Can I admit something so incredibly crazy that it's going to make Kristen look like the definition of sanity?"

Her lips tipped up at the corners, and she nodded eagerly.

"If Walt did switch the eggs, I don't hate him for it. I hate him for what he did to you. To Tessa. To everyone. But, if he gave me Tripp… I mean, it wasn't ideal. Those months knowing we were going to lose him were the hardest of my entire life. But I got twelve minutes with a little boy I'd carried inside me for nine months. It killed me to let him go, but I wouldn't give up that time with him for anything."

Her chin quivered as she asked, "Can I say something so incredibly selfish that it's going to sound like I'm the worst person in the entire world?"

I grinned. "Lay it on me."

Her tired gaze lifted to mine. "I'm glad it was y'all. I know that's shitty, but I have no idea where I'd be if it weren't for you guys and Heath. I'm sorry this is happening. I really am." A tear finally breached her lid.

Out of the corner of my eye, I saw Heath come unstuck from the jamb and stride toward her. She didn't seem to notice and kept talking.

"But I'm so selfishly thankful it was y'all. Does that make me a horrible person?"

I laughed, fighting back tears of my own. "If it does, then we can be horrible people together." I released her hand and clinked my empty glass on her beer.

Heath stopped in front of us, concern crinkling his forehead. "You good, babe?"

She shook her head and laughed, wiping the dampness off her face with the back of her hand. "I'm a horrible person. But so is Elisabeth, so I think it's okay."

I bumped my shoulder with hers as I laughed even louder.

It wasn't really funny.

It was sad. Terribly and tragically depressing.

But, sometimes in life, your only options were to laugh or cry.

And both Clare and I were way overdue for a laugh.

She handed her beer off to Heath as she fell over on the couch, howling with laughter. I was right behind her, falling over to the other side, lost in hysterics.

And we laughed.

And laughed.

And laughed some more.

Until the entire room laughed right along with us.

There would be plenty of time for crying later.

But, for one night, we drank beer and wine, spent time with family, ordered pizza, and pretended it was all so perfectly normal.

CHAPTER FOURTEEN

CLARE

"Honey," I breathed, threading my fingers in the top of Heath's hair, his head between my legs.

I'd woken up in his arms as he had been carrying me from the bed beside Tessa, into his room across the hall. He'd wasted no time before snatching the panties down my legs and dropping to his knees.

"I want you inside me," I begged.

"You come on my mouth and I'll give you my cock."

I groaned. It wasn't exactly a hardship; it was, however, early. The morning sun was just starting to peek through the windows, and it wouldn't be long before Tessa woke up.

It had been almost three weeks since the DNA results and the day Heath and I first had sex. Though, for about a week after that, it had been the *only* time Heath and I had sex.

The following day, Heath had told me that he wanted me to see a therapist before anything else happened between us. He was also concerned that we hadn't used a condom. I could see his point on the condom, but there was not one thing a therapist was going to say that was going to sway me from wanting to be with Heath.

And she didn't.

After my first appointment with the doctor they had brought in to the house to see me and Tessa, I came skipping out of the door, informing him, "She said we were both consenting adults, and if I want to have sex with you, I can."

He arched an eyebrow and asked, "Did you just spend an hour getting permission to fuck me?"

I shrugged. That wasn't the only thing we'd discussed, but it was one of the higher points.

He glowered and then shoved me back inside.

An hour later, I reemerged with red-rimmed eyes, emotionally exhausted.

He grinned and hugged me, muttering, "Thank fuck."

I didn't give up on my attempts to get him back into bed though. For a week, I tortured him with nighties and cornered him with kisses every chance I could get him alone. I never felt more alive than I was when I was in his arms—naked or clothed.

Though, the night I snuck into the shower with him, I decided I definitely liked him better naked. He wanted me. I knew he did. He was just trying to do right by me. But right for me was just being *with him*. So, as I pressed him against the wall in the shower, he finally relented with a sexy smirk and a, "Jesus Christ, woman."

And it was a really good thing, because when we were together, he made me forget the rest of the madness swirling around us.

And I desperately needed more of that.

The same day I started seeing the therapist, I started working with the DEA to take Walter down. In exchange for complete immunity for my part in any of his crimes, I spent days upon days answering questions and filling them in on everything I knew about his operations.

Tomlinson wouldn't allow Heath in the room while they questioned me, and I feared his head was going to explode the first day when I came out crying. By the second day, he relaxed a fraction, but he was always sitting in a chair on the other side of the door when I came out, an exhausted and worried look painting his handsome face.

But that was then…and now was now.

And, in the now, it was Christmas Eve and his mouth was between my legs, his tongue making tight circles over my sensitive clit.

"Yes!" I cried, arching off the bed.

"Hurry, babe," he ordered roughly, his hand sliding up my stomach to my breasts.

He thoroughly worked me with his mouth, sucking and licking as he drew me to the edge. But it was his skilled fingers at my nipples, plucking and rolling, that sent me over.

I came hard, long, and beautifully.

"Heath, honey," I moaned when he continued eating away at me. I squirmed beneath him, too sensitive post-orgasm but still wanting more. "You promised me your cock."

His head lifted, a mischievous glint in his eye as he leaned to the nightstand to retrieve a condom. "You say the word *cock* again and we're not gonna make it that far."

I spoke around a wide smile as I said, "Cock." I enunciated each letter while propping my feet on the bed and allowing my knees to fall open.

He sucked in a breath through his teeth, his eyes dipping to my core. "If I hadn't woken up this morning with dreams of your pussy, I'd fuck that mouth of yours."

"We could do both," I suggested, reaching out for him.

He grinned as he tore the condom open, the muscles on his stomach rippling as he worked it down his thick shaft. "Christmas is tomorrow, Clare. We can do both then." He winked, and my stomach fluttered with the excitement of "both" more than any gifts under the tree.

Once he had the condom in place, he kept his feet on the floor and bent his tall frame over me to take my mouth in a deep and wet kiss, the taste of my release lingering on his lips.

"What do you need, Clare?" he asked against my mouth.

I replied with the same but no less accurate answer as always. "You."

"Then take it," he rasped.

I reached between us and lined us up, and then Heath *took* it from there.

He fucked me hard and fast, but it was Heath, so it was also loving and gentle.

His hands were in my hair, his teeth nipping at my neck, his powerful body pinning me to the mattress.

Orgasm number two built within me. His pace quickened as I locked my legs at the ankle around his back, using my heels to urge him deeper.

A request he more than fulfilled.

As the first wave hit me, I raked my nails down his back and he quickly covered my mouth with his own to swallow my cry. A few strokes later, I swallowed his growl as he found his own release.

Then I took his weight as he collapsed on top of me. His mouth went to my ear as his early morning scruff scratched my cheek.

"Merry Christmas Eve, babe."

Isn't that the damn truth. "Merry Christmas Eve, Heath."

"Mama! Luke made Christmas bacon!" Tessa exclaimed as I entered the kitchen.

I laughed, going straight to her and kissing her forehead. "His name's Heath, baby," I reminded her for the millionth time.

"No. He Luke," she giggled before chomping down on a piece of bacon.

"Sweet girl, you can call me whatever you want," Heath said from the stove. "You want some, babe?"

I walked his way, snagging a coffee mug from the cabinet before pressing up on my toes and planting a chaste kiss on his lips. "What's Christmas bacon?"

"It from a reindeer," Tessa answered behind me.

I playfully lifted my eyebrows. "We're eating Rudolph?"

He stared down at me with a bright smile. "Nah. It's just regular bacon, but she told me she didn't like it. Reindeer bacon is soooo much tastier, apparently."

I laughed again. "In that case, bacon sounds ah-mazing."

"Oh good. I saved *Dancer* just for you." He kissed me again.

I went to the coffee maker and poured a cup. "Where are Roman and Elisabeth?"

A loud sizzle filled the kitchen as he added more bacon to the pan. "They went out to grab a few last-minute things for tomorrow. Oh, that reminds me. The last of the packages"—his gaze flashed to Tessa—"arrived. We're all set for tonight."

I smiled, stirring milk and sugar into my coffee.

Tessa and I hadn't left the house since we'd arrived almost a month earlier. It wasn't safe, not while Walt was still out there. So, with Christmas fast approaching, Heath had insisted we go online and do some shopping for Tessa. I felt like a mooch with no way to so much as buy gifts for my daughter, so I added exactly three items to the online cart.

Heath frowned and then took the computer from my lap, adding approximately two dozen toys before pulling his credit card from his wallet and buying them all. I bit my lip, overwhelmed with gratitude.

He kissed my temple and pulled me into a hug, muttering, "I've got you, Clare. Both of you."

And he did, so I sucked in a shaky breath and let it go.

Then I made him the biggest, best chicken masala he'd ever tasted that night for dinner.

It was a double win because Heath hated Elisabeth's food. It wasn't that her food was necessarily bad, but she was such a picky eater that she put odd flairs on every dish. Meatloaf with mustard. Pot roast with weird white gravy, and gyros made with beef instead of lamb. I was more of a traditionalist, and not to brag, but there were never leftovers.

I tried to help Elisabeth as much as I could. I'd spent hours weeding, pruning, and trimming her flowerbeds to get them back into decent shape. And I'd promised her that, as soon as spring came, I'd help her plant flowers. I also did my best to earn my keep when it came to the house. While we were relatively neat people, nine of us were living under one roof if you included Alex, Devon, Jude, and Ethan, who often rotated through. Quarters got cramped sometimes, but no one had killed anyone yet. I chalked that up as a success.

"Do you think we have enough wrapping paper?" I asked him, lifting my mug to my lips for that first glorious sip of coffee.

His attention remained on the frying pan as he replied, "I think we have enough paper to wrap the state of Georgia. An entire rainforest will be crying in the morning."

I giggled, and he aimed a panty-drenching grin in my direction, some of his hair falling over his forehead and into his eyes.

"You need a haircut. Want me to do it? I bet Roman has some clippers or something. I could clean up the sides."

He twisted his lips and flipped the bacon in the pan. "You saying my hair looks like shit?"

"No. I'm offering to do you a favor. Considering you've kind of weighted your side of the scales, I owe you at least a million favors by now."

He scowled at me. "There are no scales with us."

I set my coffee on the counter and slid up behind him, looping my arms around his hips and resting my cheek between his shoulder blades. "There are always scales, Heath. A haircut won't even them, but it'll be a start."

He shoved the bacon off the burner. Then he turned in my arms and wrapped his arms around my shoulders. "You know how to cut hair?"

"Yep. I grew up poor and in a shitty trailer park—not to be confused with the good trailer park." I grinned. "When I was twelve, I got my dad's clippers and started offering five-dollar haircuts to make some money…to, ya know, *eat*. Well, the good thing about being poor in a shitty trailer park is that *everyone's* poor. Five dollars a pop was a steal. I had to start taking appointments."

He cocked an eyebrow. "You any good?"

"I am now. I was shit at first. But hey, it was five bucks. No one complained."

His lips twitched, but he didn't smile. "You said you were a waitress when you met Noir. Why weren't you doing hair if you're so good?"

I shrugged. "I didn't have the money for school. I only graduated high school because it was free and it kept me busy. I had to get out and get a job. Higher education wasn't a luxury I could afford."

His hand glided up my back, squeezing the back of my neck as he asked, "Did you like it? Cutting hair, I mean."

I squinted one eye and looked over his shoulder, trying to remember what seemed like a lifetime ago. "Ummm…I liked the money. I liked that I was good at it. I liked that I was able to give people something they normally wouldn't have been able to afford. But no, I don't think I necessarily *liked* doing it."

He gave my neck another squeeze. "And what do you think you would have enjoyed doing?"

"I don't know. When I was a kid, I always wanted to open a little garden shop. Nothing big, but one where little old ladies could pop in and talk about what flowers were in season while their husbands bought hoses and ugly gnomes."

I got another lip twitch, but this time, it was followed by a lip touch.

He glanced up at Tessa before allowing his hand to slide down to my ass. "That's how you balance the scales, Clare. You open that sexy mouth and use it to tell me about yourself. I don't need favors. I need you."

Oh. My. God.

Heath's blanket of warmth didn't just wrap around me.

It enveloped me.

Head to toe.

Mind and soul.

My vision swam, and he brought his lips back down for another lip touch. "No crying. Your Christmas bacon's ready."

"I'm scared," I admitted.

His hands flinched. "Why?"

"Because, if you keep being this sweet, there is a really good chance I'm going to fall in love with you." I was only half joking. I was already in love with Heath; that falling crap was history.

He chuckled. "It's about damn time you caught up."

"Caught up?" I squeaked.

His shoulders shook as he dragged me into his chest. "Babe, I've been falling in love with you for months. It's not exactly a secret. Tomlinson threatened to fire me over it last week."

My heart came to a screeching halt. And not because Heath was going to get fired for being with me.

But because Heath had been falling in love—with me.

For months.

Plural.

Misreading my reaction, he stroked up and down my back. "Don't worry, babe. I assured him we weren't sleeping together. Which, technically, we aren't, considering you sleep with Tessa every night and I sleep across the hall." He winked. "But, with that said, I should probably reevaluate my career choices sooner rather than later. At this point, I got one foot in the grave with you."

"Death isn't romantic," I informed him because it was either cry or be a smartass.

He laughed and kissed the top of my head. "It is when I'm ninety years old and doing it after spending fifty-plus years with you."

Oh. My. God. I could not handle this conversation. Like, at all. I was in love with Heath, unquestionably. But I was struggling to see why he was falling for me. My redeeming qualities at the moment were spending his money to buy my daughter, who coincidentally wasn't even mine, Christmas presents all while he spent his days making sure my current *husband* didn't kill me or, worse, him.

I cleared the lump from my throat and said, "I think I need that reindeer bacon now."

He squeezed me tight and murmured, "Okay, babe. Whatever you need."

But what he failed to see was that I really needed a time machine so I could go back in time and track him down before all of this mess started. But I didn't figure he had one handy or he would have already used it to do the same.

CHAPTER FIFTEEN

HEATH

"Pass the red paper," I said to Clare as we sat on the living room floor, wrapping presents.

The house was dark, Tessa was asleep upstairs, and Roman and Elisabeth had called it a night after they'd dumped an entire toy store of flawlessly wrapped gifts under the tree. And that was on top of the half of a toy store I'd already bought, which were definitely *not* flawlessly wrapped. Clare had keeled over laughing when I'd wrapped the first one and used only one piece of tape. But Tessa was a kid. I was banking on the fact that she didn't give a damn how they looked as long as there was something pink and glittery inside.

"I feel like we need to donate half of this stuff," she replied, passing both the tape and the wrapping paper.

I cocked an eyebrow and picked up the twenty-seventh, yet somehow different, baby doll I'd wrapped that evening. "Only half?"

She giggled, cutting into one of the boxes strewn across the floor and pulled out a small, black, velvet box. "What's this?"

I shrugged. "No clue. Open it up and see."

Her cheeks pinked as she smiled, peeking up at me through her lashes, a flirty shimmer of excitement dancing in her eyes. "Right. You don't know."

But I honestly didn't. I figured it had to have been something of Roman's that had gotten mixed in with our stuff.

I peered over the mountain of presents as she pried the top up.

I'd barely made out the glint of a diamond before it went sailing across the room, slamming into the wall before dropping to the floor.

"No!" she shrieked, but she was already searching through the brown packing paper until she found another box. "No," she whispered, slapping a hand over her mouth and staring down like she'd seen a ghost.

"Talk," I ordered, shooting to my feet and then closing in on her.

"He knows where we are," she breathed, her wild gaze bouncing to me then back to the box in her hand.

There was no need for her to explain who the "he" was.

Molten lava surged in my veins as I snatched it from her hand and pulled the top open.

A tiny, gold bracelet with a heart charm that read *Daddy's girl* sat within, but that was all I could observe before it was suddenly gone from my hand.

"No!" she yelled, racing to the front door and yanking it wide. "He does not get to do this."

I marched after her just as she sent it flying through the chilly night air. The sensor lights flashed on, illuminating the darkness.

"Fuck you!" she screamed manically.

I hooked her around the waist, but she frantically spun, racing past me through the living room to the first box she'd opened. She snatched it off the floor then, rushing back to the door and hurling it out to join the bracelet. A guttural, "No!" tore from her throat as she watched it sail through the air.

"Clare," I called cautiously. I braced for her to fall apart and prepared myself for another breakdown the likes of when she'd checked out on me after the DNA results. "Come here, babe," I urged, staring at her back.

Her shoulders were rising and falling with her heavy breaths, and her fists opened and closed at her sides.

I prowled toward her, only to stop dead in my tracks as she slammed the door and pivoted on a heel to face me.

Not a tear in sight.

Her back was straight.

Her shoulders square.

Her jaw clinched.

Rage radiating off her.

And that subtle flicker of fear she wore so often when it came to Walt was gone completely.

"You okay?" I asked warily.

It was safe to assume she was *not* as she seethed, "It's Christmas for God's sake. He does not get to do that. Not today. Not fucking ever."

I caught sight of Roman and Devon storming down the hall toward us. But I lifted a hand to halt them, shaking my head as I assured them, "We're good."

Clare spun to see who I was talking to, but she was nowhere near done with her rant. "We are *not* good. We are fucking *great*!"

Roman cocked his head to the side, but he had the good sense to mutter an apology and back away.

With the hall empty, Clare turned her anger back on me. "I swear to God. I'm finally fucking happy for the first time in my entire goddamn life. He does not get to take that away from me!"

It made me an asshole, but a huge smile spread across my face, pride swelling my chest.

"What do you need, Clare?" I asked, fighting the urge to sweep her off her feet.

"To kill him," she replied without missing a beat.

Weeks ago, she would have crumbled, overwhelmed with fear and panic. She would have lost it at the thought of Walt knowing where she was.

Weeks ago, it had been, "He'll kill me."

Today, a beast emerged from within her.

Today, it was, "To kill him."

I smirked. "While that's not exactly legal, I wouldn't stop you."

She stomped past me, plucked the cardboard box the gift had been delivered in, and slung it across the room. "Why haven't they been able to find him?" she snapped. "It's been over a fucking month. I refuse to believe he's hiding in an underground bunker. He's out there, Heath. Shopping at a goddamn mall for Christmas presents while I'm locked up here, hiding like a fucking coward."

I crossed my arms over my chest and continued to smile at her.

She continued with the bitchy little attitude that had me fighting a hard-on. "Why are you smiling?"

I shrugged casually. "Oh, maybe because the man you've been terrified of since the day I met you sent you a present just to fuck with your head and, instead of allowing him that move, you exploded and threw that shit on the front lawn."

Her lips thinned, but her resolve stayed strong. "He didn't send them just to fuck with my head. It's a warning."

"How do you figure?"

"The diamonds. Those aren't new. He gave them to me after he almost killed me on our first anniversary. He thought I was flirting with the waiter. I spent a week in the hospital. It was so bad we had to tell them I was in a car accident." She sucked in a shaky breath. "We were staying in that cabin I told Tomlinson about. He took me back there every year and made me wear the diamonds as a not-so-subtle reminder." Her gaze flashed to the floor. "He knows about you."

For fuck's sake, I wanted to kill that bastard for ever having laid a finger on her. But, worse, for have mentally manipulated her with fear for so damn long. It was a miracle she wasn't a head case after everything that son of a bitch had put her through. It was a true testament to her strength.

I closed the gap between us and rested my hands on her hips. "So?"

"So?" she repeated in confusion.

"Why does it matter that he knows? Honestly? I hope that motherfucker lays awake in bed every single night knowing that you're with me." I stabbed my thumb at my chest. "Knowing it's me you chose. Knowing it's *my body* you crave. Knowing it's *my name* you call when I make you come. I hope that shit eats away at his soul because he *knows* it's happening and can*not* do one goddamn thing to change it. You aren't his anymore, Clare."

A playful grin pulled at the side of her mouth as she whispered, "It's probably destroying him."

"I'm sure it is. It used to kill me when you went home to him every night."

Her smile fell flat. "Oh, Heath."

"But you're with me now. And he will *never* get you back. Those diamonds and that bracelet was his last-ditch effort of getting in your head because he can't get to you any other way. He doesn't even deserve your anger. Don't give him that. Let's sit back down. Finish playing Santa. And carry the fuck on with our lives."

Her lips once again curved up. "You're right."

I narrowed my eyes and studied her face, searching for the chink in her armor.

But I didn't even see armor anymore.

I just saw Clare.

My Clare.

The one she gave me when we were alone with Tessa.

The brave woman whose smile could light even the darkest night.

The one who had ensnared me from the moment we'd met.

The one I would protect with my life for no other reason than she was made to be mine.

The one I'd fallen in love with before she had even known my name.

If I hadn't had to get Walter's fucking gifts off the front lawn and bag them so the lab could dust them for prints, I would have carried her upstairs and showed her how much it meant to me that she gave me that kind of trust.

I didn't have that kind of time though. We had a boatload of presents left to wrap and a little girl who was dreaming about Christmas morning upstairs.

But what I did have was forever with her.

Whether she knew it now or not, she would soon enough.

I dipped my head low and brushed my lips across hers as I arrogantly said, "I'm always right, Clare. You should probably get used to that."

She swayed away and gave me the side-eye. "Except for when you're playing *Wheel of Fortune*."

I groaned and slid a hand down to pinch her ass. "Oh, come on. Let it go already."

She giggled and pressed up on her toes to kiss the base of my neck. "Sorry, but I'm never letting that go. You guessed 'Winter Woman' on a superhero puzzle. It's just sad."

I had to laugh. It was because it was becoming abundantly clear that my *Wheel of Fortune* abilities were definitely lacking. "Okay, enough out of you, Vanna White. Let's finish this Santa gig up so we can actually get some sleep before Tessa wakes up."

"Maggie, this is Clare. Clare, Maggie."

Clare removed her arm from around my waist and extended it toward my baby sister.

Maggie looked up at me and grumbled, "This is so not fair."

I grinned. I'd threatened her with all-out retaliation of the law if she embarrassed me when she came over for Christmas. Just to make sure my point was made, she'd started her Christmas morning with a parking ticket on the windshield of her car.

She clasped Clare's hand and said, "It's really nice to meet you, but you have to understand it's against my religion not to give Heath hell. It's well deserved though. He shut down my senior prom for over an hour because he thought my dress was too skimpy. My *entire* prom. He told the principal that drugs had been found on the premises. And refused to give the all clear until I put a sweater on."

I smiled. That wasn't even the worst thing I'd done to her. But that was what she got for switching dresses after she'd left the house. My dad was worthless when it came to parenting, but that didn't mean she didn't have someone to look after her.

"I didn't break your date's legs when I caught him feeling you up in the driveway," I said. "Consider that my apology."

"He was kissing me goodnight…on the freaking cheek! That's hardly feeling me up. And he was pulled over and detained by a state trooper on his way home."

I beamed with pride at the memory. "Yeah, I had to call in some serious favors for that one."

Her voice took on that crazy monkey squeal that sent dogs into a tailspin as she shrieked, "He refused to speak to me again!"

I smiled wider. "He was touching you, Mags."

She growled, clenching her teeth as she turned to Clare. "Heath has a collection of Pokémon cards in the top of his closet at home."

Clare burst out into laughter.

Son of a bitch. I had known bringing her here was a bad idea, but the rest of the family went to Melanie's in Augusta for the holiday. And God knows why, but for whatever reason, the two of them weren't speaking. I was sure it had to do with borrowed lip gloss or something equally as trivial that my sisters found to bicker about. It wasn't like I could leave Maggie alone at home.

"I collected them when I was a kid!" I defended.

Maggie leaned toward Clare and whispered, "He was in high school."

I glared at her. "Are you done?"

She batted her eyelashes and smirked. "For now."

"Well," Clare started, barely able to speak around her laughter. "It's very nice to meet you, Maggie. And, if you happen to think of anything else you think I should know about your brother, I'd be thrilled to listen."

I turned my glower on Clare. "Don't encourage her."

Her lips curled up at the corners in a patronizing smile. "Why not? I love getting to know you better. Besides, I find it incredibly sexy that you know which card could beat a Pikachu."

I cocked my head. "That's the only Pokémon you know, isn't it?"

"That's the only Pokémon seventy-five percent of the population knows. And that percentage goes up to ninety-nine if you only count people who've actually gotten laid." She lowered her voice and teased, "Honey, I didn't realize I took your virginity."

"Oh my God! I love her!" Maggie exclaimed, pulling Clare into a hug.

Funny thing—I did, too.

But I kept that to myself and pretended to be annoyed.

I stared up at the ceiling, muttering, "God help me."

Tessa suddenly patted my leg, holding up a Barbie doll. "Luke, you open dis?"

Clare and I had gone to bed late by the time we'd finished wrapping, and Tessa had gotten up at the crack of dawn, demolishing all of our hard work in less than an hour. It was only nine a.m., and I was already on my third cup of coffee. But it was worth every minute of the exhaustion to see Tessa smiling and laughing with her mother.

Maggie's eyes twinkled as she squatted in front of her. "You wouldn't happen to be Tessa, would you?"

Tessa looked up to me then back at my sister and nodded.

"Oh good!" Mags exclaimed, digging into her purse and pulling a small gift-wrapped box out. "See, Santa accidentally delivered this to my house. It was addressed to a Tessa, and Heath told me it was probably yours. I rushed over this morning as fast as I could."

Tessa's big, green eyes lit as her mouth fell open. "Yes! Dat's mine!"

Maggie stood up and extended her hand. "What do you say

you and I go sit down and open it?"

"Yes!" she squealed, bouncing on her toes as though it were her first and not hundredth present of the day.

Before taking off, Maggie pulled another box from her purse and slapped it against my chest. "Here ya go, Romeo."

She tossed Clare a smile then took Tessa's hand and disappeared around the corner.

"What's that?" Clare asked, anxiety in her eyes.

I chuckled and curled her into my chest. Kissing the top of her head, I murmured, "Relax. It's nothing big. I had her pick it up for me a couple of days ago."

"Heath!" she scolded. "We agreed no presents."

"Babe, it's our first Christmas together."

"Right. And I got you nothing."

I smirked. "Oh, I don't know. I plan to sneak you away for a shower in a little while."

Her cheeks pinked as she swayed into me, repeating, "We agreed no gifts."

I offered her the box. "Fine. It's not a Christmas gift. But it's something I've wanted to buy you for a really long time. I finally got the chance, and here it is. Better?"

She chewed on her bottom lip and stared at the box. "You've wanted to buy me something for a really long time?"

"Too long…so do me a favor and quit bitchin' and actually open it."

She glared up at me, but a second later, she snatched it from my hand and tore it open.

"Oh, Heath," she breathed. "It's beautiful." She traced her finger over the bracelet-style silver watch with diamonds surrounding the face of the dial.

It was beautiful. That was why I'd picked it out. But I'd made a modification that had thoroughly confused the sales person at the jewelry store.

She tilted it to the side and shook it. "It doesn't quite work.

It…" And then the words died in her mouth as she sucked in a sharp gasp and looked up at me with wide eyes. "Oh my God."

I took the box from her hand and removed the watch. "I had them take the battery out."

"Oh my God," she choked out, tears slipping from her eyes.

I slid it on her wrist. "You're with me now, Clare. I'll make damn sure you don't ever need another wish again. But, if you do, it'll always be 11:11."

"Oh my God," she repeated, staring down at her watch. "I can't believe…" She trailed off and shook her head. "I know you don't believe in my silly wishes. But there is no other explanation for how I got you."

And, if it were a wish that got me her, I'd kiss that clock every fucking day for the rest of my natural life.

She stood on her toes and pressed her lips to mine, inhaling reverently. "Thank you."

I let her have her kiss, but when she was about to break away, I snaked a hand into the back of her hair and held her to my mouth as I murmured, "I love you, Clare."

Her eyes popped open, and her head jerked away an inch. "Don't say that!"

I cocked an eyebrow and reluctantly let her go. "And why not?"

"Because that's my line. You got me an amazingly thoughtful and meaningful watch. Telling you I love you was kinda all I had left."

I stifled a laugh. "And what if I hadn't gotten you the amazingly thoughtful and meaningful watch?"

She huffed and rolled her eyes. "I'd still love you, but I'd probably wait until I was absolutely sure you loved me before I told you."

"Well, nothing says absolutely sure like me *telling* you I love you. So, how about you just say it back and we'll be square?"

She adamantly shook her head. "Now, it doesn't have as much impact. You ruined it. Now, we'll just have to wait until I can catch you off guard."

"Excuse me?" I said roughly, but I was smiling, so it didn't quite pack the punch I had been hoping for.

She returned my smile and kissed me again. "Thank you for the watch." Kiss. "I love…" Deep kiss, complete with tongue and a rumbled groan. She pulled away, grinned, and finished with, "It."

"Very funny," I deadpanned, sliding my hand down to her ass, squeezing, and using it to grind her against me. "I think I'll have better luck coaxing this out of you in the shower."

She moaned her approval, but when I stepped away, she caught the front of my shirt. "I loved you when I thought you were Luke. I didn't understand it, but day after day, I felt it"—she took my hand and placed it over her chest—"right here."

"Fuck," I growled, my fingers spasming against her chest.

I went in for another kiss, but she dodged it.

"I still loved you even when I thought you were Agent Light sent to arrest me. You risked everything and saved me and my little girl's life. I'll never be able to repay you for that."

My chest expanded into entirely new realms. I brushed a stray hair out of her face and pressed my lips to her forehead. "Jesus, Clare."

"But, right now, after spending the last month with you and getting to know the real *Heath*, I can honestly say I love you more than Luke and Agent Light combined. But I never want you to think it's just because you rescued me from Hell. Or just because you were kind to me when I needed it the most. I love you because you're an incredible man who remembers something like a silly superstition from when I was at my darkest and bought me a gift so I could carry that with me into the light—with you. For that, I love *you, Heath*."

I waited a second to make sure she was finished talking before I lifted her off her feet and covered her mouth with mine. She moaned, circled her legs around my hips, and locked them at the ankle as though I were trying to get away rather than crawl inside her the way I so desperately wanted to.

How the fuck was I ever going to find words to follow that up?

There was no combination of letters in all of the world's vast languages to properly convey how I felt about her. But, as I rested her shoulders against the cool sheet rock and moved my mouth to her neck, I *gave* her all I had.

"I love you, too."

CHAPTER SIXTEEN

ELISABETH

"I can't believe you made me wear this," I whispered to Roman.

Why I'd whispered, I had no idea. Probably out of habit. Because there was not one person in the entire movie theater. Of course, that was because bajillionaire Roman had insisted on renting out the entire theater. He'd done the same thing with the restaurant at dinner. It was a far cry from date nights back in the day when we'd hit the dollar menu at a drive-thru then sneak into a movie with one ticket.

But such was life with this new, loaded version of Roman. I can't say it was a bad thing. He'd surprised me that morning with a pair of Jimmy Choos that cost more than my *first* engagement ring. (Not my second. That thing was a *rock*.)

However, this new version of him did come with some downfalls.

In addition to the heels, he'd also given me a pink Rubicon bulletproof vest to wear.

I'd attempted one of my typical fits, refusing to wear it. He'd sat on the edge of the bed, grinning at me, his sexy arms folded over his equally sexy chest. Moments later, his hand was in my hair, I was naked, and he was moving inside me while declaring that I would wear it any time I went out of the house.

Considering I was currently wearing that aforementioned

vest under a silky, white blouse and black pencil skirt with the also aforementioned Jimmy Choos, we all know how that conversation ended.

"Oh hush. That's the newest model of Rubicon. It's barely three millimeters thick. You should have seen Simon Wells's face when I showed up at his office with that batch. I'm most likely the first person in the entire world to get custom body armor made in less than an hour." He patted his chest, where his T-shirt concealed his own vest.

He wasn't wrong. It was thin. And lighter than I'd ever imagined a vest could be. But it was still bulky under my fitted top, and it basically erased my boobs.

However, the glint of pride in Roman's eyes as I'd pulled it on made having the figure of a twelve-year-old boy worth it.

I mean, it wasn't like we saw anyone else anyway.

"Where should we sit? This place is packed," I teased, surveying the empty theater.

"Smartass," he chuckled, walking up the steps.

Pointing with the huge tub of popcorn, he indicated the two seats directly in the middle.

Once settled, Roman began pulling candy from his pockets.

He knew me well.

Or so I'd thought until he handed me a bag of Raisinettes.

I stared down at the offending candy. "Are you new here?"

"They were out of M&M's," he defended.

"Um, in what world is Raisinettes the default choice when they're out of M&Ms? Everyone knows chocolate-covered almonds are the only suitable replacement."

"I hate almonds though," he replied, tossing a handful of popcorn in his mouth.

I curled my lip in disbelief. "Since when?"

"Uh…since always."

My chin jerked back. "What the hell are you talking about? You love my almond chicken."

He chuckled. "No, I love your chicken. I pick the nasty almond pieces off."

"Seriously?"

He glanced over at me and lifted the soda to his lips, a smile curling the corners of his mouth as he took a sip from the straw. He swallowed and then confirmed, "Seriously."

My jaw slacked open. "No way. You're screwing with me, right?"

He barked a laugh. "I can't believe you didn't know this. I pick them out of the trail mix and everything."

I gasped. "Oh my God. I thought you did that because you knew I loved them and wanted to leave them for me. I always thought it was so romantic."

He laughed, quickly covering it with a cough. "Right. I mean. That's exactly why I do it."

I leaned back in the chair and waved him off. "Oh, don't even try that now. It's like I don't know you at all. I'm married to a stranger."

"Well, actually, you're not married to anyone. But we've got to get that shit fixed soon. It's fucking killing me." He offered the candy my way again.

"I don't think now's the best time for a wedding," I replied, begrudgingly taking the bag of Raisinettes.

"You want another wedding?"

"I don't know. Maybe like a destination thing or something," I mumbled absentmindedly when something hit me. "Wait, do you like olives?"

He swayed his head from side to side and then grinned tightly. "Yes."

"Oh my God, you don't!"

He laughed loudly. "Not at all."

"I find not one thing funny here, Roman. You do realize you've been lying to me for our entire relationship."

Still laughing, he set the popcorn on the seat beside him and moved the drink from the cup holder between us. Throwing his arm around me, he soothed me with, "All right. Simmer down. I haven't been lying to you our entire relationship. I don't like almonds, or olives, or salmon."

I gasped, thoroughly affronted by that little addition.

He didn't seem concerned with my affronting and kept talking. "But *you* do. You hate red sauce, and just last night you made me lasagna. We both make compromises. That is not a bad thing. I can pick off olives and almonds and choke down salmon once in a while because I know you'd do the same for me. Now, chill out, eat the damn Raisinettes, and then give your man a dark movie theater hand-job."

A laugh bubbled up my throat, and I threw a hand out to slap his chest.

"What?" He feigned innocence. "It's a compromise, Lis."

"How is a movie theater hand-job a compromise?"

He crinkled his forehead. "Um, because I really want a dark movie theater blow job but I paid to rent out the entire theater because I know you've been wanting to see this movie. At least, with a hand-job, you can still watch."

I giggled, but he caught my hand and guided it down into his lap, letting me know just how serious he was.

"Annnd on that note, I need to go to the restroom before the movie starts."

He groaned and dropped his head back against the chair. "Fine. But hurry back, I hear Hemsworth takes his shirt off in the first five minutes. I'm hoping that will get you in the mood."

I stood up and stared into those silver eyes that had stolen my heart. Bending over, I dragged a seductive finger down his chest and murmured, "Hemsworth has nothing on you." I kissed him, deep and wet. And, as I righted myself, I taunted him with, "However, if this were a Channing Tatum movie..."

He swatted my butt. "Smartass."

I giggled and jogged down the stairs, but I did it contemplating how one gives a movie theater hand-job without staff or security seeing it.

When I got to the door, Ethan was waiting for me.

"Restroom?" I asked.

"Right there," he said, pointing his finger just across the hall.

Two minutes later, the novelty of an empty theater restroom had me giddy as I took my time drying my hands in the air blower.

Just as it turned off, I heard the bathroom door close.

"Roman?" I called, smiling when I lifted my head.

But it wasn't Roman.

Or Ethan.

A man I'd never actually met but would have recognized anywhere emerged from around the corner.

Panic blasted through me, but I'd barely gotten a scream out before his hand landed over my mouth.

And then I was silenced completely when he slammed me to the floor, his body landing hard on top of me, stealing the breath from my lungs.

His disgusting lips brushed my ear. "Hello, Elisabeth. So nice to finally meet you."

The feeling was not mutual. I could have lived a thousand lifetimes without meeting Walter Noir.

"Let me go!" I yelled, fighting against him, but he kept me pinned to the tile floor.

The tip of his gun pressed into my temple as he snarled, "Shut the fuck up."

I froze immediately, blood thundering in my ears.

"Good girl." His hand landed on the back of my head, where he fisted it, wrenching my head to a painfully unnatural angle. He leaned into my face, spit spraying from his mouth as he seethed, "I want my wife back!"

"I don't know where she is," I cried.

He tsked his tongue against his teeth as he furrowed his brow. "Now, that's just not true. She was at your house when you left, right?" The butt of his gun slammed down on my nose.

My vision blurred from the explosion of pain.

"Don't fucking lie to me!" He released me and pushed to his feet.

But I was helpless to try to get away. I rolled to my back, barely able to remain conscious.

"How's my daughter?" He laughed maniacally, squatting in front of me. "Or should I say *our* daughter. We did make a beautiful girl, didn't we?" He ran his gun down the side of my face.

A shiver shot down my spine as I struggled to focus. "I don't know where she is," I slurred, drunkenly lifting a hand to wipe blood away from my nose as it began to seep up into my eyes.

"I suggest you figure it out, Elisabeth."

His hand drifted down to the hem of my blouse, tugging it up as disgust awakened my senses. I batted his hands away and then scrambled across the floor until my back met a wall.

He tipped his head to the side, a slow smile pulling at his mouth. "Rubicon?" he asked, pointedly glancing down to the exposed pink vest.

I didn't reply as I kicked my feet, trying desperately to get farther away from him with no luck. My body trembled as blood poured from my nose and into my lap.

"Of course it is." He laughed. "That ball-less son of a bitch has proven himself to be somewhat of a successful businessman. Trust me. I was just as shocked as you were."

I remained silent as he began to pace the length of the bathroom.

"You know, when I paid that doctor to give me your egg, I lucked out that you resembled Clare. The truth is I picked you because I'd heard your husband was broke and worthless. I was doing you a goddamn favor." He stopped and covered his heart with his gun. "I was brokenhearted to hear about our son's passing."

"No," I croaked, acid burning in my stomach. "He wasn't—"

"He was." He grinned proudly. "I always wanted a son, you

know?" Suddenly, he swung his gun wide and leveled it on me. "But I'll settle for Tessa. Tell Light he has twenty-four hours to return my family or, the next time, I aim higher."

"No. No. No!" I yelled, throwing a hand out as though I could stop him.

His sinister smile grew impossibly wide just before I felt the agonizing crush of my chest caving in.

The deafening sound of the gun's explosion barely registered before the lights went out completely.

It could have been a second. It could have been a millennium. But, sometime later, I awoke to Roman's pained roar.

"Elisabeth."

Through slitted eyes, I saw him drop to his knees beside me. He then jostled my limp body until I was flat on my back.

"Call nine-one-one!" he screamed in a voice so agonizing that I didn't even recognize it as my husband's.

Though, as my sluggish eyes focused on his face, I didn't recognize my strong man, either. His face was pale and contorted as though he were in the final stage of death.

"Are you okay?" I asked, raising a shaky hand to his jaw.

He frantically patted my neck and my chest down and then shoved my shirt up to do the same on my vest. "Oh, thank you, God," he cried in relief as I heard the ping of something metal hit the tile. "Okay. Hang tight, baby. I'm going to get you out of here."

"It was Noir," I whispered. Even the simple act of talking was painful.

His wild gaze landed on mine. "I know. But I've got you now."

"You need to get Tessa and Clare somewhere safe. He…he wants them back."

"Okay, baby. Calm down and breathe. I'll get word to Light."

I closed my lids and forced the words from my throat. "He said

Tripp was his."

"Shhh. He was *ours.* Don't worry about the rest of it right now. Just hold on. I'm gonna get you to a hospital." He lifted my upper body and tucked my face into his neck.

The movement was unbearable, and the mixture of overwhelming pain and the comfort of knowing that he was there with me had me drifting into the darkness once again.

CHAPTER SEVENTEEN

CLARE

I perched on the edge of the bed as Heath paced a path in the carpet of his bedroom. His phone was at his ear, and a barrage of curse words streamed from his lips.

"And you decided using the APD to secure the movie theater was your best option?" he roared. "Jesus Christ, you might as well have just sent Noir an invitation." He paused and raked an angry hand through his hair. "Bullshit. A man dying and Elisabeth Leblanc getting shot *is* absolutely my problem."

My stomach rolled as a wave of nausea hit me.

Heath and I had been celebrating my latest *Wheel of Fortune* victory by cooking together. Tessa had crashed out hours earlier, and I had been admiring Heath's bare feet and shirtless chest as he'd flipped pork chops in a frying pan when Alex and a swarm of DEA agents had stormed in and forced us upstairs.

I'd panicked, fearing the worst.

But I'd never expected that the worst could actually be worse than I feared.

Ethan was dead, and we were still waiting on an update with Elisabeth's condition. The last thing we'd heard was that she was being rushed to the hospital with a possible gunshot wound in her chest.

Walt had finally come out of hiding.

And he was back with a vengeance.

At this news, I hadn't fallen apart.

I hadn't cried.

I hadn't even gotten pissed.

They were all worthless emotions that would change nothing.

And, right then, I'd desperately needed someone to change *everything*.

So, with my ears ringing and numbness cloaking my body, I'd settled on the edge of the bed and tried to make sense of a senseless situation.

"Oh thank fuck!" Heath barked. "She was wearing the vest."

I closed my eyes, my chin falling to my chest as a surge of relief inundated me.

"Clare? You hear me?"

"I heard you, honey," I whispered, doing my best to keep it together. But, as my shoulders shook and my breath shuddered, I failed.

"Yeah. Have Leblanc call me when you can. I gotta go."

The space beside me on the bed sank, Heath's blanket of warmth surrounding me.

"It's okay, babe. Let it out."

"I hate him," I told his chest as I face-planted against it.

"I know. I do, too."

I perked my head up so I could see him. "No, Heath. I *hate* him. And I hate myself too, because if it weren't for me, none of this would have happened."

He frowned. "This isn't your fault."

"No. It's not. But Elisabeth was only on his radar because of me."

"Bullshit. Elisabeth was on his radar because he's a whack-job who stole her eggs and played God so he could have a kid."

I shot to my feet. "Because I couldn't give him that!"

His eyebrows furrowed. "Do not go down this road. Do not take his actions on your conscience. You didn't shoot them, Clare.

And you know good and damn well not a single person involved in this situation blames you for any of it. So don't fucking start."

I aimed my gaze over his shoulder. He was right, and deep down, I knew that none of it was my fault, but guilt was a real bitch like that.

I opened my mouth to tell him that I hated his sensible answers, but his phone vibrated in his hand. He immediately put it to his ear while lifting a single finger in my direction.

"Roman? Shit. Yeah, we're good. What the hell is going on over there?"

I leaned into his side to hear what Roman was saying, and Heath caught the hint and put him on speakerphone.

My heart ached as Roman painfully recounted finding Ethan in the hall then finding Elisabeth unconscious on the bathroom floor with a bullet hole in her shirt and blood covering her face and chest. The devastation in his voice was tangible, and it slashed through me.

Before I knew it, Heath had scooped me up and set me in his lap. His strong hand smoothed up and down my back.

My body was nearly vibrating as I struggled to hold my rage back.

There were no words to adequately express the loathing and detest I felt for Walt.

"So, is she okay?" Heath finally asked when Roman quieted.

"Doctors are gluing the gash on her nose. She's got two cracked ribs from the bullet, but thank fuck she was wearing that vest."

Heath grunted his approval then pressed his lips to my temple.

"Listen," Roman started. "Can Clare hear me?"

Heath's gaze bounced to mine. "Uh, yeah. She's right here."

"Take me off speaker."

Heath's finger went to the button, but I was done being a silent participant in this conversation—and, really, my entire life. I'd had no control over anything when I had been with Walt. And, most recently, I'd been sitting back and trusting Heath, Roman, and the

DEA to take care of me, but I was finished being in the dark.

"Don't you dare," I hissed at Heath. "Do not cut me out of this. Roman, whatever you have to say to Heath, you can say it to me, too."

"Clare," Roman sighed. "I…ah…"

"I deserve to be involved in this. And I dare either one of you to tell me I don't. I have more than earned my place in this conversation."

"Babe," Heath warned.

"You know what? Fuck you both." I climbed off Heath's lap.

His astute gaze followed me as I began to pace.

"I spent seven fucking years being controlled by that maniac. I refuse to let you two decide what I can and can't handle." I crossed my arms over my chest and stopped to give Heath a pointed scowl.

His face was tight and his eyebrows pinched together, but when he opened his mouth, it was to say, "Talk, Roman."

"Light, I don't think—"

"Talk," he demanded, his eyes locked on mine. The muscles in his jaw ticked as his traps swelled beneath his gray T-shirt.

Roman grumbled and reluctantly said, "He told her to give you a message. You got twenty-four hours to return Clare and Tessa or, next time, he aims higher."

I sucked in a sharp breath, and my eyes fell shut. Walter's menacing, green eyes danced on the backs of my eyelids while resentment and anger swirled within me.

But I wasn't afraid.

My wounds had healed, and that included the bonds of his mental reign of terror over me.

"Clare, I won't—" Heath started, but I cut him off.

With my eyes still closed, I confessed, "I want to move out."

"No!" Roman said definitively.

My lids popped open, a new resolve settling over my shoulders.

"No offense, Roman. But you don't get a say in this. You can't make me stay here, and let's be honest—you need me gone. He'll come back for her."

Heath was instantly on his feet and striding toward me.

I held my ground. “Don’t argue with me about this.”

“You’re not fucking leaving.”

“It’s not up to you, either,” I shot back.

His head snapped back as though I’d slapped him. “Excuse me?”

“I love you. I really do. But hiding out in this house is not doing anyone any good. He knows where we are. You yourself said he can’t get to me. And I believe you. But he *can* get to the people I love to get to me. I have to leave. Me and Tessa.”

“Absolutely fucking not,” Roman barked over the phone.

“Have you lost your mind?” Heath growled.

“Yes!” I threw my hands out to my sides. “I have lost my mind. I’ve lost everything. Walt is not in hiding. He’s biding his time. He’s cold and calculating and arrogant as hell. He’s playing this game and using us all as pawns. It’s what he gets off on. There’s a reason I slept with a knife under my mattress for seven years. And it wasn’t to keep him from killing me. There were a lot of nights where death would have been welcomed. It was because I knew he was going to torture me before he ever let me escape him. Physically. Mentally. Emotionally. Nothing is off-limits.”

“He won’t touch you,” Heath swore.

I laughed without humor. “Don’t you see? He *is* touching me. Right now. He’s in this room with us. But I’m sick and fucking tired of playing his games. He killed Ethan tonight…but not Elisabeth. Why?”

Heath planted his fists on his hips and sniped, “Because he’s a fucking psychopath.”

I adamantly shook my head. “It’s all part of his little game to punish us. Do you honestly think he believes that you’re going to give me and Tessa back to him? No. He’s not stupid. But, now, Elisabeth will always be looking over her shoulder. And Roman has to live knowing that Walt got to her right under his nose. He didn’t give a damn about terrorizing Ethan. And that’s exactly why he’s dead.”

Heath crossed his arms over his chest and glowered at me. “I think you give him entirely too much credit.”

"I don't think you give him enough! He's going to come for us. And this is not me being Debbie Doomsday. This is a fact. He's going to send in his army of men and let them do the dirty work. They'll slay the agents who try to stop them. Devon, Alex, Jude. All of them. Walt will be sitting at home, not caring about the outcome, because he just enjoys the show."

"I'll give him a fucking show!" Roman exclaimed across the line.

I stopped my rant and walked over to Heath. He had a white-knuckled grip on the phone, so I reached over and pressed the end button, severing our connection with Roman.

He continued his silent glower as I stood on my toes and pecked his lips. "He's setting up his game. I can't have him storming in here. Taking the lives of all of those people."

"And what? You just expect me to let you go? Fuck, Clare. I love you."

I smiled sadly. "And he hates you. You'll be the target number one."

"I can handle myself."

I kissed him again, but his body remained stiff. "I know you can. And, if you are with us, it will draw him away from the Leblancs. I'm proposing that you let me and Tessa move in with *you*. It will piss Walter off and ruin whatever he's been planning to do here for the last few weeks. I lived with that man for too long. I know him. He's got too much pride to allow you to ride off into the sunset with his family. But he's so cocky that he'll want to teach you a lesson—personally. If we get the hell out of here, Walter *will* come after us, but he'll leave the army at home."

Careful consideration flashed in his radiant, blue eyes. He knew I was right. But making him put the protective caveman aside in lieu of a rational endgame was not going to be an easy sell.

Case in point: when he finally opened his mouth and boomed, "No fucking way!"

I'd seen Heath angry; it had just never been aimed at me. And, much to my surprise and delight, it didn't faze me in the least.

"Tough shit," I said, "because it's happening. You either come with me or—"

His face contorted with outrage. "I swear to God, you finish that sentence, I'm going to lose my shit."

"Then fucking lose it! Lord knows, I already have." I slapped my thighs. "This sucks. But you're going to have to trust me. You've done research on Walt, but you are not mentally insane. You do not know how that man thinks." I hitched a thumb at my chest. "I do. I spent years learning how to read him and figure out his next move so I could make sure I wasn't on the receiving end of his wrath. And I'm telling you we *need* to leave."

He stared down at me as he crossed his arms over his chest. "And what? You just want to go back to my house? Set up camp and wait for him to arrive?"

My lips twitched as I fought a smile back. "Um. No." I rested my hands on his forearms. "I want to go back to your house. Maybe set up an alarm or something. Take one of your fancy DEA agents with us. And, if I'm right and Walt decides to try to get to us, we cut him off before he ever has the chance. Confidence is not something he lacks, and he's going to underestimate you. We are not going to do the same with him."

His shoulders sagged as he dropped his arms and folded me into a hug. "Jesus Christ, Clare."

"We'll do this smart and safe," I mumbled against his chest. "I trust you to handle that. And all I'm asking is that you trust *me* when I say we need to leave."

"This is crazy." He groaned and rested his chin on the top of my head. "Roman's gonna flip his shit. And, as my new boss, that is not going to go over well for me."

I craned my head back. "Roman's your new boss?"

He swayed his head to the side. "Well, Tomlinson hasn't fired me yet, but I assume when I tell him I'm moving you and Tessa in with me, it's going to speed up the process."

"I'm so sorry. I never—"

"Don't. I couldn't care less about my job, as long as I get you and your girl at the end of this."

"But—"

"End of story," he snapped.

I crinkled my nose and attempted a glare. He seemed immune.

Rolling my eyes, I gave up. "So, what are you going to be doing for Roman?"

"He offered me a job as the liaison to law enforcement at Leblanc Industries. It seems, after all of this mess, he's decided to start a new division to ensure all officers of the law have access to Rubicon." He grinned. "I made that man wear a Kevlar vest one time and I think it changed his life. I swear to God I saw him doing the sign of the cross." He paused to chuckle. "He isn't even Catholic."

I giggled and snuggled closer into his arms. "So, we're really going to do this?"

He sucked in a resigned breath. "I'm gonna see what I can come up with. I need to talk to Tomlinson. I have a security system at the house, but it's not good enough for this shit. I'm not taking you and Tessa there until it's one hundred percent. But yeah, Clare. I'm gonna try. I don't necessarily agree with this move, but I see your point."

"And you trust me," I prompted.

He grinned down at me. "And I trust you."

"And you love me."

"And I love you."

"And you're going to take care of me and my girl."

He bent forward and touched his lips to mine. "Always."

I closed my eyes and nuzzled against his chest.

His breath breezed past my ear as he whispered, "But I'm gonna need you to throw at least one round of *Wheel of Fortune* so I can build my confidence back up for an operation of this magnitude."

A bubble of laughter sprang from my throat. "Of course, Winter Woman. You want to kiss my watch too?"

"I wanna kiss *you*."

CHAPTER EIGHTEEN

HEATH

I hadn't been wrong about how Roman was going to react to Clare and Tessa's moving out. He'd lost his fucking mind. We nearly came to blows after he accused me of thinking with my dick and not my head. He didn't mean it, but that didn't mean it didn't piss me off. The worry was etched in his face, but like the miracle worker she was, Elisabeth somehow managed to talk him off the ledge of insanity. She was still recovering and in a lot of pain, but never underestimate the power of a good woman when it comes to her man.

Elisabeth wasn't thrilled with losing everyday access to Tessa. But, after a private conversation with Clare, she put on a smile that did nothing to hide the fear in her eyes and acted supportive.

It took me over a week to get my security system updated. Our new security plan came complete with DEA surveillance on the outside of the house. We didn't have agents waiting at the door anymore, but they were still in and out a good bit. We were keeping things tight without being overt.

As I'd expected, Tomlinson fired me. Or, really, he told me he was going to fire me as soon as Noir was behind bars. He couldn't risk assigning someone new to Clare's case.

With the information Clare had provided the department, they were able to take a large chunk of Noir's operation down. And, slowly but surely, they were making great strides at bringing him down completely. After his little stunt with Elisabeth, he'd gone back into hiding. All it was going to take was one of his men who were now in custody to give up his location and we'd be home free.

"Oh my God, it's so cute!" Clare exclaimed, bouncing with excitement in the passenger's seat of my Explorer.

I hadn't stayed at my house in weeks, but even with the lingering unease I felt about bringing Clare and Tessa there, I had to admit that it felt really fucking good to be home.

"Heaf, dis you house?" Tessa asked.

My whole body jerked, and Clare's hand slapped down on my forearm.

"Did you hear that?" she whispered.

Oh, I'd heard it. Never had my name been so sweet.

It made me a bitch, but a lump lodged in my throat. Until that moment, I hadn't realized that I actually cared what Tessa called me. Luke was a façade, but with a simple syllable, she'd made me something real in her life. And, if I had anything to say about it, something permanent.

"Jesus," I breathed. After clearing my throat, I managed to speak. "Yeah, sweet girl. This is *our* house now."

Clare squeezed my arm and offered me a smile.

Fuck, Walter Noir was insane. That man had had it all.

An amazing wife.

A gorgeous daughter.

A beautiful life.

But, for some reason, he hadn't been able to get his shit together enough to hold on to it.

And thank God for that.

Because, now, she was *my* woman.

My girl.

My life.

Before I was forced to hand my balls over, I turned the car off and shoved the door open, saying, "Let's go in."

Tessa squealed as I unbuckled her from the car seat and again as I planted her on my shoulders.

Clare rounded the hood and took her place under my outstretched arm. "I have to confess, after seeing your yard, I'm even more excited."

I chuckled and looked down. "You're frothing at the mouth to get your hands on those bushes, aren't you?"

"Yes! I know it's January, but that's just sad. They're never going to bloom this year if you don't trim them back."

"Have at it, babe. The backyard should make you damn near orgasmic if this got your motor running."

She draped her arm around my hips, tucking her hand in the back pocket of my jeans as we strolled up the sidewalk to my front door.

I released Clare long enough to use my key to open the door.

But, after I'd swung it open, the world stopped turning.

"Take her," I growled, passing Tessa off to her mother before racing into my house.

The alarm beeped in warning as I spun in a circle, my heart slamming in my chest and ice coursing through my veins.

"You have got to be shitting me!" I growled, storming over to the bar that divided my kitchen and my living room. A vase of flowers sat on the granite countertop. I plucked the card off, read it, and then threw it on the counter. "Son of a…" I trailed off as I snatched my phone from my back pocket.

"Heath?" Clare called cautiously, her gaze flashing around the room.

"Put your code into the alarm, babe," I ordered.

I dialed my phone as I listened to the chirps of her dialing her numbers into the security panel.

"Do I need to hit the green button?" she asked.

"Yep," I snapped, lifting my phone to my ear.

He answered on the first ring.

"Leblanc? Put Elisabeth on the phone."

"She's in the shower. Everything okay?"

I gritted my teeth. "No. Everything is not fucking okay. I just got home and there are goddamn floral throw pillows on my couch."

He barked a laugh.

"This is not funny! I have a coffee table, Roman. It has *coasters* on it."

He continued to laugh.

I turned in another circle, taking in the explosion of patterns that had most definitely not been there when I'd left the day before. My gaze landed on Clare, who was biting her lips to hold her laughter back.

I pointed at her. "Did you have any part of this?"

A giggle escaped as she shook her head.

"Oh, Heaf, you house is beautiful!" Tessa exclaimed, rushing over to what could only be described as a massive vase filled with petrified branches covered in glitter.

My stomach actually churned at the sight.

I pinched the bridge of my nose and turned away only to find a table with a wicker basket next to the door. A matching pair of motherfucking *sconces* were mounted on the wall above it.

"Roman, put your wife on the phone," I demanded.

"You know Elisabeth had help. Maggie was more than willing to let the delivery people in."

"Of course she did," I grumbled.

"Maybe you should have stayed here?" he said, his voice thick with amusement.

"Is that what this is? Payback for leaving?"

"No, that's Elisabeth's way of making sure Clare and Tessa are comfortable and not living in a bachelor pad. However, when you get upstairs and find all of those scented candles in your bedroom, *that's* your payback for leaving." He laughed again before saying, "Call me if you need anything," and then he hung up.

I fisted my hands on my hips and turned to the kitchen only to wince when I saw pink-and-white-striped *dishtowels* hanging on the door of my oven.

Clare's arms wrapped around me from behind. "I think it looks nice."

I raked my hand through my hair. "This isn't going to work out. I think we need to get a divorce."

She laughed musically. "We aren't married."

"Then, for the love of all that's holy, please tell me why my house looks like we just celebrated our tenth anniversary."

Her chest shook against my back. "Maybe I can talk to Elisabeth and see if we can switch some of it out for something a little more…uh…gender neutral."

Tessa shoved past me and went straight to the fridge. "Heaf, you got chocolate milk?"

I sighed. "I don't know, sweet girl. But, from the looks of the place, I'm betting there is probably some rose water in there."

Clare laughed so loud that my smile broke before I could even stop it.

She slid around to my front. "Breathe, honey. They're only decorations."

I looped my arms around her hips and brushed my lips with hers, admitting, "I'm scared to go upstairs."

She smiled against my mouth. "How about I go up there first and get rid of anything that could possibly be construed as feminine?"

"No. My guys cleared the house right before we got here, but I should still check it out first."

Her eyes grew wide as her hands drifted under the hem of my shirt. "I won't lie. I knew she was up to something. She asked me to help her pick out a new duvet. But I remembered she'd just gotten a new one."

I curled my lip. "What the fucking hell is a *duvet*?"

"It's like a comforter. And…let's just say, the one I told her I liked had big magnolias on it."

I closed my eyes and groaned. She, of course, giggled at my

pain. If I didn't love her so damn much, I would've been offended.

Gathering up all the courage I could muster, I headed for the stairs. "Pray for me."

She smirked. "Do I get the house if you stroke out?"

"Don't look so excited. It's not paid off."

She covered her smile with her hand.

I took the first step up. "Tell my family I love them. Well, except Melanie. She's pissed at me right now for calling her job and leaving a message with her secretary that her gonorrhea test had come back positive. Maybe wait a week before contacting her."

Her mouth gaped. "You did not!"

I took another step up. "You're not praying."

"Oh, right." She folded her hands in front of her and closed her eyes.

Only then did I allow myself to smile.

Huge.

CHAPTER NINETEEN

CLARE

I was lying on my stomach on his bed, in nothing but one of Heath's T-shirts and a pair of panties. My knees were bent, my ankles crisscrossed in the air above me as I flipped through the pages of a huge plastic binder.

I'd spent over an hour soaking in his bathtub while Heath had taken on the task of getting Tessa settled in her new bed in his bright-pink guestroom that looked like Kid's Pottery Barn had thrown up all over it. I hadn't been sure Heath would survive that one. But, of all the rooms Elisabeth and Maggie had decorated in the house, that was the one that bothered him the least.

He'd peeked his head in the doorway and grunted, "Looks like her." Then went on to obsessing about the new yellow and black chevron in his bathroom. "Georgia Tech colors," he'd muttered just seconds before stripping the shower curtain down and throwing it in the trash.

"I can't decide how I feel about this," I called out to him when he came sauntering into his bedroom.

Maggie had not been lying. My man did, in fact, have a collection of Pokémon cards in the top of his closet. He also had baseball cards, football cards, and some weird Olympic cards that had apparently been popular at some point.

I knew Heath well—or so I'd thought. But being in someone

else's space is telling on a whole new level. I'd learned that Heath was a bit of a packrat. He was super neat though, so all of his random collections were organized in shoeboxes or binders and stacked alphabetically in his closet.

Yes. Alphabetically.

So perhaps neat wasn't the right word. Anal was probably more fitting. But it was cute.

Other things I'd learned:

He didn't play video games.

Loved Chuck Palahniuk novels.

He had a penchant for old guns.

And he had the most random assortment of spices I'd ever seen. Apparently, he was an experimental cook. But he hated almost all of it and ate sandwiches instead of whatever failed meal he'd attempted.

"You feel incredibly turned on and are fighting the urge to jump me," he replied, crawling up the bed on all fours until he hovered over me.

"She asleep?"

As his lips pressed behind my ear, I moaned and turned my head so he could kiss my neck.

"Yep. She was almost out before I finished the first page of the book."

"Thanks for putting her down. Your bathtub is amazing."

"That's because you're small. I tried to get in there one time and I swear my heels were touching my ass. I instantly regretted the garden tub upgrade the builder had sold me on." He kissed my neck again. "At least, now, I can consider it money well spent."

I rolled over underneath him and slid my hands up his chest. "How long have you lived here?"

"Three years. When Maggie first moved in with me, I had a little two-bedroom apartment. But, let me just tell you, that shit got small. Women are a nightmare to live with."

I bit my bottom lip. "You do know I'm a woman, right?"

"What?" He feigned surprise. "No way." He shifted his weight onto one arm, using his other to pat down my breasts. "Well, what do you know?"

I glided my hands around to his ass and dragged his hips down to rest between my legs. The friction of his denim against my barely covered core lit my system up. "I promise not to be a nightmare—all the time, anyway."

He kissed me chastely and whispered, "Liar."

"Probably," I murmured back, seductively rolling my hips off the bed.

He pressed down against me and cussed, but then he suddenly shifted to the side and propped himself on an elbow. "Before we get to that, I need you to talk to me. And I need you to be honest." He arched a sexy eyebrow. "Can you do that?"

"I can do a lot of things," I replied breathily.

He grinned. His large, callused hand brushed my damp hair off my face. "You gonna be able to sleep with her in the other room tonight?"

I cut my gaze over his shoulder as a bucket of ice water doused my mood. "Um."

No. No, I wasn't going to be able to sleep a single wink with her in the other room. But he didn't make me admit that.

"That's what I thought," he said. "So listen. Me and you, we'll hang out. Do our thing. And when you start to fall asleep, I'll go get her and put her in bed with you. I'll sleep on the couch. My dick might shrivel if I sleep in that neon-pink room of hers."

My heart lurched. I didn't want him sleeping in another room, either.

Sure, I was playing the part. Putting a brave smile on and pretending I wasn't scared out of my wits. But the fact of the matter was we were somewhere new, and only a week earlier, Walt had killed a good man in order to send me a message. I trusted Heath implicitly, and I believed with my whole heart that we'd made the right decision by leaving Roman and Elisabeth's. But that didn't mean I wasn't still worried.

"It's a king-sized bed, honey. We'll all fit," I said.

His face turned soft. "Clare, I love you. And you gotta know by now that I love Tessa too, but I don't think it's in anyone's best interest for her to wake up in a bed with me and her mom. Yeah, she's seen us hugging and kissing, and I'm okay with that because I want her to know that love can be gentle. And I want her to see how much you trust me because then she'll trust me more too. But, a couple of months ago, you were in Noir's bed—the man she called daddy."

I opened my mouth to object, but he talked over me.

"I know you didn't want to be there. And I know you were mine even back then. I'll be damned if she ever calls him daddy again. But she doesn't understand that shit. I think we need to give this thing between us a little more time to grow before she wakes up in the morning snuggled into my chest."

I sat up and crisscrossed my legs between us. "Because that's exactly where she'd be. Snuggled into *your* chest. Heath, I love you for the way you make me feel. For the way I come alive under your touch. I love you because you're smart and funny and thoughtful. You've gone through hell and even sacrificed your own job to be with me. You look at me like I'm the only woman you've ever seen. And hold me like you never want to let go. You laugh with me. And challenge me to be a better person, but at the same time, you remind me that there is nothing wrong with the person I already am. But that's why *I* love you."

He cupped my face and lazily trailed his thumb over my cheek. "Jesus, Clare."

I covered his hand at my face. "But, Heath, honey, Tessa loves you because, from the first day she met you, you were always kind and gentle with both of us. When she was terrified on that driveway, watching her *daddy* beating me while Roman yelled at her from the gate, chaos swirling all around her, she ran to *you* because she knew you'd make it okay. And you did." I sucked in a shaky breath as my vision got blurry. "For both of us."

"Come here, babe," he murmured, hooking his arms around my waist and pulling me down to lie beside him, my head resting on his bicep.

"She's young, but if you think for a single second she doesn't know what you've done for us, you're crazy." I smiled, and a tear slid down my cheek.

Using his thumb, he wiped it away.

"So, yeah," I said, "she's a kid who's been through hell in her short life, and she might be confused about a lot of it, but waking up between her mom and a man she trusts and loves is probably exactly what she needs."

"Fuck," he breathed, his mouth pressing against mine for a deep closed-mouth kiss.

I broke it all too soon. "But, if *you* don't feel comfortable with her sharing a bed with you… *That*, I'll understand. It'll suck because you two are my life. But you're right. She's not yours—"

"Yet," he quickly corrected.

My head jerked back. "What?"

"She's not mine *yet*. She will be eventually."

Oh.

My.

God.

My nose started stinging as my face contorted into that dreaded chin-quivering, scrunched-up, on-the-verge-of-an-ugly-cry expression.

"When this is all over, it's still going to be me, you, and Tessa," he said. "We're making a life together. And, in that life, she's gonna grow up. It's gonna be me teaching her how to ride a bike. Me bandaging her skinned knees. Me interrogating her first boyfriend. Me teaching her how to drive a car. Me grounding her for sneaking out. Me building bookshelves in her college dorm. And me walking her down the aisle one day when she's at least forty years old."

I hiccoughed a laugh through my tears, and he shot me a smirk.

"Right now, she's *your* girl because I haven't earned the right to call her mine yet. But I will. And, when I do, she's gonna be *our* girl. So, if you're good with her waking up with me now before I've earned that role, then I'm good with it, too."

God, he was going to make such an amazing dad, even if he was just *Heath* to her for the rest of her life.

And, with that realization, something dawned on me.

"Do you want kids of your own?" I sniffled, nerves fluttering in my stomach. "Because I…I don't know that I can give them to you."

"I do," he replied curtly. "And I want them with you." He gripped the back of my neck and gave it a reassuring squeeze as he rested his forehead against mine. "You're twenty-eight, Clare. We've got a lot of years ahead of us. If a baby comes in that time, great. But, if it doesn't, that'll be okay too. I've got you. And we've got Tessa. The rest is just bonus."

A fresh set of tears streamed down my cheeks as Heath's warmth blanketed me in a way I knew I would never lose. How had I gotten so lucky? How, after spending years of kissing the clock just to survive, had I found a man better than anyone I ever could have wished for? Maybe God hadn't abandoned me after all. Because whoever had paved our pasts that ultimately put him in that gym with me had known exactly what they had been doing.

I sucked in a deep breath and held it until my lungs began to burn.

"Are you okay?" he asked.

Yes. Utterly. Completely. Thoroughly. Entirely. And an entire thesaurus's worth of synonyms more.

And it was only that feeling of contentment that allowed a smile to spread across my face.

"Yeah, but I have a question. You're, like, eighty. Isn't your biological clock ticking?"

One side of his mouth tipped up as he wrapped his arms around me, muttering, "She's cryin', but she's still got jokes."

"It's a valid question," I squealed as he began tickling me.

"It's not a valid question, Clare. It's you being a smartass."

"And me being a smartass," I confirmed, laughing wildly and flailing in his arms.

I stilled when his hand slid under my T-shirt.

I moaned when his finger slipped inside my panties.

I cried out when his mouth found my nipple.

Minutes later, I came with his name on my lips.

Minutes after that, he came with mine on his.

And then, just before my eyelids got too heavy to stay awake, he got *our girl* and put her in bed with us.

She promptly curled into his chest.

And I fell asleep without a single worry on my mind.

CHAPTER TWENTY

HEATH

Two weeks later...

"But it's January," Clare objected, settling on the barstool on the other side of the counter.

She'd been visibly nervous all morning and spent a full hour earlier chewing on her thumbnail and staring into space. I couldn't figure out exactly what was going on, but I figured she'd come to me when she was ready.

Using a fork, I removed one of the steaks from the marinade and set it on a plate. "It's almost February in Atlanta. We're basically a week away from summer. It's perfect grilling weather."

"It's still cold," she argued.

I cleaned my hands off on the gray-striped dishtowel Clare had ordered to replace Elisabeth's pink ones. "So put on a jacket."

She tipped her chin to the plate of meat. "You know I could pan-sear those and no one would have to put on a jacket."

"I love your food, but you've cooked breakfast, lunch, and dinner every day since we've been here. After two weeks, I think I can handle a meal."

"But you've bought all the food, and Tessa new clothes, and..." She trailed off, biting on her thumbnail again.

"So?" I drawled.

"So I need to be pulling my weight."

"I'm not saying you don't. But you don't have to pull *all* the weight."

"I'm not pulling all the weight. I mean…I'm not sure cereal can even be considered 'cooking breakfast.'" She tossed me a pair of air quotes.

I arched an eyebrow. "Did I have to pour the milk?"

She shyly glanced away. "Well, no."

"Then it's considered cooking breakfast." I grabbed the plate and headed around the bar. "Besides, you put forty dollars' worth of steaks in a frying pan, we're gonna have problems. There's one way to cook a steak, and it's on a grill. End of story."

She rolled her eyes as I stopped beside her.

"Now, get up here and give me a kiss, pull on a jacket, and meet me on the deck."

She stood off the stool and lifted up on her toes to touch her lips to mine. "You want me to grab you a beer?"

I shot her a grin. "So you do understand the fine art of grilling."

She rolled her eyes again. "I'm teachable."

I chuckled before turning away and calling out to Tessa, "Sweet girl, we're going outside. You want to come, or are you waiting on pins and needles to see if he can actually find the girl to fit the glass slipper for the seven thousandth time?"

She laughed loudly. "Dis not *Cinderella*, Heaf!"

I scoffed. "Oh, well, *excuse* me. You gonna be able to tear yourself away?"

"After he kiss her," she said, turning her attention back to the TV.

I bulged my eyes over my shoulder at Clare. She was now in one of my hoodies and carrying a beer my way.

"Why is her favorite part always them kissing? This does not bode well for our future."

"She's a girl, honey. She'll be chasing boys around the playground, trying to kiss them first chance she gets."

I curled my lip and shook my head. "Hopefully, Roman pays well, because I see a private all-girls school in her future."

Clare smirked and called to Tessa, "Okay, baby. We'll be on the deck. Come out when it's over."

"'Kay," she chirped.

I was contemplating how hard it would be to check her into a convent before preschool when I felt Clare's hand on my back.

"Let it go," she said. "I'm starving."

Begrudgingly, I led the way to the sliding glass door.

"Hit the alarm," I said, shifting the plate of steaks to one hand so I could take my beer from her.

After she disarmed the alarm, she slid the door open and we both walked out.

She started to close the door as I emptied my hands on the side of the grill.

"Leave it open," I told her.

She continued to slide it shut. "All the hot air is escaping."

"Babe, leave it open so we can hear her if she needs anything."

"I'll just crack it. I need to talk to you about something private."

"What kind of private?" I walked over and caught the top of the door over her head. "Leave. It. Open."

She narrowed her eyes and thinned her lips. "Above and beyond wasting money on heating the backyard, you're going to freeze her out in there if we leave it all the way open."

I shoved the door wide open. "Good. Then she'll be forced to come out here to ask for a jacket and hopefully miss the fucking kiss."

She laughed but gave up on the door.

I twisted the top of the beer off and went to work on the grill. "What'd you want to talk about?"

"Well," she started at the same time my phone began ringing.

Tomlinson's number showed on my display.

"Hold that thought," I said, lifting the phone to my ear. "Light."

"We picked up Brock Nolan today," he stated as his greeting.

My back shot ramrod straight, and my gaze sliced over to Clare, who was lounging in the white Adirondack chair she had long since claimed as her own.

Nolan was Noir's number two. He was one of the few men he'd trusted with Clare. Which was insane even for Noir because, by all accounts, Nolan was off in the head. I wouldn't have trusted that scum with a goldfish, much less my wife and child. I had often seen him lurking around at the gym. And not just because he was keeping tabs on her. His eyes were always aimed at her ass or tits.

"He with Noir?" I asked.

Clare's attention snapped to mine.

I pushed the button to put him on speakerphone.

"Nope," Tomlinson said. "But guess what? The asshole hasn't stopped chirping since we got him in custody."

"No shit?"

"No shit," he confirmed. "We've got units headed out to where he says Noir's been hiding out."

Clare rose from the chair and took a step in my direction, her hand covering her mouth as hope and surprise mingled in her eyes.

I extended an arm and curled it around her shoulders. "Keep us updated. Yeah?"

"Will do." He hung up.

"Who'd they get?" she asked immediately.

"Brock."

Her body tensed, but just as quickly, she melted into my side. "Good. I hated him."

"I know."

"I once found him standing in the bathroom when I got out of the shower. He refused to leave until one of the recruits rushed in and told him Walt was home."

I gritted my teeth. I knew this story all too well. I'd destroyed an entire office after Atwood had reported it back through his chain of command just days before he was killed.

"The recruit was Tim Madden, right?" I asked.

"Yes!" she exclaimed, stepping out of my embrace. "That guy was an asshole too."

"He wasn't an asshole. He was a good friend of mine."

"W-what?" she breathed.

"Rob Atwood was his real name. We got to the DEA about the same time."

Her mouth fell open. "He was DEA?"

I glanced down at the wooden deck, the pain of the memory ripping the scab off. "Yep. He was the first guy we were able to get into Noir's operations. I was already under as Luke when I got word that we'd landed someone on the inside. I got a lot of my information on you from his reports."

"Oh my God. I never would have guessed that. He was such a dick."

I swallowed hard and told the ground, "It was his job to be a dick. But he was always looking out for you."

"Holy shit. What happened to him?"

I lifted my gaze back to hers. "Tim Madden landed on the APD's radar, so the DEA was forced to step in and leak his identity to get him off of it. We'd thought for a long time that Noir had someone on his payroll in the APD, but this was the final straw. A day later, Atwood was found dead."

She slapped a hand over her mouth and gasped. "Oh my God, Heath."

I shook my head and went back to the grill, opening it to find forty dollars' worth of charred steaks. "Fuck," I growled, turning it off.

Her arms folded around my waist from behind. "I'm so sorry."

"I hope you like well-done," I replied.

"I meant about your friend."

"Yeah…it wasn't exactly a good time, but—"

All further conversation was halted with the shrill of a little girl's scream.

"Tessa!" I shouted, rushing past Clare and bolting through

the door.

I made it into the house just in time to see movement at the foyer.

I couldn't make the man out, but I knew that it wasn't Noir. My body relaxed for a fraction of a second when I assumed that it had to be an agent.

And then ice fresh off a glacier flooded my veins as I saw my little girl's bare feet kicking in his arms.

"Heaf!" she cried.

That was the exact moment every decent, law-abiding part of me tore away from my soul, leaving nothing behind but a visceral need to slaughter whoever had her.

My pulse spiked as I darted after her—after him.

I reached for the gun I wasn't wearing at my hip, but I never slowed my feet. "Tessa!" I roared, pushing myself harder and faster.

He was slow—clumsy, even—bumping into the walls as he tried to escape. I lost sight of her as the bastard rounded the corner. Then I heard the front door open and my heart lurched into my throat.

"Heath!" Clare shrieked behind me.

"I've got her. Hit the panic on the alarm," I ordered as I ran out.

The unknown man trudged through the grass toward a black SUV at the curb. I knew with an absolute certainty that, if he got to that car, I would never see her again.

I also knew with an absolute certainty that he would *never* make it to that car.

Her cries fueled my system with a tsunami of adrenaline that allowed me to gain ground on him.

His chubby arm held her around the waist, her head and her legs flopping and jarring with his every step.

My long legs swallowed the distance between us. And, just feet from the car, I dove, landing a shoulder at the small of his back. I did my best to break her fall, but she went crashing down with him. I landed hard on top of his back.

Slinging him over me, I got him as far away from her as I could.

She cried again, but this time, the sound soothed me. She was okay. I could handle whatever the fuck else the asshole planned to throw at me as long as she was okay.

"Go to Mama, Tessa," I barked, wrestling with the man.

He was no competitor, and I easily got him on his stomach and wrenched his arms up his back until his fingers were nearly tickling his hairline.

He cursed in pain.

I kept my eyes trained on Tessa. She stared at me, tears rolling down her face, grass stains covering her clothes and face. But, despite the emotional trauma that would probably never heal, she appeared unharmed.

"Heaf," she whined, reaching out for me, concern and worry aging her baby face.

"I'm okay, sweet girl." I assured.

The man bucked beneath me, but I fisted the back of his hair and slammed his face into the ground, following it up with a knee in his back to pin him.

"Tessa, go."

She sniffled but scampered away.

With her on her way to safety, my body relaxed and my instinct-driven senses gave way to logic and reason.

And that was when a second wave of panic hit me.

With the exception of the man on the ground grunting and cussing, it was silent.

No screams from a relieved mother.

No alarm screeching out in warning.

No sirens blaring in the distance.

Only absolute, terrifying silence.

It was wrong.

So fucking wrong.

"Tessa, freeze!" I yelled.

CHAPTER TWENTY-ONE

ELISABETH

My ribs had still been sore, but I couldn't sit at home anymore. I was starting to go stir crazy. The only time I'd gotten out of the house over the last few weeks was in order to go over to Heath and Clare's to see Tessa. We'd been giving them time as I healed to settle in and adjust to their new life. Thankfully, Clare texted pictures nearly everyday. But it wasn't the same as having her and Tessa living under the same roof.

We'd gone over to celebrate her third birthday only days earlier. It'd been bittersweet. Tripp's birthday had been the week earlier, but watching Tessa blow out her candles was hard for me. My little boy never got to do that. It was a pain that would never completely disappear, but listening to Tessa laugh as she ripped wrapping paper open certainly eased the sting.

After that, I decided I needed to get out of the house more instead of wallowing in pity and fear.

Per Roman's requirements, I was wearing a new Rubicon vest and Alex remained close enough that he could have been mistaken as my conjoined twin, but it was a small price to pay for being able to go to the grocery store and then have lunch with Cathy and Kristen.

Alex probably disagreed now that he had been subjected to being our chauffeur to lunch and then forced to eat sushi while listening to Kristen bitch about Seth for a full two hours.

Apparently, Seth had finally called and apologized. They went out again. Hooked up again. Then he never called…*again.*

Cathy spent half of the time informing her daughter that, if she hadn't have ended the date on her back, things might have turned out differently.

Kristen spent the other half of the time informing her mother that it was Seth who had been on his back.

Alex spent the majority of the time shaking his head and groaning.

I spent the *entire time* laughing my ass off.

It was much-needed. After my incident with Noir, I'd been struggling with nightmares and anxiety. I had no idea how Clare had lived with him as long as she had and was still able to smile. I could barely breathe sometimes when the memories of that night ravaged me.

Through it all, Roman had been right there with me, holding me and reminding me that I was safe.

Unfortunately, the same couldn't be said for Ethan. And it shredded me. Leo's company, Guardian Protection Agency, had paid for his funeral, and Roman had sent a large sum of money to his parents, but I knew that that did nothing to heal the holes in their hearts. I hated the helplessness and guilt I felt about the whole situation.

I also hated that Clare, Heath, and Tessa had moved out.

I understood why—sort of. But it still stung. Clare and I had become close, and Roman and I had both fallen head over heels for Tessa. And, honestly, I even missed Heath's quirky jokes—even if he did bitch about my food sometimes.

However, it wasn't as though I'd expected them to live with us forever. I'd just expected that the threat would be gone before they finally moved out. I worried about them more often than I'd ever admit.

So yeah. A delicious lunch, good friends, and a lot of laughs were exactly what I needed after the last few weeks—or, really, few months.

"I've got the check," Cathy announced.

"No. No. I've got Roman's credit card. He's buying lunch." I leaned forward and whispered to Cathy, "Do you have any idea how much money he makes now? It's ridiculous."

She giggled. "Well, I don't know the specifics, but seeing as to how I don't have a house or car payment anymore, I'm assuming it's *extremely* ridiculous."

"Ah, yes. Here we go," Kristen said dryly, crossing her arms over her chest and reclining back in her chair. "Roman is the golden child paying off all your bills, and I'm the whore."

Cathy turned *the mom glare* on her daughter. "I never said you were a whore. God knows I have no room to talk. When I first met your dad—"

"Oh God, Mom! No!" Kristen exclaimed, plugging her ears.

I choked on a sip of water, my tender ribs aching as I coughed.

Cathy patted me on the back but kept her eyes on Kristen as she scolded, "If you don't want those details, quit being a dramatic little shit."

"Ms. Leblanc?" a uniformed police officer said, approaching our table.

We all turned to look at him, and Alex immediately pushed to his feet, brushing his coat back to rest his hand on the weapon at his side.

The officer's gaze flashed to Alex for but a second. "I'm officer Marco with the APD. I've been sent to take you into protective custody after a break-in at Agent Light's home."

I jumped out of my seat. "Are they okay? What happened?"

"Everyone's fine." He assured. "But I need you to gather your things. We need to leave immediately."

"Does Roman know yet?" Alex rumbled.

"He does," Marco replied. "An officer has been dispatched to pick him up as well. Light and the DEA are asking for everyone involved to be locked down immediately." He tipped his chin at Cathy and Kristen, who were looking on, their mouths gaping. "You get them home safely then meet us at the station."

Alex nodded, pulling a wad of cash from his pocket and tossing it on the table. Cathy, Kristen, and I all exchanged nervous hugs and whispered goodbyes before Alex herded them out the door.

Marco cautiously led me out the other. His gaze flashed around, one hand on the small of my back and the other at his weapon.

With my heart in my throat and my stomach wrenching with nerves, I climbed into the back of his police car.

CHAPTER TWENTY-TWO

HEATH

"Where is she?" I bellowed, slamming the now cuffed man against the hood of a police car.

"Light, calm the fuck down," an agent said, trying to step in front of me.

But I was having none of it.

Clare was gone.

There was no such thing as calm anymore.

In the two minutes it had taken me to go after Tessa, someone had taken her. I didn't know how. Or where they had caught her. Or how I hadn't seen it. But she'd never even made it to the panic button on the alarm.

Someone taking Tessa had been nothing more than a distraction to get Clare away from me. The cocksucker was too fat. Too slow. Too stupid. Noir never would have sent a man like that if he'd really wanted to get his daughter back. This guy was more than likely some low-level thug who owed him drug money.

"I don't know!" he yelled. "I was just supposed to grab the girl."

"And take her where?" I pressed my forearm against the back of his neck.

He grunted under the pressure. "I was supposed to call when I had her."

I slammed his head into the car again.

"Light!" Roman yelled, jogging up the driveway, Devon right behind him. "What the fuck happened?"

I released the piece of shit. He didn't know anything, and time was wasting.

I turned on a toe and marched toward my door. "I need you to stay with Tessa."

He caught my bicep and jerked me to a halt. "Where's Clare?"

Son of a bitch. It fucking killed me to have to admit it.

I'd sworn to her that he wouldn't touch her ever again.

And I'd failed her on his first attempt.

"I don't know. But I'm going to find her. And I need you to stay with Tessa."

He fell back on a foot. "What the hell do you mean you don't know?"

I gritted my teeth. "I mean Noir got her, and I do not have time to sit here and explain this bullshit to you. Take Tessa back to your house, lock it down like Fort Knox, and Clare and I will pick her up as soon as we can."

His phone rang, so he dug it from his pocket. I took it as confirmation that he'd understood me and carried on to the house.

"Heaf!" Tessa cried when I got inside.

A female officer was sitting on the floor with her, and she jumped to her feet and raced over, careening into my legs before I'd even had the chance to squat.

I scooped her up to sit on my hip and gave her a hug. "I gotta go, sweet girl. But Roman's here, and he's gonna take you back to his house so you can see Elisabeth and play with Loretta. That sounds fun, right?"

Tears welled in her big, green eyes as she asked, "But where's Mama?"

I swallowed hard. "I'm going to get her."

"Where'd she go?" she pushed.

"Listen to me, Tessi. I'm *going* to go get her. And I'm *going* to bring her home. And then all of this is going to be *over.* No more bad men. No more trouble." I swiped my thumb over her cheek after the moisture had escaped. "No tears. Everything's fine. I'm gonna take care of this, okay?"

She nodded but started full-on crying. It broke me to have to pass her off, but I needed to get the fuck out of there if I had any hopes of keeping that promise to her.

"I love you," I whispered into the top of her head as I walked her out to Roman.

"I love you, too," she cried, clinging to my neck.

Clare

I woke up at home.

Not at Heath's.

Not at Roman and Elisabeth's.

Not even that shitty trailer I had grown up in.

No, I woke up in Hell.

The only real home I'd ever had.

A man I'd vaguely recognized had grabbed me right off the back deck as I'd watched Heath charge into the house after Tessa.

On instinct, I'd screamed his name. But only once, before I'd made the conscious decision that I'd rather not distract him from getting to her. I didn't know what he would have done if he'd known we were both in trouble.

But I knew without a doubt what I'd wanted him to do—save our girl.

I'd fought against my attacker, but in the end, it had been a futile effort. He'd dragged me out the back gate and through the neighbor's yard to a waiting car.

And then everything had gone dark.

I'd woken up in a small house I recognized as the one Walt used for his "business" deals. I'd spent many nights there when he'd get in his moods and I wasn't allowed out of his sight at all. It was not a place you wanted to be with Walt. Men who went in there with him rarely left alive. I'd cleaned blood off those stone-tiled floors countless times—sometimes, even my own.

I'd also turned the address over to Tomlinson weeks earlier.

And it was only that knowledge that kept me from falling apart after I opened my eyes and saw Walt's slimy gaze staring back at me.

"Sweetheart," he purred, sauntering toward me.

I sucked in a sharp breath but showed no fear as I whispered, "You finally came for me."

He rested a fist on the bed and leaned into my face, his breath slithering across my skin and his green eyes dancing with arrogance as he said, "Did you think for a single second that I wouldn't?"

Chills prickled the hairs on the back of my neck. "No." I shook my head and scooted across the bed. *But I hoped for every second that you wouldn't.*

He prowled up on the bed after me. The flex of his muscular body under the confines of his dress shirt made my stomach churn.

He cornered me against the headboard, one hand on either side of me, and cooed, "Welcome home, my love."

I squeezed my eyes tight as he pressed his disgusting lips to my forehead.

"I've missed you so much," he said, approximately two seconds before the back of his hand landed against my face.

Heath

"I'll be back," I assured Tessa as I handed her over to Roman.

The truth was I didn't actually know where the hell I was going, but even if all I had to use was my sixth sense, I was going to find Clare.

I looked to Roman and held his gaze in an unspoken plea for him to take care of her. He lifted his chin and shifted her on his hip so she could rest her worried head on his shoulder.

My chest ached and my legs were heavy as I forced myself to

walk away, but it had to be done. That was *my family*, and I was getting it back. No matter the cost. No matter the consequence. That shit was going to end once and for all.

I didn't give a damn how much the DEA wanted to get their claws in Noir. He had taken what was mine. Scared my little girl. Put his hands on my woman. Sent his men into *my home*. Fuck that.

Walter Noir would not end that day breathing.

My only prayer was that I got to Clare in time to ensure that she would.

"Hey, Light," Roman called out behind me. "Thanks for having Elisabeth picked up."

I froze in my tracks and slowly turned to face him. "Come again?"

"Alex told me you sent APD to take her into protective custody. Appreciate it. But I'm gonna swing by the station and pick her up. I'd feel better she's with me right now."

I blinked, my distracted mind trying to fit the pieces of the day's puzzle together. But they were all corners and nothing made sense.

When I'd realized Clare was missing, I hadn't been able to concentrate on anything else. However, after Noir's attack on Elisabeth, I should have considered her safety as well.

But I absolutely hadn't, and I sure as fuck hadn't called the APD.

I took a long stride toward Roman. "I didn't…" I started only to stop when the pieces clicked into place. I snatched my phone from my pocket and ordered, "Get Alex on the phone. Now!"

I dialed a different number.

Clare

He landed another hand on my face. "What did you tell the police?"

I kicked and bucked as I hid behind my arms. "Nothing! I swear."

His assault stopped as he barked a laugh and then snatched me upright by my hair.

My hands flew to his wrists, taking some of my weight to relieve the paralyzing pain at my scalp.

His furious gaze burned into me as he brushed his nose with mine. "Do not fucking lie to me." He gave my hair a hard snatch, wrenching my head to the side. "And what about Agent Light? I've heard you think he's your new man." He inhaled deeply and released it on a growl. "You are *mine*!"

With the slice of his arm, I went sailing backward off the bed.

I landed hard, which knocked the breath out of my lungs. I gasped for air as he got to his feet, and then, using my hair, he dragged me across the floor to the nightstand. My body went stiff and a sob tore from my throat as he retrieved a gun from the drawer.

"Walt, please!" I cried as he pressed the metal tip between my eyes.

"Tell me the goddamn truth, Clare. Now or fucking never."

Suddenly, a noise caught his attention and he quickly aimed the gun to the door.

Relief blasted through my body as I saw a uniformed officer—a savior—filling the doorway.

That relief died along with part of my heart when I saw who was beside him.

"Elisabeth?" I breathed.

HEATH

"Rorke," he answered.

"Where the fuck is Officer Marco?" I barked as soon as he picked up.

"Interesting. You want us on the case now that your precious Clare is missing?" he sniped.

I had no time for his bitchy little feelings over jurisdiction. "I found your fucking mole," I snapped. "He currently has Elisabeth Leblanc, and I'd wager my life that she's headed to Noir."

"What?" he asked in outrage. "No fucking way. Anthony Marco is a well-respected cop. You've got this wrong."

I clenched my teeth and searched deep within myself for even a fragment of patience. There was none to be found. "Bullshit!" I boomed. "He used my name in order to convince her bodyguard that I'd ordered him to take her into protective custody. That was twenty minutes ago, and she has not made it to the station yet. Now, *where* the fuck is he?"

"I, uh…" he stammered. "Shit."

I stormed to my car, Roman nearly exploding as he followed behind me. His phone was at his ear with Tomlinson on the other end.

"Where is he?" I repeated.

"The DEA has everyone out clearing Noir's known properties, looking for Clare."

I slammed the door to my Explorer closed behind me. It echoed as Roman did the same.

"Is he out clearing houses alone?"

"Shit," he repeated. "Goddamn it. I want you to be wrong here. But fuck, yeah, he's alone. He was on patrol when we got the call."

"Okay, I need you to fucking listen to me here. Do not alert anyone. I have no idea who else Noir's got buried in your ranks. But this stays between us. Track his car. Get me the address. Alert no one. You hear me. Not a single person finds out about this. Yeah?"

"Son of a—"

"Say you got me, Rorke."

"Light, this needs to be reported. He could be—"

"You tell no one!"

Roman finally detonated, slamming his fist down on the dash

before trying to rip the phone away from my ear.

"Let me fucking handle this," I barked, throwing a hand out to stop him from all but climbing through the phone.

"He has my wife!"

"He has mine too!" I snarled back. "We will get them back. But chill the fuck out and get your head together."

He stared at me for several beats before curling over and burying his face in his arms. He rocked back and forth in his seat, physically unable to sit still as adrenaline ravaged him. A feeling I knew all too well.

I turned my attention back to Rorke. "You've met Elisabeth Leblanc, and I know you've heard what Noir did to Clare. Now, that fucking monster has them *both.* I'm gonna get them out, and you are going to grow a fucking pair of balls and keep this quiet from your chain of command. Get me the GPS location of Officer Marco's cruiser, and then, when we have both of those women home safe, you can report whatever the fuck you want. But, for right now, you keep your fucking mouth shut unless you are talking to *me.* Now, say you got me."

He sighed. "I got you."

"Good. Get me the damn address." I severed our connection and dropped my phone into my lap.

I threw my arm around the back of Roman's seat and started to back out of my driveway, but then I caught sight of Tessa peeking over Devon's shoulder as he carried her into the house.

Her scared, green eyes were like a rusty knife to the gut. She should have been oblivious to this kind of drama for at least another…forever. She should be playing with Barbie dolls and watching fucking princes kiss their princesses, not living with the knowledge that someone had tried to snatch her from the safety of a place I desperately wanted her to call home. And then knowing they had succeeded in taking her mother.

I watched until the door closed behind them, a slew of agents and officers still flooding my lawn.

I couldn't change her past, but I could—and would—change the future.

No more.

This life was done for her.

ELISABETH

Blood trickled down Clare's ashy, white face as her gaze locked on mine.

"We're even now. I can't do this shit anymore, Noir," Officer Marco said.

"You're done when I fucking say you are."

"I'm going to lose my job over your obsession with this bitch," Marco returned, shoving me into the room.

I stumbled on my heels before falling forward and landing on my knees. Clare climbed to her feet and hurried toward me, but Walter caught her by the back of the shirt at the last second.

"Oh God!" I cried, extending my arms toward her as she crashed to the floor.

She jumped up again, clawing her way toward me, only to be forced back down.

Shoving his gun into the back of his pants, he planted a foot on either side of her and bent at the hip as he barked, "Enough!" And then he backhanded her so hard that I had to fight back a dry heave.

"Clare, don't!" I cried while praying that she would listen to him.

She didn't.

She spit in his face and shouted, "You bastard! She has nothing to do with this."

He stabbed a finger into her face. "I warned them, Clare. They kept you from me. You take a man's wife—*my* wife—you *will* lose your own. It's time Leblanc learns that lesson. And, if you don't shut up and remember who the fuck your husband is, you're going to learn a lesson, too."

Another round of vomit threatened to escape my throat as twin streams dripped off my chin. Yet, somehow, in the face of evil, Clare appeared to collect herself. Her hunched shoulders rolled back, and the color returned to her cheeks. I'd known that Clare had to have been strong to have lived with Noir for so long, but until that moment, I hadn't realized how strong she truly was.

I watched in awe as an eerie calm washed over her.

"Clare?" I whispered.

"You still want to be my husband?" she asked him weakly.

Walt seemed oblivious to her sudden change. His face remained hard as he growled, "You're a Noir. No fucking pig is going to change that."

She blinked her doe eyes at him and slowly pushed up onto her knees. "I'm still a Noir?"

He gently reached down and threaded his fingers through the top of her hair. "How can you even ask that? What the fuck did they do to you?"

Her chin jerked to the side as if something had struck her.

And I supposed it had, because not even a second later, she fell apart.

A strangled cry bubbled in her throat, and she scooted on her knees to hug his hips. "Oh God, Walt. I was so scared without you. I thought you hated me. That…that's what they told me. They said you didn't love me. And that you were planning to kill me. Heath and the police made me stay away." Her voice caught as tears rolled down her face. "I thought… I just… They kept telling me that they would take care of me. But they didn't. All I wanted was to come home." She rose to her feet and gripped the front of the beast's chest. "They're awful people, Walt!" she cried.

His malevolent gaze softened as he brushed the blood-streaked hair away from her face.

She dropped her forehead to his chest as her entire body trembled against him.

I had never in my life been more confused—or impressed. I

glanced around the room, hoping for an answer, but Marco was the only one there. He was wearing a similar perplexity as he narrowed his gaze on Clare.

"Noir, you're not buying this shit, are you?" Marco said.

Oh, but he was. Hook, line, and sinker.

The taut muscles under his white button-down visibly relaxed as he folded her into his arms. "I would never kill you, sweetheart," he murmured as if it were a romantic sentiment. "Don't worry. They'll pay for what they did."

She sniffled and used the back of her arm to dry her eyes. "We need to get Tessa."

Oh hell no.

"Clare," I hissed.

"We could trade Elisabeth for her," she continued. "If you kill Heath, Roman will trade Tessa for Elisabeth. We'll have our family back."

I slapped a hand over my mouth as my pulse skyrocketed. No way was Tessa getting near this. And even suggesting something like that left me questioning everything I knew about Clare.

"What are you doing?" I interjected into their conversation.

Walter's hand snapped in my direction to silence me, but he kept his gaze leveled on *his wife*. "I couldn't agree more."

"Noir, seriously?" Marco called. "This bitch is playing you. She's been shacked up with Light for weeks."

She held Walter's gaze, sliding her hands up and down his chest as she jerked her head to Marco. "I don't like him. He scares me."

An arrogant grin tipped one side of Noir's mouth as he nodded almost imperceptibly.

As she cuddled into his chest, her gaze landed on mine. But she wasn't there. At least, not the woman I knew.

She didn't even blink as Walter suddenly retrieved the gun from the back of his pants.

"What the..." was all Marco got out before Noir pulled the trigger.

Heath

Marco's cruiser had pinged at one of Noir's known properties, less than ten miles away. Tomlinson and a team of agents were already on the way over. Rorke had once again been banished from the investigation, but this time, for obvious reasons, he didn't voice any complaints.

The windows had nearly fogged from the molten anger rolling off Roman as we sped through town.

"How the fuck are you so calm?" he asked.

I kept my eyes on the road as I stated definitively, "Because I'm going to get her back."

He curled his lip. "You don't fucking know that. I swear to God, if he so much as—"

"Nope," I interrupted, shaking my head. "Don't do that. Don't let your mind go there. They're gonna be fine." I cracked my neck. "Clare can handle Noir."

I felt his incredulous gaze jump to me.

"Are you fucking crazy?" he asked. "I've seen the shit he used to do to her."

My knuckles turned white as I gripped the steering wheel. I'd seen that shit too, but I refused to think about it. She'd asked me to trust her weeks ago, and I'd be damned if now was the moment when I broke that promise.

"He could have killed her every day for seven years," I said. "He never did. She's lived in that lion's den before and come out on the other side. She'll do it again."

Roman scoffed, clearly not sharing my confidence. "And what about Elisabeth?"

"She'll take care of her, too."

"Jesus Christ, I fucking hope you're right." Roman banged his head back against the headrest. "You need to take my vest," he told the ceiling.

"Keep your shit," I grunted, weaving through traffic.

He peeled his shirt over his head and unstrapped the Velcro on his vest. "He'll be gunning for you, Light."

I turned off the highway, opting for a side road with less traffic. "He's a sociopath. He's gunning for civilization in general."

He dropped his Rubicon vest on the center console between us. "You know what I mean. He's got my wife, but it's you he's gonna be after." His eyes darkened, and his jaw ticked. "Besides, anything happens to me, Elisabeth will be taken care of. Clare needs you. Tessa too."

My chest tightened. He was only partially wrong.

"I need them, Leblanc. I'm going to get her back. Elisabeth too. But you're putting that fucking vest back on or I'm shooting you myself."

"Come on. Don't be a dumbass. The DEA is not going to let me storm in there this time. You need this shit more than I do. Kevlar will slow a bullet, but Rubicon will *stop* it."

I turned to look at him. Roman and I had butted heads more often than not. He was stubborn as a fucking mule and didn't have any problem letting you know when he thought you were wrong. Which was basically any time you disagreed with him. But, with all of that said, he was hands down one of the best men I'd ever met.

He'd waded into the middle of this mess from the very start. Blood, sweat, and tears, he'd been there from the moment he'd found out about Tessa. He didn't give a damn that she wasn't his child. He'd never backed down or cowered from what seemed like the impossible task of keeping both of our families safe. The world needed more men like him. And, if it hadn't been for his woman being at Noir's place, I would have pulled over and left his ass on the side of the road just to ensure he woke up the next morning.

As it stood, I didn't have *that* choice.

I did, however, have the choice to put him in that fucking vest to make sure he at least didn't go home full of bullet holes.

"Then we better hope my aim is better than his."

"Light, don't be stupid," he objected.

I ignored him. "We're two minutes out. Suit up."

Clare

Elisabeth screamed and frantically crawled away, but I felt not one ounce of remorse as Marco's lifeless body hit the floor.

Maybe I was just as ruthless as Walt after all.

Or maybe I was just happy to rid the world of one more maniac.

It didn't take a rocket scientist to figure out that he was the APD's mole who had gotten Heath's friend killed. But, worse than that, I knew for certain he was the worthless piece of shit who had somehow gotten to my friend—my *only* friend—and hand-delivered her to the Devil himself. He'd more than earned his spot in Hell as far as I was concerned.

Something had broken inside me when Walt had reminded me that I was his wife.

Or, more accurately, something had been reborn.

No matter how much I hated it, I was Mrs. Walter Noir.

He'd spent years emotionally terrorizing me, but in that time, I'd learned how to manipulate him to stay alive.

I hadn't thought I'd had any of that left in me after I'd lived in the light with Heath. But, the moment Elisabeth had walked through that door, an all-too-familiar darkness had consumed me. And, as long as Walt was alive, I'd never fully escape it.

Jail was no longer good enough. I wanted him wiped from the face of the Earth.

For the first time, I had a life to fight for.

A daughter who depended on me—and for more than just to keep her alive.

A handsome, kind, and warm man who loved me—and not in the warped and disgusting way Walt had.

And, lastly, I had a baby I hadn't even had the chance to tell Heath about yet growing within me. I'd only found out earlier that morning. I didn't know how far along I was. Or even if it would be a viable pregnancy, given my history. But, for that one moment, as I'd cried tears of joy on the floor in Heath's bathroom while staring down at those two pink lines I'd tried so hard to avoid when I had been with Walt, it was a baby—a piece of me and a piece of Heath. Conceived in love and not fear. The way it always should have been.

I would not allow Walt to take that away from me.

Or take *me* away from *them.*

"Will you get me something for my face?" I asked softly.

He leaned away and cupped a hand on my jaw. "When are you going to stop being so damn difficult? You don't have to fight me on everything."

"I know. And I'm sorry. I'll do better. I swear."

Bile crawled up the back of my throat as his lips swept across mine. "Lie down. I'll get you some ice."

I held my breath as I seductively trailed my fingers down his arm to the gun held tightly in his palm. "Here. Give me this and I'll keep an eye on Elisabeth."

He chuckled and opened his hand.

I kept the surprise hidden from my face, but hope slammed in my chest as I reached for the gun.

And then I froze when his hand shifted from my jaw down to my throat. He gripped impossibly tight, cutting my air off. Panic tore through me, but I forced myself to stay calm. It was the only way to stay alive.

Guiding me with my neck, he walked me backward until I hit the wall. My lungs burned and my vision started to tunnel, but I didn't fight. I remained perfectly still as he brushed his nose with mine, whispering against my lips, "I love you, Clare. But don't press your luck. I'm not oblivious to your games. I just happen to like playing them with you."

He studied my eyes, but I showed him nothing. And, after a few beats, a filthy grin pulled at his lips. He slammed my shoulders against the wall one last time before finally releasing me.

My legs had become weak, and I folded over, resting my hands on my knees as I gasped for air.

He stroked the top of my head and ordered, "Sit your ass on the bed. And don't even think about pulling any of your bullshit."

I kept my head down as I watched his feet disappear. He kicked Marco's lifeless body all the way into the room before closing the door.

As soon as it clicked behind him, I moved. And I did it fast. "Stop crying. You're making it worse. He's a leech who thrives on the fear," I whispered to Elisabeth as I began searching the room.

I hadn't been to that particular house in a while, but everything looked the same as it always had. Walt's desk sat in the corner, covered by paperwork and a laptop that reminded me more of an attorney's than a drug dealer's. I snatched the drawers open, but they were completely empty.

"What are you doing?" Elisabeth asked, climbing to her feet.

"I need a weapon. Help me look," I said, moving to the nightstand, but that drawer was empty too. "Shit."

"Clare, no," she pleaded. "Don't be the hero here. Let's wait. The guys have to know we're missing by now."

"Maybe. But that's not going to end well for any of us," I said, continuing to search the room. "I can keep us alive. But, if they show up, I can't promise the same for them."

"You can't do this," she begged. "Please just think about Tessa."

Oh, but I was. She had been living that life right alongside me.

I was going to end it for both of us.

Suddenly, I stopped as my gaze landed on the bed.

That room was exactly the same. Time hadn't touched it at all. Same bedspread. Same pillowcases. Same sheets.

Everything was just as I'd left it.

Everything.

Every. Thing.

I sucked in a deep breath and lifted the watch Heath had given me to my lips.

Closing my eyes, I conjured up images of Heath and Tessa playing in the backyard. There was a dog we didn't yet have racing around and barking as I stood on the deck, my stomach swollen with life, a content smile on my face, and a peace I had never experienced filling my heart.

Free of fear.

Free of pain.

Forever.

Kissing 11:11, I made the very last wish I'd hopefully ever need.

My heart pounded in my ears as I reached under the edge of the mattress.

HEATH

By the time Roman and I arrived at Noir's hideout, federal agents had it surrounded. Marco's patrol car was parked in the driveway beside a shiny, black BMW that I assumed was Noir's.

"Talk to me," I barked at Tomlinson, crouching next to him behind a black SUV.

"From what we can tell, both of the women are still alive. We have two distinct movements in the south bedroom and another in the kitchen. However, our concern is it seems to be only one male. We're trying to get eyes on the inside to see if it's Marco or Noir."

Dread pooled in my gut. "Son of a bitch," I bit out. "If it's Noir, you're going to try to take him alive, aren't you?"

"We need him, Light."

"You have got to be shitting me. You're gonna play this out and send in a fucking *negotiator* while he's holding two innocent women?"

"I will repeat: We need him alive, Light. What the fuck are you even doing here? I told Leblanc not to show up here."

I didn't even humor him with an answer. I pushed to my feet and drew my weapon. "I'm going in."

"The fuck you are!" he shouted back, catching my arm in an

attempt to drag me back down.

"Get the fuck off me." I snatched my arm away, and then we were suddenly interrupted.

A woman's scream rang through the air.

My entire body went taut. "Let me go!" I roared.

"We've got activity inside!" an agent yelled. "It's coming our way."

"Don't do this, Light. Do not fucking do this," Tomlinson begged as chaos broke out around us.

At least a dozen agents took cover, locked and loaded, all aimed at the door.

Time stood still as that front door swung open.

I held my breath, shamefully hoping for Clare to appear.

A frantic, blood-covered woman ran out.

But she wasn't mine.

"Elisabeth!" Roman yelled, taking off at a dead sprint after having shoved his way through the line of agents.

"Help her!" she cried, flying into his arms. "Please. Oh God. Help her."

My feet were moving before my mind could even process the dangers on the other side. Clare was in there. Nothing could stop me.

Not Tomlinson. Not the DEA. And sure as fuck not Noir.

I battled the urge to call her name as I made it into the house but thought better of announcing my presence.

I held my breath as I cleared the den before making my way through the house, toward the south bedroom.

And, as I turned the corner, my gun drawn and extended out in front of me, nothing could have prepared me for the scene in front of me.

Blood.

Entire fucking oceans of it covering the floor.

Please. God.

My hands tensed around my gun, her words from weeks ago

replaying in my mind. *"You're going to have to trust me."* And that trust was the only thing that kept my knees from buckling right then and there.

I stepped over Marco's body as I cautiously crept inside. Motion from the other side of the bed had me swinging my gun.

"Oh fuck," I choked.

I was vaguely aware of agents flooding in behind me. Mumbled curses filled the air as they took in the massacre around us.

However, I saw but one person.

She was kneeling beside Noir's body. Covered head to toe in blood. A knife in her hand. Her feral eyes locked on me as she tracked my movement.

It was a sight straight out of a horror movie.

And still somehow the most beautiful thing I'd ever seen.

She was alive.

Still breathing.

Still mine.

Still…

"Clare," I said gently, squatting several feet away and bringing us to eye level. "I'm here, babe. Tell me what you need."

She blinked and then opened her hand, sending the knife clattering to the floor. "I couldn't let him ruin our future."

"I know, babe. Come here."

She shook her head and flashed her wild eyes down at the blood covering her chest and her arms. "This isn't who I am. I'm… I'm not him. I just…" She looked back up. "He was never going to stop."

I kept my gun aimed at Noir's motionless body. Despite the massive amounts of blood pooling around him, I didn't trust that he was really gone.

"Clare, I know who you are," I replied, curling two fingers in her direction. "Come here."

"It's just—"

"Clare," I growled. "Listen to me. Everything is going to be okay. But I need you to come on over here and step away from him. Just in case."

She drew in a shuddered breath and rose to her feet. Emotionlessly, she stepped over his legs as she walked toward me.

I stood to my full height and opened my arms in an offer she had never refused. This time was no different. Plastering herself to my front, she hugged me tighter than ever before.

She remained completely collected as she asked, "Tessa?"

"She's fine."

Her voice remained steady as she pleaded, "Tell me it's over."

"It's over, Clare," I vowed, tucking my gun away as agents got their hands on Noir.

The tears finally appeared on her red-streaked face as she struggled with trembling hands to undo the watch I'd given her for Christmas.

Holding my gaze, she dropped it onto the floor. "That's what I wished for."

My arms spasmed around her, and emotion lodged in my throat.

"I want to go home, Heath."

Without words, I bent down, caught her at the backs of the legs, and lifted her into my arms. "Whatever you need," I replied as I carried her away from Noir for the very last time.

CHAPTER TWENTY-THREE

CLARE

When we arrived at the hospital, Heath carried me straight into an unused room and flipped the shower on. Methodically, he removed every piece of my blood-soaked clothing and dropped them into a nearby trash can before tying the bag up and tossing it in the hall. I wasn't sure if the police wanted them as evidence or if he couldn't get the remnants of Walter Noir far enough away from us.

"Am I going to be in trouble?" I asked as he climbed into the shower with me.

"No," he replied without expounding.

But that was enough for me. I trusted him.

As water poured over us and red circled in the drain, Heath held me. However, in a lot of ways, I was holding him. He was visibly distraught. His hands repeatedly traced and washed every inch of my body, but there was not one thing sexual about that shower. He was struggling, and if a quiet shower where he convinced himself that I really was okay was what he needed, I'd give it to him.

When I was finally clean, he dropped his forehead to mine and breathed, "Jesus, Clare."

"Are you going to ask me what happened?" I asked, looping my arms around his hips.

"No. You're standing here with me and he's dead. I don't need anything else."

I swallowed hard. It was important to me that he knew. He'd eventually get curious. Maybe he'd assume the worst of me. Maybe the best. Neither would be accurate. Though, knowing Heath, he'd never ask for fear of upsetting me.

"I think I want to tell you," I admitted.

He curled his hand around the back of my neck and leveled his gaze on mine. "Then I'm gonna listen."

I nodded and took a minute to rinse my hair while gathering my nerves. "I used to sleep with a knife under my mattress. I remembered it when he left the room to get me some ice for my face."

He closed his eyes and tilted his head back to look at the ceiling, his hands tensing at my hips.

"Do you want me to stop?" I asked in a whisper.

He turned his sad, blue gaze back to mine. "What I *want* is for you to have never been in that house with him."

I slid my hands up his chest. "Me too. But I'm okay, honey."

His eyebrows pinched together. "Are you? I mean…are you really?"

I wasn't. But I knew I would be. And the promise of that was more than I'd had in years.

I found the bar of soap and lathered it in my hands before setting it aside. Silently, I went to work cleansing his hard planes and straining muscles of the blood I'd transferred all over him.

When he was finally clean, I found the courage to continue. "I asked him to lie down with me." I peeked up at him through my lashes. "And, when he turned to set his gun down on the nightstand, I stabbed him in the neck and screamed for Elisabeth to run."

His Adam's apple bobbed as he stared down at me—despair marring his handsome face.

"He struggled at first, gurgling blood as he fought to get the knife." My voice broke.

"You don't have to do this," he whispered.

I shook my head, needing him to hear me. "I don't know how many times I stabbed him. I couldn't stop until he was dead. Even if the police had swarmed in to arrest him, I would never have been able to escape if he was still alive." My voice hitched. "I couldn't stop. I would have been stuck in that house, living under the weight of his captivity, for the rest of my life regardless of if I got out or not. I needed him dead. And, honestly, I'm afraid of what that says about me as a person."

He blew out a ragged breath and cupped each side of my face. "It's okay to be confused about this right now. You've been through a lot. And we're gonna get you someone to talk to who can help you through this." Tipping my head back, he swept his lips across mine. "But you need to hear me now and really take this shit in. You did what you had to do in order to survive. And, as pissed off as I am about you taking that risk, deep down, I'm so fucking proud of you."

My breathing shuddered. "You're proud of me for killing a man?"

Palming the back of my head, he tucked my face into his neck. "No, Clare. I'm proud of you for being strong enough to bring my woman home to me when I couldn't."

My nails dug into his shoulder as I murmured a sad, "Heath."

"Shhh. That's enough talking for now. We need to get out of here and let a doctor check you over. While they're doing that, I'll give Devon a call and have him bring Tessa up."

My whole body sagged in his arms. "That sounds amazing."

He stood there for several beats before saying, "You gotta let me go, babe."

"I know," I said without releasing him.

And then Heath being Heath muttered, "Whenever you're ready." And then stood in the water that was starting to chill for at least another five minutes.

"I said back the fuck up," Heath growled.

Lifting his hands in the air, the young emergency room doctor backed away, his eyes wide. "Sir, it's just a sedative," he defended.

Heath took another angry step toward him. "Yeah. And she said she doesn't want it."

That wasn't exactly what I'd said, but I figured he was paraphrasing.

I wasn't scared of needles, and I desperately needed something to help slow my racing heart, but I'd yet to mention that I was pregnant to anyone.

And weren't we a fucking pair, because the second I lost my shit, Heath lost his too.

Only my shit had been clawing up the bed, repeating, "Wait, wait, wait."

Heath's was much scarier.

"Do not make me repeat myself," he snarled, taking another step forward.

I grabbed Heath's arm. "Okay, let's just take a deep breath." I turned my gaze to the doctor. "Can I have a minute alone with my… um…guy?"

"Yeah. Sure. Whatever." He pocketed the shot as he headed for the door, peering over his shoulder as if he were afraid Heath was going to attack him from behind.

And, as I looked back up at Heath, I understood the man's fear.

"Honey," I purred, tugging on his arm.

His irate gaze jumped to mine.

"Breathe. There's no reason to be upset."

"Bullshit. I'm pretty sure the word *wait* means the same as it always has. You don't want that medicine—he does not get to continue. Plain and simple."

I grinned and scooted over in the bed. "It's just—" *Shit. Why is this so hard?* "Come here, Heath. We need to talk."

He folded his tense body to sit on the edge of the bed and stared at me expectantly.

But I said not a single word.

I could have danced around this conversation for nine months. Part of me was nervous to tell him. Part was excited for him to know. Part was terrified that there was nothing to know.

"What do you need, Clare?" he whispered when I started chewing on my thumbnail.

"I'm pregnant," I blurted.

His already tense shoulders turned to stone. "I'm sorry. What?"

"I'm pregnant. Well, at least I was this morning."

His face paled. "How…how do you know?"

I wrung my hands in my lap. "I ordered a test on Amazon. Also, coincidentally, I stole your credit card to buy a test on Amazon."

"But we used protection," he argued.

"Except for those couple of times in the shower. And I'm pretty sure that still counts."

He shot to his feet. "Oh, Jesus."

"Heath, it's okay. We don't even know if it will stick."

He began to pace. With one hand on his hip, he raked the other through his hair, repeating, "Oh, Jesus. That's not better."

Oh shit. So maybe Heath didn't share my excitement about us having made a baby in love. I guessed it was pretty quick for us to be starting a family. And I had just killed my husband after having been kidnapped.

Okay, so it was definitely bad timing.

"With my history…it's probably nothing."

He stopped and blinked at me. "Probably *nothing*?"

"I just mean, I've never gotten pregnant without medical intervention. Maybe the tests were wrong."

He cocked his head to the side. "Tests? How many did you take?"

"Well, they came in a two-pack. So…." I bit my lip and squeaked around it, "two."

He gripped the back of his neck.

And, just as I decided to crawl under the blankets and never show my face again, he boomed, "That motherfucker. Took *my woman* while she was *pregnant* with *my baby*!"

Alex came barreling in the room. "Everything good?" he asked, surveying the otherwise empty room.

Heath stormed past him and out the door. "Yep. I'm just about to light a body from the morgue on fire."

"Heath, stop!" I scrambled after him. "Stop him," I told Alex.

But Heath was gone.

I'd barely made it to the door when he reappeared, his arm around the bicep of the same frightened doctor.

"Tell me if my baby's okay," he ordered at the doctor as if he had ultrasonic vision.

"You're pregnant?" the doctor asked, snatching his pencil-thin arm from Heath's grasp.

"I'm so sorry," I apologized to him before turning to scowl at Heath. "You have to calm down. My nerves cannot take this."

"You can forget about calm. You're carrying my baby. That ship has officially sailed," he smarted back.

"You get back in bed while I grab an ultrasound cart." That order had come from the doctor.

I apparently didn't obey fast enough, because Heath started herding me to the bed.

Grabbing a chair from the corner and dragging it over, he ordered, "Pull your dress up."

"It's not a dress. It's a hospital gown, Heath," I snapped because, really, my nerves were *shot*.

I was beyond frustrated. However, it all melted away as I felt his hand land on my stomach. His touch was gentle but his finger flexed, biting into my flesh.

"Oh, Jesus," he whispered.

Only then did I notice the tiniest tremble of his hand.

"Talk to me," I urged, covering his hand with mine.

He cleared his throat. "If anything happened because of him…" He shook his head as he trailed off.

I intertwined our fingers. “Then we'll deal.”

“Fuck. I don't want to deal,” he growled. “Not about my child. I want everything to be okay.”

And God, I wanted that too, but life didn't always work like that.

But, then again, as I stared down at the nervous man I didn't deserve but was selfishly going to keep for the rest of my life, I realized that, sometimes, it did.

We sat in silence until the doctor came back in with an ultrasound machine and a nurse.

I giggled at Heath's appalled face as the doctor prepared the internal ultrasound wand.

And then, minutes later, we both gasped as a whooshing sound flooded the room. Tears pricked my lids as I witnessed my rock, big, tough Heath Light's eyes become watery too.

“Is it okay?” he asked urgently.

The doctor kept his eyes on the screen but smiled. “It's got a strong heartbeat.”

I laughed, and the tears finally escaped.

Heath rocked in his chair, muttering, “Oh Jesus.”

I laughed even louder and squeezed his hand.

The doctor finished up and then turned to face us both. “I'm going to send you over to ultrasound for a full workup, but as far as I can tell, everything looks good. I'd put you at around nine weeks, but they can give you a better estimate on your due date over there.”

“Nine weeks?” Heath exclaimed then raked a hand through his hair. “Oh Jesus.”

I laughed again.

“I'll give you two a minute alone. I'll be back shortly to finish my exam on the rest of your injuries.”

“That'd be great. Thanks,” I said, sitting up and pulling the blanket over my lower half.

Heath remained frozen at my side. His face filled with so many emotions that it was almost unreadable.

"You have to talk to me, honey."

"How the hell am I going to ever relax with you pregnant? And, if it's another girl… Oh Jesus."

"Should I chase down the doctor and see if he'll give you that shot of sedative?" I teased weakly.

He grunted something that sounded like a laugh, but he went back to staring off into space.

I decided to take a move from his playbook. It had always worked so well for me.

"What do you need, Heath?"

His gaze bounced to me, and a familiar grin pulled at the side of his mouth as he replied, "You."

"Then get over here and take it." I smiled, lifting the sheet in invitation.

It was an offer he did *not* refuse. His large frame barely fit in the small bed, but he wound his arms around me and held me to his chest.

"You're having my baby," he murmured reverently against my temple.

I was.

It was the most perfect moment of my entire life.

Well…almost.

There was a short knock at the door before it swung open and *our girl* came running in.

"Mama!"

"Hey, sweetie," I choked.

Heath sat up and scooped her up off the floor, placing her in my arms before dragging us both back down to the cramped bed.

My body was aching. I had a little girl's knee in my ribs and my head resting awkwardly on Heath's elbow.

But, on the flipside, I was alive. Free. My little girl was safe in my arms, a baby safe in my stomach, and the man who had made it all possible holding me safe in his arms.

That was the most perfect moment of my entire life.

Well…almost.

"Heaf, move! You too big!" Tessa complained, squirming between us.

"Son of a…" Heath grunted as her foot caught him in the balls.

I stifled a laugh as I lifted my head to see over Tessa. "You okay, honey?"

He shook his head and coughed out, "Never been better."

And, even as he writhed in pain, I knew he was telling the truth.

CHAPTER TWENTY-FOUR

ROMAN

"Wake up, baby," I murmured, sweeping her long, blond hair off her face.

We were still up at the hospital, and even though a night had passed since I'd seen her running out of Noir's house, my pulse had yet to return to normal. I wasn't sure it ever would.

I hadn't thought that anything could ever be more terrifying than finding Elisabeth on the bathroom floor after Noir had put a bullet in her Rubicon vest.

But, when I'd found out she was missing and once again in the hands of a lunatic, a terror rooted so deep inside me that I knew I'd been permanently changed.

There was no recovering from something like that.

But all I could do was make sure *she* did.

When we'd gotten to the hospital, Elisabeth had been a wreck—understandably so. After two hours of me trying to comfort her, Clare, Heath, and Tessa had stopped by. They'd hugged and cried as it seemed Elisabeth and Clare did all too often when they were together. But, within minutes, as Tessa sat in her lap, pressing buttons on the hospital bed, while Clare sat close beside them, I saw Elisabeth smile.

And, finally, the pressure in my chest started to ease.

I'd died a thousand deaths over the last few months.

But, with Walter Noir in a body bag, it felt like we could finally take the first step on the road to recovery.

And, for me, that first step was finishing what I'd started years earlier.

I pressed my lips to her forehead then sat on the edge of the bed and repeated, "Wake up, baby."

She moaned sleepily, stretching her body before curling around me. "Mmm," she purred.

"I've got a surprise for you, but I need you to wake up."

"If it's hospital food, I'd rather sleep. The nurses were in and out all night."

She was not wrong. Thanks to Clare, Elisabeth hadn't sustained any substantial injuries during her ordeal. The doctor had only kept her overnight for observation as a precautionary measure. Thankfully, the nursing staff seemed to have missed that memo. It was usually my job to be overprotective when it came to Elisabeth. It was nice to finally have a team at my back. She argued with me about damn near everything, but she was too polite to argue with them. So I'd gotten to sit back and watch them do my dirty work.

"The doctor will be around in a little while to sign your release papers, but first, we have to take care of something."

She pried one eye open. "What kind of something?"

I smiled and ran my finger through her hair. "Making you Elisabeth Leblanc—with an S and a lowercase B—again."

Her forehead wrinkled. "What?"

"Reverend," I called over my shoulder.

"What?" she repeated louder, sitting up.

"Ms. Keller," the hospital chaplain greeted from the doorway, a Bible tucked in his hands in front of him.

"I'm sorry. Who are you?" Elisabeth said in a sugary-sweet tone before turning an angry scowl on me.

"I'm Reverend Potter. I understand you'd like to get married today?"

She blinked once.

Twice.

Thrice.

And then she opened her mouth to speak only to close it and blink again.

Closing her eyes, she shook her head and said, "Can you give us a minute, Reverend Potter?"

"Of course," he replied, backing out of the room.

I remained impassive, sitting on the side of the bed. I knew what was to come. I also knew how'd it end. And that was the only part I cared about.

"Roman," she started in the faux calm she used so often right before she lost it.

"Lissy," I purred back in a *real* calm I used so often when I knew she was gearing up for an explosion.

"Why is there a reverend in my hospital room at six thirty in the morning?" More of her faux calm.

"Well, I didn't expect him to be here at six thirty, but I guess you get VIP treatment when you donate two hundred thousand dollars to the hospital chapel." More of my real calm.

Tick.

Tick.

Boom!

"Two hundred thousand dollars?" she accused. "What the hell, Roman!"

"Calm down. It's not a big deal. I needed a last-minute chaplain. Besides, I can write it off on my taxes."

"Your taxes?" she scoffed. "You think I'm concerned about your tax shelters right now?"

So fast that she didn't have time to react, I thrust a hand into the back of her hair and then I hauled her toward me until our mouths were less than an inch apart. Her breathing sped, and her eyes flashed wide. I rued the day she'd lose that heated surprise every time I got close. The way her mind fought the attraction but her body melted at the first touch.

I nipped at her bottom lip. "I figured it had to be the money because I *know* you couldn't be upset about becoming my wife again."

"This isn't the right time," she whispered, her attitude already fading.

"No. It's the *perfect* time," I replied. "I could have lost you yesterday, Lis. I never would have recovered knowing all of the memories I missed out on with you. I wasted two years I could have been waking up with you. Holding you. Living at your side. Two fucking years I can never get back. Two years I will regret for the rest of my life. Two years I will spend a lifetime trying to make up for. And the first step in that is not wasting another second without you being my wife. This is a new day. And we're starting a new life. When we walk out of this hospital, we're doing it together—the way we were made to be. Marry me, Lissy. Right here. Right now."

Her green eyes sparkled as she lifted her hand to my cheek. "Why do you always have to piss me off? Why can't you just start with the romantic speech?" She hooked her arm around my neck and pressed her lips to mine.

"Because then I'd miss your attitude," I murmured, pushing her back onto the bed and following her down.

She giggled against my mouth.

"Is that a yes?" I asked.

She stared up at me like the innocent angel I'd met all those years earlier.

And then she gave me back my life. "It's always a yes, Roman."

EPILOGUE

ELISABETH

Five years later…

"Don't forget to pack the bottles!" I yelled down the stairs to Roman.

"I said I've got them already!" he yelled back.

"You don't have to be so rude, you know?"

"You don't have to micromanage everything I do, either."

I rolled my eyes. I was *not* a micromanager. Far from it.

Well, kind of.

"Did you actually put the formula in them?" I shouted.

A very unhappy Roman suddenly appeared at the base of the stairwell with a pink, floral diaper bag draped over his shoulder. "I swear to Christ, Lis. I said I'd pack the baby's bag so you could get dressed while she takes her morning nap. But, if you are just going to scream down all the crap I've already packed, then I'll gladly unpack it so you can do it your damn self."

"You did not just say that," I spat.

He planted a hand on his hip and glared at me. "Oh, I said it. And, if you don't knock it off with the attitude, I'm gonna do it too."

Being a parent was *hard.*

Like *really* freaking hard.

But throw in a bossy, overprotective father, a baby with colic, and a grand total of ten hours of sleep in two weeks and it became exponentially harder.

I loved Roman more than anything, and I believed with my whole heart that he was my soul mate. But *damn*, parenting with someone was enough to make you question the universe's matchmaking skills.

"I dare you," I whispered ominously.

His silver eyes narrowed on me as he reached into the bag and very slowly pulled a purple swaddling blanket out before sending it fluttering to the floor.

I breathed in through my nose and out through my mouth, praying for patience that would never be found.

After a few years of healing both physically and mentally, Roman and I had decided to try to start a family—again. However, this time, we had gone into it with a different mind-set and took a different path.

Neither of us had had any desire to attempt IVF again. As far as we were concerned, that was a bridge better left burned. I'd never regret the family we got out of our first attempt—Tripp, Tessa, Clare, and Heath. But that was the end of it for us.

Adoption became the obvious avenue. It was an expensive and time-consuming process, but the good news was money was no longer a factor for us and I got to spend that time waiting with Roman. Even if it was arguing.

"Pick it up," I ordered.

He cocked his head to the side. "Drop the attitude."

"What's wrong? I thought you *loved* my attitude," I smarted

A sinister smirk curled his lips as he dropped the bag to the floor. "Oh, I do. Mainly because I enjoy fucking it out of you." He took a step up.

Oh shit.

I knew that glint in his eye all too well.

"Roman, no! I have to get dressed."

He took another step up, his smile growing.

"Mom!" Parker yelled from the playroom.

Roman froze, but his heated eyes remained locked on me as he replied, "Yeah, buddy?"

Parker Tripp Leblanc had come into our lives three years earlier via international adoption when he had been eighteen months old. I would never, for as long as I lived, forget the day we'd brought him home. Wounds I hadn't known were still inside me had suddenly healed. I'd told myself I could have lived a lifetime with only Roman, and it was the absolute truth. But that was before we'd experienced life with Parker.

Watching Roman as a father was one of the most fulfilling experiences of my life. He was amazing with Parker. Patient, loving, and gentle as he helped our little boy adjust to a new life and culture. It only cemented the fact that I wanted more children with him.

And, only six weeks earlier, after a year of waiting, a three-a.m. call had come, matching us with a newborn baby girl via domestic adoption. By four a.m., we'd dropped Parker off with Kristen and her husband, Seth (yes, *that* Seth), and we were on our way to Savannah, Georgia, to meet our daughter. With her dark-brown hair and even darker eyes, Alissa Cathleen was perfect. How a person could instantly fall in love with a tiny, wrinkly thing that did nothing but scream in their face for hours on end was beyond me. But, oh my God, how we loved that little girl.

And we started our life as a new family of four.

After years of being a workaholic, Roman had finally hired a CEO and turned the reins of Leblanc Industries over. He still worked a lot, but he'd become strict about keeping a nine-to-five schedule. I even went back to work, too. I gave up real estate and started working part time as an interior designer. It was my true passion, even if my clients did drive me crazy with their outlandish requests sometimes. (I'm sorry, but cowboy chic was not a real thing—or, at least, it shouldn't be.)

"Can I watch a movie?" Parker asked.

"No!" I replied.

At the same time Roman yelled, "Yes!"

"Yay!" he squealed, apparently only having heard his father.

I frowned and crossed my arms over my chest. "We have to leave in thirty minutes. We don't have time for him to watch a movie. We have to drive the kids all the way to your parents' house, and Clare is going to lose her mind if we're late!"

Roman took another step up. "A movie could buy us fifteen minutes alone before we have to leave." He smirked. "The baby's asleep. Li'l man is watching Lego people save the world. We could shut the door and discuss your attitude the proper way."

"The proper way?" I asked, tilting my head to the side.

"Mmmm," he groaned, taking the last four steps two at a time.

I backed away, but I did it *wanting* to be caught.

And Roman was never one to disappoint. He shoved his hand into the back of my hair just as my back hit the wall. His lips went straight to my ear, where he explained, "Naked. With you apologizing by coming on my cock."

A shiver traveled down my spine.

He traced a hand up my thigh and under my skirt. My breath hitched as his finger brushed over my core, igniting me.

"What do you say, Lis?" His teeth raked over the base of my neck. "You got fifteen minutes to spare for your man?"

I was sleep deprived, cranky, and in a rush.

But it was Roman.

"Yes," I breathed.

HEATH

"Get out!" I barked at all four of my sisters as I herded them to the door.

"That is not fair. Clare loves us," Melanie defended, flashing a smile at Clare.

Clare did love them. But she also loved to join them in their ruthless attempts to harass me. It was never a good day for me when the five of them got together. Or so I pretended as I smiled, secretly listening to them laugh like a bunch of old hens.

Maggie moved to the front of the huddle, her engagement ring twinkling on her finger as she patted my chest. "We got it. You're a big, bad tough guy and she's your wife. But I'm going to need you to put away your loin cloth and let us give her a hug before we go."

I had proposed to Clare about two months after Noir died. I would have done it sooner, and it had killed me to watch her stomach swelling without my ring on her finger, but I hadn't wanted her to associate that happy moment in our life together with the memories of that day at his house. So I'd performed the damn near heroic feat of waiting.

One day, after she had come home from a day of shopping with Elisabeth, Tessa and I surprised her with a homemade version of *Wheel of Fortune*—complete with me in an ugly brown Pat Sajak suit and Tessa dressed in a gown, acting as my Vanna White. On a poster board covered with sticky notes were the words Will You Marry Me. Per the game rules, I'd given her R, S, T, L, N, and E, so it wasn't exactly hard to figure out. However, as she cried, staring at me through bright-blue eyes, she guessed every single letter that we both knew was not on that board. After she'd gone through most of the alphabet and finally guessed an X, I laughed and dropped to a knee, muttering, "Jesus, you are terrible at this."

She said, "yes."

And, one month later, in a small ceremony at the botanical garden, we both said, "I do."

And, then a few months after that, a doctor announced the magical words that changed my life all over again: "It's a girl."

Shelby Grace Light was born via C-section, looking just like her mother. While she hadn't exactly been planned, in a lot of ways, she healed us all. She was beautiful, and the way Tessa's face lit up when she held her baby sister made me believe in divine intervention.

They shared not a strand of the same DNA, but those were my girls. Through and through.

I tore my gaze from my sisters and looked over my shoulder to Clare. An infectious smile split her face, and her eyes danced with a heart-stopping combination of happiness and love. It was everything I'd ever wanted for her. And, because she was my wife, I got it all too. I clenched my jaw to suppress my grin and stepped out of the way for my sisters to pass.

After hugs, jokes at my expense, and then more hugs, they finally left.

But, no sooner had my shoulders sagged in relief than the door swung open again.

"We're here!" Elisabeth called, rushing into the room, her heels clicking on the hospital floor.

"Oh, thank God," Clare sighed. "I didn't want them to start without you. I literally had to fight off the doctor a minute ago."

"Aunt Elisabeth!" Tessa exclaimed, jumping off the edge of the bed. "Can you take me to the barn? Pleeeeeease! There's a baby goat that's about to have a baby. My horseback riding trainer said she'd let me watch!"

I groaned. "For the seven billionth time, you aren't going to the barn today, sweet girl."

"Dad!" She stomped her foot. "That's not fair!"

"Sweet Jesus." I stared up at the ceiling. "Deliver me from the estrogen."

Roman sauntered into the room. "I can take her."

"Yes!" she shrieked.

"She's not going to the barn," I declared. "Your mother is having a baby, Tessi. I'm not really concerned with goats today."

"Heath, honey," Clare called, her voice filled with humor.

But Tessa was too busy complaining like only an eight-year-old girl knew how for me to pay her mother any attention.

"I've never seen a baby goat before. And Mom's baby is going to look just like Shelby," she argued. "And I've seen her, like, every day for four years." She walked over and hugged my hips. "Please, Daddy."

I'd been "Dad" to Tessa for several years, but the "Daddy" was relatively new. It was my kryptonite, and she knew it.

When Shelby had been around two, Tessa had started randomly calling me Dad. She'd slip it in occasionally, always peeking up at me or her mom to see if we were going to correct her. I had to struggle to breathe every time I heard her say it. One night, after a long talk with Clare, I'd sat Tessa down before bedtime and asked her if she wanted to start calling me dad all the time.

Her emerald eyes had filled with tears as she'd peered up at me and asked, "Does it mean you'll really be my dad?"

I'd nearly passed out from the lack of oxygen in that neon-pink room. I nodded at least seven thousand times but couldn't choke out a single word.

The very next day, I'd hired an attorney and legally filed for adoption.

Tessa Noir would forever be Tessa Light.

Well, until she turned forty and got married. Or I convinced her to become a nun and marry Jesus. Whichever came first.

"Give it up, kid," Roman said, fluffing Tessa's hair as he went straight to Shelby and scooped her into his arms. "You ready to be a big sister?" he asked, tossing her in the air.

She squealed with delight.

Roman and Elisabeth were fixtures in our life. We all went to Tessa's horse shows each weekend and spent nearly every holiday together. Our kids played—and fought—like siblings, Tessa acting as the bossy big sister to them all.

While Roman and I were tight, Clare and Elisabeth were inseparable. If they weren't together, they were texting or talking on the phone. She'd been the only one Clare trusted to keep the kids when it was finally time for her scheduled, repeat C-section.

"So, are we finally ready in here?" a nurse said as she came through the door.

A unanimous, "Yes!" came from the entire room, except for Tessa, who cried into my stomach, "But it's a baby goat!"

"All right! I'll call down and let the OR know," the nurse said, backing out of the packed room.

"Okay. We'll be in the waiting room." Elisabeth leaned over the bed to give Clare a hug. "Let me know if you need anything."

"Thank you for doing this. I know Alissa is still so little. But I really wanted the girls to be here as soon as she's born," Clare said, releasing her.

"He," I corrected. "When *he's* born."

Roman shot me a who-are-you-kidding glare.

We'd decided not to find out the gender at the ultrasound, but I was holding on to hope for a boy.

"Don't you dare apologize," Elisabeth said. "Cathy has been praying you'd go into labor early so she could get her hands on that baby. I'm surprised she hasn't been delivering you dinners laced with castor oil."

Clare laughed.

Shelby froze, her big, blue eyes flashing wide. "Is Grandma Cathy coming?"

"Nah. She's at home with Parker and Baby Lis. She'll come see you tomorrow though, I'm sure," Roman said, setting her back on her feet.

"Girls, go give your mom a kiss," I ordered.

Tessa might have still been upset about missing the coveted goat birth, but she did love her mama and quickly went to her side for a long hug and a kiss. Shelby fell into line behind her.

"Come on, girls," Elisabeth said, taking both of their hands. "Let's go raid the vending machines."

I kissed both the girls on the top of their heads before they left.

Roman squeezed my shoulder. "Good luck. We'll be in the waiting room. Keep us updated."

"Thanks, man."

Once we were finally alone, I made my way over to Clare's bed. She scooted over so I could sit beside her.

"You okay?" I asked.

She smiled and began picking invisible lint off the blanket. "Nervous, I guess. But I'm okay."

"I love you. You know that, right?"

Her eyes lit. "I definitely know that."

"Any chance you gonna return that love by giving me a boy?"

She reached for my hand and rested it on her stomach. "I'll do my best."

We both fell silent, but Clare continued to fidget.

After several minutes, I whispered, "Lean on me, babe. You don't have to be brave right now."

Her gaze shot to mine, and her chin started to quiver. "I'm scared."

But, even at her weakest, Clare had always been brave. I wasn't completely sure she knew how to be anything else.

I shifted toward her and tucked her hair behind her ear. "We'll wait until you're ready."

She smiled weakly and wrapped her arms around my neck. "Maybe just a minute?"

"Whatever you need, Clare."

A minute turned into twenty.

However, with Clare in my arms, I would have waited a lifetime.

Fortunately, I didn't have to.

An hour later, at exactly 11:11 a.m., Noah Heath Light was born.

I didn't even have to use a wish.

Transfer
The Retrieval Duet

THE END

OTHER BOOKS

The Retrieval Duet

Retrieval

Transfer

Guardian Protection Agency

Singe

Thrive

The Fall Up Series

The Fall Up

The Spiral Down

The Darkest Sunrise Duet

The Darkest Sunrise

The Brightest Sunset

Across the Horizon

The Truth Duet

The Truth About Lies

The Truth About Us

The Wrecked and Ruined Series

Changing Course

Stolen Course

Broken Course

Among the Echoes

On the Ropes

Fighting Silence

Fighting Shadows

Fighting Solutude

ABOUT THE AUTHOR

Originally from Savannah, Georgia, *USA Today* bestselling author Aly Martinez now lives in South Carolina with her husband and four young children.

Never one to take herself too seriously, she enjoys cheap wine, mystery leggings, and baked feta. It should be known, however, that she hates pizza and ice cream, almost as much as writing her bio in the third person.

She passes what little free time she has reading anything and everything she can get her hands on, preferably with a super-sized tumbler of wine by her side.

Facebook: www.facebook.com/AuthorAlyMartinez

Twitter: twitter.com/AlyMartinezAuth

Goodreads: www.goodreads.com/AlyMartinez

Bookbub: www.bookbub.com/authors/aly-martinez

www.alymartinez.com

Made in the USA
Lexington, KY
05 February 2019